CLOSE
ENCOUNTERS
OF THE
MAGICAL KIND

JEFFREY POOLE

Jeffrey Poole's Epic Fantasy Books
Bakkian Chronicles:
The Prophecy
Insurrection
Amulet of Aria
Disneyland Debacle (short story)
Winter Wonderland (short story)

Tales of Lentari
Lost City
Something Wyverian This Way Comes
A Portal for Your Thoughts
Thoughts for a Portal
Wizard in the Woods
Close Encounters of the Magical Kind
The Hunt for Red Oskorlisk (short story)
May the Fang be With You (Pirates trilogy #1)
The Hammer is Strong with This One (Pirates #2)
These are Not the Stones You're Looking For (Pirates #3)
Blast from the Past

Dragons of Andela
Harness the Fire
Strike the Spark
Clear the Water

Mysteries by J.M. Poole
The Corgi Case Files Series
18 delightful cozy mystery novels featuring corgi
sleuths, Sherlock and Watson

CLOSE ENCOUNTERS

OF THE

MAGICAL KIND

Tales of Lentari, Book 6

JEFFREY POOLE

Secret Staircase Books

Close Encounters of the Magical Kind
Published by Secret Staircase Books, an imprint of
Columbine Publishing Group, LLC
PO Box 416, Angel Fire, NM 87710

Book layout and design by Secret Staircase Books
First Secret Staircase paperback edition: August, 2023

First Secret Staircase e-book edition: August, 2023

* * *

Publisher's Cataloging-in-Publication Data

Poole, Jeffrey
Close Encounters of the Magical Kind / by Jeffrey Poole.
p. cm.
ISBN 978-1649141507 (paperback)
ISBN 978-1649141514 (e-book)

1. Lentari (Fictitious location)—Fiction. 2. Epic fantasy fiction
3. Dragons and mythical creatures—Fiction. 4. Time travel—Fiction.
I. Title

Tales of Lentari : Book 6.
Close Encounters of the Magical Kind
Poole, Jeffrey, Tales of Lentari epic fantasy series.

BISAC : FICTION / Fantasy/Epic.

813/.54

For Giliane, without whom this story would have never come to be. You are my inspiration, my dear. Thank you for being by my side!

Love you always & forever!

Acknowledgements

This marks the 10th book that I have published, and at the risk of sounding like a broken record, I do have some people to thank.

As always, I have to thank my wife. Most especially her. This story is the direct result of Giliane waking up one morning, looking at me, and saying, "Get a notebook. I have an idea for a story." This is essentially her story, which is why you'll notice the main POV throughout this book is Sarah's.

I'd also like to thank my beta readers, and this time around I handled the beta readers a little differently. I created *The Posse*, which is family, friends, and readers who are willing to sacrifice their time to make sure I don't look like an idiot. Thanks for spending so much time helping me, offering suggestions, advice, and so on. Therefore, many thanks go out to the following Posse members:

Diane Bowlin, Elizabeth Davis, Dawn Nolder, Caroline Craven, Sarah Rice, Jody Kahiapo, Toni Trick, Wendy Egan, Jason Harvill, Amanda Barrow, Debbie Davis, Marie Howells, Kate Craven-liu, Krista Jasper, Amanda Jean, Tracey Bryuette, Deb Shapiro, Dorothy Roberts, Hellen Mcneil, and Tanner Erb.

There's a second set of readers I'd also like to thank. This one is from Secret Staircase Books. They are: Sandra Anderson, Paula Webb, and Susan Gross. Thank you!

I've saved the best for last. I need to thank you, the reader, for continuing to keep the magical land of Lentari alive and allowing me to continue bringing you more stories! Happy reading!

J.

Table of Contents

Prologue

Don't you just love our new cabin? I think it's perfect. No neighbors, no noise, and no interruptions." An attractive woman in her mid-thirties sank blissfully down onto the tiny, comfortable bed. With a small flourish, she flopped over onto her back and opened her eyes to take in the simple furnishings of the tiny, one bedroom cabin.

Just as her eyes settled on the bedroom's only window, which afforded her a spectacular view of the surrounding forest, she heard a loud bang, followed immediately by a muffled curse. Wanting to see what her husband was doing, the woman rolled to her right and instantly got a mouthful of hair for her trouble. The small elastic band that had been holding her ash blonde hair in a braid had come loose, flinging itself directly in her face.

"Ack-pbth."

She felt around on the bed, came up with the black rubber band, and coaxed her hair into a ponytail. Her husband was nowhere to be found. Concerned, she sat up on the bed.

"Steve? Where are you?"

"Out here."

Sarah walked into the tiny living room and found her six-foot-three husband down on his hands and knees with his head thrust into the fireplace, looking up. He was muttering to himself as he poked around the chimney's innards, presumably to find the flue. Sarah waited a few moments longer than she deemed was necessary and finally cleared her throat. Her husband jerked upward, cracking his head on the top of the fireplace. A resounding clang echoed throughout the small cabin. Sarah suppressed a giggle. It was the same clang she had heard earlier.

"I'm sorry. That had to hurt."

Steve sat back on his haunches and rubbed the top of his head. "That'll leave a mark."

"Can't find the flue?" Sarah guessed.

"Right. I was thinking about building a fire. The skies are overcast, and it's starting to drizzle. This is too good of an opportunity to pass up."

"Isn't this place just perfect?" Sarah asked, sighing contently. "No one knows about it. We can finally take a proper vacation. We owe him, you know."

Steve nodded. "I wonder what Mikal had to do in order to secure his parents' permission to have this place built. I mean, do you hear that? We can actually hear the waterfall from here."

Sarah shook her head. "Mikal has some pretty impressive powers of persuasion, no doubt about it. I don't know what he had to do, nor do I want to know. This is our cabin. It's hidden, and it's by our waterfall."

Steve rose to his feet. "It was very nice of the king and queen. How long have we wanted to spend some quiet time here without getting mobbed by the people? Too long, if you ask me."

The waterfall was the one Steve and Sarah had stumbled onto when they had first found their way onto another world. It was also the first time husband and wife had encountered a live griffin. Two live griffins, for that matter. Now, they regarded the waterfall, and the tiny lake it created, as their own private retreat in Lentari.

Sarah knew that it was sometimes difficult to stay in their home in the capital city of R'Tal because they were treated like celebrities. Between the royal family and the Lentarian subjects, they had no privacy. Therefore, it had been a nice surprise when Mikal had convinced his parents to have a secluded cabin built just for the two of them. After much debate, the king, along with significant input from the queen, decided the best location would be by Greenquill Falls, referring to one of more than two dozen small waterfalls scattered throughout the Selekai Mountains. This particular waterfall, Mikal knew, was one both of his former bodyguards knew very well.

"I think we ought to go explore the waterfall."

Caught in mid-yawn, Sarah froze. "What? Why?"

"Well, you never know what we might find out there. We already know there's a secret cave behind the water. Who knows what else might be out there waiting to be discovered?"

"Whatever's out there can certainly wait until morning," Sarah informed him. "It's been a long day. I'm looking forward to a technology-free night. No cell phones, no tablets, and no television."

"It's awfully quiet out there," Steve observed, as he pulled some clothes out of his suitcase and transferred them to a small dresser. "Don't you think it's too quiet? I think we're going to need some white noise of some sort."

"No, we don't," Sarah contradicted. She slipped her arm through his. "Not as long as I have you. You are the perfect source of white noise. Just try to keep the snoring down to a minimum, okay?"

"Hardy har har."

Extinguishing the two lit oil lamps, Sarah climbed into bed and snuggled next to her husband. Hundreds of pictures of their day flashed through her mind. She closed her eyes and thought of her favorite moment, their late-night swim. She drifted off to sleep with a smile on her face.

* * *

Sarah awoke slowly, feeling more relaxed than ever in her entire life. She cracked an eye open and noticed that it was still dark inside their cabin. She fervently hoped sunrise was still hours away. Her eyes closed and she rolled onto her side. The next thing she noticed was that her bedding vanished and had been replaced by grass.

Grass?

Sarah gently swept an arm around her body. Yes, it was true. She was lying on a patch of plush, dew-covered grass and she was most definitely not inside her cozy cabin.

Sarah instantly shot up and carefully looked around her new surroundings. It was a cloudless night, and the full moon was providing more than enough illumination to allow her to see what was around her. One thing became disturbingly clear: Steve and the cabin were nowhere in sight. In fact, she wasn't even certain she was still in Lentari. What if she had inadvertently activated her jhorun and teleported herself to someplace else, while sound asleep?

She frowned. While plausible, it was unlikely. Her jhorun, her magical ability, could instantaneously teleport her from one locale to the next in literally the blink of an eye. However, in order for her jhorun to work properly Sarah had to be thinking of a destination.

With wide, unblinking eyes, Sarah slowly stood and stared at her unfamiliar surroundings. She shook her head. There was no way her jhorun could have teleported her here.

She took a few hesitant steps. She could sense something. It felt as though she was being pulled toward the trees in front of her. Something wanted her to start moving. Not sensing any malice, Sarah began to walk. Within a few minutes she knew without a doubt that she hadn't ever been to this place before.

In front of her was a dense coniferous forest city. The trees were like skyscrapers in the most amazing urban forest she had ever seen. Intricately carved structures rose hundreds of feet into the air. Walkways ran from each tree to the next, allowing movement from one building to the other without stepping foot on the ground. Her eyes were drawn to a huge pine tree in the center of a large clearing. The tree was so massive that it easily dwarfed all the other wooden structures. Determined to find answers, Sarah headed toward the gargantuan tree.

As she approached the huge evergreen, she could see that the tree's prolific root system formed a canopy over the glowing path that led toward the center of the tree. Sunken into the base of the huge pine's trunk were two exquisite amethyst gemstone doors. She studied the sparkling doors for a few moments before craning her neck to look up at the huge trunk that rose hundreds, if not thousands, of feet above her head.

Sarah squinted. There appeared to be windows, many with flickering lights, all across the grand trunk. Many of the windows had lights that were sporadically turning on and off. She saw there were no other signs of people or inhabitants of this fantastic city.

Sarah looked back at the sparkling gemstone doors and timidly approached. Both majestic doors silently opened, allowing her access to the heart of the tree. Sarah peered through the opening and paled with wonder.

The center of the tree appeared to be the inside of a beautiful castle, complete with verdant light filtering down from the leaves above to illuminate every corner with a soft, emerald glow. The air itself seemed to glitter and sparkle, as if infused with thousands of tiny fireflies. Sarah reached out to try and grab a handful of the lights but discovered the tiny sparkles moved like water through her fingers.

"Lady Sarah," a voice announced, breaking the silence. "Please come forward."

Sarah froze. The female voice appeared out of thin air and spoke with assurance. It was strong, powerful, regal. This was someone that was used to giving orders, Sarah decided. A queen, perhaps? If it was, how did she know her name?

Sarah looked down. A pathway appeared, leading into the depths of the tree. She placed a foot on the path. Deep down, she knew she should be afraid but she wasn't. She knew with absolute certainty that no harm would befall her.

The light seemed to get brighter with every step she took. She blinked with surprise. There were now people lining either side of the path. In fact, every person she passed, be it man or woman, bowed to her, as if she were their queen. That couldn't be right. These people didn't know her, did they? And she certainly wasn't a queen!

At the end of the path were two jewel-encrusted thrones, occupied by a man and a woman. Both rose to their feet as she approached. Sarah fidgeted. Should she bow? Curtsy? Do nothing? Deciding a curtsy would be the most appropriate Sarah gave it her best attempt. Feeling awkward, seeing how neither the strange king nor queen had yet to say anything, Sarah glanced up at the royal couple. Both were smiling, which made her feel better. Somewhat.

The queen stepped forward to take Sarah's hand. Sarah stared, awestruck. A thin pair of gossamer wings flicked up and fluttered once. Speechless, Sarah turned to the king. He, too, had a pair of glittering translucent wings. How had she not noticed them before?

They were faeries, only they were the biggest faeries she had ever seen. Weren't they supposed to be small? Like pixie-small?

"Lady Sarah, I am so glad you could come," the queen said, leading Sarah through a doorway to the left of the thrones. The queen gently escorted Sarah to a perfectly round granite table and indicated one of the chairs. "I am Ria and this is my husband, Tivan."

Sarah turned to see that the king had followed them into the smaller antechamber. He took a seat next to his wife and took her hand in his own. He nodded at Sarah.

"I'm sorry," Sarah began, "but could you tell me where I am?"

Tivan replied with a slight grin, "You are in the Fae city of Dynwe."

"Dynwe," Sarah slowly repeated, as if that alone answered all her questions. "Where exactly is that? Am I still in Lentari or is this another world?" She watched the Fae king and queen give each other a coy grin. "Will you at least tell me how I got here?"

"Please join us for a meal," the queen replied, "and we will explain everything."

All of a sudden, the lights in the room brightened considerably and the table was magically filled with an abundant feast. Roasted meats, steamed vegetables, huge platters of colorful fruit, and enough examples of freshly baked bread to make a baker green with jealousy, filled the table. Servants appeared and began filling goblets, serving the food, and offering quiet answers when asked what certain dishes were. Satisfied that Sarah was being well cared for, Ria began answering questions.

"First, to ease your mind, I can tell you that you are still in Lentari. We are presently located on an island off the western coast of what the humans call Capily. However, technically speaking, you are not here. Using a mixture of our magic, and your own teleportation jhorun, we have brought your *essence* here. Your body is still lying next to your husband's."

"I wasn't aware that could be done."

"The humans know very little about Fae magic," Ria explained. The Fae queen noticed her husband's decisive nod of agreement and laughed. "It's a notion we have no desire to dispel."

"I guess my next question would be, why would you bring me here?"

The smile faded from the queen's face.

"We need your help, Sarah. Both yours and your husband's. We are dying."

Chapter 1 — To Fae or Not To Fae

S arah awoke with a start. She sat up in bed and looked at the sleeping form of her husband. He was snoring, as was the norm for him. At least it wasn't too loud. She looked around the small room, noting that the light was growing steadily brighter. Sunrise had to be only minutes away.

Sarah quietly slipped out of bed. She made her way to the tiny kitchen and carefully opened the wood burning stove so she could light the fire. Setting a kettle of water onto one of the burners, she made herself a steaming cup of tea.

Her dream had been so vivid! Could it have been an actual plea for help? Could there actually be faeries in Lentari when thus far, she had heard no mention of them at all? Or was this just an example of an overactive imagination?

Sarah sipped her tea and watched the sunrise out the window. Bright streaks of golden amber appeared on the horizon as the sky grew steadily brighter. As if someone had pressed the 'unmute' button on a remote, the sounds of the forest started filtering in—birds chirping, animals scurrying through the treetops, and an occasional squawk from a griffin.

Sarah shook her head in exasperation as she gazed back through the open doorway of the cabin's only bedroom to see her husband still snoring contentedly away. Unlike her, that man could sleep through World War 3, she thought with a smile.

"It's a curse," Sarah murmured.

She gave her husband another fifteen minutes before she gently tapped his shoulder. Steve rolled onto his back and cracked an eye open. He looked at her and smiled. "Hey, babe. What's up? What are you drinking?"

"Tea. Want some?"

Steve made a face. "Thanks, but I'd rather drink dishwater. I don't know how you drink that stuff. I'll take orange juice any day over tea."

"You prefer juice because it is sweet," Sarah told him yet again. "You've got to have the biggest sweet tooth I have ever seen."

"You have met my mother, right? That woman could live and die by a slice of chocolate cake and have no regrets."

Sarah nodded. "True. Hey, listen, I think I need to tell you about the dream I had last night."

"As long as it didn't involve dragons asking for help, I'm all ears."

Sarah grinned. "Now that you mention it, Rinbok Intherer was there, and he had a…" She broke off laughing as she caught sight of her husband's concerned face. "Relax. It wasn't about dragons."

Steve's frown disappeared. "Good."

"It was about faeries."

"Faeries? As in tiny little humans with wings? Like Tinkerbell?"

"These faeries weren't tiny," Sarah replied. "They were the same size as me."

Her husband was silent as he studied his wife.

"What?" Sarah demanded.

"Nothing. I'm just waiting for you to continue."

"I thought you were going to accuse me of being crazy."

"Well, now that you mention it—"

"Don't even go there, Paco," Sarah warned. "I have my glitter spray here."

Steve paled and held up his hands in surrender.

"Now," Sarah continued, "where was I? Oh, yes. The faeries. They brought me to their forest city."

"They had an arboreal city?" Steve asked, as she took a breath. "How cool!"

"Arboreal? Someone's been using that word-a-day calendar I bought him, hasn't he?"

Her husband smiled at her. "As a matter of fact, I have. Been trying to impress my wife with my newfound vocabulary. I reckon I'm doin' purty good, dontcha think?"

"Doofus. Can I finish? As I was saying, they took me to their *arboreal* city. They—"

"What'd you see? What did it look like?"

"Stop interrupting me and I'll tell you."

She began with her impression of the forest, and her delighted discovery of the tree-shaped skyscrapers. She moved on to describe the tree that dwarfed the tallest sequoias, and how she was able to walk into the heart of it. Steve sat, perfectly quiet, as she talked about her encounter with the king and queen, and the history they imparted.

"That city is something I won't ever forget. And the food!"

Steve perked up, interested. "Oh? Do you remember what the food tasted like?"

"What? Of course, I do. Why would you ask me that?"

"In all the years I've been dreaming, not once have I ever tasted something, in a dream, and thought it was remarkable enough to remember. If you're telling me you can still clearly remember what it tasted like, I'd say that's another point leading to the credibility of your dream."

Sarah took another sip of her tea and considered. Placing the mug on the counter she pulled out a small notebook from her suitcase and began taking notes.

"Let's see. The first thing I saw that I wanted to sample was what looked like a teal kiwi fruit that was the size of a cantaloupe. Thankfully it didn't taste anything like a cantaloupe."

Steve smiled. Everyone in their family knew how much Sarah detested cantaloupe.

"It tasted like a strawberry-kiwi mix. It was very light and so refreshing. I loved it. Then I saw the queen being served a salad filled with vegetables. I knew instantly that you'd hate it but I wanted to try it." Sarah made a few more notes. "It was wonderful. Then I had…"

"Alright, alright," Steve laughed, raising his hands in surrender. "The court will acknowledge the defendant dutifully remembers each and every thing she ate while in the company of her faerie friends."

Sarah swatted his arm. "Once we finished eating, the queen finally told me why she had brought me there."

"Oh? Go on."

"She said they were dying."

"Was the king there? Did he say anything?"

Sarah nodded. "Yes. Tivan didn't say much, only that we were in the Fae city of Dynwe. He wasn't nearly as talkative as the queen."

"Dynwe, huh? I've never heard of it."

"Up until last night, neither had I."

"They're dying," Steve repeated, thinking hard. "It sure does sound like a plea for help to me."

"That's what I was thinking, too," Sarah admitted.

"What do you want to do?" Steve asked, knowing full well what the answer would be.

"I want to go to R'Tal."

"Hon, we're in this teeny tiny cabin 'cause we wanted to have some quiet time to ourselves. Only Mikal knows we're here right now. This is our chance to finally explore the kingdom as unknowns."

"I can't ignore this dream," Sarah answered. She splashed some water on her face and pulled her hair back into a ponytail. "It was too real. Ria and Tivan asked me for help. Actually, they asked the two of us for help."

"They mentioned me?" Steve asked, surprised.

"Not by name. The last thing Ria said before I woke up

was, and I quote, 'we need your and your husband's help'."

"Alrighty. R'Tal it is. Let's go see what's happening at the castle today."

* * *

"You're sure you reactivated that charm Shardwyn gave us?"

Sarah sighed, "I'm sure. I know how to work it just as well as you."

"I don't want anyone to find our place."

"No one will ever find it," Sarah assured him. "I'm actually surprised at how well his spell worked. Not even the Romulans' cloaking shield could have hidden that cabin any better." Sarah groaned. "I don't know what's worse. Your constant reference to nerdism or the fact that you've gotten me to sound like one of them, too."

Her husband slung an arm over her shoulder and laughed. "That's my girl!"

Sarah pushed his arm off. "*Star Wars. Star Trek. Lord of the Rings.* Do you have any idea how much useless information you have crammed into my head?"

He gave her a proud look. "You're welcome."

"I wasn't thanking you."

"Close enough."

They approached the West Gate and were more than halfway across the bridge when Sarah noticed three guards exit the gate keeper's office. Before they could ask a question, her husband waved at them with a lit hand. Wordlessly, all three guards spun on their heels and headed back to the keeper's office.

"They don't treat me like that around here," Sarah remarked.

"That's only because they don't recognize you at first. I guarantee if I hadn't lit my hand on fire, then they'd have stopped us to ask us what we're doing. If you had lifted all three of them into the air, I'm pretty sure you'd get the same treatment."

Sarah shrugged as she conceded the point. She took

her husband's hand and pulled him past the open portcullis and into the castle's outer keep. People were milling about everywhere. Squadrons of guards were practicing drills. Half a dozen housekeeping staff were beating on rugs Judging by the flying dust and debris, it must have been spring cleaning.

They approached the castle's inner keep and ducked through a second portcullis. The heavy iron grate gently clinked against the grooves in the stone as an easterly breeze picked up. One guard looked questioningly at them as they passed through. Her husband tilted his head, indicating this would be the perfect opportunity to give a small demonstration of her jhorun to see if she'd be recognized. Sarah shook her head.

Steve ignited another hand and gave a mock salute. The guard promptly returned the salute and turned his back on the visitors. When he was sure he wasn't being watched, the young guard pulled a set of dice from his pocket and resumed his game.

Sarah guided them straight toward the Great Hall. This was where the Kri'yans, the king and queen, held court. Their gilded thrones were here, as were a number of nobles and high-ranking soldiers. Noticeably absent, unfortunately, were the king and queen.

"Aww, great," Steve grumbled. "Where do you think they are?"

An arm draped itself around each of their shoulders as someone suddenly appeared standing between them. Sarah barely refrained from teleporting the newcomer straight into the moat. Steve turned, noticed who had surprised them, and broke out into a grin.

"Rhenyon! It's good to see you, buddy! How are you?"

Sarah visibly relaxed. She smiled at the Commander of the Royal Guards and the king's most trusted advisor.

"Sir Steve! Lady Sarah! What a pleasant surprise. I didn't know you were in town."

"We're here for a little R&R," Steve told him.

"R&R?" Rhenyon repeated, puzzled. "I'm not familiar with that term."

"It means 'rest and relaxation'. We're here to enjoy some

quiet time."

"Ah. Are you looking for their majesties?"

"Yes," Sarah told him. "Are they busy?"

Rhenyon nodded. "As a matter of fact, they are away on business. They should return shortly. You are more than welcome to wait in the Antechamber."

Sarah nodded. A meeting with the Kri'yans in their jhorun-proof private room was actually much better than trying to explain the true nature of their visit out here in the open. They bade Rhenyon farewell and headed toward the small room adjacent to the Great Hall. A set of guards recognized them and rushed to open the doors.

Stepping inside the luxurious chamber, Steve instantly gravitated toward one of the half dozen plush chairs set in a semi-circle around the large hearth. He noticed that Sarah had moved over to the wall that concealed the king's private safe.

"What are you doing? You know the griffin safe is there, right?"

"Yes. I don't care about the safe." Sarah pointed at the huge parchment on the wall directly to the left of the hidden panel.

"Do you remember seeing that in here before?"

Steve joined her and stared admiringly at the highly detailed map of the kingdom. Rivers, mountains, peaks, and grasslands, everything they had ever seen was labeled and represented on the map. Steve leaned forward and tapped a spot on the Bohani Mountains in the north. There was a sketch of a two-bladed axe on the valley southeast of Lake Raehón.

"I wonder if that is supposed to be Bohragg," Steve mused. "It's not that far from the dwarf door hidden in those boulders."

"Are those boulders on the map?" Sarah asked, amazed.

Steve leaned forward for a better look. "No."

"There's another axe over here," Sarah told him, pointing to another location about a foot to the right. "Look. There are two more over here."

"One of these must be that new Kla Guur city," Steve

surmised, noticing the closest axe to Bohragg. "Foronlir. Remember when we attended the ceremony marking the dragons and dwarves becoming allies? There were several dwarf clans there. I wonder which ones are which. You know what? I didn't know the king had a map like this."

"We were just in here a few months ago," Sarah reminded him. "It wasn't here then. I'm guessing he just had it made."

Her husband appeared at her side and leaned close to the map, squinting as he did so. Sarah noticed and put her hands on her hips.

"I am *so* getting you some reading glasses for your next birthday."

Steve shot her a dirty look. "Snot. Can I not study it without getting an age joke?"

"Would you perhaps like a magnifying glass? I could probably teleport you one from home."

"Aren't you a barrel of laughs?"

"So, if you claim to be *studying*," Sarah added air quotes around Steve's supposed excuse, "then what are you looking at?"

Her husband tapped one of a dozen or so tiny lakes, buried in the heart of the Selekai Mountains. "Do you see this? What do you think that means?"

Sarah studied the graphic and shrugged. "Maybe it's a swimming hole. Why else would they put a picture of a woman's head in the water? Wait. Hmmm. The ears are pointed. Why would they make a human's ears pointed? It must mean something else."

Steve made sure he wasn't being watched as he studied the teeny tiny figure on the lake's surface. He shook his head. He couldn't tell if the woman's ears were pointed or not. Maybe his eyes weren't working as well as he thought, although he'd never admit that to her. Ever.

Steve tapped a few more places on the map. Sarah noticed he touched tiny figures of griffins, dragons, and even a small two-headed dragon in the southeastern section of Anakash forest. She quickly found Capily on Lentari's western shore and was surprised—and dismayed—to see that small islands were everywhere around the seaside village. She easily counted more than two dozen before she gave up.

Voices sounded behind her. She and Steve turned to see Kri'Entu and Ny'Callé enter the Antechamber. Both were wearing traveling cloaks and were outfitted in leather armor. They clearly had just returned from some type of excursion. The king's face lit up as he saw who their visitors were. He unfastened his cloak and tossed it over the nearest chair. The queen cringed and quickly gestured to one of her ladies-in-waiting. Once both of their cloaks had disappeared, tucked safely away in the arms of a maid, the queen turned to Sarah and smiled.

"Lady Sarah! Sir Steve! What a pleasant surprise! What brings you to the castle today?"

Sarah turned back to the new map and pointed at it. "Is there a map which displays everything? What I mean is…" She hesitated as she tried to correctly formulate her question. "Is there a map which shows where all the nine dwarf clans live, where Nevir lies, where the many flocks of griffins call home, etc."

Kri'Entu unbuckled his leather gauntlets and let them plop onto his private desk. He nodded his head. "Aye. You're looking at it. Why do you ask?"

"This map is new, isn't it? It wasn't here the last time we were in here."

Ny'Callé nodded. "Aye. Our cartographer finished it last month."

"When will it be updated?" Sarah asked, curious.

"That map is less than a month old, Lady Sarah," the king pointed out. "It took nearly a year of research between the cartographers and the team of archivists to include everything you see on the map. Everything they know is there. Why do you ask? Did they miss something? If only that were so. Commander Rhenyon would be eternally in my debt if I told him that the new map was incorrect."

"Does Rhenyon not get along with the cartographers?" Steve asked, surprised. "He strikes me as the type of guy that could get along with anybody."

"His issue is with Miss Andra Alwyn," Ny'Callé said with a giggle. "Commander Rhenyon was one of her first pupils and she still treats him as a boy, much to his chagrin."

Kri'Entu walked over to the map and gave Sarah a questioning look. "Is there something missing from this map, Lady Sarah?"

"I don't see any mention of the Fae on here. Why is that?"

The king regarded her silently for a few moments before turning his back on the map and heading toward the semi-circle of plush chairs. He sank down into one and began unbuckling more pieces of his leather armor.

"That's because you won't. The Fae have been absent from our history for many years."

"Why?" Sarah wanted to know. "I never knew Lentari had any faeries."

"Please tell us why you're asking about the Fae," Ny'Callé prompted. "You've never brought them up before. Why now?"

"Did the Fae have many cities?" Sarah pressed, hoping the Kri'yans wouldn't notice that she had yet to answer their questions.

"The Fae only had one city," Kri'Entu slowly answered. He rose from his seat and returned to the map. He touched a spot in the northwestern section of the Bohanis and turned expectantly to Sarah, who hurried over to the map to see for herself.

Sarah's eyes narrowed. The king was pointing at a very specific location, only it wasn't anywhere near Capily. Perhaps this was where the former city was? Or had been. Whatever. Kri'Entu's finger was resting on a skillfully drawn illustration of a noble fir. A quick check of the surrounding map revealed there were no other intricately detailed illustrations of trees anywhere in the area. Sarah's pulse quickened. That tree had to mean something!

"This was where Vineelm used to be," the king softly told her. "I'm told it was an elegant city. Elegant and sophisticated. Very secluded. The Fae lived their lives in peace, not bothering anyone nor asking for anything in return."

"They left you alone so you left them alone," Steve guessed.

The king nodded. "That's right."

"The tree is wrong," Sarah said. "The top wasn't pointed, like a fir. It was more rounded, like an ash tree."

"It was a different city," Steve whispered to her. "Different city, different tree."

King and queen stared at each other for a few moments before the king held out an arm and invited Sarah to sit down. Once they were seated, the two monarchs joined them. The king, Sarah noted, had resumed removing pieces of leather armor from his body. The queen elected to leave hers in place.

"What do you know about the Fae, Lady Sarah?" the king inquired, as he wrestled with a stubborn buckle on one of his greaves. "You say the tree is wrong? How would you know? The Fae faded into obscurity hundreds of years ago."

"I, er," Sarah cleared her throat and started again. "I may have been approached by the Fae king and queen."

Surprised, both Kri'Entu and Ny'Callé's eyebrows shot straight up. The king dropped the piece of armor he had been holding and sat back in his chair.

"Please, continue."

"Either they asked me for help or I have a very vivid imagination," Sarah decided. "Until I see evidence which proves otherwise, I'll assume it wasn't my imagination. The dream was too real. I still remember it like I was just there five minutes ago."

Kri'Entu cocked his head. "Just there? Where? The Fae city?"

Sarah shook her head. "Not Vineelm. That's not what they called it."

The queen sat forward in her chair. "What were their names, Lady Sarah? Did they say?"

"The queen's name was Ria and the king's was Tivan."

"And they were the Fae?" Ny'Callé asked. "You're sure?"

"I saw their wings with my own two eyes," Sarah confirmed. "The problem is, I always thought the Fae were tiny humans with wings."

The king gave her a quizzical look. "They *are*, Lady Sarah. Were they not so when you saw them?"

"They were the same size as me, Your Majesty."

"They were the same size as you, or were you the same

size as they?" Ny'Callé curiously asked.

Sarah's eyes opened wide. Had she been their size?

"It certainly didn't feel like I was shrunk," Sarah began, "but I wouldn't put it past them. I guess it's possible I was their size."

"Did they say what they wanted?" the king asked.

"Only that they were dying and they wanted our help. Mine and my husband's. Those were their words."

The king glanced briefly at Steve before looking back at her. Kri'Entu waited patiently, as though he was expecting her to elaborate why the Fae decided to ask them, and not the Kri'yans, for help. Steve cleared his throat, causing both the king and queen to look at him.

"Can I ask you why the Fae aren't in any of your history books? Was there some type of disagreement between the two of you?"

Kri'Entu shrugged. "All that is known about the Fae is that there was some type of falling out between our two species. The Fae parted ways amicably, and respectfully went their separate ways. I had always assumed the Fae were still out there but if I were asked, I couldn't begin to say where they were now."

"You've never looked?" Steve asked.

Kri'Entu shook his head. "Not once. I've always felt that I should honor their decision to go, and I have not once broken it."

"Have any of your predecessors?" Sarah wanted to know. "Are you aware of any attempts to reestablish contact with the Fae?"

"Not that I'm aware of, Lady Sarah," the king answered. "I always figured if they needed help all they had to do was ask. Now I learn that they apparently need the help but chose to ask someone else. This concerns me."

"Don't read too much into it," Steve cautioned. "Maybe it's something that only we can do. You are the king. I don't think you're allowed to get involved, even if you wanted to."

"But I *do* want to," the king muttered. The queen took his hand in hers and squeezed it reassuringly. "How can I help?"

"By not helping," Sarah advised. "I think you're right.

You should honor their request. If we determine that you're allowed to help, we'll let you know."

Kri'Entu nodded. "If permission is given, then I expect to be notified at once."

Chapter 2 — Validated Vision

S o where do we start?" Steve asked, eyeing the waterfront. Visible in the distance were at least a dozen islands, each looking as identical as the next. The last time he had seen that many islands in such close proximity was when he and Sarah had visited Puget Sound in Washington State. The Evergreen State had a popular ferry system that was frequently used by the locals whenever they wanted to go island hopping. Too bad a system like that didn't exist here. "We need a plan."

"Well, ordinarily I'd say we should see if we can find a map and go from there."

"We just came from R'Tal," her husband pointed out. "They had one mother of a map. Why do you need another one?"

Sarah turned on her heel and headed toward the busy coastal village. "You saw what I did. There are a ton of islands out there. I'm willing to wager there's more than what the cartographer has selected to be on the map. I counted twenty-five. We're going to need some way to find out which ones we've searched."

Steve groaned. "Do you plan on searching them all?"

"If we have to, yes. Dynwe is on one of those islands. We have to find it. We need to see if we can help the Fae."

"So, you're thinking there might be a local map that shows more islands than the king's map?"

Sarah nodded. "I hope so, otherwise we'll have to sketch each island as we go, so we know we don't end up searching the same island twice."

"Too bad they don't have a tourist center," Steve mused. He glanced around the busy street and watched as several fishermen unloaded their hauls. A number of birds were circling about overhead, which instantly caused Steve to seek shelter. He and his feathered adversaries had a longstanding arrangement: they wouldn't poop on him and he wouldn't use them as targets for his fire thrower jhorun. Not that he ever would use a live animal as a target, but if the right circumstances presented themselves, namely a certain substance appearing on his head or his clothes, he might be tempted.

Sarah took his arm and pulled him down the street toward a large building. Villagers could be seen ducking in and out of the structure, some clutching items tightly to their chest, and others escorting sullen children away from the building. Steve looked back at her and raised an eyebrow. He hooked a thumb in the house's direction.

"Are you heading toward that? Are they giving away maps?"

"That's the constable's office," Sarah told him. "If anyone would know about the islands around here it would be the constable. Besides, we know him."

"We do? How?"

"That is Constable Fensham's office. He's Lissa's father, remember?"

Steve snapped his fingers. "That's right. I had forgotten. Well, let's see if he's there."

Husband and wife stepped inside the open doors and followed an older man and a boy down a hallway on the right. The boy couldn't have been more than fourteen years old, and from the way he hung his head, and the way the older man was glaring at him, they must have been father and son. The boy must have been there to answer for some type of trouble.

The hallway abruptly dead-ended into a spacious room occupied by a large desk, walls of bookcases stuffed with papers, and a long counter which ran the length of the room. The counter was against the far wall and was filled with all manner of things. Dirks, a quiver of arrows, figurines, several sacks, three helmets, and a stack of books could be seen. A brawny man in his mid-forties, replete with a short, trimmed beard and a thick head of auburn hair, sat behind the desk, staring impassively at two older gentlemen who wouldn't stop glaring at one another. With a sigh, he turned to the man on his left.

"Remus, I'm waiting."

The man on the right turned to his companion and cackled at him. "You heard him. He wants to know where it is."

"Sunk it, I did."

The first man shook his head and scowled. "You know you didn't, Remus. You got just as much at stake in her as I do."

"You shut your mouth, Boris."

"Make me, Remus."

"Enough," Fensham snapped, silencing them both instantly. "Remus, you need to produce the vessel or you'll be spending tonight, and every consecutive night until it's located, in irons. Is that what you want?"

The old man stubbornly crossed his arms across his chest and scowled. Thankfully he didn't say anything. Satisfied, as though Remus had just admitted his guilt, Fensham nodded.

"Good. That's what I thought. I'm glad you came to your senses, Remus. It's his boat just as much as it is yours. Now, you and your brother divide up your haul, evenly and fairly like you always do, and go about your business."

The two old men pushed by them, muttering darkly as they passed. Steve suppressed a smile and winked at Sarah, who smiled back at him. She eyed the pair directly in front of them. What problem could they have had? Fensham, who had been scribbling some notes on a piece of parchment, glanced up as the father and son approached and sighed heavily. He tossed his quill onto his desk and deliberately capped his bottle of ink.

"Bertram. Would you care to take a guess as to why you and your son have been summoned to my office again?"

"Whatever you think my son has done," Bertram hesitantly began, "I can assure you he's innocent. My son told me he's innocent and I believe him."

Fensham pushed back from his desk and studied the father and son pair. "Is that so? Do you even know what he did? Has he admitted it to you yet?"

"I have no idea what he *allegedly* did," Bertram hastily fired back.

"Pratt, you have precisely five seconds to come clean with your father."

A look of defiance fluttered across the young man's face.

"I have witnesses, Pratt."

In less time than it takes to blink an eye, the youth's face transformed from defiance to sheer terror.

"Time's up."

"Alright!" the boy shrieked out. Pratt's face was so red that it was practically glowing. "I did it! I'll take my punishment. Now can I go?"

Bertram placed a hand on his son's shoulder and spun him around, looking him in the eye. "You told me you had stopped stealing, boy. I'll tan your hide if I find out otherwise."

"I didn't!" Pratt protested. "I didn't steal anything!"

"Then what did you do?"

The boy's face colored. He mumbled something but it was much too soft to overhear. Bertram cuffed his son on the back of his head.

"Try that again, boy, only louder this time."

"Your son was caught defacing the school," Fensham announced, keeping his voice neutral.

Bertram started sputtering with rage. "What? You did *what*, boy? I didn't raise you to be disrespectful. How did you do it? When? What kind of damage are we talking about?"

"The damage is minimal," Fensham coolly responded, seeing how the boy had clammed up and was refusing to lift his eyes from the ground. "It's nothing a bucket of soap and water can't remedy."

"What the blazes did you do, boy?" Bertram was so angry that flecks of spittle were flying out of his mouth. "Why would the constable imply something needed to be cleaned? Did you vandalize the school? Since when do you like getting your hands dirty?"

"He didn't use his hands," Fensham added. This time the constable's mouth quivered, fighting to keep a straight face.

"Oh, please don't," Pratt pleaded in a soft whisper.

"You didn't use your hands?" Bertram exclaimed, confused. "Do I want to know what you used?"

The constable cleared his throat. "I can only hope either he was trying to mark his territory or else had consumed too much water. Class was still in session and the entire younger class was witness to everything. Quinn, the schoolmaster, believes young Mister Pratt has suffered enough but would like him to clean the affected walls."

"The school will get a new paint job," Bertram vowed, glaring at his son. "The entire school. Are we clear, son?"

Pratt nodded sullenly.

Fensham took up his quill and reopened the bottle of ink. He dabbed the point inside a few times before making notes on another piece of parchment. He looked up and nodded at Bertram.

"I will consider the matter closed. Do keep an eye on your son for me. I grow tired of his impertinence."

"This will be the last time we're in here, rest assured." Bertram grabbed his son by the arm and forcibly pulled him out of the room.

Sarah's eyes were watering so much from trying to hold back her laughter that she was unable to answer when Fensham asked a couple of questions. He wanted to know who they were and what the nature of their business was. The constable's eyes locked onto Steve's and he slowly stood. He looked back at Sarah and nodded his head.

"I thought I recognized you. You're the Nohrin. You two

are the reason my little Lissa returned to me. I wasn't aware you were in our village. What can Capily do for you?"

"We need to check out your islands," Steve cheerfully explained. "I don't suppose you have a map which shows them all, do you?"

Fensham stared at the two of them for a few moments before gesturing to a map tacked up on the wall closest to his desk.

"Are you looking for something or someone? Do you require assistance?"

Sarah shook her head. "We would just like to take a look at them. Do you know how many there are? Have they all been properly mapped?"

Fensham sadly shook his head. "I've been petitioning the king for years to have a cartographer properly chart them all. To answer your question, no; there isn't a map that shows them all because they number too many. Last year a fisherman strove to be the first to visit them all. He claimed he visited over fifty different islands."

"Fifty?" Steve exclaimed, dismayed. "I had no idea there were so many."

Fensham grunted once and turned to the map on the wall. He started tapping places. "There are over a dozen, large enough to require three days to explore. You can see them here. Then there are close to a dozen half that size, and of course there are some even smaller. What really is worthy of being plotted? A piece of dirt or rock sticking up out of the water? If that were the case then I couldn't even begin to guess how many actual islands are out there."

Steve shared a look with her. "This is going to take a lot longer than either of us originally thought."

"What choice do we have?" Sarah asked helplessly.

"So you *are* looking for something?" Fensham interjected, nodding. "I suspected as much. Perhaps if you tell me what it is then I might be able to help you."

Steve laid a friendly hand on the constable's shoulder. "I'm sorry, pal. We have to keep this quiet."

Fensham shrugged and pulled the map from the wall. He folded it and reverently held it out to Steve.

"Take this. May it be of use to you."

Steve took the map and immediately handed it to Sarah, who pocketed it and smiled at the constable.

"Thank you. We'll return it as soon as we can."

"Take your time. There is no rush. I haven't looked at that map in months."

An hour later, after purchasing some supplies from the all-to-eager vendors, husband and wife approached one of the many piers along the shore and stopped. They consulted the map and saw that the closest plotted island was somewhat southwest of their present location, but a quick glance out at the open water confirmed what they already suspected. In reality there were far more. In fact, there was a small island about half a mile away. It was heavily treed and gave every indication there wasn't one bit of open land anywhere. Both of them stared silently at the island for a few minutes.

"Well," Steve began, as he scratched an errant itch behind his ear, "you said we're looking for a tree. That one has a whole mess of 'em. Want to start there?"

Sarah shrugged, folded the map, and handed it to Steve. "We might as well. Here, you're a better artist than I am. You get to start sketching out which islands we've been to."

"Oh, swell," Steve grumbled. He took the pencil Sarah was holding out to him, unfolded the map, and seeing that there wasn't a place for him to work, dropped down to the ground. He started to sketch out the island's shape when Sarah smacked the pencil out of his hand. Confused, he looked up and saw that she was holding a blank piece of parchment out to him.

He unfolded the large piece of paper and set it next to the map. Next, he quickly sketched out the coastline, taking into account the curve of the land and the huge peninsula that was jutting out into the water, and placed an X where he thought the island would be. He'd have to wait to sketch the actual shape once they were on it.

Fourteen Xs and four hours later, Sarah watched Steve rise painfully from the ground of the latest island they'd explored. Her husband tried to rub the kinks out of his aching back. This island, just like the dozen or so they had already checked, was completely covered by trees. On a side note both husband and wife were pleasantly surprised when they learned the islands weren't nearly as large as they looked from the water.

Thanks to Sarah's jhorun, they were easily able to jump from one side of an island to the next, and then to jump anywhere else Sarah could see they needed to go. The tiny chunks of land were sometimes so close together that they could have waded through shallow water to get to the next one. Other times the next nearest island was at least ten miles away. With her jhorun, it was no effort to jump from one island to the next. It was just time consuming.

Sarah retrieved the map from the ground, folded it, and tucked it back into a pocket. She waited until her husband had folded his rudimentary map and had shoved it into his back pocket. She looked around the secluded glade and decided this was as good a place as any to have lunch. Thanks to an arrangement with the queen, and consequently with the chief cook, whenever she and Steve went out on an excursion, a picnic lunch would be packed and waiting for them on a table in the Antechamber.

She held out her arms and teleported their lunch to herself. She smiled the instant the old pack appeared in her arms. She shouldn't have been able to do what she just did, since the Antechamber was specifically designed and enchanted against jhorun. Even so, there were a small handful of people who had jhorun strong enough to defeat the protective enchantments cast upon the king's private chamber. She and her husband were two of them.

Sarah set the pack on the ground and settled beneath the shade of a large pine tree. About to object, Steve saw that she was setting out containers of food and wisely refrained from saying anything. Sarah unwrapped a chedra—a meat and cheese roll—and handed it to her husband. She did the same for herself.

They ate their lunch in silence, each reflecting on the events of the day. Steve grunted once and held out a hand to Sarah, all without looking up. Sarah's eyes narrowed. She looked around their makeshift campsite, selected a broken twig, and dropped it onto his outstretched hand. His hand automatically closed, but then sprang open as if he thought he had latched on to a bug.

"What'd you give me that for?"

"Well, what did you expect? You grunted, so I assumed we just reverted back to caveman days. I figured you must want a slab of meat or a big heavy club. The stick was the best thing I could find."

Steve regarded her as though she had finally lost her mind. "I wanted the map, you goofball."

"Then ask me for the map. I don't speak caveman."

Once the map was spread out on the ground, Steve compared it to the one he had created. He pointed at the last half dozen islands they had visited.

"You have to admit that most of the islands we've seen so far could have been prime candidates for your Fae Island."

"None of them had that tree," Sarah reminded him. "It's kind of a deal breaker, dear. No huge tree then no faerie city. It means wrong island."

"Don't you think if this tree is as big as you say it is, we'd be able to see it without stepping foot on the island? These islands aren't that big. We'd see it."

"Not necessarily," Sarah countered. "Do you remember when you mentioned something about the faeries being as big as me and then suggested maybe I had been shrunk?"

Steve nodded. "Yeah, what about it? Do you think that you had been shrunk when you were on that island?"

Sarah shrugged. "It's hard to say. How would I have known? Everything looked like it was on the right scale."

"Except for that big tree," Steve added.

"Right. With the exception of *that* tree, I'd say I was normal sized."

Steve suddenly stood and started pacing. "Maybe we're looking at this the wrong way."

"What do you mean?" Sarah wanted to know.

"If the faeries were living on an island within eyesight of Capily, I think it's safe to say they would have been noticed."

Sarah nodded. "I'll go along with that."

"Now," Steve continued, warming up, "using that same

logic, if what the queen told you is true and they *are* living on an island off the coast of Capily, I'd say we need to focus our attention on islands that are farther away from the coast." Her husband looked off to the west, out over open water. "We should be looking for islands that are as far away from the coast as possible."

Sarah shook her head. "No, I don't think so. Ria, the Fae queen, specifically told me that their island was off the western coast of Capily. She didn't say that it was way out to sea, but off the coast. It can't be as far away as you're suggesting."

"Hmmph," Steve grunted, silently disagreeing. "Then where do you want to search?"

"I think you're partially right," Sarah told him, as she also turned to face west. "I say we should look for islands close enough to be visible from the coast but far enough away to discourage people from trying to explore."

"That's where I disagree," Steve argued. "If someone in Capily can see this island, they're gonna wonder what's on it. I still say it has to be out of range from the coast."

Sarah was silent as she studied the open water. She held a hand over her eyes and studied the western horizon. Then she looked up at the clear blue sky for a few moments. She pointed out at the water. "What does that look like to you?"

Her husband looked where she indicated. He held a hand over his eyes and squinted. Sarah shook her head and sighed.

"I'm so getting you in to see the eye doctor. Or getting you glasses."

"Bite me."

"Well? What do you see?"

"A fog bank. So what?"

"A fog bank," Sarah repeated. "On a warm sunny day like today?"

Steve's brow furrowed. He glanced up at the cloudless sky and then returned his gaze to the distant bank of clouds. It was more than five miles out to sea and, judging by the size of it, at least a few miles long.

"That doesn't necessarily mean anything. You need humidity for fog to form. You may have noticed, but that huge body of water out *thataway* would accomplish just that."

"That is a lot of water," Sarah observed. She saw her husband smile victoriously. "However…"

His smile vanished.

"In order for fog to appear, the humidity has to be extremely high. Yes, there's water out there, but believe it or not, it's not enough to cause fog. There are no clouds. There's no water in the air. It's too warm and sunny for that."

"What are you trying to say?"

Sarah pointed at the distant fog bank. "What do you want to bet that fog is hiding something?"

"Oh, come on," Steve protested. "Do you really think if that fog was hiding something, it wouldn't have been discovered by now? That's gotta be the oldest trick in the book."

Sarah turned to look east, toward the distant shore.

"I'll bet we're far enough away so that people on the shore wouldn't be able to see the fog, let alone know it was there."

"Again, what's your point? You want to teleport out to a bank of fog? What if there isn't a hidden island there? What if there's no land? You'd be dropping us right in the water."

"So what if I do? You can dry us, can't you?"

"Well, yeah, I suppose."

"Steve, it's an anomaly. I think we should check it out."

"How are you going to teleport there? You can't see anything but the fog. If there's land, it's completely hidden from sight."

Sarah clasped his hand tightly in hers. "Just trust me."

Steve screwed his eyes shut, "Just tell me when you're gonna do it. I'll take a deep breath. I would recommend you do the same, Ms. Smarty-pants."

"We're not getting wet. There's an island there. I just know it."

"Mm-hmm. Deep breath."

Sarah smacked her husband on the arm. With his own hand. Hard.

The coast of the island they had been on vanished, replaced instantly by a fog-covered wooded glade. Narrow beams of sunlight filtered in through the treetops, giving the glade an ethereal appearance. Husband and wife stood silently, hand in hand, in the middle of the clearing. It was deathly quiet. There weren't even any birds chirping.

"Told you," Sarah whispered.

"You were lucky, lady. I was totally expecting to get dumped in the water."

"If you still want to go swimming, then you're talking to the right person. Say the word and I'll drop you out in the ocean."

"You love me too much to do something like that."

"I love you just enough to keep you in line."

"Snot. So, what's the word? Is this the right place?"

Sarah released his hand and started exploring the glade. "I'm not sure. It certainly feels right. I won't know until I look around for a bit. Come on. Let's see how big this island is."

They turned to the left and headed south. At least Sarah thought it was south. She might not be able to see the sun, but she was fairly certain south was to the left. She could never fully explain to her navigationally impaired husband how she always seemed to sense which direction was which. She just *knew*. Just like she knew south was to the left. Besides, something was pulling her that way. Until she knew for certain it was the Fae, then she was going to keep that little tidbit to herself.

Thirty minutes later, they emerged from the thick of the trees into another clearing. This one was larger, almost perfectly spherical in shape, and devoid of anything but soft grass. Sarah approached a spot in the center of the knee-high grass and bent down to run a hand along the tops of the grass blades.

"This is it. I was right here. This is where I woke up."

Steve joined her to stare down at the indicated patch of grass.

"If you were sleeping on the grass, then shouldn't it have been tamped down? I don't see any bent blades, or depressions, or anything else that would indicate you were here."

"It was a dream, remember? They said that my 'essence' was here but in reality, I was still lying next to you. So, physically, I was never here."

"Like that clears anything up," Steve muttered.

Sarah took his hand and pulled him close. "When I woke up, I went *that* way. Come on. Let's see what's there."

"What made you go that way?" Steve asked, curious.

"The only thing I remember was being pulled, firmly, in one direction. I didn't think I was in any danger so I didn't object."

Steve shrugged as he looked all around. "Alrighty then. We go that way."

"What are you looking for?"

"Well, if this was the place you were at before, then I was checking to see if anything looked different."

"You mean you're checking to see if we shrunk?"

"Right."

"I haven't seen any huge trees yet. I think we're good."

Sarah closed her eyes as they walked. This was definitely the right place. Her skin was tingling. Her pulse was racing. There was something here, something in the air that made her feel more alive than she had ever felt in her life. She looked over at Steve. His face appeared guarded. She was pretty sure he didn't believe her when she said that she had been there before. She stopped three steps later.

"What is it?" her husband asked, alarmed. His hands had turned red. "Is something the matter?"

Sarah turned to him and smiled. "Do you believe I was here before?"

Steve stared at her. Sarah could just picture him wondering what her reaction would be if he answered her honestly.

"I believe that you believe," he finally answered.

"And if I can prove it?"

"How?"

"See those three trees? All lined up in a row?"

"Yeah. What about 'em?"

"Directly on the other side will be a path."

"Mm-hmm. You sound sure of yourself."

"Because I've been here before," she reiterated.

They walked to the three trees growing side-by-side and paused. Steve leaned around the closest trunk and noticed a well-cared for cobblestone path.

"Okay, you're making a believer out of me."

Sarah stepped onto the path, pulled her husband to her side, and headed off. Knowing which way to go was easy. All the memories from her dream were still fresh in her mind. Sights, sounds, smells--as though she had just woken up from that dream a few minutes ago.

Guiding her husband deeper into the wooded island, Sarah drew up short. The trees! The trees had tiny little dots of light on them! She was certain Steve would claim it was light reflected by something, but she knew otherwise. She had found the city. All she had to do now was...

"Whoa!" Steve exclaimed, interrupting her thoughts. "Check that out! What's causing that, glowing bugs?"

Rushing forward, confident the tall majestic pine tree was where she remembered it, Sarah guided them toward the trees she knew was the Fae city. The *arboreal* city, Sarah remembered, using Steve's word-of-the-day.

"This is it!" Sarah excitedly told him. "This is the city! Do you see the lights? Running up and down the trunks?"

"I thought you said they'd look like skyscrapers."

"Look! Look at the tree from this side!"

Together they walked around the trunk to inspect the opposite side. Steve whistled with amazement.

From the forest side of the city, the tree was just that. A tree. But, entering the city and gazing at the other side of the tree, a whole different scene appeared. The tree had been carved, from the base of the trunk an inch or two above ground level, all the way up as high as they could see. Doorways, windows, intricate stairways that spiraled in full loops up the trunk, everything had been painstakingly carved onto the surface of the tree.

"Man, those carved trees are everywhere!" Steve whispered.

Sarah slowly turned. It was just as regal and wondrous as she remembered.

"Welcome to Dynwe," she reverently announced. "I knew it was real. I just knew it!"

"Okay, okay, you were right and I was wrong."

"Again," Sarah added. Her husband grumbled at her. She continued to stare at the closest carved tree. "The city is so pretty, don't you think?"

"Umm, I can't help but notice how small those windows and doors are, not to mention the stairs," Steve announced. "I definitely don't think you were shrunk, my dear. I think the opposite. The king and queen must have increased their size to talk to you."

Sarah started to respond when her eyes landed on a trunk much larger than its neighbors. In fact, the trunk easily dwarfed every other tree. Together, they stared at the base of the gigantic tree and slowly lifted their gaze to peer at the distant canopy far over their heads.

"That's one mother of a tree," Steve observed. "How did we not see this from that other island? Look how tall this thing is. I swear the top would be touching the clouds, if there were any up there. There's no way we missed that."

Sarah's gaze dropped back down to the ground. "Speaking of things we're missing, what happened to the fog? Why isn't it foggy in here? Look around the city. No fog. However, I can still see it through the trees right over there. Outside of the city, fog. Inside, nothing. Why do you think that is?"

"At this point, it's anyone's guess," Steve muttered. "It's probably their doing."

The path sloped downward as they approached the base of the enormous trunk. As before, the mammoth evergreen's prevalent root system became a canopy over their heads as they descended lower. And there were the two amethyst gemstone doors. Both doors were closed but silently swung open as they approached.

"It doesn't look as healthy as it did last time," Sarah recalled. As if on cue, several pine needles bounced off her shoulder and fell to the ground. The ground, she was dismayed to see, was already covered by a thick blanket of the needles. That couldn't be good.

"Maybe it's the light," Steve suggested.

"What about it?"

"The light isn't the greatest in here. Maybe it'd look better if the light was brighter. As soon as this fog passes, we should take another look."

Sarah scuffed the ground with the toe of her shoe.

"And the needles? Look how many there are. The ground is covered with them. I think the tree is sick. I didn't see all these needles before. I'll bet you if I swept the needles away from those doors, we'd find a glowing path."

"Didn't you say that the queen told you they were dying? Is that what they meant? Could they have been talking about the tree?"

"It's the only tree that doesn't look so hot," Sarah observed, studying a few nearby. "Maybe you're right. Come on. I want to see if the king and queen are here."

Confident and unafraid, Sarah strolled through the open gemstone doors. She turned back in time to see Steve swallow nervously and edge out after her.

"There's nothing to be afraid of," she assured him. "Had they wanted to do something to us, then they would have by now."

"That's comforting."

The exterior of the tree might have been looking less than stellar, but the interior was still as spectacular as she remembered. The walls had richly colored tapestries hanging on pegs. Thick, woven rugs practically covered every square inch of the stone floor. Several hearths, one on each wall, had bright, crackling fires in them. Resting in their holders, spaced evenly ten feet apart, were torches lining the walls. The torches were unlit. The green glow she remembered seeing the first time was also mysteriously absent.

"Where is everyone?" Sarah wondered. "There were tons of people here before."

"Could they be hiding from us?" Steve wanted to know. "I'm sure they must know we aren't here to hurt them."

"You know that and I know that. I guess they don't. Come on. The thrones are just through that door over there."

The hall leading to the throne room was just as devoid of personnel as the rest of the castle. Their footsteps echoed loudly throughout the tree's interior as the two of them transitioned from the rug-covered entry into a large arched hallway. Visible at the end of the hallway was an archway that opened into another large room. It was the throne room. There, just as they had been before, were the two jewel-encrusted thrones. This time, however, they were empty. Sarah pointed at a closed door to the left of the thrones.

"Last time they took me in there. You'll find a large round granite table. It's where I had that dinner I told you about."

"Want to check it out?" Steve asked.

Sarah nodded. "Yes. We've come this far. I want to see if the king and queen are in there."

Sarah tried the door handle but it refused to budge. It wasn't locked, no. A locked door handle will usually allow the handle to slightly wiggle back and forth. This handle refused to move, almost as if it had been carved directly into the door and was never designed to be used as a method of entry.

Sarah suddenly smiled. It was a test. They wanted to see if it was really her. Without asking first, Sarah grabbed her husband's hand and immediately teleported the two of them to the other side of the door.

The large granite table was there. Its surface was completely empty. However, the room wasn't unoccupied. Ria, Queen of the Fae, was sitting in the same seat as the last time Sarah had seen her. Ria turned to Sarah, smiled, and slowly stood.

"Lady Sarah. I was wondering when you were going to turn up. You're late!"

Chapter 3 — Aftershocks

"What do you mean, I'm late?" Sarah demanded, growing angry. "We got here just as soon as we could! Do you know how many islands we had to check before we found this one? You could have made it a little easier for us."

"Why didn't you simply teleport here?" the Fae Queen asked with a twinkle in her eye. "That's what I assumed you would do."

"Why *didn't* we teleport here?" Steve asked, turning to her. "If the memory was that fresh in your head, then why couldn't you have taken us straight here?"

Sarah stared at her husband; surprise etched all over her face. "I didn't even think about that. Wow. That would have saved a lot of time, wouldn't it?" Sarah giggled. "I guess deep down I still thought it was just a dream and figured I could only teleport to a place that was real."

Ria rose from her seat at the table and approached them. She smiled warmly at Sarah before turning to look at Steve.

"I do not believe I have had the pleasure of making your

acquaintance. Lady Sarah, would you kindly introduce me to your husband?"

"Oh. Of course." Sarah performed the introductions and looked around. "Umm, I don't see the king anywhere."

"Tivan is away, I'm afraid. He is ensuring all of our people are safe and accounted for. Ordinarily he would have returned by now, only journeys now take us much longer since all Fae have been grounded." Ria's wings snapped up, fluttered once, and slowly lowered until they were hidden from view. She sighed heavily and gave Sarah a *what-can-you-do* smile.

"All the Fae have been grounded?" Steve asked, confused. "If you don't mind me asking, why? Did something happen to your wings?"

"A Fae is a complex creature," Ria explained, as she slowly sank into her chair, prompting husband and wife to join her. "In order for us to fly, we must be in constant contact with our Tree, be it mental or physical. It sustains us, nurtures us, and protects us. The Tree also supplies us with all the jhorun we'll ever need. All Fae need jhorun."

"Speaking of all the Fae, where are they?" Sarah asked. "I could see Fae everywhere the last time I was here. Now it's like a ghost town out there."

"My Fae are hiding deep beneath the roots of the Tree. They are frightened and worried. Tivan and I have apprised our people of our present plight. As you may have imagined, it didn't go over well."

Steve leaned forward to rest his elbows on the table, earning himself an instant frown of disapproval from Sarah.

"You told my wife that you're dying. Why? I assume this tree you're talking about is the big one we're in now? We can see that it doesn't look healthy. Is that the problem?"

Ria nodded. "All Fae share a symbiotic relationship with their home tree. Their lives are forever linked. Whatever affects the tree affects us as well. To answer your question, Steve, no. Our Tree isn't sick. It's dying. As a result, we're dying."

"Save the tree, save the Fae, huh?" Steve quipped.

Sarah elbowed him in his gut, "It's not a laughing matter. We have to find out what's wrong with their tree."

"We already know what's wrong with our Tree," Ria clarified. "All its jhorun has been siphoned away. We, the Fae, have channeled what jhorun we have left back into the Tree. That's why the Tree hasn't died yet. It's struggling to keep us alive, but it's also why the Fae are grounded. The Tree has lost its ability to supply us with jhorun, which means once we've used what we have left, our jhorun will be gone, too. That's why the Fae will not fly."

"You want to conserve your jhorun as much as possible," Sarah observed. "For your tree. I get it."

Ria nodded. "Aye. For our Tree."

"You mentioned that you know what is wrong with your tree," Steve recalled. "Do you know how to heal it? Do you know what it will take to reverse the effects of whatever it is that caused it to lose its jhorun?"

Ria finally smiled. "Aye. There is but one solution to save our Tree."

Sarah eyed her husband. Why did she get the feeling that this wasn't going to be easy?

"Okay, I'll bite. What will … wait a minute. Did anyone else hear that?"

"What?" Steve asked, looking first at Ria, and then at the rest of the room. The Fae queen looked just as confused as Steve felt.

"Did anyone else hear it?" Sarah wanted to know as she pushed back from the table and stood. "It sounded like someone was ringing a school bell, but from a great distance."

A look of alarm passed over Ria's beautiful face. She closed her eyes for a few moments and remained motionless. After nearly ten seconds, the queen's eyes opened. Once more they filled with tears.

"My love, tell me it isn't so," the Fae queen softly whispered, breaking the silence. "Are you certain? Where are you?"

About to tell the queen that there was no one else in the room, Steve snapped his mouth closed as soon as he noticed Sarah holding a finger to her lips.

"I will be right there. Wait for me." Ria gave them an apologetic look. "I'm sorry. I must go. I am surprised you heard that bell, Lady Sarah. Only Fae are supposed to be able to hear it. That bell is only to be rung under dire emergencies. Again, I'm sorry. I must be off!"

Ria gathered her skirts and rushed out of the room. Sarah grabbed her husband's hand, and pulled him along as she bolted after the fleeing queen. Sarah had noticed Ria said 'my love,' which meant she was talking with Tivan. The queen was going to join him, wherever he happened to be. It didn't take a world-famous sleuth to figure out that Ria was headed outside. A quick glance at the slowly closing gemstone doors confirmed her suspicions.

"Where are we going?" Steve quietly asked, increasing his pace to a rapid walk.

"Something has spooked Ria. Come on. I want to see if we can help."

Once they had passed through the sparkling amethyst doors, Sarah cursed silently to herself. Ria was nowhere to be found. Outside, it was dead quiet. Sarah helplessly looked at her husband.

"Which way did she go?" Steve demanded. "She wasn't running that fast."

"I guess she could still be inside the tree," Sarah suggested, turning to look back. "She … no, wait. There she is!"

Steve looked at where Sarah was pointing and discovered why neither of them had spotted Ria. The Fae queen was already past the outskirts of Dynwe, rapidly approaching the thickest part of the forest. In only a few moments she'd be swallowed up by the trees. Steve prepared to sprint after her when Sarah pulled him to a stop.

"There's no need. Did you see where she's going? The glade. I'll bet you she's heading toward the water."

Bringing up an image of the familiar glade, Sarah teleported the two of them. They were just in time to see Ria, now much closer, again vanish deeper into the woods.

Steve groaned. "She's a nimble little minx, isn't she?"

"Something's scared her," Sarah reminded him. "It has to do with Tivan. I'd say she has a right to be upset."

Sarah's next jump placed the two of them at the water's edge, looking at the distant shores of Capily. Ria and Tivan were standing nearby, embracing. Ria was softly sobbing while Tivan stared impassively at the distant shore. Passing alarmingly close was one of Capily's huge three-masted galleons, returning from a trading trip overseas. Its bow was facing east as it sailed away from them.

"What is it?" Sarah softly asked. "What's wrong?"

Tivan's grim expression focused on her. He slowly pointed at the open water.

"Perhaps if you could be a little more specific," Steve suggested, trying valiantly to keep the sarcasm out of his voice. "It's just a ship. I've sure you've seen 'em before."

Tivan turned to Steve and raised a questioning eyebrow. Steve started to extend his hand when he paused. He opted for a bow instead.

"I'm Steve. I believe you know my wife, Sarah?"

Sarah's face colored. She apologized and made the introductions.

Tivan bowed. "A pleasure. You are welcome here."

Steve kept his guarded smile plastered onto his face. Sarah couldn't blame him. Tivan might have given him his welcome, but the tone of his voice was anything but welcoming. The Fae king was worried, but Sarah didn't understand why. The ship was harmless. It was sailing away from them. She was told the Fae couldn't fly, so maybe Ria was worried her Fae would have nowhere to flee if suddenly faced with a group of humans? Could the Fae even swim?

"Hey, where's all the fog?" Steve suddenly asked, as he looked around the rocky shoreline. "The sun's out. Perhaps it burned off?"

Surprised, Sarah looked at the Fae monarchs. Each of their faces bore a troubled expression. Comprehending, Sarah nodded. The fog, which must have acted as their protection from the outside world, was gone. That must mean they could be seen from Capily. Was that why the ship passed so close? She turned to look back toward Dynwe and the center of the island. A ghostly outline of the gargantuan tree was becoming visible. She gasped with shock.

"Dynwe's enchantments are failing," Tivan answered miserably. "The last of the Fae magic is almost gone. When that happens this place will be seen for what it is. An island. Humans, as they are wont to do, will want to investigate and explore."

"How much longer before your tree becomes fully visible?" Steve asked.

"It's only a matter of time. The fog has disappeared. The spell that concealed our Tree is failing, too. A day or two, no more. Sooner or later, we will be spotted."

Sarah stepped up on a large boulder and shaded her eyes with her hand. She peered intently at the distant shoreline. "I think it'll be much sooner than that."

Alarmed, Tivan hurried to Sarah's side. "What is it? Why would you say that?"

"The ship has changed course. It was headed to Capily. Now I believe the ship is turning around. Guys, I think it's coming back this way."

"Oh, come on," Steve complained, looking back at the ghostly image of the huge tree. "There's no way they could have seen that."

"No," Tivan agreed, "it is unlikely they have spotted the tree. However, they have probably noticed that there is now a large island where there wasn't one before. That, unfortunately, would bear further investigation."

Steve held a hand over his eyes and stared at the distant ship that was slowly turning around. There was no doubt about it. The ship was headed their way.

"Is there anything you guys can do?" Steve asked, turning to the Fae king and queen. "Can you bring the fog back?"

Tivan sadly shook his head. "Our jhorun has been exhausted. Until our tree has been restored, we will be utterly defenseless."

"I could sink it," Steve mused aloud as they watched the ship sail closer, "but I really don't want to do that. They didn't do anything wrong. It's just a ship full of curious humans."

"And I wouldn't want you to sink their ship," Ria added with a frown.

"I could try to scare them off," Steve suggested. "However, as soon as they see my flames, they're going to know who's responsible for them. Unfortunately, my jhorun is very well known around these parts. Besides, that would damage the relationship we have with the Lentarians and that's something I don't want to risk."

"That's definitely out," Sarah agreed. "I may have an idea. Come on, we really should hide. If anyone on that ship pulls out a spyglass, and points it at this island, they're going to see us."

"Lady Sarah is right," Tivan announced. He pulled Ria back toward the safety of the trees. "We can hide in our Tree. With luck they won't be able to find us."

"Hide, schmide," Sarah scoffed. "No one is stepping foot on this island. Not today."

She peered intently through the trees at the approaching ship. At the rate it was sailing, it would be within range within ten minutes. Sarah cracked her knuckles. She would make certain that ship wouldn't get close enough to launch a landing vessel.

Closing her eyes, Sarah brought up a vision of the ship. She had to push them back to Capily, but how? Well, that was the easy part. She had learned several years ago that she could use her jhorun to move an object without having to teleport it. In this case, she could push a massive quantity of air directly at the oncoming ship. What would happen as a result? The ship, with three masts full of sails, would catch the wind and propel them in the opposite direction.

That ship has no business coming here, she told her jhorun. *We're going to push air into its sails and guide it back the other way.*

Her hands started to tingle. She clenched her fists, ordered her jhorun to move enough air to create a strong, powerful wind, and then directed it at the ship. Her hands sprung open.

A breeze appeared. The nearby trees rustled noisily as the wind increased in strength. Within moments, a powerful gale blew along the water's edge. Pebbles, leaves, pine needles, and a slew of other objects rose into the air and swirled about. The flying detritus showed Sarah the overall shape and size of the wind gust and she was impressed. She was definitely getting better at manipulating air currents.

She briefly recalled the last time she had used her jhorun to create a breeze. It had been just about a year ago when she had helped Steve's ancestors make the townsfolk of nineteenth century Coeur d'Alene, Idaho, think her mansion was haunted. Sarah smiled. It had worked then just as well as it was working now.

Cute and impressive. However, we're trying to drive that ship away, not clean up their shore, remember?

She sent the blast of air roaring straight toward the large ship. Its sails caught the wind and brought the ship to a sudden stop. She imagined tackle, fishing gear, crates, and personnel alike, all slammed forward. Muted curses came across the water.

I really should have turned it around first, Sarah scolded herself as she watched the ship get hammered by the wind. *If that boat capsizes, then people could get hurt. I don't want that. At all.*

An errant gust rammed the bow from the port side. The huge galleon shifted, turning around.

That's it, Sarah instructed, concentrating on the ship. *A little more. Once it's pointed east then let them have it.*

A minute later the ship, having been hammered mercilessly by the winds until the bow was facing east, began to move as the sails filled. Two minutes later the ship was already halfway across the channel on a direct intercept to Lentari's western shore.

Sarah smiled as she heard the dismayed shouts of the sailors trying valiantly to turn the ship back around, but to no avail. "That'll hold them," Sarah announced, emerging from the forest. She approached the water's edge. "The problem is, I don't know how long that will hold them. If they turn around and head back this way once the wind lets go, then we're sunk. Best case scenario is that they try again in a few days."

Steve beamed a smile at her, "Nicely done, babe. They don't know what hit 'em."

Ria pulled Sarah into a hug, "You have given us some time. You have my eternal thanks."

"It doesn't solve your immediate problem, though," Sarah pointed out, once Ria had released her.

Ria hooked her arm through her own and turned her around until she was facing away from the water. "Let us return to Dynwe. I have yet to tell you what we require of you."

"Require?" Steve repeated, frowning.

"You must forgive my wife," Tivan murmured, increasing his pace until he was walking side-by-side with Steve. "It is rare for the Fae to ask outsiders for help, and even more so for those outsiders to be human. She's exhausted. She means no ill will toward you humans."

"Are humans that bad?" Steve asked, curious. "What exactly happened between the Fae and the humans to cause you to go your separate ways?"

Tivan deliberately slowed in order to increase the gap between the men and the women. Steve slowed his own pace to match the Fae king.

"The specifics are unclear to me," the Fae king whispered to Steve, "as these events are before my time, what I can tell you is the humans abused our trust."

"How?" Steve asked, insanely curious.

"Lentari wasn't always the peaceful kingdom it is today," Tivan explained. "Dwarves warred with the dragons, the humans warred with the griffins, and essentially any other species you could think of warred with the other."

"Unpleasant times," Steve commented, with a grunt. "Got it."

"We, namely our ancestors, determined that our Fae princess was threatened by one of our own. Back then we even fought amongst ourselves, but that is a different story. We beseeched our human allies for help in protecting our princess."

"And they refused?" Steve exclaimed, annoyed. "What jerks."

Tivan smiled. "As a matter of fact, the human king agreed to help."

"Oh. So, what happened? They didn't do a good job and the princess ended up kidnapped, or hurt? Tell me she wasn't killed."

"Worse. The king married the princess to his only son."

"Oh, snap. I'll bet that didn't go over well."

"It didn't," Tivan agreed. "Both the princess and the

human prince swore it was true love but the Fae king of the time, my ancestor, disagreed. Thankfully, neither side declared war, but sadly, the alliance was broken that day."

"What happened to the princess?"

"What?"

"What happened to the princess?" Steve repeated, curious. "Did she stay with her human husband? Did he decide to live with the Fae? If you tell me that the parents made them split up, then I'm gonna be pissed. I hate lousy endings."

Taken aback, Tivan chuckled. "Honestly, I have no idea. I don't believe anyone has ever thought to ask before."

They arrived at the Tree and walked into the antechamber. Once they were all seated at the round granite table, Ria cleared her throat and began again.

"Now that we are all here, let me continue my narrative. I believe I was just about to reveal what it would take to restore our Tree to full health."

"That's right," Sarah agreed. "Please continue."

"We need pollen."

"Pollen?" Sarah repeated, frowning. "*Any* pollen or does it have to be a special kind?"

"Do you really think it would be something easy?" Steve chided. "If it were, they could have gotten it themselves."

Sarah, holding one of Steve's hands in her lap, dug her nails in as she clenched her hand. Steve whimpered, but dared not say anything.

"Only the pollen processed from a recently harvested pontal—specifically, the *orbsceia*—will resuscitate our Tree."

"A *what* flower … er, pontal?" Sarah asked, frowning. That was one she hadn't heard of before. Then again, she was in Lentari and not her own world. It wasn't that surprising.

"An orbsceia," Ria slowly repeated.

"Where can we find one?" Sarah immediately asked.

"What's it look like?" Steve asked at the same time.

Ria smiled fleetingly. "Lady Sarah, your answer is 'unknown' I'm afraid. The answer to your wonderful husband's question is a golden multi-petaled pontal of such beauty that anyone who gazes upon it will find themselves reduced to tears."

Steve snorted. "No offense, ma'am, but when I do see this thing, I can guarantee you that I won't be collapsing into tears."

Ria gave him a dazzling smile. "Only time will tell, good sir."

Sarah raised a hand. "Umm, excuse me? Did you say you didn't know where this flower can be found?"

Ria sighed heavily. Her eyes filled with tears, prompting Sarah to immediately reciprocate. The Fae queen dabbed at her eyes with a delicate square of lacey fabric.

"I wish I could say otherwise but I cannot. I'm sorry, Lady Sarah. You heard me correctly. We do not know where the flower is. We have been searching for it for months now. In fact, we began searching for it before we even realized the danger our Tree was facing."

Steve groaned. "So, you're telling me this flower, er pontal, is rare."

Ria sighed. "Aye."

"And it's clearly hard to find?"

Tivan nodded. "Extremely. Now, if you will excuse me, I must be off. I have not completed my search of the city."

Ria bowed. "Of course, my love."

Once the king departed, the conversation resumed. Steve held up a hand and waited until he had the queen's attention. Sarah could only smile watching her husband patiently wait for the queen to look his way.

"So, allow me to venture a guess," Steve began again. "There's only one of these super rare flowers left?"

Surprisingly, Ria shook her head. "As a matter of fact, no."

Husband and wife shared another look with each other. Steve smiled and nodded. "That's good to hear."

"The last time they were located, it was said there were three plants remaining which were bearing flowers."

Steve's smile faded. "Three? That's it? Well, I guess it's certainly better than one, only not by much. Wait. If you don't know where to find these things then how do you know there are only three left?"

"You're right," Ria conceded. "I should clarify. The last

time the pollen of an orbsceia was needed, and one was harvested, the Fae who located it reported seeing two others, both bordering pools."

"And how long ago was that?" Steve asked, exasperated.

"A long time," Ria admitted. "Over fifteen hundred years ago."

"How do you know someone hasn't found these other flowers by now?" Sarah asked as she felt her concern growing. It sounded as though the Fae wanted to send her and her husband on a wild goose chase. "How do you know they haven't all been picked? How do you know these plants are even alive? We're talking about an incredibly long time."

"Because of where they were found, Lady Sarah."

"Didn't you just say you didn't know where they could be found?" Steve protested, growing more and more frustrated with each passing second.

"Again, you are correct," Ria patiently told him. She placed a hand over his on the table.

"What are you not telling us?" Sarah pointedly asked. "What is it you're afraid of saying?"

Ria placed her other hand over Sarah's. "Allow me to finish and you'll see our dilemma. Now, where was I?"

"You were telling us what would save your Tree," Sarah reminded her.

"Of course. We need the processed pollen from an orbsceia flower. Difficulty in finding the flower notwithstanding, once the flower has been harvested, then it must be properly processed within one hour."

Steve whistled. "Talk about your major time crunch. I wouldn't worry about that, though. Thanks to Sarah we can be pretty much anywhere and be able to get back here lickity-split."

"That is the primary reason we approached Lady Sarah in the first place," Ria agreed. "Her remarkable jhorun will allow her to return here in a matter of a few moments. That will allow us the maximum amount of time to prepare the pollen. Frankly, we are going to need it. I personally have never done anything like this before."

"Then how do you know what you need to do?" Sarah asked, confused.

"Because my grandmother did. She told me stories about what she tried to do to save her Tree many years ago."

"The exact same thing happened to your grandmother's tree, too? Do you know what happened to it? I mean, what's the point of going through all of this when there's a chance it could happen again?"

"Because the creature that attacked our Tree was destroyed."

Curiosity piqued; Steve leaned forward. "Creature? What creature?"

"To the Fae, it is the Mist," Ria explained, frowning as she recalled what she knew of her Tree's attacker. "It was an ancient being that had been imprisoned deep beneath the sea for over two thousand years."

"Mist?" Steve scoffed. "You guys were attacked by a mist? How bad could that be?"

"It has other names. I believe the wyverians called it thriper. I know the humans had their own name for it, but it escapes me at the moment."

"Why did the dragons call it a thriper?" Steve repeated, puzzled. He looked over at Sarah for confirmation. "Wait a minute. Isn't that the name of the thing that Mikal said he and Lissa helped destroy?"

Sarah nodded. "That's right, only he said something about it having to be changed into something else in order for it to be killed. I think he said … wait. Wait a moment. Ria, didn't you say the Mist thing had been imprisoned for thousands of years?"

"Aye. What of it?"

"Could it have been responsible for attacking your grandmother's tree?"

"The creature fed on jhorun," Ria answered. "While theoretically possible we would be unable to validate such a claim."

Sarah suddenly shook her head. "That can't be right."

"What isn't right?" Steve asked.

"We're suggesting that the same creature that attacked their tree this time is the same one from Ria's grandmother's time."

"Yeah, so?"

"So, if that were true, then that'd mean Dynwe, this city, has been here for thousands of years."

Ria's lips curved upward in the beginnings of a smile.

"Do you remember what the king said in the Antechamber?" Sarah continued. "He said the other city, Vineelm, was in the northwest part of the kingdom."

"That's right," Steve recalled. "There was that special illustrated tree symbol on the map."

"Based on that I'd say Vineelm is older than Dynwe," Sarah finished. "If the mist monster is the same one that attacked both trees, and killed the first one, then Vineelm must be considerably older than Dynwe."

Ria clapped her hands delightedly. "Very well done, Lady Sarah. You are correct. Vineelm was the home of our ancestors. It was abandoned after Vineelm's Tree perished. Thank the Maker they were fortunate enough to have collected a seed from Vineelm's Tree before the catastrophe fell. We planted the seed here, and this Tree is the result. Dynwe was born."

"Why do you say you were fortunate to have collected a seed?" Sarah wanted to know. "You make it sound like the tree only produces one seed."

"Because it does, Lady Sarah. Only one seed every millennia, and only then will it be produced under special circumstances. The seed is so unremarkable in appearance that it was almost overlooked. Fortunately, my grandmother recognized the seed for what it was."

"How long ago was that?" Steve wanted to know.

"Over two thousand years," Ria answered.

"So, if my math is correct," Steve said, "then there should have been two seed pods, correct?"

"Didn't you hear her?" Sarah asked, annoyed. "She said the right circumstances have to exist before the tree will produce a seed. How it does that, I don't know."

"Nor do I," Ria admitted. "I've never seen a seed before. The last was before my time."

"Does everything that lives in Lentari live longer than humans?" Steve asked, feeling exasperated. "We know that wyverians can live at least a thousand years. Same for the dwarves. Humans? Hell, I'll be lucky if I make it to a hundred."

"You are but a young babe in the eyes of a Fae," Ria agreed.

Sarah groaned. She knew instantly, and immediately, how her husband would respond to that. She looked at Steve and saw that he was grinning.

"Did you hear that? Did you? She called me a 'babe'. She's not wrong, you know."

"Is that why you're blushing?"

"Am not."

"Your face is as red as a Coke can."

Steve held the back of his hand to his forehead. He shrugged.

"It doesn't feel any different to me. Speaking of the king," Steve said, raising a hand, trying to change the subject, "are we allowed to get the human king involved?"

Ria shook her head. "Tivan and I are aware you have already discussed our plight with the human king."

"How could you possibly know that?" Steve asked, amazed.

"Our jhorun is almost exhausted, aye," Ria admitted, "but it isn't exhausted yet. We have our ways."

"Can we tell Kri'Entu what's been going on here?" Sarah timidly asked. "I know he can keep a secret and he desperately wants to help."

"Humans and Fae are not allies," Ria quietly informed them. "I know not what distrust exists between our two species, only that it does. Ownership of the fault matters not."

"I couldn't agree more," Sarah muttered to herself.

"What does matter is that human and Fae parted ways. You would like to see the ancient alliance restored? So would I, Lady Sarah. I ... hmm?"

"I didn't say anything," Sarah answered automatically.

"I'm sorry, I'm talking with Tivan. He has been monitoring our conversation and he ... Tivan, slow down. I cannot carry on two conversations at the same time. Lady

Sarah, a moment, if you please."

Sarah took her husband's hand and waited, companionably, for Ria to resume their conversation. After a few minutes of listening to the Fae queen give monosyllabic answers, Sarah watched the faraway look disappear from Ria's eyes. The queen shifted her attention back to her.

"My apologies. It would seem Lord Tivan is also interested in renewing the ancient alliance."

Sarah's face lit up with a smile. "Really? That'd be wonderful, Ria!"

"There are provisions, I'm afraid."

"Of course, there are," Steve added.

"What are they?" Sarah asked. "Does it have to do with your present predicament being solved?"

Ria nodded. "Aye. That's it, in its entirety. You must prove to us humans are to be trusted again. Only then will we consider the notion of reforming the alliance."

"By solving this dilemma?" Sarah stammered. "That's a bit one-sided, don't you think?"

"I'm not sure I follow, Lady Sarah."

"You said it yourself. You, the Fae, are dying because your tree is also dying."

"That is correct."

"If we're able to solve this for you and find that orbsceia flower, it would mean the Fae would be in our debt. That is to say, the Fae would then be indebted to the humans, wouldn't you agree?"

Ria regarded her for a few moments. She tapped a delicate finger on her lips as she considered. The queen briefly closed her eyes, no doubt relaying what she had said to her husband. Several seconds passed. The queen opened her eyes and smiled at her.

"What do you have in mind, Lady Sarah?" Ria finally asked.

"While I'm not certain what transpired between the humans and the Fae to lose trust in each other, I think this quest should go in our favor. If we are able to solve your dilemma, then I'd like you to do everything in your power to rekindle the alliance between our two species."

"While admirable," Ria began, "it ... pardon me for a moment."

The queen's eyes closed once more. Apparently Tivan was relaying another message.

"Her terms are acceptable," Ria announced. "My husband has spoken. He has agreed to Lady Sarah's terms. However, since the Fae are incapable of telling a lie, I should also inform you that we were already prepared to do just that."

"Oh."

"Should you and your husband prove to be successful in restoring our Tree to full health, we will commence negotiations at once."

"Negotiations for what?" Steve wanted to know. "If you're brokering a peace treaty, then what details need to be worked out? I mean, all you have to do is admit that each side is better off working together rather than separately."

"If only it were that simple," came Ria's response.

Sarah, still holding her husband's hand, pulled him next to her.

"Very well, Your Majesties. Steve and I hereby promise to do what we can in order to save your tree."

"We will be forever grateful for your assistance," Ria formally answered. "Regardless of the outcome, let it be known our human friends have been more than accommodating in our time of need."

Bidding their farewells, husband and wife slowly retraced their steps back to the glittering amethyst doors. Steve pulled Sarah to a stop.

"Did they answer the question?"

"What question?"

"Are the Kri'yans allowed to give us help in solving this dilemma?"

Sarah paled. "Damn. I forgot to ask."

Steve started to chortle when Sarah shot him a dangerous look.

"You forgot to ask, too, so don't get cocky."

"You're the teleporter," Steve pointed out. "Just go back and ask them."

"I'd feel foolish teleporting back in there unannounced.

You go ask."

"No way."

Sarah held up a fist, challenging him to do the same. With a sigh, Steve curled his fingers into a fist and held it up.

"Fine. Let's get this over with. One … two … three. Damn. I should've known. I'll be right back."

Chapter 4 — Sorcerer's Apprentice

The Fae king and queen are allowing us to aid in your quest? This is most excellent news, Lady Sarah." Kri'Entu looked hopeful.

"That's not what I said," Sarah hastily reminded the king. "I said they never *specifically* said one way or the other."

"But you informed King Tivan about my desire to help, did you not?"

Steve raised a hand. "I did, yeah."

Kri'Entu's eyes shifted to Steve's. "And he didn't immediately forbid it?"

"Well, no," Steve hesitantly admitted. "But he…"

"Then it's settled," Kri'Entu decided. "I'm not ashamed to say this news pleases me greatly. Very well. What do we have to do?"

Sarah looked helplessly at the queen. Ny'Callé turned to her husband and laid a reassuring hand on the king's arm.

"My love, this task is theirs. While it is true the Fae king did not forbid you from interfering, I really do think this is something Lady Sarah and Sir Steve should be doing themselves."

"Tell you what," Steve hastily interjected as he noticed the frown forming on the king's face, "if we are stymied by anything and need your assistance, then we'll definitely ask for your help."

Sighing dejectedly, the king nodded his head and sank back down into his chair. Kri'Entu was quiet a few moments before he turned to Sarah. "If there is something I can do, anything, then you are to let me know as soon as possible. Agreed?"

Sarah nodded. "Agreed."

"What do you have to do?" the king asked, curious. "Are you allowed to tell us?"

"We have to find a rare flower," Sarah answered. "Apparently there are only three left somewhere in Lentari."

"A flower?" the king asked, cocking his head slightly to the left. "Allow me to venture a guess. The pontal's whereabouts are unknown."

"Naturally," Steve agreed.

"And you were given no clue how to find it?"

Steve nodded. "You're two for two."

"That's all the Fae need? This one type of pontal? That really doesn't sound too bad."

"No, it doesn't," Sarah agreed. "And that's what scares me most of all. What if we can't find it? The Fae and the humans won't ever be friends again."

"The Fae and the humans haven't been friends for a very long time now," Kri'Entu reminded her with a smile. "If the mission fails then we'll be no worse off than we were before."

Sarah groaned. "That's reassuring."

Kri'Entu gave her a fleeting smile. "That's not what I meant, Lady Sarah. The Fae have lived their lives away from human influence for centuries. While not ideal, I'm sure we would be given another chance sometime in the future."

"Umm, except they'll be dead," Steve pointed out.

Kri'Entu's head lifted. Alarmed, he glanced at Steve.

"The lives of the Fae rest with the success of this quest?"

Steve shrugged. "That's one way to look at it."

Kri'Entu looked at the queen and gave her a look of sheer defiance. "I will *not* allow the Fae to perish, not when there's a chance that working together could possibly save their lives. If the Fae disagree, they can continue to live their lives in isolation. I can live with that decision."

Surprisingly, the queen nodded. "I concur. While unfortunate, the Fae were once our allies. How can we, as a compassionate, civilized species look the other way when someone needs our help?"

Steve took Sarah's hand in his own and held it tightly. "They asked you for help, babe. This is your show. What do you want to do?"

"I will not let them die, either," Sarah vowed. "Not when they only have a day or two left."

Emboldened, Kri'Entu motioned for everyone to follow him over to his desk. He, the queen, Sarah, and Steve all huddled around the king's private desk. His voice dropped as he addressed Sarah.

"This flower. Once you find it, what then? What has to happen?"

"Ria only said that the flower must be processed and that it has to happen within an hour of being harvested."

"Thankfully your jhorun will allow you to return the flower to the Fae queen well within those parameters," the king observed.

"It is part of the reason why they asked me to help," Sarah confirmed.

"Without knowing where this flower is," Ny'Callé quietly whispered, "I would suggest the two of you begin your search in the north wing."

Kri'Entu nodded. "Our Archives are unparalleled. If this flower exists, it will be catalogued somewhere within its shelves. I will inform Miss Alwyn that you are to have complete access to anything you require."

Sarah nodded appreciatively. "Thank you. Hon, we should get going. We'll let you know if we find anything."

* * *

"I don't think I've been in here before," Steve admitted less than an hour later. "In fact, I didn't even know this was here."

Husband and wife were standing just inside the open archway leading into the Archives, located in the castle's entire north wing. Smooth slate stones lined the floor and extended through a second arch into a multi-floored chamber. Situated just inside the first archway was a large wooden desk that had seen better days. Scratches, dents, and small burns showed from beneath the surface clutter.

Sitting behind the desk, peering suspiciously at them from between two stacks of small slips of paper, was a tiny old lady with frizzy white hair. She was wearing a thick rimless pair of square spectacles and a long white robe with purple butterflies festooned all across it. The old lady's arms were crossed and she wore a scowl on her wrinkly face. Her nose was scrunched up, from squinting or from trying to keep her glasses from sliding off her nose. Steve couldn't tell which.

"Alrighty," he softly whispered, pulling Sarah close, "that's a look that should strike fear in the hearts of children everywhere."

"Hush," Sarah scolded. "She'll hear you."

"You're the Nohrin," the tiny, frail lady announced, as though reminding them who they were. "I am Andra Alwyn, head of the Archives. I was instructed to make available all areas of my precious Archives for you and your research."

"Great," Steve smiled, as he patted his wife's hand reassuringly. "We really app…"

"I wasn't finished," Andra interrupted. "I *may* have to open my Archives to two unregistered, inexperienced visitors but I *don't* have to like it. You take care when you handle the books and documents in my collection. You treat them with the same care and respect as if they belonged to you, is that understood? Just imagine. His majesty allowing visitors full access. He must be losing his mind."

Sarah noticed her husband had crossed his arms and was scowling. She quickly decided to intervene before he could undoubtedly further annoy the tiny head of the Archives. She stepped in front of Steve and adopted the friendliest smile she could muster.

"Don't you worry, Mrs. Alwyn," Sarah soothed, infusing kindness into her voice. "We'll treat everything here as though it was worth its weight in gold."

"It *is* worth its weight in gold," Andra snapped. "And you may address me as *Miss* Andra Alwyn."

"There's a shocker," Steve muttered, deliberately keeping his voice loud enough to be certain Andra heard him.

The archivist returned Steve's scowl with an equal amount of malice. Sarah frowned. Her patience with the cantankerous old hag had just run out. No one scowled at her husband but her.

"Well, as much fun as this has been, we have work to do. You have yourself a good day."

"I haven't finished explaining the rules," Andra snapped.

"Noted," Sarah coolly told the archivist. "We'll be careful and we'll be on our way. Have a nice day."

The wizened old lady stepped in front of Sarah as she started to walk by the desk on her way to the large chamber beyond the second archway. Andra puffed out her chest.

"No one touches my Archives without my permission."

"Except the king," Steve said.

"Except for the king," Andra reluctantly admitted, "and he's not here."

"We're here under his orders," Sarah smoothly told the quietly fuming archivist as she side-stepped around her. "Again, have yourself a nice day."

They entered the main floor of the Archives and took in the huge atrium with neatly lined up tables and chairs everywhere. Sarah blinked her eyes in amazement. The entire facility seemed to be wall to wall books. Huge tomes, many times the size of the largest encyclopedia she had ever seen, were on the racks to her left. Sarah looked straight ahead and saw racks with the exact same book on it. Or, she figured, they could be multiple volumes in a series. Liking that explanation better, she nodded. One series, she noted, spanned several cases. Each book was the same width, had the same dull green spine, and had gold lettering identifying the title. As good as her vision was, she couldn't make out the titles.

Off to her right were the rest of Lentari's vast collection. Wall after wall, rack after rack, the ground floor alone must have at least five thousand titles. Sarah glanced up. The ceiling rose at least thirty feet. She could see that the second floor contained even more racks and cases. Most of these contained stacks of papers, loosely bound bundles of parchment, and the like. They could also see that the second floor stretched out and away from the atrium itself. Sarah could only imagine how far back the racks must extend.

Steve slowly spun in place and grunted with frustration.

"What?" Sarah wanted to know. "What's the matter? We finally got away from that horrible old lady. I thought you'd be happy."

"Happy? Do you see a computer in here? How the hell are we supposed to find anything? We could search for days and not make a dent."

Sarah hesitated, got an evil gleam in her eye, and cleared her throat. "Mrs. Alwyn? Would you come here for a moment, please?"

"You deliberately called that crone *Mrs.*?" Steve quietly asked. "Ballsy. Stupid, but ballsy. Aren't we going to want her cooperation?"

Sarah grinned at her husband. "And we'll get it. Trust me, I know what I'm doing. Women know how to seriously aggravate other women without openly admitting to doing anything. I cannot abide rudeness. So, I'm going to fight fire with fire. Er, pardon the pun. Watch and learn, dear." She cleared her throat and tried again. "I know you're listening, Mrs. Alwyn. We need your help. I really don't want to go back to the king and tell him you were being uncooperative."

The tiny archivist stepped out from behind a rack of books, her hands clenching and unclenching. She glared at Sarah and waited, expectantly. Sarah looked over at Andra and gave a little jump, as though she had been startled.

"Ah! There you are. Alright, here's what we need. We're looking for a very specific flower called an orbsceia. We don't know where…"

"There's no such flower," Andra flatly stated.

"Oh, but there is," Sarah contradicted. "There are three out there. I need to know where to look. Kri'Entu says that the Archives have everything we'd need to locate that flower. Let's find out, shall we? Now, where should we look first?"

Andra reached into her robe's pocket and withdrew a small slip of paper. "You'll need to fill this out to make it official."

"Why don't you fill it out?" Steve suggested, keeping his voice firm but neutral. "You'd know what we're looking for, right? Thank you in advance for your understanding."

Andra's lips thinned, scowling at Steve. The slip of paper was returned to her pocket. Grumbling to herself Andra disappeared into the shadows.

Fifteen minutes later, Steve pulled a couple of tables together and spread out the myriad of selections Andra had pulled from her collection. Books of varying size, covering everything from basic horticulture to hand-raising exotic orchids, to a few titles covering 'plummon', the Lentarian equivalent of creating exquisite floral arrangements, had been plunked down on their tables.

Sarah pulled a chair over to the closest stack of books and began to sort through the titles. Steve pulled a chair next to hers and did the same. Thirty minutes later, Sarah knew they were in trouble. There simply wasn't any mention of an orbsceia anywhere. On top of which, a new problem had manifested. A crowd of onlookers had formed and was growing steadily larger. Sarah gave Steve a worried look and quickly glanced at the crowd of people that were edging closer.

"We need to do something about this," she whispered. "It's getting out of control."

"I'll handle this," Steve assured her.

"How?"

"Like this."

Steve slid over one of the small slips of paper which Andra had deliberately left on their table, flipped it over, and composed a short message. He folded it in half and gave it to a nearby guard whom he was certain had been tasked with keeping an eye on them.

"Give that to the king, would you?" Steve quietly told the soldier.

The young guard nodded and disappeared.

"What did you say?"

"I asked him to give that to the king."

"I know, I heard you. I meant the message. What did you say?"

"The king wants to help. I sent him our first request."

"Which was?" Sarah prompted.

"Privacy."

"Nice."

Thirty seconds later, a half-dozen guards had appeared and quickly escorted everyone from the Archives. Everyone but the ever-popular archivist, of course. Steve waved at her from her position in the front entryway. She didn't wave back. Just then another guard appeared and hooked his arm through the elderly woman's own arm and gently pulled her away.

"Unhand me this instant, you simpleton. No one manhandles me in my own Archives."

A second guard appeared and took Ms. Alwyn's other arm. They effortlessly hoisted her up and exited the room. The old woman's cries of indignation eventually faded away, leaving the huge chamber eerily devoid of all noise. Sarah smiled at her husband.

"Nicely done. I wish I'd thought to do that. Where do you think they put her?"

"I'm sure she was returned to her desk," Sarah said, without looking up from her book. "And, I'm also willing to bet there's now a guard stationed nearby to keep an eye on her. She doesn't strike me as the type of person to be easily intimidated."

"That lady needed a reality check," Steve muttered darkly, returning his attention to a stack of books before him. He selected one from the stack and opened it. "Someone needed to tell her that she's not the grand-high poobah of the universe."

"I don't think we'll be able to count her as an admirer of

ours," Sarah mused, selecting her own book. "I'm sure she's writing her own message to the king right now, complaining—bitterly—about us."

"Let her. Grouch."

Their silence lasted about fifteen minutes. That was when they noticed Ms. Alwyn put in another appearance, only this time, she didn't interact. She simply passed them from a distance, glaring at them as she did. Shadowing her were two guards.

For the next hour, the cantankerous elderly record keeper made a point of walking by to spy on their progress. After they didn't complain, the records keeper became bolder, and moved progressively closer. First, it was a well-timed act of clumsiness. Several large tomes fell to the ground with a large bang. Echoes of the impact bounced noisily around the quiet room for nearly ten seconds before fading back into silence. Both husband and wife had looked over at the tiny woman who was taking her time retrieving her books from the ground.

"Whoops. Clumsy me."

"Perhaps you should have more care with your precious books," Steve instantly quipped. "After all, didn't you say that they were worth their weight in gold? You have a funny way of showing it."

Sarah quickly looked away before she could burst out in giggles. Ms. Alwyn glared at him before retreating in a huff.

The second instance happened fifteen minutes later. A loud clattering began and grew progressively louder. Sarah had looked up from her book about the care of exotic orchids when the ruckus began. She looked over at her husband and rolled her eyes.

"What do you think Ms. Congeniality has got planned for us this time?" he mused.

Andra Alwyn appeared, dragging a cart laden with books behind her. If Sarah didn't know any better, she could have sworn Andra, judging from the noises coming from her cart, was angling to hit every rut on the floor. The tiny archivist ignored the two of them and concentrated on the contents of her cart. She methodically moved around the room, placing books back on various shelves.

Husband and wife ignored the intrusion.

When the fourth interruption occurred less than five minutes later, Steve reached for the small stack of request slips Andra had left on their table. He flipped it over and composed another message. Watching from the shadows, a uniformed guard appeared the moment Steve finished writing. The slip of paper was folded in half and handed to the guard, all without either of them saying a word.

"I sure hope you just did what I think you did," Sarah whispered as she changed books. Her discard pile was growing and she was nowhere closer to learning where to find the elusive orbsceia flower, let alone it even existed.

"Wait for it," Steve told her, adding another book to their discard pile.

Exactly thirty seconds later, a loud shriek shattered the tranquility of the peaceful Archives.

"Unhand me! I will not be treated in this manner!"

Ms. Alwyn, now intent on polishing every brass placard on the rack of books closest to the husband-and-wife team, hadn't noticed the same two burly guards from before approach. Together they easily lifted the tiny sputtering woman from the ground and quickly left the room.

"Now what?" Steve asked, as silence returned to the large chamber. He snapped the book he had been skimming closed and pushed it across the table to join the mountain of discards. "This is getting us nowhere. We've been at it for hours and we are no closer than we were when we first stepped foot inside this place."

"What about asking Shardwyn?" Sarah suggested. She noticed the frown on her husband's face and sighed. "I know it isn't ideal, but we are running out of options. Hopefully he knows something about it or can point us in the right direction."

"Fine. We'll play it your way. Let's go see what that goofball has to say."

Sarah heard a distant snort of laughter. It had sounded like Andra Alwyn. She knew the batty old record keeper had been confined to her desk. Could she have possibly heard

Steve's comment about Shardwyn? Maybe the old goat had a personality after all.

Leaving the Archives behind, much to the archivist's delight, Sarah led her husband out of the castle and toward Shardwyn's tower. This tower, Sarah knew, was both home and workshop to Lentari's resident wizard. The location of Shardwyn's tower, away from the castle proper, was not a matter of convenience but by kingly decree.

"I have to wonder when was the last time he blew something up," Steve mused.

"Does it matter?" Sarah asked, curious.

"Sure. If it's been a while then that means he's due. I don't suppose we could get him to come out here, could we?"

Sarah grabbed her husband's hand and forcibly pulled him inside the large stone tower. "Stop being a baby. There's nothing in there that could hurt us."

Unbeknownst to her, the tower's next explosion was less than five minutes away, and for once, Shardwyn would actually be able to say that he wasn't responsible.

Climbing up several flights of stairs Sarah knocked three times on the heavy oak door. Sniffing loudly, she leaned toward the door and frowned. She could detect a number of different scents, the most prevalent reminding her of a potion gone wrong. She eyed her husband and gently opened the door.

"Shardwyn? Are you in? Is anyone home?"

A bright-eyed boy of sixteen rounded the corner and smiled at them.

"Hello. Can I help you?"

Steve shook his head. "Not unless you took an anti-aging potion, kid. Is Shardwyn here? We need to talk to him."

"He's up in the loft, looking for some book he insists is up there. I tried to remind him he burnt it up two weeks ago but he wouldn't listen."

"Who are you?" Sarah asked, genuinely curious. "I didn't know Shardwyn had an assistant."

"I'm his new apprentice," the teenager proudly declared. "I'm Gareth."

Sarah held out a hand and waited for the boy to grasp her

forearm in the manner Lentarians used to greet each other.

"I'm Sarah. This is my husband, Steve. We're pleased to meet you, Gareth."

The dark-haired boy blinked with surprise. He looked over at Steve and his eyes opened wide. "You're the Nohrin, aren't you? Lady Sarah, the teleporter, and Sir Steve, the fire thrower. I can't believe I finally get to meet you! Although, if I'm going to be honest, we kinda met a few years ago."

Steve repeated the Lentarian method of grasping forearms and raised an eyebrow at the friendly boy. "We've met before? Really? Under what circumstances?"

Gareth suddenly appeared suspicious, nervous even. "Umm, let's just say the conditions were less than favorable."

Jumping to the conclusion that her husband must have given the boy one of his trademark scowls at some point in the past, Sarah frowned. She crossed her arms over her chest, glaring at her husband, wondering what he could have possibly done this time.

"Steve, is there something you need to tell me? How could you have…?" Sarah turned to Gareth and smiled apologetically. "You know what? That's an argument for another time. I'm so very sorry for whatever he did. Believe it or not he's a really a nice guy."

"Now wait a moment," Steve began, giving Sarah an imploring look. "I didn't do anything!"

"I'm the one who should be apologizing," Gareth corrected, coming to Steve's aid. "I'm the one who did some stuff a few years ago that I probably shouldn't have."

Curiosity piqued, Steve cleared his throat. "Like what? You would have been, what, ten years old at that time? What could you have possibly done?"

"Well, for starters, I was twelve when this happened. I, uh, might have been responsible for forcing you to experience what it was like to be a dragon for a while."

Sarah's eyebrows shot straight up. This boy was responsible for the time she, Steve, and Pryllan had switched bodies? That could only mean … Alarmed, she glanced at her husband. Steve, much to his credit, knew instantly who he was facing. His face paled. Sarah swallowed nervously. This wasn't going to be good.

"You're the renegade wizard," Steve accused.

Time slowed to a crawl. Her husband threw an arm around her waist and yanked her backward, placing himself physically between Gareth and her. His hands ignited and Sarah watched, mesmerized, as he raised both arms. Steve blasted a huge jet of fire straight at Gareth, intending to wipe the smile right off his face.

Gareth let out a cry of alarm, made an arm gesture of his own, and leapt back. The full brunt of Steve's blast hit Gareth head on, but instead of frying him to a crisp, the fires bounced harmlessly off the young wizard's hastily created protective shield. However, Gareth was knocked off his feet by the sheer brute strength of the blast. He hastily scuttled behind a large threadbare sofa in the middle of the room.

"Wait!" Gareth pleaded. "I'm not the same person anymore. I won't hurt you, I promise!"

Holding Sarah tightly against his chest so that she'd be protected from his flames, Steve concentrated on the sofa. In seconds it had been reduced to ash, forcing Gareth to dive behind a large wooden bureau a few feet away.

A thick tentacle of water broke through the nearby window, singled out Steve, and tried to wrap itself around his body and extinguish the flames. Sarah felt her husband tense and risked a glance up at his face. His eyes were screwed shut and he had a frown on his face. She felt him trembling and instantly knew what was about to happen. She pressed her face tightly against his chest and waited for the inevitable.

The concussive blast vaporized the water tentacle instantly. It also, unfortunately, blasted out the glass in every single window in Shardwyn's tower. Sarah heard a loud bell begin to toll. It was the castle's alarm. Clearly someone in the castle had noticed a few peculiarities coming from Shardwyn's tower.

Sarah coughed. There was smoke everywhere. She didn't know the extent of the damage inside Shardwyn's workshop but she also knew it couldn't be good. Her spinning mind focused back on the problem at hand. Gareth was the renegade wizard? Did Shardwyn know? Had Gareth overpowered the castle wizard in an attempt to usurp the eccentric old wizard's powers? Well, not if she had anything to say about it.

Sarah cast her eyes around the destroyed room. The smoke was starting to thin and she was able to make out a few pieces of broken furniture. She could certainly pick those up and use them if she needed to, but first, she wanted answers. And judging by her husband's body language, if she wanted answers then she'd better act now. Steve looked as though he was preparing to finish the job.

"Gareth, I would suggest you come out," Sarah hurriedly suggested. "Peacefully."

"Peacefully?"

Sarah could hear him but couldn't see him. He must be either crouching inside the curved hall that led to Shardwyn's personal bedchamber or that overturned chest of drawers.

"He's trying to kill me!"

"Congrats, pal," Steve scowled as he readied his next blast of fire. "Now you know what it feels like. Doesn't feel too good, does it?"

"I said I was sorry!" Gareth tried again. "I'm not the same person I was before! I'm not going to hurt anyone!"

Sarah suddenly thought of her last conversation with Mikal. Hadn't the young prince said he had made a new friend? Hadn't he mentioned something about a wizard?

"By chance are you a friend of Mikal's?" Sarah cautiously asked, deliberately stepping in front of her husband, blocking his shot.

"Aye! Mikal is the one who found out who I was. He helped me see the error of my ways! Please, can we cease this nonsense? Can I come out now?"

Sarah laid a reassuring hand on her husband's shoulder. "Let's hear what he has to say. I do remember Mikal saying something about this a while ago."

"I sure don't," Steve muttered, keeping both hands ignited. He scowled at Gareth as the boy's head appeared over the overturned—and scorched—bureau.

"What have we here?" a familiar voice asked. "Pleased, I am, to know that this time it wasn't my fault."

A thin man in his seventies had appeared, wearing robes

of pale green. He inspected the burnt walls, furniture, and his destroyed racks of potion ingredients. Smiling, he turned to Steve, but then frowned as he noticed Steve was scowling. Turning, Shardwyn's eyes widened.

"I do believe I see what the problem is. Allow me to venture a guess, m'boy. You were not aware of young Gareth's identity and most certainly weren't aware of his status as my new apprentice. Am I right?"

"You put my wife in danger, pal," Steve accused, pointing a flaming finger at Gareth and completely ignoring Shardwyn. "That's not something I can overlook any time soon."

"You are well within your rights to be angry with me," Gareth quietly agreed, hurrying to Shardwyn's side. "I have been thoroughly admonished by many people. I am trying to make amends for what I've done. That's why I'm here."

"You're telling me this is community service for you?" Steve asked, his frown still plastered across his face.

"While not completely familiar with those terms, I do believe I understand the gist of what you're saying. Aye. I am performing this service as an act of atonement. Besides, Shardwyn could use the help."

"I most certainly do not need your help," Shardwyn grumped, turning to face his apprentice in what was clearly an ongoing debate between the two of them. "There's nothing wrong with my potions and spells. I had everything sorted into appropriate piles. My potions were all labeled correctly."

"Labeled correctly, but misfiled," Gareth reminded him with a sigh. "And practically all your ingredients were so old that they were growing mold on them, Shardwyn. Mold! Is that what you really want to use in your potions?"

"There's nothing to be done about it now, dear boy," Shardwyn mused as he inspected his charred table and the shattered bottles of his cherished ingredients.

"No, this is perfect," Gareth countered. "Now we have a chance to collect everything again, and to make sure everything is fresh. You'll have better results with your work, I promise you."

Steve approached and eyed Gareth coldly. "Tell me something. Were you the one who created that water snake thing and then tried to kill me with it?"

"I wasn't trying to kill you," Gareth argued. "I was trying to put out your flames. I was just trying to get you to listen."

The heavy wooden door banged open, three floors below. They all heard shouts as dozens of feet clambered up the stairs. Gareth rolled his eyes.

"I've got it this time, Shardwyn."

The boy hurried out the singed door and disappeared down the stairs.

"What does he have?" Sarah asked Shardwyn.

"We each take turns assuring the guards that we're all right," the wizard explained.

"How often does that happen?" Steve curiously asked.

"Typically, once a week."

"You have an accident in here once a week?" Steve repeated, appalled.

"It's not nearly this extreme," Shardwyn admitted with a smile. "Last week I accidentally summoned Bredo. To say he was less than thrilled is an understatement. He made quite a mess in here before we were able to get him back to the moat."

Sarah chuckled to herself as she imagined the huge snake appearing in their midst. Gareth reappeared. There was someone accompanying him. Someone tall.

"Shardwyn," Captain Pheron began in an exasperated tone, "what was it this time?"

"This time it wasn't me," Shardwyn chortled with glee. "It was Sir Steve."

"Sir Steve did this?" Captain Pheron then noticed that Shardwyn and his assistant weren't alone. "My apologies, Sir Steve. Lady Sarah. I did not know you were in here."

"Sorry, buddy," Steve began as he looked around at the destruction in the room. "Turns out the renegade wizard I've come to despise was in this very room. Had an unfortunate reaction, that's all." Steve gave the young boy a neutral look. "Whether or not that happens again remains to be seen."

"Ah," Captain Pheron knowingly said. "That explains much. I had forgotten no one had bothered to explain to you that the renegade wizard had been found. So, do you require assistance?"

Sarah stepped between her husband and Shardwyn's apprentice and then turned to face the captain. "We're good, Pheron. I think we all got off on the wrong foot here."

Mollified, Pheron nodded. "Very well. If you find that you require assistance, please do not hesitate to let my men know."

The tall captain headed for the stairs just as Sarah turned to Steve.

"I don't trust him," Steve muttered, staring hard at Gareth, who refused to look his way.

"I know you don't, and I'm not asking you to," Sarah quietly answered. "At least not yet. But, I do think you need to know something. You realize that you now own him, right?"

"What?"

"If what he says is true, and I'm inclined to believe him, that poor boy will do practically anything to make up for what he's done to us. Let's use that to our advantage. Let's see if he can shed any light on a certain matter we need help with."

Overhearing the last part of their hushed conversation, Gareth eagerly stepped forward and gave a slight cough. "Did I hear that right? Do you need some help?"

Steve shrugged and nodded toward the youth, indicating Sarah should do the talking.

"As a matter of fact, we do," Sarah admitted, smiling at the nervous boy. "Do you think you could help us out?"

Gareth's mouth opened to answer, but instantly closed as a bony hand dropped on the teenager's shoulder and pulled him away.

"Perhaps I could be of assistance, dear girl," Shardwyn crooned, rubbing his hands together. The wizard turned to his assistant and indicated his destroyed rack of potion ingredients. "You have a lot of work to do, young Gareth. I do believe I will take you up on your offer of obtaining fresh ingredients for my potions. Now, where was I? Oh, yes. Lady Sarah. You mentioned you require assistance? You have come to the right place. How may *I* assist you on this lovely day?"

Sarah explained only enough to convince Shardwyn that they desperately needed to get their hands on an orbsceia flower. As to why they needed it, she refused to elaborate.

The elderly wizard was silent as he sat back in his chair, looking thoughtful.

"And you found no mention of this particular species of pontal in the Archives, dear girl?"

"Not a word," Sarah confirmed.

"Hmm. I believe I could brew a potion that would help us find this pontal, wherever it may be hiding."

"You're unable to make any potions at the moment," Gareth reminded him, not bothering to look up as he scribbled notes on where to find certain plants and minerals on a large piece of parchment. "Not until I start replenishing our stock, that is."

Shardwyn rose to his feet and waved off his assistant's concerns. "Bah. I have a spare cauldron and an emergency kit full of supplies up in the loft. I just saw it up there, before I came down here. Let me see what I can do."

After he left, Gareth looked up and found Sarah's eyes. "I know full well what he has up there," the boy murmured. "I'm the one who suggested we should have a backup since he's so prone to accidents whenever he's in front of a cauldron. I do hope he doesn't try anything up there. There's more wood than stone in the attic."

"Do you think he can find one of those flowers?" Sarah asked.

Gareth shrugged. "I won't say it's impossible, but I will say that it's highly unlikely. A locator spell is best performed by just that, a spell, not a potion."

There was a loud thump, followed immediately by a muffled curse.

"Well, he found the cauldron," Gareth sighed. "I predict in less than twenty seconds there will be a crash."

Sarah giggled. "You sound so confident."

"You haven't been cooped up in here with him as long as I have." Gareth scowled, returning his attention to his list of potion ingredients. "It's a wonder he hasn't blown up the castle."

Steve snorted, drawing a smile from Shardwyn's apprentice.

"You think you're good, huh?" Steve finally said.

"I can hold my own," Gareth answered, returning Steve's smug look.

"Prove it," Steve challenged. "See if you can find this flower we're looking for faster than he can."

Gareth sighed. "I really shouldn't. It isn't my place. This is Shardwyn's workshop and he's entitled to…"

There was a loud crash. They all heard the telltale sound of broken glass falling to the floor. Sarah laughed.

"You called that one. What do you think he broke?"

"There was a crystal tea set up there, on a small table in the far corner. Shardwyn said it was a gift from the queen last year. I'm guessing he's knocked it over."

"Are you sure you don't want to help us?" Sarah asked, giving the boy her friendliest smile.

Gareth walked over to an open doorway with a flight of narrow stone steps visible through it. He stuck his head in and looked up.

"Shardwyn," Gareth called, raising his voice, "do you mind if I give it a try while you're working on your potion? I thought maybe I could approach it from a different angle."

"How are you going to make a potion without any ingredients?" Shardwyn's voice asked, mystified. "There are enough supplies up here to allow me several tries. I'm sorry, dear boy, I don't think I have enough for you."

"Oh, that's alright. I suppose I could try something else. That is, if you don't object."

"No objections, dear boy, no objections. I think you're wasting your time, though." They all heard the wizard chortle. "I should have my potions ready soon."

Gareth immediately turned from the doorway and strode purposefully back toward a row of shelves loaded with books. "You two are my witnesses. He gave me permission to try."

Intrigued, Steve followed the boy to the closest shelf. "What are you going to do?"

"As I said, you use a spell to locate something, not a potion. Let's do this the right way, shall we?"

Gareth selected a few books, approached a stack of folded papers and selected one. He then knelt down to move several stacks of books off a large trunk. Realizing his hands were full, he wordlessly turned to Sarah to hand her the books he was holding along with the folded parchment. She immediately handed them to Steve, who frowned.

"Admit it," Sarah whispered to her husband. "You're liking him a little bit more now, aren't you?"

Steve grunted, but didn't say anything.

After rooting around in the trunk for a few seconds, Gareth came up clutching a small stone figurine, something like the king from a chess set. Gareth walked back by Steve and, without breaking step, took the parchment from him. He spread it open on an undamaged table and set the figurine in the middle of it.

Shardwyn's apprentice then reclaimed possession of the books he had selected and began skimming through them, mumbling to himself. Sarah leaned over the table to see what was on the paper. It was a map of Lentari. Steve joined her and gazed impassively at the document.

"What are we doing now?" Steve wanted to know.

"We're waiting to see what Gareth is going to do."

"There're some things on this map that I didn't know existed," Steve remarked, gazing down at it.

Sarah tapped the water off the western coast of the kingdom.

"I remember hearing the name of this ocean somewhere, but had forgotten it. The Erudian Ocean. It has a nice ring to it."

"Look at this," Steve murmured, tapping the country to the south of Lentari. "Straosia. I never knew what this was called."

Gareth batted Steve's hand away from the map. "Don't touch. I'm about ready."

"Dude, tell me you didn't just bat my hand away."

"Hmm? Of course, I did. You just watched me do it."

Hoping to defuse the situation, Sarah tapped Gareth's book.

"What are you going to do? Can you explain it to us?"

"I've created a locator spell and have tied it to this map," Gareth explained. He picked up the stone figurine and placed it over R'Tal. "The castle will be our starting point. As soon as the spell finds this flower, provided it exists…"

"It does," Sarah assured him.

"…then it'll move the figurine to its exact location on the map. Then you'll know where to go."

"Do you think this will really work?" Steve wanted to know.

Gareth shot him a look. "Look, I know you don't trust me. I even understand why and cannot fault you for that. But when it comes to spells, I can safely say that I know what I'm doing."

"How long will this take?" Sarah asked.

Gareth shrugged. "I don't know. It could be instantaneous or it could take a while longer. I've never done a search for this pontal before so I don't have any other information than that."

The teenager closed his eyes, drew an invisible symbol in the air with his right hand, and softly chanted. The stone figurine started to emit a soft glow, as though lit from within. Gareth smiled as he pointed at the figurine.

"There. You see? It's working. As long as the figurine is glowing, you'll know the spell is searching. Once it completes the search and finds this plant, then it'll move the figurine to its location."

Steve nodded appreciatively. "Beautiful. Think you'll find it before Shardwyn?"

Gareth cast a quick glance at the ceiling. "Without a doubt," he quietly whispered.

Steve finally cracked a smile at the boy and headed toward the closest window. Sarah followed.

"Watch out for the broken glass," Steve cautioned. "Damn stuff is everywhere."

"Hey, you're the one who set off the explosion in here," Sarah pointed out. "The broken glass is your fault."

"I didn't see you objecting," Steve countered. "In fact, I was pretty sure I saw that dresser over there, the one that looks like a charcoal briquette at the moment, start to move. It looked to me like it was in the process of rising from the ground. You wouldn't happen to know anything about that, would you?"

Sarah grinned. "Nope. You can't prove a thing."

"Uh-huh. My point is, you were just as surprised as I was to learn Gareth was the renegade wizard. I just happened to attack first. My reflexes are just better than yours."

Sarah's eyes widened.

"Excuse me? Just because you got off a few lucky shots doesn't mean you have better reflexes."

Her husband grinned at her. "I do believe I have been challenged. Well, my dear, challenge accepted."

Sarah felt a tap on her shoulder. Gareth was there and he was smiling at her.

"Told you I could do it."

"What? You found it already?"

"It was just pontal," Gareth scoffed. "I knew it wasn't going to be hard to find. Come on, I'll show you."

The boy led them back to the table with the map. The figurine was no longer glowing and was still sitting directly on R'Tal. Gareth stared at the figure in shock.

"What? What happened? It moved; I swear it!"

Gareth picked the small stone figure up and set it over an area of the forest east of Avin.

"It was right about here. You have to believe me!"

"I knew it wasn't going to be that easy," Steve muttered. "Nothing ever is."

Gareth replaced the figurine and began chanting once more, only this time it was in a forced rush. Trying her best not to smile, Sarah headed back toward the open window. There were too many nasty burnt smells lingering in the air from the explosion and she craved fresh air. She took her husband's hand in her own.

"Do you think either of them will be able to find the flower?"

"Gareth seemed pretty sure that he found it," Steve told her. "He may be a kid but he clearly knows what he's doing. I'd like to think it's only a matter of time before…"

"Hah!" Gareth exclaimed, rushing over to their position by the window. "I found it. Again. I made sure of it this time."

"Alrighty then," Steve said, turning back toward the map and the table. "Let's see where this thing is."

However, by the time they had returned to the map they were dismayed to see the stone figurine had reverted back to its inert self and was once more over R'Tal.

"What is going on?" Gareth cried, dumbfounded. "That's twice now!"

"Let's assume you did find it," Sarah began. "Was it..."

"I *did* find it," Gareth grumbled, glaring at the stone figure. "Several times."

"Did it move to the same place as before?" Sarah wanted to know.

Gareth shook his head. "That's the odd thing about it. My original spell must have been off. The figurine was in a slightly different place. It's almost as if ... if ... wait. Wait a moment."

"What?" Sarah asked, curious. "What is it?"

Gareth didn't answer. He returned to the shelves of books and selected another title. He was skimming through its contents as he walked back to the map table.

"That has to be it. It's the only explanation. Well, there's only one way to find out."

"What's going on?" Steve whispered in Sarah's ear.

"I'm not sure. I do think Gareth is on to something. Look, he's chanting. I think he's trying again."

Sure enough, the tiny stone figure began glowing. This time husband and wife decided to wait by the table. After thirty seconds of uncomfortable silence, the stone chess piece started to move. It finally stopped at a point several inches west of Avin.

"Didn't you say it was to the east of Avin before?" Steve asked, curiously.

Gareth nodded. "Aye, I did. That's because it was. I saw it!"

"Well, it's not there now, so we should..."

Steve trailed off as he and Sarah stared at the map with a look of astonishment on their faces. Gareth, on the other hand, had a smug, victorious look on his.

The figurine was moving.

"I added a locomotion layer to the spell," Gareth explained as they watched the stone figure slowly inch its way across the map. "I suspected that maybe the flower was moving and that was what's been causing my spell to fracture apart. So, I updated the locator marker—the stone figure—to keep moving should the target also be on the move. I really should have done that the first time."

"How in the world can a flower be moving?" Steve demanded. He pointed at the map. "When's the last time you saw a plant traipse across the countryside? There's gotta be some explanation we're overlooking here."

"Maybe it was eaten by an animal and we're now watching its progress across the kingdom?" Sarah suggested.

Steve shook his head. "Nuh-uh. Look at that thing go. It might be only inching across the map for us, but if you think about it in scale, that speed looks to be faster than a dragon can fly. I don't think anything can move faster than a dragon."

Shardwyn reappeared, holding a metal chalice with a bubbling liquid in it. He held it victoriously up in the air.

"Behold! This will not only locate your elusive pontal, Lady Sarah, but will also conjure it here, all in one fell swoop!"

The liquid in the goblet continued to boil away, as though it was suspended over a hot fire. Sarah gave the goblet a wary glance.

"Is it safe, Shardwyn? It doesn't smell very good."

"Good potions are always known by their scent, Lady Sarah. The more foul the smell, the more powerful the potion."

Gareth frowned and leaned forward to inspect the contents of the goblet. "Shardwyn, that's not exactly true. I, er, what is that smell? What did you use?"

"Firtendril, luchfern, blacklarch, and a pinch of algallocust."

"Blacklarch? We don't have any. It was all old. Too volatile. I threw it out. How did you get it?"

"Found it in the rubbish bin, dear boy. It still has plenty of potency left in its leaves."

Gareth groaned. "Shardwyn, that's the problem. Blacklarch gets stronger as it ages. It will get to the point that it becomes too strong. That's why I threw it out!"

Right on cue, the goblet in Shardwyn's hand began

frothing harder. With a look of surprise, the wizard stared at his goblet.

"Well, I'll be. Look at that! If I didn't know any better then I'd say it was about to—"

Gareth snatched the goblet out of Shardwyn's hands and thrust it into Sarah's.

"Get it out of here! Hurry!"

The goblet vanished. A few seconds later they heard a distant explosion. Steve looked out the window at the nearby eastern shore. The Sea of Koralis was visible, as was a large plume of dark gray smoke.

"You sent it out over the water," Steve said, nodding. "Nice one, babe."

"I didn't know what else to do with it," Sarah admitted. "Spontaneous teleporting is not something I'm good at."

"I'm sorry, Lady Sarah," Gareth apologized. "I wasn't too sure what to do with it, either. Can you imagine what would have happened to us if you hadn't been here?"

"I would have just tossed it out the window," Shardwyn harrumphed. "These walls are strong. My tower can withstand practically any blast."

"Dude, what if there had been someone out there?" Steve protested, growing angry. "Soldiers are always on patrol. How would you have felt if you had hurt someone?"

Shardwyn poked his head out the window and peered down.

"Hmm, perhaps you have a point, young sir. I should have considered that possibility. I will be careful in the future. Fear not, dear boy. All I need to do is find some fresh blacklarch and we're back in business. In fact, I do believe there's some by…" Shardwyn trailed off as he spotted the map with the stone figurine inching across the surface. "What have we here? Mister Gareth, what is all this mess?"

"This *mess*," Gareth sputtered, trying valiantly to keep from losing his temper, "is a multi-layered spell. I have found Lady Sarah's plant, only it appears to be on the move. What do you think, Shardwyn? Could someone else have found it and harvested it before us?"

Shardwyn pulled a chair over to the table to study the

phenomenon closer. He pulled his pale green pointed cap off his head, wiped his spectacles on the hat's soft velvety surface, and replaced both items. He turned to look at his apprentice and shrugged.

"Truth be told, my very young apprentice, I'm not really sure. Perhaps I could write a spell that could check to see if any other organisms are nearby. That would indicate whether or not it's been harvested."

"Or eaten," Steve added, nodding his approval.

Gareth laid a hand on Shardwyn's shoulder and gripped it tightly. "Tell you what, I've already got my spell working. It's presently using four different layers. With your permission, I'll add a fifth layer to see if the pontal has been compromised."

"Why yes," Shardwyn smiled, beaming his approval and patting Gareth's hand patronizingly, "you do that. That would be good practice for you."

Sarah giggled softly and glanced at the teenager. Gareth shot her a look, rolled his eyes, and set to work. The stone figure stopped inching across the map and quickly slid over to R'Tal, where it fell still. Gareth's eyes closed and he took several deep breaths. A few seconds later he started to softly chant.

Sarah leaned forward, but the words were too soft to hear. She took her husband's hand, blew him a kiss as soon as he looked her way, and settled down to wait. She was uncertain how long it would take Gareth to make the change. She could always…

Gareth's eyes opened. He looked over at Sarah and smiled at the two of them. Then the youth's eyes found Shardwyn's and a look of disgust swept over his features. Gareth noticed he was being watched and quickly composed himself.

"I'm finished. Are we ready to get started?"

"So what have you done?" Steve wanted to know. "How will you know if something has happened to the flower?"

"If the flower has been compromised," Gareth explained as he rotated the stone figure to face west, "the eyes will glow. If the flower has been eaten, the eyes will be blue. If it's been harvested, the eyes will be green."

Sarah nodded. "Got it. Let's see what it does."

Gareth activated the spell and stepped back. Together the four of them watched the stone figure slide across the table to land a few inches from where it had previously been. As before, the figurine began to slowly inch across the map.

Gareth leaned over the map so he could see the eyes for himself. He frowned. There was no color. The figurine's eyes weren't glowing.

"So what does that mean?" Steve demanded. "If the flower wasn't picked, and it definitely wasn't eaten, then what does that leave us?"

Gareth sank down into a chair across from Shardwyn. He stared hard at the map and its moving locator. He looked up at Steve.

"It means it's moving. It hasn't been eaten. It hasn't been harvested. That could only mean wherever that flower is growing, the land it's growing on is moving along with it."

"Impossible," Steve snorted.

"If I didn't know any better then I'd say that…" Gareth trailed off as he quickly sat up straight in his chair. "Wait. Wait a minute."

"You're on to something," Sarah observed. "Care to share?"

"When everything else has been ruled out, then whatever is left, however illogical, must be the answer."

Sarah risked a glance at Steve before tapping Gareth's shoulder.

"That's the sort of thing Sherlock Holmes would say, although how you would know that is beyond me."

Gareth gave Sarah an approving stare. "Sherlock Holmes is my favorite literary character! Is he yours, too?"

Steve spun the teenager around until he was facing him. "How in the world do you know anything about Sherlock Holmes? He's a fictitious character from my world."

Gareth was nodding. "I know! I love reading all about his exploits in the foggy kingdom of London. I really need to return that book to Mikal. He's the one who lent it to me."

"And *we* lent it to him," Sarah dryly recalled. She winked at Gareth. "Why don't you keep it? With our permission. We can always pick up another copy back home."

Gareth looked at Sarah with wide, wondrous eyes. "Really? You're gifting me your precious book? Thank you! I'll cherish it always!"

Sarah pointed back at the map. "Okay, back to the problem at hand. What were you saying about whatever was left, no matter how illogical, had to be the answer?"

"I was going to say that if I didn't know any better," Gareth continued, "then I would say that the flower, and whatever piece of land it was growing on, was floating, although I have no idea how that could be."

Shardwyn rapped his knuckles on the table and let out an exclamation of surprise.

"Of course! Why didn't I think of it? I should have known!"

"What, Shardwyn?" Steve asked, genuinely curious. "What should you have known?"

"I know of only one possibility, Sir Steve," Shardwyn proudly answered, thrilled that he knew something his young apprentice did not. "It would seem we're looking for the floating isle of Ranal."

Chapter 5 — An Empyrean Enigma

"Would you care to elaborate?" Sarah asked, looking at Shardwyn and offering the wizard a friendly smile. "I've never heard of Ranal, nor have I ever heard of a floating island." She looked at her husband, who shrugged and shook his head. She glanced over at Gareth, who also shook his head. Evidently, he knew just as much as she did.

"Whereas I wish I could tell you everything you want to know," Shardwyn began, "I cannot. Little is known about the floating isle. What I can tell you is that Ranal is to the griffins as Nevir is to the wyverians."

"So, this floating island is a griffin graveyard," Steve surmised with a groan. "And naturally this flower is indigenous to that island only. The Fae can't fly, so they can't reach it."

Gareth looked up with surprise. "The Fae? What does this have to do with the faeries?"

"Better forget I said that, dude," Steve warned, under his breath.

Gareth nodded. "Consider it forgotten."

Sarah frowned. "Now that we know the flower is on this floating island, how is this going to help us?"

"Are you kidding me?" Steve asked, confused. "We finally have a break! We should easily be able to spot a floating chunk of land. Our problems are solved!"

"Not so fast," Sarah disagreed. "If it were that easy, wouldn't it have been spotted by now? Why is it we've never heard about this Ranal place? I think we're missing something else here. We need more information."

"I'm not going back to those Archives," Steve vowed, crossing his arms over his chest. "I'd rather do battle with a horde of trolls than see that nasty old crone again."

Gareth, in the process of taking a large gulp of water from his goblet, spewed his drink all over himself. He hastily wiped a sleeve across his mouth and smiled sheepishly. Steve looked over at the teenager and noticed the water still dripping down the front of his tunic.

"Let me venture a guess. You've met Ms. Congeniality before?"

Gareth nodded. "I haven't been that tempted to break the rules in a long time. Do you have any idea how easy it is to turn someone into a toad?"

"You'd probably be doing her a favor," Steve muttered, eliciting a smack on the arm from Sarah.

"Are you talking about lovely Ms. Alwyn?" Shardwyn asked, picking up the thread of their conversation. "What a wonderful, intelligent, and charming woman. She's run the Archives for decades. Decades! I've admired her tenacity for years."

Sarah looked away before she could burst out laughing. Steve shuddered at the idea of the old wizard and cantankerous archivist getting cozy, closed his eyes, and shook his head in a futile attempt to erase the mental image.

"Gross," Gareth softly muttered. "I could have done without hearing that."

Steve snorted once, coughed twice, and then cleared his throat. "Well, with that bit of unpleasantness out of the way, what's our next step? Where do we go from here?"

"If we're looking for a griffin graveyard," Sarah began, "then we should be talking with the griffins. They must know how to find this island."

"That should be easy enough," Steve decided. "I think we can take it from here. Shardwyn, thank you for your help. Gareth, you, too. Sorry I tried to blast you."

Gareth smiled appreciatively. "Don't be. Based on my history, I would have done the same. If you ever need help again, please let me know. I'll get you on the—cough—right path."

Shardwyn nodded, wished them luck, and sank down into an armchair near the window. The chair, unsurprisingly, was battle scarred and creaked heavily in protest. The elderly wizard leaned back, closed his eyes, and appeared to go to sleep.

"We're sorry we blew up his workspace," Sarah whispered to his apprentice. "Thanks to us, you have one heck of a mess to clean up, not to mention having to restock all of Shardwyn's potion ingredients."

Gareth waved a dismissive hand. "Don't be. I've been harassing him for some time now to throw everything away and start from scratch. This is the perfect opportunity to get him organized."

"Just do me a favor," Steve called back as he and Sarah started down the stairs.

"Anything!" Gareth called back.

"Go to the Archives. Introduce Shardwyn to our favorite old lady. Let's see what happens."

It was Gareth's turn to shudder. "That's not even funny."

"You must visit the Pools…"

Sarah froze in mid step. She snagged Steve's arm and drew him to a stop.

"What? What is it?"

"Did you hear that?" she quietly asked.

"No. Did you hear something?"

Gareth's head appeared in the doorway. "You should hear this," the teenager quietly informed them. "Hurry. He keeps repeating the same thing over and over. I thought he was just talking in his sleep but he seems to be in some type of trance. He keeps saying 'Ranal.' I thought you should know."

Sarah hurried back into the room and timidly approached the prone form of the wizard.

"Shardwyn?" she coaxed. "What were you saying?"

"You must visit the Pools of Ranal," Shardwyn murmured.

Frowning, Steve leaned close and studied Shardwyn's wrinkled face.

"It looks like he's sleeping," he whispered.

"What about the pools?" Sarah asked, hoping she could keep the conversation going. "Are there pools on Ranal?"

"Only in His hands," Shardwyn continued, after being silent for nearly a full minute, "will you find that which you seek."

"Whose hands?" Steve asked. "How are we supposed to—?"

"Hush," Sarah scolded. "Shardwyn, can you tell us whose hands you're referring to?"

"You must visit the Pools," the wizard intoned.

"The Pools of Ranal?" Steve guessed, holding back a smile and leaning forward.

Shardwyn's wrinkled face suddenly broke out into a smile. His eyes opened. "I'm so sorry."

Taken aback, Steve straightened. "What are you sorry for?"

"I was only napping, Sir Steve," Shardwyn insisted. "Did my apprentice ask you to do it?"

"Do what?" Steve asked, completely confused.

"Check for a pulse. Young Mister Gareth fancies having a sense of humor. He's constantly checking my pulse whenever I happen to doze off."

"Better safe than sorry," Gareth muttered. The teenager turned back to the charred potion rack and continued his inventory.

Sarah hooked her arm through her husband's and pulled him from the room. "Thanks again, Shardwyn. You, too, Gareth. We'll see ourselves to the door."

Emerging into the bright sunshine, and—thank

heavens—fresh air, Sarah led Steve back toward the castle.

"What was that all about?" Steve asked. "Do you think he was talking in his sleep?"

Sarah shrugged. "I have no idea."

"Do you think Pheris is here today?" Steve wondered.

"That's what I'm hoping," Sarah answered. The two of them walked through the Northern Gates and headed toward the Great Hall. "If he isn't, maybe someone will know where he is."

"If we can't find him, we can always try his son, Phane," Steve suggested. "At least we know where he lives."

"We *did* know where he lived," Sarah corrected. "That was years ago. You're assuming Phane didn't move his flock after the battle with Celestia. After all, she did send a large number of trolls to his island."

"True, but we did take care of the trolls for them."

They found the Great Hall full of people and both thrones occupied. Kri'Entu's head jerked up the moment they were spotted. Steve nodded toward the Antechamber, prompting the king to all but leap out of his chair. The queen, not wanting to be excluded, followed at a more comfortable rate. Only when they were all inside the king's private chamber, and the doors were sealed, did Steve ask their question.

"Is Pheris around today?"

Kri'Entu shook his head. "Pheris retired from his position at the beginning of the year. Is this urgent? I can send for the current griffin liaison, if you'd like."

Sarah nodded. "Yes, please. We need to talk to a griffin."

The king was curious. Sarah could see it on his face.

"May I ask why?"

"Not yet, I'm afraid," Sarah reluctantly told him.

"Ah. Very well. You may use the Antechamber."

Sarah smiled. "Thank you, Your Majesty."

With a sigh, the king departed just as the queen appeared in the doorway. Kri'Entu took his wife's hand, spun her around, and the two of them quickly left. They could hear the queen talking as her voice eventually faded away.

"What if this new griffin doesn't know where to find Pheris?" Steve asked.

"Then we'll have to just ask him how to find this floating island," Steve decided.

"And if he doesn't know?" Sarah pressed.

"It's the griffin graveyard. There's gotta be at least one griffin out there who knows how to find this place. Otherwise, we will…"

Steve trailed off as he heard a tapping noise, coming from a closed door. Sarah made it there first and opened it to find an adult griffin staring back at her with as much fascination in its avian eyes as she had in her human ones. The griffin bowed just as Sarah moved to the side, allowing him to come inside.

"I'm Sarah, and this is my husband, Steve," Sarah told the griffin.

"I am called Raben," a distinctly feminine voice answered. "How may I be of service?"

Sarah shot her husband a surprised glance before giving the griffin a smile. "We were hoping to talk to…"

"Wait," Raben interrupted, rustling her wings against her back. "You're the teleporter, aren't you? Our Prime has told us all about you." Raben turned to Steve, cocked her avian head, and regarded him for a few moments. "And you! You must be the fire thrower. Aye, I've heard about you, too. I know you were responsible for burning most the feathers off my father's wings during your first encounter."

Steve jammed his hands in his trouser pockets and stared at the floor.

"Ooookay. Awkward. Look, I, er, that was a long time ago. If you want to get technical about it, I was the one who proposed helping you griffins. Once we stopped trying to kill each other, that is."

Surprisingly, Raben extended one of her aquiline front legs and bowed again, dropping her head close to the floor. "I know, Fire Thrower. All griffins know the story. I meant no disrespect. I am just protective of my sire."

"As you should be," Sarah told her. "What happened is in the past. You mentioned 'prime.' Is that the leader of the griffins?"

"There is no leader over all griffins," Raben clarified.

"Our Prime governs and protects our flock. We will come to the aid of another flock, should the need arise, but in essence all flocks are self-sufficient."

Sarah nodded. "Got it. Listen, do you know what happened to Pheris?"

"Of course. He retired from his position here. Pheris recognized the importance of having a griffin presence here amongst the humans, so the call went out for a replacement. I am proud, and honored that I was selected to take his place."

"Where is Pheris now?" Steve asked.

"Why do you want to know?" Raben suspiciously asked.

"He's a friend," Sarah quickly answered. "We'd like to say hello."

"Pheris is with the flock."

"Is your flock still living in the same place it was when I, er, had the run-in with your father?" Steve asked.

Raben nodded. "Aye. There is no need to relocate our nests. Our numbers are too great. Nothing challenges us, save the wyverians, and there has been no discord for many years. We all live in peace."

Sarah held out her hand and waited for her husband to take it. She turned back to Raben and offered the griffin another smile.

"Thank you. You've been incredibly helpful. Would you please tell the king that we've left?"

"You're leaving?" Raben asked. "Are you planning on visiting my flock?"

Steve nodded. "Yep. Not for long though. Don't worry, I'll be on my best behavior."

"Just don't—" Raben stopped and sighed as she noticed she was now in the room by herself. "...arrive unannounced. Griffins hate surprises."

* * *

"This place hasn't changed much," Steve observed as he glanced around the large clearing they were standing in.

"At least the burn marks have gone away," Sarah remarked.

"Burn marks? There never were any. All the blasting I did

was aimed up."

"Oh."

Steve was silent as he studied the quiet clearing. "I can't believe it's been, um, how many years has it been since we were first here?"

Sarah shrugged. "It's been a while."

"I don't see any nests. Do you?"

Sarah stared at her husband for a few moments. "You're joking, right?"

"What?"

"Tell me you're kidding."

"Hon, look around," Steve instructed, pointing at several trees. "Do you see any nests? I sure don't. I think Raben sent us on a wild goose chase."

"Steve, they were never here to begin with."

"What? Yes, they were. Trust me, I know. I fought with them right here."

"Don't you remember what happened afterward? Once the griffins stopped attacking and you stopped shooting fire at them?"

"Of course, I do," Steve snapped, growing angry. "I was there. You weren't. Not at first, that is."

Sarah silently counted to ten.

"When I arrived, I administered aid to the adult griffins that were injured. Remember?"

"Yeah. With you so far."

"Good. Were the griffin cubs there, too?"

"Yes, you healed them. I watched you do it."

"Gingko. You're getting gingko for Christmas."

"Bite me," Steve scoffed. "What's your point?"

"The babies didn't arrive until after I did, which means?"

Steve sobered as his smug smile vanished from his face. "Oh. Damn. I forgot about that. I guess that means their nests weren't around here."

"Very good, Einstein."

"There's no need to be rude," Steve grumped.

"You were rude to me first," Sarah pointed out. "For no reason. You owe me an apology."

"Fine. You were right, I was wrong. Happy?"

"And?"

"And what?"

"What did we agree would happen when you deliberately act like an ass?"

Steve sighed. "You'd get a ten-minute back massage."

"It was twenty. Nice try."

"Fine. So where are their nests? Do you remember?"

Sarah shook her head. "No. They never did say, only that they were nearby."

"So how do we get their attention?" Steve asked. "How can we get them to come to us?"

"I don't know," Sarah admitted. "Maybe I could just teleport around a few times and see if I can spot them."

"Don't waste your jhorun," Steve told her as he strode by. "I'll get their attention."

Alarmed, Sarah grabbed her husband's arm and pulled him to a stop.

"What are you going to do?"

"Watch."

Her husband ignited both hands and moved at least fifty feet away. A large fireball swirled into existence in his right hand. Steve cupped the fireball with his other hand and began moving his hands apart, stretching the chaser like pizza dough.

Sarah watched the fireball grow larger. As soon as it was the size of her inflated exercise ball, he released it into the air. It sped straight up and exploded, ten seconds later. The forest fell silent. Kytes retreated to their nests. Insects sought shelter. Sarah was certain she would have been able to hear a hushed conversation from the other side of the clearing.

"That's your plan? Scaring the crap out of every living thing around here? Were you planning on making the griffins faint right out of their trees?"

Steve clasped his hands behind his back and slowly walked back toward his wife. "Give it a moment. They should be here shortly."

"In your dreams, buddy boy. The only thing you just did was drive them away."

"I'll bet they make contact before I can make it back to

you," Steve challenged.

Sarah smiled, thinking instantly of the massage she would be receiving tonight. Wouldn't it be nice to make it forty minutes instead of twenty? This was like taking candy from a baby. Perhaps she shouldn't take advantage of him? Then again, she was in the mood for a little candy.

"I'll take that bet. Double or nothing tonight."

"For the massage? It's a bet."

"A forty-minute massage," Sarah breathed, smiling profusely. "That's going to feel wonderful."

"I still have about fifteen feet to go," Steve cautioned. "Don't get cocky."

"I still have some of that lavender-scented oil in our cottage back in R'Tal. I think that will do nicely."

However, a second later, they heard the tell-tale squawk of a griffin.

"Damn," Sarah softly swore. "You got lucky. Boo. I was totally looking forward to a massage tonight. My back has been aching."

Steve approached and squeezed her shoulders. He leaned down to peck her on the cheek. "Don't worry, babe. I'll give you one anyway."

"And that's why I love you so much. How did you know the griffins were on the way?"

"Because I saw them in the distance before I detonated that large chaser. There's no way they didn't see it."

Sarah laughed. "You cheater. No wonder you were so confident. I should have known you had a trick or two up your sleeve."

She and her husband spotted the griffin circling high above their heads. Then a second. And a third. Within moments, more than a dozen griffins were circling high overhead and from the sounds of their squawks, they weren't happy.

One of their number, a griffin that was larger than any they had seen before, tucked its wings and dove straight for them. Sarah dropped to the ground while Steve leapt to the right.

"Oh, *hell* no," Steve spat as he rolled to his feet. "We aren't doing this again. We need to… Look out!"

A second griffin swooped by, dangerously close, causing them to once more dive to the ground.

"They're supposed to be our friends," Steve grumbled. "Why are they attacking?"

"They're diving again!" Sarah cried. "What do we do? I don't want to hurt them."

Steve looked up at the diving griffin, ignited his hands once more, and blasted a huge wall of flames straight up. Sarah watched the diving griffin flap its wings in a frantic attempt to avoid the blast of fire. However, there was nowhere for it to go. No matter how it twisted and turned, it would not be able to elude Steve's flames.

Just before contact, the wall of fire poofed out. The griffin that was about to be deep fried scrambled away, squeaking like a frightened mouse the entire time. Sarah breathed a sigh of relief. Her husband hadn't wanted to hurt the griffins any more than she did, so…

A large shape fell from the sky and zipped by her. She stumbled to the ground and let out an alarmed scream. Steve was by her side in a flash.

"The dumbasses are still attacking! Even after I snuffed out my flames so I didn't toast that griffin. Did they hurt you? I swear, if they did—"

Sarah held out a hand and waited for her husband to pull her to her feet. She glared angrily up at the circling griffins before she came to a decision.

"You tried it your way. Now let me try it mine."

"What are you gonna do?"

"Watch and learn, dear."

Sarah quickly glanced up and watched three of them dive straight for her. All three griffins suddenly squawked with surprise and froze in midair, wings extended. Sarah gave her husband a victorious smile and gently lowered the immobile griffins to the ground.

They heard a challenging shriek. The rest of the flock were preparing to attack when a loud squawk silenced them all. A new griffin had appeared on the scene and from the looks of it, this newcomer was livid. It flew from griffin to griffin, angrily squawking and trilling the entire time. After a few moments, it gently spiraled and touched down on the grass in front of Steve and Sarah.

It was Pheris. The griffin was definitely older, had a few white feathers here and there, but remained sprightly. Pheris turned to the two of them and bowed once.

"My most humble of apologies. Friend Steve. Friend Sarah. Please tell me no one was hurt."

"I didn't touch 'em," Steve began, holding both hands up, palms out. "Sarah will vouch for me."

"I'm not talking about *them*," Pheris snapped, glancing irritably at the three immobile griffins staring back at him with pleading expressions. "I'm talking about the two of you. Are you uninjured?"

"We're fine, Pheris," Sarah assured him. "We couldn't figure out why we were attacked."

"There was a large explosion and Brennus, our scout, claimed we were under attack. I should have known better than to take his word."

"No harm done, my friend," Steve told him.

"Can I let them go?" Sarah asked, pointing at the three frozen griffins.

"Please. I do believe I'd like to speak to them privately."

Sarah motioned with her hand. The three frozen griffins finally rose to their feet and stretched their wings. They warily eyed Pheris. One of them let out a tremulous squawk. Pheris, on the other hand, or wing, looked up at the griffins circling about overhead and squawked loudly at them. The remaining airborne griffins grudgingly landed.

For the next five minutes Pheris berated them with squawks, chirps, trills, and probably every other expletive in the griffin language. Every single griffin, aside from Pheris, stared at the ground.

From a nearby log, Sarah rose to her feet and pulled Steve up. Pheris was moving back toward them.

"Sounds like you ripped them a new one," Steve observed.

"I am not familiar with that phrase," Pheris returned.

"It means, uh, it means you scolded them."

"Aye. They needed to hear it. So, friend Steve, friend Sarah, what brings you here? Is there something I can do for you?"

"We need to ask you for a favor," Steve began. He noticed the disgraced griffins were still within earshot and all had cocked their heads, listening. Sarah noticed, too.

"Can we speak privately?" she asked their griffin friend.

Pheris let off another series of unfriendly squawks and trills. With a mad flapping of wings, their attackers scrambled to put distance between themselves and Pheris. Steve glanced up at the receding griffins and noticed a few with red feathers.

"Out of curiosity, how long do griffins live?"

"That's what you wished to speak to me privately about?" Pheris asked, bewildered.

"No, I was just wondering. Several of those griffins had red feathers on their wings, but not many. Most were adults."

"Aye, and they should know better than to act like juveniles," Pheris angrily agreed. "To answer your question, a lifespan of one-hundred-fifty years is not unheard of."

"And how old are you?" Steve inquired. "If you don't want to say, that's fine. I was just curious."

"I am well past my century mark," the griffin told them. "Why do you ask all these questions?"

"We need to ask you about Ranal," Sarah confided, lowering her voice to a whisper.

Pheris' eyes widened with surprise. He hurriedly checked the skies to assure they were alone. He clucked his tongue disapprovingly.

"That subject is considered taboo," Pheris answered, also lowering his voice. "Why do you want to know about it?"

"Is it a floating island?"

Pheris' eyes narrowed suspiciously.

"Aye. I should warn you that talking about Ranal is considered bad form. I answer now only because you are friends. Everything I tell you about that island is to be held in the strictest confidence, is that understood?"

Sarah automatically nodded, as did her husband.

"Good. Now, what is it you wish to know? I am uncomfortable with this subject so I will only answer that which you ask and will not volunteer more."

Sarah smiled. "We understand. Thank you for agreeing to talk to us about this."

Pheris nodded and waited quietly.

"Why is the island considered taboo?" Steve asked in a quiet voice.

"Ranal is where griffins go to die," Pheris hesitantly answered. "I cannot even begin to fathom why you wish to know this."

Sarah steeled herself and took a breath. "We have to find this island, Pheris."

The griffin's eyes widened and he squawked with alarm.

Sarah shrugged and helplessly held up her hands. "I'm sorry, but we have to. Somewhere on that island is an incredibly rare flower, er pontal. We *must* find it in the next day or two."

Pheris squawked again. Their griffin friend was staring at them as though they had each grown a second head. After a few moments, the griffin found his voice. His human voice, that is.

"This pontal," Pheris began, "…it can only be found on Ranal?"

Sarah nodded. "Yes. It's the only place. Is it that hard to find?"

Pheris began pacing back and forth in front of them. "You must understand Ranal. It is not hard to find…"

"Awesome," Steve whispered, giving Sarah a smile.

"…if you feel the *Pull*. Only griffins can see it…"

"Figures," Steve mumbled.

"Only griffins can find it," Pheris continued.

Steve groaned. "Of course. Why wouldn't they?"

"And, most importantly, as I've already mentioned, only those who feel the *Pull* will be able to find it."

Steve shared a look with Sarah. "Pull? What pull?"

Sarah suddenly deduced what Pheris meant. "He means only those griffins that are dying will be able to find the island."

"I ask again, is this your desire?" Pheris said, coming to a stop before Sarah. "You wish to find Ranal?"

"We don't have any choice. I'm sorry. We have to."

"This puts me in an uncomfortable position," Pheris admitted.

"Why?" Steve asked, growing cautious. "Are you going to try and stop us?"

Pheris shook his head. "No. What it means is that I must find a griffin who is about to die and ask if he or she is ready to make their final journey."

"Does that mean they're making a journey to find the pull?" Steve asked, still confused.

"No. A griffin will not feel the *Pull* until they've accepted it is their time to die. Only then will they be compelled to begin their last journey."

"Oh. So that means…"

Pheris squawked with disgust.

"It means I must discreetly inquire within the flock to see if anyone wishes to die."

Steve whistled. "That doesn't sound like fun at all."

Pheris leveled a gaze at him. "Sarcasm?"

Steve laughed. "Yes. That was sarcasm."

Pheris snorted once. "Good. All those years in the human castle were not wasted in vain after all."

"You didn't enjoy being in the castle?" Sarah asked, appalled.

Pheris chuckled. "*That* was sarcasm."

"No," Sarah corrected, "*that* was a bad joke."

"Oh."

"Will you help us?" Sarah asked.

"Aye. This won't be easy. Follow me."

"We can't fly," Steve pointed out. "We can't follow you."

"We might not be able to fly," Sarah said, "but we can follow along the ground. I can keep teleporting to keep you in sight."

"That will do. Let us be off."

Pheris took to the air and flew northeast. Sarah took her husband's hand and teleported them as far as she could see in that direction. They appeared in the midst of huge, towering trees. Thankfully they could still see the sky. Right on cue, Pheris flew over their location. Sarah nodded and prepared for their next jump.

"Don't forget, I don't have Mythrin with me," Steve reminded her, referring to his green-bladed Lentarian broadsword. "No Mythrin means no mimets. No power crystals, no recharges. If we run out of jhorun out here then we're on our own."

Sarah nodded. "Got it. I'll be careful. Besides, it's just the two of us. A two-person jump is a piece of cake."

Thirty minutes later husband and wife materialized in a deeper, darker part of the forest. The trees were as tall as before, but were spaced a little farther apart. There were a few locations where they could barely find the room to navigate between the trees, let alone being able to watch for Pheris to fly overhead, but thankfully, Sarah never lost sight of him.

"Do you see him?" her husband asked, looking up at the bright blue sky.

"Yes. It looks like he's descending."

"He's coming down to talk to us?"

Sarah gently turned Steve's head until they were both looking in the same direction.

"He's right over there. See how he's slowly coming down? Maybe his nest is over there. It looks like it's no more than a quarter of a mile away."

"Good. That means we're close." This time Steve took her hand and started pulling her through the trees. "Come on, let's go find him."

After ten minutes they came to another stop. There, directly ahead of them on the forest floor, were half a dozen griffin cubs. They were running circles around each other, leaping, wrestling, and even flapping their tiny wings. One of the small creatures, no bigger than a German shepherd, tripped over an exposed root and fell beak first into the lush grass. It quickly regained its feet, stared straight at the two of them, and let out a shriek of pure alarm.

It began raining griffins. Adults and juveniles seemingly appeared out of thin air and advanced angrily on them. One griffin, larger and missing a quarter of the feathers from its left wing, dropped out of the sky and squawked angrily at them.

"Who are you?" the griffin demanded. The high, somewhat nasal tone prevalent in all griffin speech threatened to make Steve laugh, but thankfully he kept his face comfortably parked in neutral. "What is the meaning of this intrusion? How did you find us?"

"I am responsible," Pheris' voice called out. Their griffin guide landed nearby and pushed his way through his flockmates to present himself before the griffin who had to be their Prime. "I brought them here."

"Why?" the Prime demanded. "I know you're fond of humans, Pheris, but escorting a pair of humans into our nests is unheard of, even for you. I am not pleased."

"Please, sire," Pheris pleaded. "These aren't just any humans. Other of their kind refer to them as Nohrin. I've told you about them. May I present the fire thrower, Steve, and his mate Sarah, the teleporter?"

The big griffin rounded on Steve. "You're the fire thrower? You look like a puny human to me. Prove it."

"You don't like humans," Steve casually remarked as he ignited both hands. "I get it. I don't have a problem with that. You want me to prove I'm the fire thrower? In the middle of the forest? Come on. Even you aren't that crazy." He held up his flaming hands. "Have you met many humans who can do this?"

The Prime eyed him for a few seconds before purposefully striding up to him. Her husband, Sarah noted, had yet to extinguish his hands.

"Why are you here, human? What do you want?"

Sarah, prepared for this particular question, stepped up to her husband's side.

"We've been all across this kingdom," Sarah casually explained, hoping her excuse sounded sincere, "and we've yet to ever come across an actual griffin village, or community, or whatever you call it. We're friends with Pheris here, so we thought we'd stop by and see if we could look around your home. Er, is that okay?"

The Prime rustled his wings irritably. "Fine. You're here. You saw our nests. Now you can go."

Surprised, Steve looked around the quiet patch of forest. Their nests were here? Where?

Sensing his thoughts, Sarah started studying the trees. Her gaze traveled up over a hundred feet of the nearest trunk to the canopy high above their heads. She squinted. Nothing looked out of the ordinary. Where were the nests?

Three trees away she saw one, she supposed. Less than twenty feet below the tree's canopy a large irregular mass stuck out in all directions from the trunk. The mass was at least as large as her SUV. Sarah checked the surrounding area. Half a dozen trees away she spotted another. Then another. She suddenly turned to the Prime and gave him her friendliest, most disarming smile.

"You know what? You're right. That was awfully rude of us, just barging in on you guys like that." Out of the corner of her eye she saw her husband give her a quizzical look. "Pheris, would you show us your nest before we go?"

She felt the Prime's eyes on them as they hurried away. Sarah risked a glance back. There he was, shaking his head as if he had decided all humans were just as imbecilic as he thought them to be. No doubt the Prime was wondering why Pheris was so fascinated with humans. Sarah shrugged. It wasn't her concern.

Once they were well away from prying eyes Steve pulled Sarah aside, forcing Pheris to stop and look back at them.

"What the hell was that all about? Why did you just give up like that?"

"Who said I was giving up?" Sarah countered.

"Okay, so what are we doing now?" Steve wanted to know.

"We need an excuse to hang out here for a little bit so that Pheris can discreetly check their elderly members."

"So that's why you wanted to see my nest," Pheris guessed.

Sarah nodded. "Right. How long do you think you'll need to check with the elderly?"

Pheris paused to consider. "Perhaps an hour, maybe more."

"Where is your nest?" Steve asked.

"We're nearly there. My tree is the one with the split trunk."

Sarah stared at Pheris' tree. Sure enough, the trunk looked as though someone had split the tree from top to bottom, leaving only a few feet near the roots intact. The split tree flowed around other trees nearby, forming a veritable net of interlaced branches. Perhaps that was why Pheris had chosen it?

"I was very surprised you didn't give the Prime a proper demonstration," Pheris lamented. "I really wanted to see the look on his face when he saw the full extent of your jhorun."

"I didn't think it'd be a good idea," Steve explained, walking around the trunk of Pheris' tree. "A huge blast of fire, in the middle of the forest? That's just asking for trouble."

"You're the fire thrower," Sarah reminded him. "Couldn't you have extinguished any fires that popped up? I know you can do it. I've seen you do it before."

"Smartass. Yeah, I could have, only how bad would that have made us look? 'Hey, thanks for showing us around your nests. Now let's see if I can set the whole damn place on fire.' No thanks. It wasn't worth it. I wasn't going to put Pheris in that position."

Pheris nodded. "Appreciated."

"Will you go find us a griffin who's willing to look for Ranal?"

They heard a loud squawk of surprise. Unfortunately, it didn't come from Pheris. A large shape moved out of the shadows and into the light. Sarah groaned. It was the Prime. It advanced on the three of them with its wings spread and marched by Sarah and her husband to confront Pheris. Their griffin friend, Sarah noted, was remarkably holding his ground, although his feathers did appear ruffled, as though he was trying to look as intimidating as possible.

"I knew something wasn't right," the Prime accused, eyeing Pheris dangerously. "Why else would you bring two humans into our midst?"

Steve snapped his fingers twice, causing the Prime to look his way. "Nuh-uh. If you have a problem, you come to us, or me specifically. I was the one who suggested we go to Pheris in the first place and therefore bring us here."

The Prime abandoned his advance on Pheris and rounded on Steve. "Humans have no say here. This is a griffin matter. Kindly keep your flat, ugly nose out of our affairs. If you … what are you doing?"

Steve raised his hands and now pointed both palms at the griffin. Sarah noticed both of her husband's hands had turned dark red and began inching behind Steve, motioning Pheris to do the same.

Steve released his jhorun into his hands, blasting out jets of fire. His flames, lacking a target, became whipping tentacles of fire that snaked through the air like an unattended fireman's hose. Steve blasted even more jhorun into his hands, and instructed the fire ropes to dance around the Prime's body.

You can scare, Steve instructed his jhorun, *but do not touch.*

The Prime remained motionless as the jets of fire whizzed by close enough to singe a few feathers. The old, grizzled griffin eyed them a few moments more before he snapped his wings closed and let out a loud squawk.

"Enough. You have made your point, Fire Thrower."

Steve allowed the fire ropes to extinguish and returned the Prime's defiant look. Sarah stepped forward and inserted herself between her husband and the griffin leader.

"I'll admit we should have contacted you first. However, we've known Pheris for years. He was the natural choice."

"What do you want here?" the Prime demanded. "Why do you seek Ranal?"

"Because there's a special pontal growing on that island I desperately need to get my hands on," Sarah answered.

"Pontal? You seek pontal? Look around you. Pontal grows everywhere."

"Not this flower, er, pontal," Steve pointed out. "Trust me, we've checked. This damn flower only exists on that island."

"Why do you need it?" the Prime asked, slowly pulling his wings back to his body.

"I'm afraid that part must be kept secret," Sarah answered.

The Prime looked back at Pheris. "What are your intentions? Ranal can only be found under the right circumstances. I know you know this."

"I am aware, sire," Pheris meekly said. "I was hoping to circulate amongst my flockmates and see if there's anyone who'd like to, that is to say, if there's anyone who, uh, er…"

"You are actually planning on asking the members of my

flock if they are ready to start their last journey, is that it?"

"Yes, sire."

"That's a very sensitive subject to bring up, don't you think, Pheris?"

"Yes, sire. I am sorry, but it must be done. Our flock numbers over two hundred. There must be someone who is ready to undertake the Journey."

"Try Achelous," the Prime suggested in a quiet whisper.

"Excuse me, sire?"

"Try Achelous," the Prime repeated, marginally raising his voice. "That cantankerous old buzzard does nothing but bitterly complain."

"Sire! He may be ornery but he appears to be in good health."

The Prime lowered his head and sidled up to Pheris. "What about Nessus? He hasn't left his nest in weeks. Or perhaps Arden?"

Pheris' eyes practically bugged out of his head. "Sire, you've just named three of your most outspoken foes! Was that intentional?"

The Prime chuckled with amusement. "Surely you jest. I do not know what you're referring to."

Steve stifled a chuckle.

The Prime glanced his way. "If I allow this, I do believe you will, as you humans would say it, owe me a favor."

Steve glanced over at Sarah, who nodded. "Fine. We'll owe you a favor, provided you help Pheris with his search."

The Prime looked at Pheris and nodded in the direction of the nests.

"Very well. I like the notion of the humans owing me a favor. This ought to be interesting. Pheris, let's go ruffle a few feathers, shall we?"

An hour and a half later they had their answer. Or, more specifically, they had their griffin. Tesur, an elderly griffin whose once tawny fur was now streaked with silver and whose wings were practically covered with white feathers, had agreed to open his senses tomorrow at sunrise to see if he could feel the Pull. It hadn't taken much convincing at all, Pheris told them later.

"He wanted to know why we wanted to go there," Pheris reported. "I told him it was important to the humans. He agreed almost immediately. He doesn't know if the Hand of Ranal will guide him, but at least he's willing to try."

Surprised, Sarah looked over at their griffin friend. "The Hand of Ranal? That's an interesting way to describe it."

"Do humans not feel a desire to undertake a journey when their time nears?" the Prime asked, curious. Sarah noticed Pheris had cocked his head in their direction, anxious to hear the answer.

She shook her head. "No, we don't."

"Not unless a ride in a hearse qualifies," Steve muttered to himself. Sarah elbowed him in the gut to shut him up.

"I certainly hope Tesur is ready," Sarah added, looking up at the rapidly disappearing sun. "We're running out of time."

Chapter 6 — Gateway Arch

Sarah awoke well before dawn. There was so much to do today that her spinning mind wouldn't stop pestering her with questions. What if Tesur didn't feel the Pull? What if he did feel the Pull, but they didn't find the island in time? What if they found the island in time but couldn't find the flower?

Sarah groaned and rolled on to her side. She and her husband were back in their small cabin after she steadfastly refused to spend the night out under the open stars. That was what their cabin was for, she had argued. Why run the risk of sleeping with insects—and who knows what else—when they had a perfectly comfortable bed *indoors* that she could instantly teleport them to?

Sleeping with bugs. Sarah shivered. She couldn't think of a worse way to wake up. For that matter, she was fairly certain she'd never be able to sleep knowing there was a chance *something* could crawl into bed with her.

Sarah gently crept out of bed and made her way to their tiny kitchen. She was desperate for a cup of hot tea. She pulled out a box of tea bags, brought from her expansive kitchen back home in Idaho, filled a mug with water, and dropped the tea bag in. As she silently headed back to the bedroom, she grabbed a towel that had been left on the small dining table. Entering the bedroom, she approached her husband, who was currently snoring like a lumberjack.

Recalling an often-used trick she had learned, she used her jhorun to create a small breeze to tickle her husband's nose, which resulted with him changing positions. Sleeping on his side, with his left arm jammed up under his pillow, Steve's right hand was sticking out from the covers, as Sarah knew it would be.

She walked around the bed and quietly knelt by his side. She gently placed her cup of cool water in his open hand and then in a practiced motion, readied her towel. She leaned close so that she could whisper in his ear.

"There's a guur getting ready to bite your right hand" Sarah whispered, referring to the heavily armored ten-legged insect that they fought during their first trip to Lentari.

Steve's hand instantly flamed up, bringing her water to a boil in seconds. Sarah waited a few moments then used the towel to carefully pluck the cup from Steve's hand, being careful not to slosh the hot liquid.

"You got 'em, honey. Good job."

The flames snuffed out. She let her husband sleep an additional twenty minutes while she enjoyed her tea before she decided they needed to get going.

"What happens if our griffin guide doesn't feel this *pull* thing?" Steve wanted to know as he munched on a granola bar. "That's going to cause a few problems, isn't it? Do we have a backup plan?"

"Think positive," Sarah instructed as she finished her tea. "Tesur will feel the Pull. I know he will."

"How is this going to work?" her husband asked as he wiped a crumb of granola from his face.

"How is what going to work?" Sarah wanted to know. "Are you asking about the Pull? I guess once the griffin decides he, or she, wants to die, then some unknown force guides them to wherever they need to go."

"That's not what I was asking. What I mean is, this griffin. Tesur? He's old, right?"

Sarah nodded. "I would assume so."

"So, he's old and definitely not in his prime. How is he going to carry the two of us? Wouldn't our combined weight be too much for him?"

Sarah stared at him, aghast. He was right, of course. There was no way that poor old griffin would be able to carry their combined weight.

She glanced out the nearest window. The sun hadn't come up. Yet. However, it was close.

"You didn't think of that one, either," Steve guessed.

"No, I didn't. What are we going to do? We're due back at the nests in ten, maybe fifteen minutes!"

"Take us to R'Tal. We're going to let the king figure this out."

Sarah took her husband's hand. "The king probably isn't up this early."

"Then we're gonna wake him up."

* * *

"I'm very glad you're an early riser, Your Majesty."

Sarah and her husband had just been ushered into the Antechamber where the king had sunk into his chair.

Kri'Entu nodded. "As am I. I wouldn't want to miss any opportunity to render assistance. Now, what can I do? What do you require?"

"We need to find a way for the two of us to safely ride on the back of a griffin," Sarah told him. "And I cannot even begin to tell you how much of a rush we're in."

Kri'Entu's eyebrows shot up. "The two of you? On the backs of griffins?"

"Just one griffin," Steve corrected. "And an elderly one at that. Even if the griffin were in perfect health, he'd still be unable to carry the two of us. Therefore, we need to find some way where we can both ride this same griffin at the same time."

"Without wearing him out," Sarah added.

"That is a dilemma," the king agreed. He pulled a familiar small gold device the size of a pocket watch out of a desk drawer and tapped its surface. When there was no immediate response, the king scowled and tried again. Shardwyn's tiny disheveled face appeared on the surface of the small device.

"Your Majesty? This is an odd time of the day for you to call. What can I do for you this fine morning?"

"Come to the Antechamber at once. I have a dilemma that needs an immediate resolution."

The elderly wizard's face sobered. "I will be right there, Your Majesty."

Steve coughed. Both Sarah and the king glanced his way.

"Yes, Sir Steve? Do you have something to say?"

"Perhaps we should, ah, bring in Shardwyn's apprentice, too."

Kri'Entu smiled. "You've noticed as well, haven't you?"

"What?" Steve asked, in mock innocence. "That there's a wizard in the tower who doesn't blow things up on a weekly basis?"

A smile briefly formed on the king's face. "Do you know that, since young Gareth has become Shardwyn's apprentice, the number of explosions coming from that tower has dropped by over ninety percent?"

Sarah giggled. "Wow. That's impressive."

Kri'Entu summoned a guard. "Find Mister Gareth, Shardwyn's apprentice. Have him report here on the double."

The guard bowed. "Aye, Your Majesty."

Sarah tapped her husband's shoulder. "You know what? I'm worried about missing our friend up north. I'm going to go back. I can have him wait while I come back here to get you. Are you okay with that?"

Steve nodded. "It's a good idea. I really don't want to have to find another candidate."

Sarah blew him a kiss and vanished.

"Find another candidate for what?" the king wanted to know.

"Oh, just a very specific task we need someone to undertake for us."

"Ah."

A few minutes later Shardwyn strolled through the door with an air of importance. He angled straight for the king and bowed. "Your Majesty. How may I be of service?"

At the same time, a very sleepy teenager, complete with tousled hair and sleep lines etched across his face, appeared in the doorway. Kri'Entu noticed the boy's arrival and waved him in.

"Mister Gareth, it's good of you to come."

Shardwyn, in the process of emptying his pockets on the king's personal desk, looked up with surprise.

"Your Majesty? Why is my apprentice here? I assure you I can deal with whatever needs to be done."

Gareth shrugged, grunted once and spun on his heel. He managed to take a few steps in the opposite direction when the king called out to him.

"Mister Gareth, hold please," Kri'Entu commanded.

Gareth froze in mid step. The boy yawned as he slowly turned back around.

"I need you here for this, son. Please have a seat and listen."

Gareth nodded sullenly and headed toward the closest chair. Just as he was lowering himself into one of the plush armchairs in front of the hearth, the young apprentice noticed Steve watching him. Gareth's eyes cleared.

"What are you doing here?" Gareth muttered. "For that matter, why am I here?"

Steve glanced over at the king, who nodded in Gareth's direction. The king, in turn, pulled Shardwyn aside and explained the nature of the problem. Steve leaned conspiratorially forward, prompting Gareth to mimic him.

"We have a problem," Steve quietly explained. He then outlined the problem as quickly as he could, stressing the importance of not pushing their griffin steed beyond his limits.

"What's the rush?" Gareth asked.

"We're supposed to be back in the glade, meeting this griffin *right now*. That's where Sarah is, stalling for time."

Gareth sat back in his chair. "Hmm."

"Think you can do it before him?"

Gareth snorted once. "Once I figure out the specifics, of course."

The teenager fell silent. Steve heard Shardwyn ask permission to brew yet another potion. Thankfully the king dismissed the idea, citing a lack of time. Kri'Entu turned to look directly at the young wizard.

"If you've got an idea," Steve whispered to the boy, "now's the time to voice it."

"Still considering ideas," Gareth returned, closing his eyes and leaning back in his chair.

"What about increasing the griffin's strength?" Shardwyn suggested, pacing in front of the king's desk. "That way the poor beast would be able to handle the burden of two riders."

"You'd overburden the griffin," Gareth murmured quietly. "It'd be a bad idea."

"Umm, wouldn't that hurt the griffin?" Steve asked, raising his voice so Shardwyn could hear him. "You don't want to overtax the poor fellow, do you?"

Shardwyn nodded. "A valid point, I must confess."

Gareth's eyes snapped open. "I have it. Weightlessness. We'll make one of the riders lighter than a feather. That way the griffin would be able to carry the two of you with ease."

"That's what I was going to do," Shardwyn announced, turning to his apprentice with a sad smile, "only we don't have the time to properly brew the potion."

"You and your potions," Gareth muttered, rising to his feet. He stretched his back, yawned again, and faced his master. "A simple spell would do it. Null the weight of the invoker and make certain it won't wear off until the appropriate counterspell is activated."

"I don't think we have the time to do that, either," Shardwyn pointed out. "A proper spell would take hours to properly craft."

"If you were doing it, sure," Gareth quietly muttered. Steve let out a snicker. Shardwyn's apprentice turned to point at the king's desk. "What is that, Your Majesty?"

Kri'Entu turned to stare at his desk. "What are you referring to, Mister Gareth?"

"That wooden thing by the corner of your desk. It looks

like a tiny castle."

The king strode to his desk to pick the item up. He nodded. "It's a replica of the East Tower, given to me by a school child earlier this year. Why do you ask?"

"May I borrow it? I need something to use in my spell."

Curious, the king passed the crude, hand carved model to Gareth. Kri'Entu moved closer to Steve and stared at the boy, who had just closed his eyes.

"What is he doing?"

"I would imagine he's working on that spell," Steve answered.

Sarah appeared a few feet away. She smiled at the king and hurried to her husband's side. "Tesur is there and is waiting for us."

Steve stared at her, waiting to see if anything else was forthcoming. "And?"

"And what?" Sarah wanted to know.

"Did he feel it? The, uh, you know."

"Oh. Yes, he did."

"That's good. Or bad, depending how you look at it. So he's waiting for us?"

Sarah nodded. "Yes, although I can tell he really wants to get going. Now that he's felt *it* he is anxious to start his, uh, journey."

"Got it."

"No, *I've* got it!" Shardwyn declared, causing everyone in the room to jump. "It doesn't have to be a potion. It can be a charm!"

"That would do what, Shardwyn?" the king asked.

"Well, the charm would keep the griffin well supplied with energy, as though the stout fellow had a full belly of food for the entire journey. That way he shouldn't tire, even if he's carrying a heavier than normal load. Fear not, Your Majesty. It shouldn't take that long to create."

The king looked over at Steve to see if it was a viable idea. Steve quickly shook his head while Sarah stared at the old wizard as though he had finally gone off the deep end. Kri'Entu put a reassuring hand on Shardwyn's shoulder and gave him a friendly shake as he firmly turned the wizard around so that he couldn't see their expressions.

"I have an idea," Kri'Entu announced.

Everyone in the room, save Gareth, turned to look at the king.

"Why don't we make this a learning exercise?"

Shardwyn looked quizzically around the room.

"A learning exercise for whom, Your Majesty?"

"For Mister Gareth, of course."

Gareth finally opened his eyes and looked over at the king.

"Mister Gareth is your apprentice," Kri'Entu continued. "Why don't we see if he can come up with a viable option for solving this problem? If not, perhaps you could offer a few feasible alternatives that would guide him in the right direction?"

"Of course, Your Majesty. Of course. I'm surprised I didn't think of that myself."

"Did the king just do what I think he did?" Gareth quietly asked Steve. "Does he want me to handle this and not Shardwyn?"

"You're here because I suggested it to the king," Steve whispered back. "Don't make me regret that decision, kid."

"You won't. Besides, I'm done."

"What? Already?"

"Contrary to popular belief, composing a proper spell really isn't that time consuming."

"He's done," Sarah announced, overhearing the hushed conversation with a pair of sensitive ears only a woman could possess.

"Is he now?" Shardwyn exclaimed, delighted. "I'm so proud of him. I taught him everything he knows. Well done, boy. Well done. So, let's see it!"

Gareth held out the model of the tiny wooden castle to Steve.

"Hold this. It can be invoked twice. The first time will render you weightless, Steve. You're the larger of the two so it would make sense to have the griffin carry the lighter rider. Now, the second time it's invoked it will revoke the spell. You do not want to invoke it a second time while airborne. Do you understand?"

"So how do I invoke this thing?" Steve asked, curious. Two seconds later, he let out a cry of disbelief as he floated up off the ground.

"Just like that. The only prerequisites are to be in physical contact with that castle and to say the word 'invoke'. And, I should mention it's attuned to your voice, so Lady Sarah wouldn't be able to invoke it, even if she wanted to."

Steve snorted. "Thank you, Captain Obvious. And thanks, about the bit about who can in- wow, almost said it. I'll shut up now."

Sarah reached out to grab her husband's hand as he floated by her. She stared at the hand, which looked and felt like a real hand only the texture was… different. It was as if she was holding a balloon-shaped hand, only the surface felt like real skin. There was absolutely no weight to the hand. She looked up into her husband's eyes and smiled at him.

"How does it feel?"

"Really freakin' weird."

"You have the counter spell?"

Steve patted his trouser pocket. "Got it right here."

"Good. We're off. Kri'Entu, Shardwyn, thank you. Gareth, thank you very much for the spell."

Gareth blushed as he nodded. "You're welcome."

Kri'Entu indicated the Antechamber's main door. "You may go back to sleep now, Mister Gareth."

"I don't think so," the teenager told the king. "I'm wide awake now. I might as well stay that way."

Shardwyn clapped his hands together excitedly and grinned at his apprentice. "Excellent. I have several potions I need to brew today. Have you finished restocking my potion ingredients? If you started now, you should be able to finish by lunch. Why don't you…"

"Do you know what?" Gareth suddenly interrupted. "I *am* feeling rather tired. Perhaps I will go back to bed."

"Good night, kid," Steve told him as the boy hurried out the door.

They bid farewell to the king. Sarah, still clasping her husband's hand, pulled him close. Suddenly they were standing back amidst the nests of the griffins. There was only one griffin present, and he was presently lying in the soft grass. At their appearance, the griffin, with silver-streaked fur and white wings, slowly regained his feet. The old fellow took one look at Steve and then turned to give Sarah an alarmed look.

"I am sure I can carry you, milady, but I fear I will not have the strength to carry your mate."

"Now don't you worry about a thing," Sarah assured Tesur. "We consulted a wizard and were given a spell. Steve is presently weightless. Look. He's not even touching the ground."

Sarah put a hand on each of Steve's hips and effortlessly hoisted him high in the air. Next she gave him a slight spin and watched, amused, as he spun around like a spinning top.

"That's just great," Steve grumped, once Sarah had stopped his spinning. "Let's start this out with a bang by having me puke over everything."

"You're fine. Don't be melodramatic."

Tesur approached and stared at Steve with wide, unblinking eyes.

"You took measures to ensure I wouldn't be overburdened for my journey?" Husband and wife nodded. Tesur bowed again. "You have my thanks. I never knew humans could be so thoughtful. Are the two of you ready? If so, let's be off. I have waited long enough."

Sarah approached the griffin and swung a leg up and over the griffin's back, finding a comfortable spot just ahead of Tesur' wings.

"Uh, dear? I could use a little help here!"

Sarah glanced back at her husband. Without realizing it she had released his hand and, as a result, he was being carried away by the gentle breeze. Sarah hurried off the griffin's back and leapt up into the air, managing to snag Steve's foot before he could rise any higher.

"Thanks. That could have been awkward."

"Don't let go of me," Sarah instructed as she made her way back to Tesur. "You have to make sure you hold on to me at all times."

"Yeah, yeah, I got it."

Sarah twisted in place and stared back at him.

"I'm not kidding, honey. We're going to be flying through the air with winds whipping by us. Look what that little breeze just did to you! Do you want that to happen once we're up there?"

"I won't let go," Steve promised.

"See that you don't. Tesur, we're ready when you are."

The old griffin broke into a trot. Tesur navigated his way through the huge trees with such ease that Sarah momentarily forgot he was the oldest griffin she had ever seen. Ten minutes later they made it to the same clearing where Steve had been attacked before. Tesur increased his pace until he was practically sprinting along the ground. Suddenly his wings snapped up and he began beating the air.

"If we're too heavy then you need to say so!" Sarah shouted, leaning forward to bring her face as close as possible to Tesur's.

Tesur squawked once. Even though Sarah didn't understand a single syllable of the griffin language, she knew the old griffin had indicated she shouldn't worry, and that he'd be fine.

The ground fell away. Higher and higher they rose into the air until Sarah felt as though she could reach up and run her fingertips along the undersides of the cloud's belly. Realizing she wanted to do just that, she stretched an arm up and watched the gaseous substance of the cloud swirl around her fingers.

"What are you doing?" Steve hissed, fidgeting in place. "Stop moving around. Are you trying to dislodge me?"

"Oh, cool your jets, Sparky. I'm just enjoying the ride."

"At least one of us is."

"You're not enjoying yourself?" Sarah asked, turning to look back at her husband. Steve was pale, his eyes intense, and was clutching her waist so hard his knuckles were turning white. However, she couldn't feel a thing.

"Imagine this," Steve suggested. "Someone has come up behind you and has decided to play tug-of-war with your belt. You know you have enough strength to be certain the other team doesn't win, but the problem is, the other team isn't letting go. There's this constant force trying to pull you away."

"Wow. Is it that windy?"

"For you, probably not. To me, it feels like it's a category four hurricane. I'm not enjoying myself. I wish you could have just teleported there."

"I told you, I already tried. Tesur said he has to be guided in. Even he doesn't really know where he's going. This Pull, or whatever it's called, is, well, pulling him a certain direction. All he can do is to go to wherever he's led."

"This sucks."

Sarah turned to look back at him once more. "Would you stop complaining? What's the worst that could happen? What do you think would happen to you if you fell off? You certainly wouldn't fall to your death, would you?"

"Well, no, I guess not."

"Try and enjoy the ride. I know you're not happy, and I'm sorry about that. There's nothing I can do. Just hang in there, okay?"

Steve grumbled something and buried his face in her back.

Two hours later Tesur announced he had spotted a human village.

"Where?" Sarah asked, curious. She leaned out over the griffin's side so she could see the ground far below.

"It's gotta be Donlari," Steve guessed. "Wow. I've never seen it from this perspective before."

They were flying at an altitude of one thousand feet. Below them, Sarah could see the sprawling river village of Donlari. The vast majority of the buildings may have been spread along the mighty river's banks on both sides of the river, but she could see that there were houses and cottages scattered all across the flat, featureless plains. She could see farmlands with fields of various crops, complete with tiny workers moving amongst the rows of plants.

"I never knew Donlari was so big," Steve remarked.

"Tell me about it. I never noticed how many farms and houses were outside of the city's limits."

Ten minutes later Donlari had disappeared, replaced by acres and acres of open grassland. The mighty Zylan River had fallen behind them and now they could see the beginnings of the rugged southern Selekai Mountains. The closer they flew to those desolate mountains the colder the air became.

Sarah shivered, which drew an immediate response from her husband. "Are you okay?"

"I'm just cold. I don't think that has ever happened with you right beside me."

"Hardy har har."

"Is something wrong with your jhorun?" Sarah asked, concerned.

"No. I deliberately pulled it back and tried to keep myself as cool as possible."

"Why?"

"I'm not sure how Tesur would handle it," Steve answered. "Besides, I didn't know how it'd affect me in this state."

"As for me, I can assure you that I'd handle it just fine," the elderly griffin assured them. "A bit of warmth right now would be most welcome."

Sarah was instantly sympathetic. "You poor thing. You're cold, too?" Sarah twisted in place to give her husband a stern look. "Honey, you need to do something about this."

"I've got it," Steve assured her.

Sure enough, less than five seconds later her back had warmed, as though she had turned on the seat warmer in her car. Sighing contentedly, she leaned back and rested her head on Steve's shoulder. He looked down at her and smiled.

"Better?"

"Absolutely. Thank you. I could do this all day now."

"What about our griffin friend?"

Tesur's head turned to the left. The griffin fixed his eye on his two passengers and nodded.

"You are the fire thrower we mistakenly fought all those years ago, aren't you?"

Steve nodded. "Yeah, I am. Sorry if I ended up hurting you."

"You didn't hurt me but you did injure my eldest offspring. Most of the feathers of his left wing were burned off during the attack. He also said that a human female, you I presume, miss, administered an elixir which forced his wing to sprout new feathers."

"That was just one big misunderstanding," Sarah assured the griffin. "We really didn't want to hurt anyone."

"I know. Had the situation been reversed I doubt I'd have been as reserved as you two."

Steve snorted. "Reserved? I've replayed that particular episode in my head quite a few times and never once did I think I acted reserved. Quite the opposite. I think I was too brash. I had just started getting a handle on my fire thrower jhorun and was eager to try it out. You griffins, I'm sorry to say, paid the price for my arrogance. So, from me to you, I'm sorry I hurt your son. I didn't want to."

"You misunderstand, fire thrower," Tesur clucked, chuckling to himself. "You put my son in his place. *He* was the one that was acting foolishly. Never once did he or his friends stop to consider that perhaps they had been fooled into attacking the wrong party. For that, you have my sincerest apologies."

Sarah leaned to the right and patted Tesur's flank. "Don't worry about it. It happened years ago, and there was no harm done. Well, no lingering harm was done."

"How is your son?" Steve asked, curious. "I've always wondered about griffin families. How many, uh, offspring do you typically have?"

"Two. Always two cubs. One male and one female."

"Never two males, or two females?" Sarah asked.

"There have been dual males or dual females," Tesur admitted. "But it is rare."

"Do griffins mate for life?" Sarah asked.

Tesur squawked once. "Do humans?"

Sarah shrugged. "I'd like to say that most do, but unfortunately, a lot don't."

"Does one gender have a shorter life span than the other?" Tesur asked, confused.

"No, not really," Sarah told the griffin.

"Then why won't human mates stay together?"

"Uh, irreconcilable differences?" Steve suggested.

"I'm not familiar with that phrase."

"It means the two humans couldn't get along," Sarah translated.

"Ah."

"Do griffins ever have fights?" Steve asked.

"With our mates? Never."

"Really?" Steve asked, amazed. "Not ever?"

"Why would I want to fight with my mate?" Tesur asked, puzzled.

"Don't you ever have disagreements?" Sarah asked.

"Sometimes, but not often. Humans have disagreements and the decision is made to dissolve the union? This makes no sense."

"There are times when I'd be right there with you, pal," Steve said.

"What types of disagreements could humans possibly have that would drive two mates away from each other?" Tesur wanted to know.

"Cheating is one of the most common reasons to, well, dissolve a union," Sarah offered after she had given the matter some thought.

"Cheating? I do not understand."

"It means if the male were to, uh, spend time with another female," Steve clarified. "That'd be grounds for trouble."

"There are numerous females in my flock," Tesur recalled. "I am familiar with them all. By your definition, would that make me a cheater?"

Sarah smiled, as her husband gave her an imploring look.

"Nuh-uh," she said, shaking her head. "You gave that lousy definition of cheating. Now you get to clarify. Good luck."

"Thanks," Steve sourly answered. He thought for a moment. "If you were to have intimate relations with another member of the opposite gender, then that would constitute the type of cheating we're talking about."

"Why would I want to dally with another female?" Tesur asked, genuinely confused. "I already had a mate."

"You asked," Steve told the griffin. "I'm just answering."

"Do humans practice this absurd behavior?"

Sarah sighed. "Sadly, many do."

"Have you?" Tesur continued.

Sarah frowned at the griffin. "Have I cheated? Never.

Not once. That'd dishonor the vows I took to my husband, just like I know he'd never do that to me. When two humans truly love one another the last thing either of them would consider is being unfaithful."

"Humans are complex creatures," Tesur decided.

"You got that right, pal," her husband agreed. Sarah elbowed him in the gut. She squinted and pointed left, at the eastern horizon.

"What's that?"

"Hmm?"

Sarah felt her husband twist left. She had just happened to be looking east when she saw a small black cloud materialize above a section of the passing trees. It almost looked as though something had caught fire and was emitting dark smoke, only this smoke was behaving in a manner she hadn't ever seen before. Smoke typically rose up into the air and then spread out, dissipating into the sky as it mixed with the air. This cloud, however, wasn't dissipating. It retained its original shape and began to rise higher into the air.

"Is something burning?" Steve asked.

"You're the fire thrower," she reminded him. "You tell me."

Her husband fell silent as he undoubtedly sent his jhorun to investigate. After a few moments, she heard him grunt with surprise.

"What is it?"

"I don't know what it is, but I can tell you what it isn't. It isn't smoke. I can't sense any fire whatsoever."

"Well, that's good, right?"

"Could they be some type of animal?" Steve asked.

"They'd have to be really small animals," Sarah said. She watched the small dense cloud rise higher into the air. "Tesur, can you tell me what that black cloud is and why it appears to be heading toward us?"

Tesur squawked with alarm. "Emberlichs! We must rise higher!"

"What's an emberlich?" Sarah asked, growing concerned.

"Carrion feeders! We mustn't let any of them touch us!"

"Birds, bugs, tiny dragons… what are they?" Steve asked

from behind her.

Tesur banked hard to the right. "Insects. They're no bigger than the talon on my claw. However, an emberlich horde can consist of thousands. They'll eat us!"

Sarah eyed the rising, pulsating cloud that continued to gain on them. "How many would you say are in that group?"

"Tens of thousands. I'm afraid our journey is going to end here. I lack the resources to evade an emberlich horde. I am sorry, my friends."

Sarah stared at the approaching swarm of creatures. She still couldn't make out any individual creatures, so she had no idea what these tiny little carrion eaters were supposed to look like. The black swarm reminded her of the huge schools of fish she had seen on underwater documentaries, which were predominantly harmless. Thanks to Tesur, she knew this particular mass of creatures was anything but friendly. She pointed at the cloud.

"Honey, would you care to do the honors?"

She felt her husband tense up and saw that his hands had ignited.

"Be careful that you don't light up anything that isn't supposed to be incinerated, okay?"

"Piece of cake," Steve assured her.

Sarah watched his left arm rise, blasting out a jet of flames. She then screamed with surprise as the three of them were wrenched to the right, as if they had been sideswiped by a passing locomotive.

Tesur furiously beat his wings in an attempt to right himself. The griffin turned to look at her with an incredulous look.

"What happened? What was that?"

Sarah groaned. "That was my husband. I never realized how strong Steve's jhorun blasts are. Now that his mass has been reduced to zero, they can be readily felt."

"Let's not do that again, agreed?" the griffin implored.

Steve pointed a flaming finger at the swarming horde.

"Look! It worked! The horde scattered, as though I hit 'em with a bowling ball."

"I'm not familiar with…"

"Forget about it, Tesur," Sarah hastily informed him. She looked back at her husband. "Any chance you could scale that back a bit? You practically knocked us out of the sky with that shot."

"But I *did* tone that down a bit," her husband protested. "I was only trying to scare them off, not do any major damage."

"Something you should know about emberlichs," Tesur added, banking again and flapping like crazy to increase their velocity, "is that they are attracted to heat."

Steve groaned. "Great. Are they immune?"

"No."

"Good. Brace yourself. They're getting closer. I'm going to fire another shot."

Inspiration struck. Sarah patted Tesur's side to get his attention.

"Point yourself directly away from the swarm. Steve will shoot at them from behind us."

"Pushing us in the direction we want to go," Tesur deduced. "Excellent. One moment."

The griffin's right wing dipped until the southern mountains were straight ahead. Tesur squawked his readiness. Sarah patted her husband's leg.

"You're up. Let 'em have it!"

Steve's left arm gripped her tightly as his right arm targeted the silent black mass edging ever closer. She glanced down at the arm holding her in place when a thought occurred. "Honey! Wait!"

Too late. Steve blasted a powerful shot directly at the heart of the emberlich horde. The jet of fire had the positive effect of scattering the emberlichs in all directions. However, with only one arm doing the blasting, with nothing to counter the off-balance shot, the three of them suddenly found themselves spinning helplessly out of control through the air.

Disoriented, Tesur pulled his wings in as close to his body as he could.

Now, they were spiraling *and* dropping like a rock. Sarah screamed, hugging Tesur's back. Steve cursed and fought a wave of nausea. They plummeted toward the trees.

Steve leaned forward, spreading his arms wide. In the

process, he hooked his legs under Tesur's wings. He took a deep breath and blasted jets of fire from both hands.

The plummeting stopped almost immediately. If Steve hadn't locked his legs under Tesur's wings, then he would have blasted himself off the griffin's back. Once they started to rise then he began shooting off quick bursts of flames in the opposite direction they were spiraling, which thankfully enough, managed to stop them from spinning around.

"Ooooo, I want to get off," Sarah moaned, still hugging Tesur's back. She started to rise when she felt her husband push her back down.

"No, stay there. Keep your eyes closed. We're not out of this yet."

"What's the matter?" she asked, trying to keep her mind from spinning.

"I have good news and bad news. The good news is we've stopped dropping and spinning. The bad news is those damn emberlich things are much closer. I think they're trying to surround us."

"What are we going to do?" Sarah cried.

"Tesur, are you okay?" Steve hastily called out.

"Aye. I have finally regained my senses. Now that I have, I wish that I hadn't."

"Can you steer?"

"Can I *what?*"

"Listen, you steer and I'll push."

"What are you…?"

They were blasted forward as Steve repositioned slightly so that his legs remained hooked around Tesur's wings and blasted jhorun through both hands. They managed to punch through the last remaining piece of the sky that hadn't turned black. Something hard smacked into his shoulder. Without moving his hands, Steve quickly located the thing. It was an emberlich. It was momentarily stunned and on its back.

To Steve, it looked like a black grasshopper-sized beetle with a pair of elongated front pincers, much like he'd seen on stag beetles. The emberlich quickly righted itself and scuttled over to Tesur's flank, preparing to take a bite of fresh griffin. Steve eyed his hands. He couldn't risk moving either of them until they were well away from the voracious mass of bugs, so blasting it was out. His eyes narrowed.

Just as the emberlich spread its front pincers, it stiffened with surprise and then was reduced to ash. Steve, who had watched the entire scene unfold, grunted with satisfaction and returned his attention to the rapidly passing scenery. Lucky for him, and Tesur for that matter, he had learned long ago how to make an object burn just by looking at it.

Steve looked back. The emberlich swarm was growing rapidly smaller. Five minutes later it had disappeared completely, so he finally extinguished both hands. Tesur resumed beating his wings as they decelerated to a normal velocity.

"How are you holding up?" Sarah asked.

"Not too bad. I can feel the drain on my jhorun, but it's not depleted. I think we're good."

"Just remember we don't have any mimets here with us," Sarah reminded him. "We have no idea what we might be facing. The word of the day is conserve, okay?"

"Yeah, yeah, I know."

They had been gliding on air currents for the past hour. Tesur hadn't beat his wings once, but now that they had crossed into the Selekais, the currents dropped in strength. They began to descend, which prompted Tesur to begin flapping his wings in order to increase their altitude. A large peak was rapidly approaching and they needed to pass over it.

Sarah detected another drop in temperature. The higher they flew the colder it became. Just then she felt her back's temperature rise by a few degrees. Steve had apparently noticed the decrease in temp, too, and had compensated by increasing his jhorun. Sarah checked their griffin guide and was shocked to see flecks of ice and snow coating his already white wings.

"Tesur! Are you okay? You have ice on your wings!"

"It is getting quite cold," Tesur admitted.

"Are you sure we need to fly this high?"

Tesur nodded. "I'm being pulled south. That mountain is sitting directly between us and where we have to go. I have no choice, miss. I cannot deviate our course."

Sarah turned to her husband. "Can you help? Can you keep Tesur warm?"

Steve nodded. "I can try. I have to let go of you so I'll need you to hold on to me this time."

Sarah nodded. "Got it."

She leaned back, hooked her arms around her husband's legs, and leaned her full weight against him. Steve stretched out his arms and laid a hand on each of Tesur's wings. Both of his hands turned red. Moments later the ice was gone and the griffin informed them that he was feeling much better. Invigorated, even.

"You definitely come in handy," Tesur observed, turning his head so that he could see the two of them. "My wings are no longer numb and I am no longer cold."

Steve grinned. "I've been told that before. I'm glad to help out."

"We've already passed several mountains," Sarah observed as she watched the passing landscape beneath them. "Can you tell us what we're looking for? Are we getting close?"

"We are headed for the Arch," the griffin promptly answered, as if he had been waiting for this particular question to be asked.

"The Arch?" Sarah asked, confused. "Can you elaborate?"

"You know," Steve automatically answered. "An arch. Kinda looks like this?" He drew a half circle in the air with his finger.

"I'll do it. I'll push your butt right off of Tesur's back."

Steve grinned. "You love me too much to commit murder!"

"Murder? Hah. You'd simply float away. No one would know I had anything to do with it."

"Tesur would," Steve said, patting the griffin's side. "You wouldn't do that to me, would you?"

"If you're asking me to take sides," Tesur slowly began, "then … Hmmm. That's a tough decision."

"Who's your friend?" Steve jovially asked. "Who made you all warm and tingly inside? Wait. That came out wrong."

"I'll side with Miss Sarah," the griffin decided.

"What? That's gratitude for you."

"Hah!" Sarah beamed her victorious smile back at her husband. "Admit it. He likes me better than you."

Steve started to let go of Sarah's hips when a gust of air threatened to send him careening off the griffin's back. Sarah frowned.

"Let me guess. You wanted to fold your arms across your chest. Hmmph. Serves you right, mister."

Steve fidgeted in place. Sarah felt his hands clench into fists. Alarmed, she looked back at him.

"Is everything okay?"

"Um, er, no."

"What's wrong?"

"I have to go."

"Go?"

"You know. Go to the bathroom. We've been up here for hours now."

Sarah stifled a giggle.

"Do you mean to tell me that you have to go before I do?"

"You don't have to go? At all?"

"Well, it's been a while, but I'm still good."

"Is all well?" Tesur inquired, turning his head to observe them.

"We need to land," Sarah instructed.

"What for? Are you well, Miss Sarah?"

"I am, but my husband isn't."

"Is he sick?"

"It all depends how you look at it," Sarah smugly replied.

"Thanks a lot," Steve grumped.

"He needs to go, uh, water a tree," Sarah explained.

"Water a tree? Why would he wish to do this now?" the griffin inquired, confused.

"Let's just say that I have to relieve a little pressure," Steve added.

"You need to urinate?"

"I was trying to avoid saying that, but yeah, I do."

"Very well. I will land. Will this take long?"

"Not at all," Steve assured the griffin. "Just find me a tree."

"All this talk about having to go has made we want to go, too," Sarah confessed.

Steve laughed out loud. "Hah! I knew it!"

"I was fine until you said something. This is your fault."

"Better find us two trees," Steve told the griffin.

"You think I'm using a tree? You'd better wake up, buster."

Tesur landed and Sarah hopped off his back. Steve, still gripping Sarah's hips, was pulled along with her. Steve started to inspect the nearby trees when Sarah turned to face Tesur.

"Don't go anywhere. We'll be right back."

"Where are we going?" Steve asked, puzzled.

"Why in the world would you think I'd go to the bathroom out here when the one in our cabin would work just fine?"

Before Steve could protest, Sarah had teleported them back to their cabin. She pulled her husband's hands off of her and wedged him in a chair at their dinner table.

"Don't go anywhere, either. I'll be right back."

"Very funny."

As soon as she had done her business, Sarah returned to the table, eyed Steve, and laughed.

"You're on your own. I love you to death, honey, but you're gonna have to take care of this one yourself."

"I'll manage."

As soon as Sarah teleported them back to Tesur, and were airborne once more, Steve finally laughed.

"Everything okay back there?" Sarah asked, turning to look back at her husband.

"Yep, it will be."

"Will be?"

"I'm going to have to clean the bathroom."

"What? What did you do?"

"Well, I'm weightless, remember?"

"Yes, obviously. Oh, no. You didn't!"

"I guess all parts of me were weightless."

"Honey, you can't be serious!"

"I'll clean it when this is all said and done, okay?"

"That's ... gross."

Sarah noticed that Tesur was now angling toward a

mountain that looked no different from any of the others they had seen. This one was barren; no trees, no discernible features, and had only bare rock to meet their eyes. The griffin dipped his wings and brought them lower.

"Is that the one?" Sarah asked. She peered intently at the looming mountain. "I really don't see anywhere to land."

"Nor do I see any type of arch anywhere," Steve pointed out.

Tesur ignored them and continued his descent. He banked left and began to slowly circle around to the mountain's western face. Sarah could see that they were heading toward a small plateau nearly three quarters of the way up the side of the mountain. As they neared the plateau, they could also see that parts of the western face were concealed by a dense shroud of mist.

"I don't remember seeing any fog as we approached," Steve commented as they drew nearer.

"Neither did I," Sarah admitted.

Instead of coming in for a landing, Tesur began beating his wings and climbed higher. He continued to circle around the mountain, approaching the southern face in just a few minutes. There, appearing where it hadn't been before, was a second plateau. This one was also covered in mist, which began to clear as they came closer.

As before, Tesur flew higher. The southern plateau fell away as they continued their trek around the mountain. They approached the eastern face and were surprised to see another plateau appear as they neared. Steve tapped her shoulder and nodded back the way they had come.

"Look! That last plateau has vanished! What do you think it means?"

"That we're on the right track," Sarah quietly answered. "Shh. I think we need to be quiet."

"Gotcha."

The third plateau appeared and was quickly passed. As they continued flying around the mountain's circumference, approaching the northern face, they were startled to see that there wasn't a fourth plateau. Bewildered, Sarah looked up and noticed that they were several hundred feet from the mountain's peak. However, the peak was hidden from sight by a thick cloud that she hadn't noticed before. Had it always been there? Wouldn't they have noticed that the mountaintop was shrouded by a blanket of clouds?

Sarah shook her head. No, probably not. After all, the plateaus didn't appear until they had followed the correct path around the mountain.

Sarah felt Tesur increase the tempo of his wings. He was trying to reach the peak! Was that where this mysterious arch was?

Rising higher, they pushed their way through the thick clouds to see what they'd find at the top of the mountain. The clouds suddenly cleared and they saw that they had reached their goal. The top of the mountain was inexplicably flat. It was, Sarah realized with a start, the fourth and final plateau. Only when Tesur had landed and was facing due north did they find what they were looking for. Directly before their eyes the air shimmered, as though waves of heat were emanating from deep within the mountain.

The Arch materialized in front of them.

It was a strangely organic looking formation, as though it had sprouted up and out of the rock. The Arch stretched from one side of the mountaintop to the other, and was nearly fifty feet tall at the apex of the arc.

"This is it," the griffin breathed with excitement. "The Arch. We found it!"

Sarah, with Steve virtually attached at the hips, dismounted, and stared up at the spooky stone curve rising above their heads. She glanced over at their griffin guide and saw that Tesur's eyes were wide open and his head was slowly pivoting in place.

"What now?" Sarah asked. "We found the Arch. What do we have to do next?"

"Now we wait."

"What are we waiting for?" Steve wanted to know.

Tesur gasped and pointed a wing at a point visible through the Arch.

"That."

Husband and wife turned to see what the griffin was

looking at. Seeing nothing out of the ordinary, Sarah turned back to Tesur and gave a slight cough.

"We don't see anything. What are you looking at?"

"Do you not see it?" Tesur asked as he strode closer to the Arch. "Only visible through the Arch and only for those who have a need to find it."

Steve looked back through the Arch and raised an eyebrow. "I see a cloud, dude."

"Only it isn't a cloud," Tesur corrected. "That's Ranal!"

Chapter 7 — Eyes of the Beholder

Y ou're telling me that you see an island?" Steve began, looking skeptically back at their griffin friend. "You actually see a floating island and not some insignificant cloud?"

Tesur nodded. "Of course. Trees, rocks, grass. I see it all."

"I don't see anything, either," Sarah confided to her husband. "It must be because we're not looking for it."

"But we *are* looking for it," Steve argued.

"True, but we have no reason to, only Tesur does."

"We must be off," the griffin impatiently told them. "Look. The island is on the move. If we don't get moving, we won't be able to catch up to it. Let's get our feathers in the air."

As soon as both Sarah and Steve had returned to Tesur's back, the old griffin surprised them by retreating as far from the Arch as he could.

"What are we doing?" Steve whispered.

"Hush," Sarah whispered back.

Tesur broke into a run. His wings extended and they lifted into the air, but not by much. Sarah eyed the approaching Arch. It looked as though the old griffin was deliberately adjusting his course so that they could all fly *through* the Arch.

"What'd you do that for?" Sarah inquired as she looked back at the curved formation of rocks. "Why did you fly through it?"

"Passing through the Arch constitutes my acceptance of the final leg of my journey."

"You can't turn back now," Sarah guessed. "Even if you wanted to, right?"

"Correct. I am committed."

"Were you having your doubts?" Steve asked.

"No," the griffin answered. He beat his wings as they rose higher into the air. "I wish to see my beloved Salana. I know she awaits me on Ranal."

"Was she your mate?" Sarah softly asked.

"Aye. We mated young, nearly a hundred-twenty years ago. She felt the Pull almost ten years ago this winter. Words cannot begin to describe how much I miss her."

Once they were within a hundred feet of the large cloud, they began their approach. Sarah stared at the wispy outlines of their target and shook her head. Tesur claimed he saw the cloud for what it was: an actual floating island. However, had he shown any amount of hesitation, then Sarah would never have believed. However, their griffin guide convinced her, insisting he saw the elusive floating island.

Sarah eyed the cloud from underneath as they had ascended. She had halfway expected to see stone crags protruding from beneath the cloud's underbelly, but she hadn't. She thought, perhaps, the cloud was nothing more than some type of concealment spell and by getting up close to Ranal, she would be able to see it for what it was.

Wrong on all counts.

The closer they flew to the island the more her doubts grew. She could only hope that Tesur knew what he was doing. Whether his eyesight was strong enough to penetrate the cloud cover, or else only he saw a floating island, she didn't know. She only … Sarah eyed the cloud and frowned. They had been flying toward the island for several minutes now and they were no closer now than they were when they first flew through the Arch. Coincidence? Were they caught in some sort of air current?

She turned to look back at the mountaintop. There it was, fading rapidly from sight. That proved they were still moving forward. She returned her gaze to the cloud. Island. Whatever.

Ranal still wasn't getting any closer.

Alarmed, Sarah tapped Tesur's shoulder. "Why aren't we getting closer? Is the cloud moving faster?"

"I feel the Pull diminishing," Tesur answered. He squawked angrily. "I cannot explain it. The Pull has remained strong through my entire journey."

"Until now," Steve guessed.

"Correct."

Sarah swallowed nervously. "It's us. We're the problem."

"What about us?" her husband wanted to know.

"We're not supposed to be here. This journey is supposed to be for griffins only. Ranal is keeping us from approaching."

"You're telling me that island is conscious?"

"I'm telling you there are rules in place," Sarah exclaimed, frustrated. "And we're not following them. If we don't get off Tesur's back then we're going to prevent him from reaching Ranal."

"Can't you just teleport us there?" Steve asked. "You can see where we need to go. Surely you can see enough to make a jump, right?"

Sarah closed her eyes and concentrated. The only image she was able to see was the swirling mists within the cloud.

"No. I don't see any land, and you don't want me trying to teleport into a mist."

"You are correct," Tesur confirmed. "Ranal is preventing my approach. If you try to force your way into that sacred place, you will fall to your death."

"Couldn't you risk it?" Steve pressed. "If you teleport us and solid land isn't there, couldn't you just teleport us back to the Arch?"

Tesur squawked angrily. "Approaching the Arch must be done properly. You will dishonor all griffins if you simply *appear* before it."

"When will it stop being a cloud and start being solid land?" Sarah asked.

"I suspect Ranal will present itself only when you step foot on its surface," the griffin answered.

"Why would the Fae send us to a floating island if we can't even step foot there?" Steve grumbled. "What good does it do to tell us the flower we want is on that island, get us within reach of it, and then yank it away from us?"

"The Fae never said it could only be found on a floating island," Sarah patiently explained. "We didn't find that out until later, when *we* did the research. Right now, it doesn't matter. We're here. Ranal is just over there. There *must* be a way."

"Maybe we just weren't meant to find it," Steve said.

"And doom the Fae? I don't accept that," Sarah snapped.

"We're running out of time," Steve pointed out. "You heard Tesur. He's losing the Pull. Clearly Ranal doesn't want us to … wait. What if Ranal is trying to protect us?"

"Protect us from what?" Sarah asked.

"From our own folly. What if we, as humans, aren't allowed to touch Ranal? Or maybe it's like the Underworld in Greek mythology. Once you get there you can't get back."

"I think that's why the Fae chose me. I alone, with my teleportation jhorun, can get us back safely. No, I don't accept that we've come this far only to fail now. There's gotta be a way. Think!"

Sarah suddenly spun in her seat to stare back at her husband. Somehow, and she didn't know how, she could sense that Steve was smiling. Had he thought of something that would work?

"What? What is it? Do you have an idea?"

Her husband pointed at the cloud. "We just have to get Tesur on that island, right?"

Sarah nodded. "Right. Do you have a plan for getting us over to that cloud?"

"As a matter of fact, I do. I have an idea."

"What's your plan? I'll tell you if it'll work."

"The Pull is almost gone!" Tesur cried out. "Please hurry! If I can no longer feel the Pull then I will lose the ability to see Ranal."

Sarah watched her husband climb over Tesur's wings and hook his arms under the point where the wings joined with the griffin's back. He extended his arms as far as he could on either side of his body and opened his hands, palms facing backward. He looked up at her and grinned.

"I'm going to do my Iron Man thing again. I'd hold on to something if I were you."

Sarah lunged forward to grab Tesur around his neck.

"What is..." the griffin began but then saw Steve angling his hands to deliver a powerful blast.

"Same as before, pal. You steer and I'll push. Are you ready?"

Tesur nodded eagerly. "Aye!"

Steve released jhorun into both hands at the same time, blasting out twin jets of fire. They were propelled forward way faster than Tesur could ever fly. Within moments Steve could tell that it was going to work. The island was finally approaching.

"Ranal is beginning to fade!" Tesur squawked with dismay. "We will not reach it in time!"

Sure enough, from their perspective the cloud was beginning to disappear. At the rate it was dematerializing they only had about thirty seconds before it would be completely gone. Sarah quickly sat up and took stock of their situation.

"Give it all you've got, honey! Hurry!"

Sarah heard her husband grunt with the strain of holding his arms in place under Tesur's wings. She didn't know how much more he'd be able to take since his arms had to be under a considerable amount of strain. She glanced back and gave him a reassuring smile. Steve didn't notice. She could tell he was focused on getting the three of them to the island just as quickly as possible.

Sarah felt the heat increase. The jets shooting out of Steve's hands, which were about twenty feet long, had increased to thirty. Even though she knew Steve was in considerable pain, she couldn't help but giggle. Steve was flying like Iron Man! The look on her husband's face was priceless. If only she had her camera. Eyes wide open, huge grin, and that telltale smug look on his face.

Sarah smiled and shook her head. How many people could say they were able to propel themselves by blasting out jets of fire? In fact, Sarah wondered if his fire jets had enough power to lift him off the ground when he wasn't rendered weightless. Did she dare ask him? If she did, she knew full well her husband would want to try.

She decided to leave that discussion for another time.

Sarah heard an excited whoop, which was completely out of character for the situation they were in. Did Steve find something funny? Did he not know that Tesur would be doomed if they didn't make it to the cloud in the next fifteen seconds? She risked another glance back and stifled a giggle. Steve had a look of sheer joy on his face as he blasted jets of fire out of his hands.

Yes, she grudgingly admitted, he kinda *did* look like Iron Man. A look of concern appeared on her husband's face. Alarmed, Sarah faced forward.

"We're almost there! Tesur, Steve can't see the island. If you see a suitable landing point then you'd better let him know!"

"Angle for that mound of rocks!" Tesur squawked, dipping a wing to turn more to the left.

"I see clouds, dude," Steve called out. "Just say left or right, faster or slower. Let me know when you need me to stop."

"Angle to the left," the griffin instructed. "A little more. Just a little… no. Too far. Too far! Back to the right! Hurry!! There, that's better. We're nearly there. Give it another five seconds and then stop. Our momentum will take us the rest of the way in."

Sarah felt the exact moment Steve extinguished his hands. Their speed diminished and she was thrust forward. Alarmed, she noticed the swirling substance of the cloud's interior grow closer. She closed her eyes and told herself over and over that the griffin knew what he was doing.

A gust of wind buffeted them, forcing her to close her eyes. She had seen them rapidly descending into the heart of the cloud and decided she didn't want to watch. Until she could feel solid ground under her feet she had no desire to see what was transpiring around her.

Sarah grunted with surprise as Tesur collided with something. Something solid. Were they on land? Had they arrived safely? She cautiously cracked open an eye to see for herself.

Both eyes snapped open. Tesur had been right. This was no cloud. The watery mists had finally disappeared, revealing that which Tesur had seen all the way back from the Arch. Sarah whistled with amazement.

The floating island of Ranal stretched endlessly in all directions, with no discernible borders anywhere on the island. She turned to look behind her. Jungle seemed to stretch on and on. Ranal was, by Sarah's estimate, several thousand feet up in the air, but it looked and felt like they were back on the ground.

Sarah dismounted. She watched her husband reach into one of his trouser pockets and pull out the small wood carving he'd been carrying. Gareth had given it to him with the explicit instructions not to use until they arrived at their destination. The spell he placed on Steve, the young wizard had explained, was a one-time shot. Once the spell was invoked for the second time, his full weight would return. Her husband clutched the tiny wooden castle to his chest, mumbled something, and immediately stumbled to the ground. Alarmed, Sarah rushed to his side.

"Are you okay? What's the matter?"

Steve glanced up at her and winced. "Wow, I'm more of a lard-butt than I originally thought. Have you ever been on a trampoline?"

"What?"

"A trampoline. Ever been on one?"

Sarah nodded. "Yes. Why?"

"Do you remember what it felt like when you jumped off?"

Smiling, Sarah nodded again. "Ah. Gotcha. You need to

get acclimatized to the presence of gravity again."

"Exactly. Gravity. Thou art a heartless b—"

"Hey!" Sarah interrupted, cutting her husband off. "I don't like that word."

"Bully. I was gonna say 'bully'."

"Sure you were."

Her husband finally rose to his feet and looked around. He gasped with surprise. "I don't know what I was expecting, but this sure wasn't it."

Sarah gazed wordlessly at the expanse before her and had to agree. Never in her wildest dreams had she ever seen a setting as beautiful as this. A single word sprang to mind: utopia.

Directly in front of them was a large pool of clear azure water. She could see every detail inside the pool, all the way down to the swaying bed of lush green underwater plants. The pool, Sarah noticed, was being fed by the runoff from a second pool, located at a slightly higher elevation and a little further back. That pool, in turn, was being fed by three different pools, each at higher elevations.

Sarah slowly spun in place. Pools and lush foliage were everywhere! Since the landscape's topography fluctuated drastically, small bodies of water had collected everywhere they could and, as a result, created dozens of pools in their line of sight. Due to the abundance of water on the island, thick lush foliage was everywhere. The closest Sarah had ever come to seeing greenery like this was when she and Steve had taken a vacation to Hawaii a few years ago and even then those tropical rainforests were nothing compared to this. She turned to her husband. Steve's mouth was moving but no sound was coming out. Sarah leaned close.

"What was that?"

"I was saying that we have our work cut out for us. We're supposed to find a specific flower amongst all that? Can we say needle in a haystack? Babe, this is impossible!"

"Nothing's impossible," Sarah corrected. "We're here. The flower is here somewhere. We just need to find it. Perhaps if we…"

Sarah trailed off. She noticed they weren't alone. Large

prone figures blended in with their environment, lying so still that Sarah's eyes had skipped right over them.

Griffins. Dozens, if not hundreds, of avian eyes were watching them. They were everywhere. The magnificent winged creatures were lying next to pools, resting in trees, and even sitting complacently on the ground. All of them, Sarah noted with dismay, were watching them.

Sarah turned to Tesur just as their elderly griffin guide hurried past them. Tesur was angling for a thick, multi-branched tree that had one large limb in particular stretching out over a nearby pool. Resting comfortably on the limb, gazing down at her, was a silver-winged griffiness with streaks of dark charcoal gray running through her fur. The female griffin was tracking their movements, without moving a muscle.

"Why aren't they moving?" Steve whispered.

Sarah noticed his hands had turned dark red and instantly she took his hands in hers. "Absolutely not. You will not torch anything here. We are the intruders. Remember that."

"You just make sure you tell that to them," Steve grumbled. The exact moment Tesur arrived at the tree, the reclining griffiness finally stirred. She silently jumped down to the ground and placed herself directly in Tesur's path. Sarah wiped tears from her eyes as she watched Tesur gently touch his beak to that of the griffiness.

"Salana. It's you. I've waited so long."

The griffiness bowed. "Tesur. I was beginning to lose hope. I feared you would be denied passage. We all did."

Tesur ruffled his feathers nervously. "Why?"

Salana took a step to the right and peered around her mate's body. She locked eyes on Sarah and stared, unblinking, forcing Sarah to take a few steps back. Steve automatically pulled his wife behind him and stepped in front, shouldering Salana's withering look.

"If you want to get mad at someone then you can be mad at me," Steve announced. "I'm the one who got us here. I'm the fire thrower. If you want to pick on someone then pick on me."

"Be at peace, fire thrower," Salana gently told him. "You

are in no danger from us."

"But we are in danger from someone else?" Sarah asked, peering around Steve's body.

"In a matter of speaking," the griffiness informed her. "All here can feel it. You have violated the laws of Ranal. This island is for griffins only. Humans were never meant to step foot on this sacred land. I fear doing so may have caused irreparable harm."

"We were told to come here," Sarah insisted. "We have to find a flower. As soon as we do, then we'll go. We wouldn't be here if it wasn't important."

Steve held up his hands in mock surrender. "Hey guys, we come in peace. Look, you don't want us here. We don't want to be here. We get it. This place is for griffin eyes only. However, we are here on some friends' behalf. We have to find a flower that will restore a tree. As luck would have it this flower only exists somewhere on this island. Will you let us look for it?"

"It is not for us to decide," Salana coolly informed him.

"Who should we talk to?" Sarah asked.

"I do not know," the griffiness admitted.

"Then how do you know someone else is calling the shots?" Steve countered.

"You are not a griffin," Salana answered, as if that simple statement explained everything.

Sarah nudged her husband's shoulder. "I think I have it. There's a power governing this place. We saw proof of its existence during our arrival. It kept us from approaching, remember? That power dictates what will and will not happen here."

"What if this power decides it doesn't want us here?" Steve asked. "What do you think it could do to us?"

"Are you kidding?" Sarah exclaimed. "What *couldn't* it do to us? We're on a floating island populated by griffins, remember? The griffins could attack us…"

"Unlikely," Tesur quietly added, drawing a neutral stare from his mate. "And please lower your voice."

"Or Ranal could revert back to a cloud for us," Sarah suggested, dropping her voice to a whisper. "We're up in the air, remember? It's a long way down to the ground. Don't you get it? Things we aren't even aware of could do us in."

Steve clasped his hands behind his back and began to pace. "Let's look at this logically," he began.

"In that case," Sarah interrupted, "perhaps I should do the talking?"

Steve snorted. "Cute. Look. We're here. We're on Ranal. And we're *still* here. What does that tell you?"

Sarah shrugged. "That it has decided to let us stay?"

"Or it hasn't decided what to do with us," Steve finished.

"What are you trying to say?" Sarah asked.

Steve shrugged. "I think as long as we behave ourselves, and don't intrude on any of the griffins, we'll probably be allowed to look around."

"And when we find that which we're looking for?" Sarah asked.

"Then I'd say we should be ready to depart before we do anything, if you catch my meaning."

Salana and the rest of the griffins continued to stare silently at the two of them. Sarah swallowed nervously. She recalled the instructions Ria had given her. The orbsceia flower had beautiful golden petals. Two of the plants were allegedly situated by pools. Sarah sighed loudly. This wasn't going to be easy. This island was far larger than expected, there were pools of water everywhere, and no matter where she looked, she could see griffins dubiously eyeing her back. Complicating the situation was this *power* governing the island.

Sarah glanced up at the sun. Less than three hours of sunlight left. They were running out of time.

Chapter 8 — Needle in a Haystack

This place is huge," Steve grumped. "I swear, if I didn't know any better, I'd say we were on the ground. I mean, look!" Sarah watched as her husband pointed south. "There's no way this is an island. That cloud was nowhere near this big."

"Are you sure?" she challenged. "We don't know how it works. For all we know Ranal could act just like Mary Poppins' purse."

"Huh?" Steve asked, turning back to her. "Care to run that by me again?"

"You know what I'm talking about," Sarah said. "Do you remember when she first arrived and began unpacking? She was pulling all kinds of things out of her bag that would not fit otherwise."

"Okay, yeah, I do remember that," Steve admitted, remembering that the beloved fictional character had pulled potted plants, hat racks, and all manner of items from her small carpet bag.

"What if the island is like that? The cloud could be just a doorway, or an opening, to much more."

Steve frowned. "Do you remember what Tesur said? He didn't see a cloud but an actual island. Your theory couldn't possibly be right."

"Regardless of what the *doorway* may look like," Sarah said, adding air quotes around 'doorway', "it's still just a way to enter. Clearly there are powers at play here. Powers way beyond our control. Who knows what could happen here?"

Steve groaned and ran a hand through his short hair.

"Ok, let's assume you're right. This island is much larger than either of us expected. How can we expect to find a single flower in this mess?"

Sarah gazed thoughtfully at the expansive, lush tropics before them. Her husband was right. Thanks to the abundance of water in pools everywhere she looked, her mind's eye classified her immediate surroundings as a tropical paradise. Lush green grass ringed many of the pools. Exotic orchids and flowering plants were everywhere. Huge trees with trunks covered in dense, green moss were scattered here and there. Even the trees, Sarah noted with dismay, had flowers and plants growing in the soft moss covering their trunks.

She sighed again. This wasn't going to be easy. She took her husband's hand and pulled him away from the disquieting eyes of the nearby griffins.

"Come on. We might as well get started. We only have a few hours to search and we have a lot of ground to cover."

"Only a few hours?" Steve sputtered, casting a quick glance behind to verify they weren't being followed by the griffins. "Where'd you come up with that?"

Without breaking her stride, Sarah pointed up at the sun. "It won't be long until sunset. Once the sun goes down, so does our light. We won't be able to search. And, you will recall, this is day two. The Fae won't make it another day. This is our last shot."

"Great," Steve grumbled. "No pressure there."

They pushed their way through the thick foliage of low-lying tree branches, waded through hip-deep grass that was so soft and luxuriant to the touch that Sarah was thoroughly tempted to stop, and circumnavigated at least a dozen of the pools before they finally came to a stop. Recognizing the hopelessness of the situation, Sarah's eyes filled. Steve approached and rubbed her back tenderly.

"This isn't looking good, is it?" he whispered.

"No," Sarah admitted. "It's freaking me out. Steve, we've come so far. We can't fail now! We have to find that damn flower!"

Her husband suddenly straightened and looked behind them. Then he pivoted in place and stared up at the nearby trees. The hairs on the back of Sarah's head suddenly stiffened.

"What is it?" she asked, certain she wasn't going to like the answer.

"I feel like we're being watched." Her husband turned to a second nearby tree and clenched his fists. Much to Sarah's dismay, both of Steve's hands had turned dark red.

"No!" she hissed, snatching her husband's hands and wrapping hers around them. "Are you kidding me? No fires!"

"There's something out there," Steve insisted. "I can just feel it."

"Fine. Let whoever, or whatever, it is watch us. Whatever you do, mister, do not use your jhorun. Remember the power of the island? The simple fact that we're still here suggests it's okay with our presence. All that goes out the window if we disrupt anything."

"You don't know that for certain," Steve accused.

"You're right," Sarah conceded. "I don't. However, we're going to assume it's true because we don't want to take any chances, right?"

Steve scowled and jammed his hands into his pants pockets. "Fine. No jhorun."

Mollified, Sarah smiled with relief. "Thank you."

"But…" Steve interrupted.

Sarah groaned. "But what?"

"We need to have some sort of game plan in place in case something happens. What if something does jump out at us? You don't want me torching it. I'm inclined to agree with you.

It'd be in everyone's best interests if I keep my hands in my pockets. What about you? Do you think you can use your jhorun here?"

Sarah nodded. "I know I can. That's why the Fae contacted me, remember?"

"No, I don't mean teleporting. I'm talking about self-defense. Could you use your jhorun to protect us?"

"Oh." Sarah thought for a moment. "I think both of our jhoruns would work here, but if we use my jhorun for self-defense, much like you'd use yours, then we'd be in the same pickle. We'd incur the wrath of whatever power controls this island."

Steve shrugged. "Got it. No pissing anything off. I guess if anything shows up you'll just have to teleport us out of the way, huh?"

That was a good point, Sarah thought. In case something *was* lurking in the trees and tried to attack them, she ought to have a couple of safe zones ready. She thought back to the clearing where Tesur landed. That should make an adequate…

She frowned. No mental image was forming within her mind. Concentrating harder, she willed a mental picture to form. It shouldn't be hard. They were just there half an hour ago. How could she have forgotten what their landing point looked like?

Try as she might, Sarah was unable to get any mental picture to form. Unfortunately, her jhorun's prerequisite for a successful teleportation jump was a clear image of where she wanted to go. If she couldn't imagine the destination then she couldn't teleport there.

Growing angry, Sarah pulled her husband to a stop, held a finger to her lips before he could protest, glanced directly behind her to study the small grassy knoll they had just traversed, and closed her eyes. The trail of flattened grass was still visible on the small hill. She had just seen it with her own two eyes. Surely, she'd be able to recall that image and teleport back to that hill, shouldn't she?

Once more she was denied. No matter how hard she tried, she couldn't picture any locale on Ranal. That couldn't be a coincidence.

"Is everything okay?" Steve asked, concerned.

Sarah opened her eyes and gave her husband an exasperated look. He automatically took a step back from her and raised his hands in the universal *I surrender* gesture.

"What are you doing?" Sarah asked, stifling a giggle. "I'm not mad at you."

Steve's arms dropped back down to this sides.

"Good. Okay, so if it's not me, and assuming it's not the fact that this flower is practically impossible to find, what's the matter? Why did you stop?"

"I can't teleport here."

"What? Are you serious? You can't get us off Ranal?"

Sarah closed her eyes. She hadn't thought to pick a location off of Ranal. She ordered her jhorun to bring up an image of their hidden cabin in the quiet woods. A picture immediately formed. She switched locations and brought up the throne room in the Great Hall. Sure enough, an image formed there, too.

Her eyebrows shot up. Kri'Entu was there, leading Constable Fensham, Lissa's father, away from the thrones, presumably heading toward the Antechamber. Mikal was following close behind. The queen, on the other hand, had an arm draped across Lissa's shoulders and was leading her and an older woman Sarah didn't recognize in the opposite direction. What was going on?

Well, she'd have to inquire later. At least her jhorun was working, it just wasn't working *here*, or more specifically, it would only allow her to teleport *from* here, not *to* here. That was definitely something she needed to know.

"Okay, what's going on?"

She gave Steve the quick rundown of her discovery.

"Ah. You can teleport off but not on. I would deem that important, need-to-know information. Er, how does this help us?"

Sarah stepped close and hooked her arm through her husband's. "It means that you and I are going to remain side-by-side for the remainder of our time on Ranal. We aren't going to separate for any reason whatsoever."

"We could cover more ground if we split up," Steve

reminded her.

Sarah strengthened her grip on his arm. "I know, but I can't take that chance. And I won't. Will you?"

Steve gave her hand a reassuring pat and they moved off.

"If we're going to find this flower we're going to have to be smart about this," Steve told her. "We just don't have the time to search this place from top to bottom."

"I have a feeling that even if we *did* have the time, we'd be unable to search this whole place," Sarah observed.

"Suggesting what?" Steve asked.

"I have the feeling this place is infinitely large. We could spend years wandering around. You're right. We need to figure out the clue."

Steve pulled her to a stop. "What clue?"

"The one Shardwyn gave us. Remember?"

Steve shrugged. "Oh. That. It wasn't very helpful. He wanted us to find the pools. Trust me, we found 'em. The damn things are everywhere."

"I'm talking about the second part," Sarah clarified.

"Umm, what part was that again?"

Sarah shook her head. "Not only am I making you take daily gingko supplements when we get home, I will also be signing you up for some of those online brain stimulation courses."

"Hardy har har. I'm doing no such thing."

"Mm-hmm. We'll see. Anyway, the second thing Shardwyn said during his trance was the part about the hands. Remember now?"

"Oh, riiiiiight, the hands." Steve studied the palms of his own two hands. "Something about water falling through open hands would point us to … to … care to help me out here?"

Sarah laughed. "You're just proving my point, Sparky. As I was saying, Shardwyn said 'only in his hands will you find what you seek'."

Steve's brow furrowed. "Whose hands?"

"Yep. That's what you said earlier."

"Uh huh. And what was the answer?"

"Wow, you really don't remember, do you?"

Steve sighed and gave her a speculative look.

"That's when Shardwyn woke up," Sarah reminded him. "He wasn't able to answer your question. So that's the answer we need to figure out. Whose hands was he referring to?"

"And you think if we can figure that out, we'll be able to find the flower?"

"We've had to solve puzzles and clues practically every step of the way," Sarah recalled. "This shouldn't be any different. Shardwyn presented us with this puzzle. We just have to solve it."

"You mean we have to figure out what he meant," Steve translated. "Got it. So, what's it mean? What do we have to do?"

"Do you think I have a magic wand that I just wave around, which will automatically point out which way to go?" Sarah demanded, growing angry. "That's the whole point of a clue. We have to figure it out. Shardwyn said 'in his hands'. What does that tell you? Do you think we're looking for a pool in the shape of a hand?"

"I thought you said 'hands'," Steve recalled. "Plural."

"Fine. Maybe we're looking for two pools that look like hands?"

"Why two pools?" Steve asked.

"What?"

"Why two pools? Why not just the one? How could a flower be in two separate locations?"

"Well, there *are* three flowers left," Sarah argued. "Maybe he means we can find two flowers in the same spot?"

"It's possible, I guess," Steve said, reaching up to push a low hanging branch out of the way. "What else could it mean? What else could look like hands?"

They both stopped as soon as they pushed their way through a line of slender moss-covered trees resembling willows. Steve reached up over Sarah's head to part the dangling branches and allowed Sarah to enter first.

"This place just keeps getting prettier," Sarah observed.

The island of Ranal, it would seem, had more than one biome. They were now staring at a mountain forest, starting as abruptly as if they had just walked from one movie set to another. A large lake stood directly before them, and in the distance, they could see two smaller bodies of water. Curious, Steve poked his head back through the line of willow trees and saw the jungle sitting right where they left it.

A blast of frigid arctic air appeared from the north. Steve wrapped his arms around his wife and increased his jhorun, effectively warming them both. Seemingly out of nowhere a mountain range appeared, stretching from the north all the way past the western horizon. Of the three small peaks, two were covered with snow while the third was barren rock, devoid of vegetation. A deciduous forest consisting of a variant of oak, hickory, and maple trees began about a quarter of a mile away, ringing the back half of the lake. The trees grew progressively thicker the farther away they looked.

"Still think we're on an island?" Steve asked, in a quiet voice.

Sarah nodded. "I do. I still think there's some logical explanation."

"That would mean this *island* has snow," her husband pointed out. "Did you catch that? Snow. We just came from the tropics back there. The climate just changed as quickly as walking from one room to the next."

"It is odd," Sarah agreed, turning to look back the way they had come. "The only theory I can come up with would concern the griffins."

"What about them?" Steve asked.

"Well, we know there are mountain griffins living in Lentari. Wouldn't Ranal need to have a place for those griffins to, uh, well, rest?"

"That would suggest somewhere in Lentari there is a tropical jungle," Steve pointed out. "We've been all over the kingdom. I'm pretty sure we would have noticed had we walked into a jungle."

Sarah was silent as she considered. After a few moments, she shook her head.

"Not necessarily." She carefully picked her way down the ridge where the willow trees bordered the jungle setting and marveled at the drastic change of scenery. She shook her head with disbelief. They were just walking through a jungle not five minutes ago! Now it almost looked as if they were walking around the Coeur d'Alene National Forest back home in Idaho. "You're assuming that Ranal is the resting place for all the griffins in Lentari, right?"

"Yeah, you could say that."

"What about the others?"

"What are you talking about?" Steve asked. "What others?"

"Griffins aren't indigenous to Lentari, are they? What about that country to the south? What was it? Straosia? What if there are griffins living down there?"

Steve was silent as he considered.

"I think that's why Ranal moves," Sarah continued. "This is where griffins go to die. *All* griffins. So it makes sense that this island can accommodate griffins from every climate."

"Okay, I'll buy that," Steve finally decided. He held a hand over his eyes and gazed at the distant mountains. "I wonder how big this place really is."

"Oh, *please* don't start up with me again," Sarah groaned. "Regardless of our present situation, we are still on an island."

"No way," her husband argued. "We've somehow stepped into another realm. The cloud/island thing we saw was just... how did you put it? A doorway."

Sarah suddenly smiled.

"Would you like to make a wager?"

Steve nodded. "Fine. You're on, milady. What wouldeth thou liketh to wager?"

"Dork. Alright, if *I* win, and this turns out to be an island, then ... hmm ... let's see. What kind of insidious task can I make you do?" She was silent for a few moments before she snapped her fingers. "I have it. You have to paint the master bathroom."

Her husband scowled, as she knew he would. Steve hated to paint. He had the right temperament for the job, being meticulous and patient, but there was just something about the possibility of getting paint on his fingers that he absolutely detested.

"Fine."

"What? Really? You're agreeing? Awesome! Oh. It's gonna be purple."

"What?"

"The paint will be purple. You will hereby withdraw all objections to me making our bathroom purple."

Steve groaned.

"You're wagering one paint job, is that it?"

Sarah nodded. "Right. And the paint you'll be using will be eggplant purple."

"What are *you* wagering?" Steve wanted to know. "You're gonna have to come up with something good in order for me to even consider picking up a paint brush."

"Well, if you'd like to up the ante, I just thought of something."

Steve's left eyebrow slowly lifted. "I'm listening."

"If you add the kitchen to your list of rooms to be painted…"

"I'm not painting the kitchen purple," Steve vowed. "I don't care what you wager."

"Not even for one full-size upright arcade machine of your choice? For your man cave?"

"Ohhh. You fight dirty."

"I'll withdraw my objection to getting a completely useless, money-wasting arcade machine that belongs back in the '80s. Well? Do we have a deal?"

Steve glanced back at the line of willow trees marking the end of the jungle and slowly turned to study the distant mountains.

"Fine. You have yourself a bet."

"Fool," a new voice chimed in. "You just lost. This *is* an island."

Sarah stiffened with surprise and whirled to look behind her. There wasn't anyone there. She looked over at her husband.

"You heard that, right?"

Steve nodded. "Yep. I thought I heard someone tell me I had lost the bet. In record time, I might add."

They both heard a small thump, as though an acorn had fallen. Steve whirled back around; fists clenched. Sarah grabbed his hands and held them tightly.

"Relax. No fires, remember?"

"Sage advice," the mystery voice agreed.

"Where are you?" Steve demanded. "Show yourself."

"I'm right here," the voice insisted. "In front of you. Look down, imbecile."

Sarah squatted down, prompting Steve to mimic her. There, sitting on a broken branch, was a miniature man. It was a Fae! The tiny figure's thin gossamer wings briefly appeared, fluttered once, and then disappeared from sight. As soon as the two of them were on his level the Fae, dressed in a dark green tunic and matching green trousers, jumped to his feet and took a few cautious steps back. He was also wearing a flowing black cloak, presumably to keep his wings hidden when he had them folded flat against his back.

"Who are you?" Sarah asked. "What are you doing here?"

"Forget about that," Steve interjected. "I want to know how you got here in the first place."

Sarah swatted her husband's arm. "Excuse me, but I'd like to know who he is first."

"I am Thinian Silver Oak," the Fae proudly declared. "I am on a secret mission for my king. What are you doing here, human?"

"Would that be King Tivan?" Sarah asked. She had to stifle a giggle. The look of surprise on the Fae's face was priceless.

"How is it you know my king's name?" Thinian demanded.

"Because your king asked me for help," Sarah answered.

"Lies," Thinian flatly stated, crossing his arms across his chest. "My Lord King Tivan would never ask a human for help."

Sarah shrugged. "Technically correct."

"Hah!" Thinian exclaimed, pleased. "I knew it."

"It was Queen Ria's idea to transport me to Dynwe," Sarah explained, smiling with satisfaction as Thinian's smirk disappeared. "She used what little magic she had left, mixed with some of my own jhorun, to bring me to your city. That's where I met the king and queen. They officially asked for my help, Thinian. Obviously, my husband and I agreed. Here we are, trying to find a special flower, er, pontal."

"You seek the orbsceia," Thinian breathed. "You know

about that?"

"So, you're here looking for this flower, too?" Steve asked, confused. "How did you get here? I thought the Fae were grounded."

"We *are* grounded," Thinian confirmed. "Do you have any idea how difficult it was to find a dying griffin, sneak a ride on its back, and make it here unobserved? Five of us set out from Dynwe to accomplish this task. As far as I'm aware, I'm the only one who made it."

"How long have you been here?" Sarah asked.

"Nearly two months."

"And you haven't been able to find the flower in that time?" Steve asked, dismayed.

"Think I have it hidden in a pocket, do you?" Thinian asked, staring at the two figures towering above him.

Ignoring the Fae's sarcasm, Steve turned to Sarah. "If he can't find it, and he's been looking for two months, how the hell are we supposed to find it when we only have a few hours left?"

"A few hours?" Thinian repeated. He cocked his head as he studied them. "Why, if you don't mind me asking, do you humans say you only have a few hours left?"

"First off," Steve declared, "she's Sarah and I'm Steve. We have names, just like you."

Shamed, the Fae bowed. "My apologies. I have gone for some time without company in this accursed place."

"The reason Steve said we only have a few hours left is because it's true," Sarah told the Fae. "There are only a few more hours of daylight before it's too dark to search. According to the queen, the tree will not survive another day."

"But," Thinian sputtered, "should the Tree die, that means... the Fae will..."

"We know," Sarah gently told him. "That's why we're here. We're doing everything we can to help."

"There's no time to lose."

Thinian sprang to his feet and in less time than it took for the two of them to straighten up from their crouch, the tiny Fae had leapt toward Sarah, latched on to her pant leg, and scrambled upward. Before she knew what was happening,

Thinian was sitting on her right shoulder, resting a hand on her right ear lobe to keep from falling off. The Fae's touch, Sarah noted, was reminiscent of a very slight caress. Thinian's touch made her want to rub her ear, as though something had tickled it. Unfortunately, the sensation made her think a bug had landed on her ear. The first swipe of her hand almost knocked the faerie off his perch.

"Be careful!" Thinian scolded. "Are you trying to dislodge me?"

"You're holding on to my ear," Sarah told the Fae. "It felt like a bug on me. I'm sorry. It's an automatic reflex."

"You are forgiven, hu … I mean, Sarah. We should be off."

"Where to?" Sarah wanted to know.

"North," Thinian answered, pointing at the distant mountains.

"How do you know that?"

"Because that's where I was headed next, before I stumbled upon you two."

"So are you telling me you think this is an island?" Steve asked, after ten minutes walking in silence.

"Indubitably," Thinian agreed.

Sarah clapped her hands excitedly. "I'm getting my purple bathroom! Yay!"

"Now hold up there," Steve argued. "How do you know? You're telling me you've found the borders and were able to look down at the ground far below?"

Keeping a hand on Sarah's ear, Thinian looked at Steve.

"As a matter of fact, I have. I had my doubts, as did you. However, make no mistake about it, this is an island and it is floating above the ground. We will pass through Lentari in just a few hours."

"And then where will we be?" Steve asked. "What country will we be over then?"

Thinian shook his head. "We won't be over any land. We will be over water."

"The Erudian Ocean?" Sarah asked, appalled. "How long before we'll be in Lentari again?"

"Nearly a full week," the Fae answered with a sigh.

"That will never do," Sarah decided. "Either way you look at it, our search ends once the sun goes down."

"So how big is this place?" Steve wanted to know. "How much area have you covered since you've been here?"

Thinian began. "I have thoroughly explored the tundra, grasslands, and desert. I had just finished the jungle and was working my way toward the last area I've yet to explore: forest."

"You'd think that the forest would be the first place you'd check after the jungle," Steve quipped.

"Do you see those mountains?" Thinian countered. "Please remember, I am unable to fly. Fae and mountains are not a good mix."

"You've been saving the best for last, is that it?" Steve guessed.

"Aye."

"Have you encountered griffins in all the areas you've searched?" Steve asked.

Thinian silently regarded him for a few moments. "What kind of question is that? Obviously. This *is* Ranal after all."

"I don't buy it," Steve muttered.

"What?" Sarah asked. "What's the matter?"

"If what Thinian says is true, and he's searched all of the other sections of Ranal, then that means the three flowers will be found in this forest section?"

"Make that two," Thinian quietly remarked. "Only two flowers remain."

Sarah froze in mid step and whirled about, forgetting Thinian was sitting on her shoulder. The tiny Fae had to grab hold of Sarah's ear to keep from tumbling to the ground. "What? You've found one of these orbsceia flowers?"

"I found what was left of one of the plants in the grasslands," Thinian corrected. "I can only assume it had been eaten."

"By a griffin?" Steve asked, incredulous.

Thinian groaned and shook his head. "No, the wyverians are to blame."

Steve blinked in surprise. "Really? Dragons don't eat flowers, do they?"

"No, of course not," Thinian grumped. "Obviously it was a griffin. Only they are allowed on Ranal."

"Yet you are here," Steve observed.

"As are you," Thinian countered.

The three of them approached the lake and moved east to circle it.

"You mentioned five of you set out?" Sarah asked. "If you don't mind me asking, what happened to the other four?"

"I can only assume they didn't survive," Thinian sadly reported. "Five of us snuck onto the backs of a mated griffin couple set to make their final journey together. I'm sorry to say that during the approach to Ranal, the male griffin noticed they were carrying passengers."

"And?" Steve prompted.

"And it's a long way down," Thinian finished.

"How did you manage to survive?" Sarah asked, curious.

Thinian fidgeted uncomfortably on her shoulder. "I'd rather not discuss the matter any further, thank you very much."

"My guess is the male griffin warned the female and both took measures to ensure they rid themselves of their unwanted guests," Steve mused. "Of the five, you alone made it here. You must have either really hung on when the griffin tried to dislodge you or else you found a really good hiding place. Where—"

"By all that is sacred, stop talking," Thinian begged. His wings must have fluttered because his cloak suddenly whipped upward, as though the Fae had been hit with a blast of air from below. "I've been trying to suppress that horror for two months now. Please, let us not speak of this anymore."

Husband and wife shared a look. Steve bit his lip and looked away.

"So, have you found any hands?" Sarah asked, hoping to keep their Fae friend talking.

Thinian looked down at his own appendages. "Hands? That is a strange question to ask. Why would I be looking for hands?"

"So, you didn't know to look for hands?" Steve asked, picking up the thread of conversation.

Puzzled, Thinian stared at the two of them. "Whose hands are you referring to?"

"Before we left R'Tal," Steve began, "which is, uh, the castle where the human king lives, we…"

"I know where R'Tal is," Thinian interrupted with a scowl.

"Right. Anyway, we spoke with our wizard. He said that in order to find what we seek, we must find some hands."

Sarah shrugged. "Close enough."

"Hands?" Thinian repeated, puzzled. "What does that mean? Someone has harvested one of the flowers and we must therefore steal it?"

Steve shook his head, but before he could say anything, Sarah cut in.

"No. I believe it means we need to find something that resembles hands. It could be a pool that looks like hands. It could be rocks shaped like hands. I honestly don't know."

"I have covered many areas of this island," Thinian told her, tightening his grip as Sarah stepped over a fallen log. The Fae ducked just as Sarah brought up her hand to absently rub her ear. "I have observed many pools, peculiar trees, strangely shaped shrubs, but I have yet to encounter anything that even closely resembles hands."

"Excellent," Steve breathed.

"Excuse me?" Sarah sputtered. "Would you care to explain yourself?"

Steve shrugged. "If Thinian hasn't come across it yet then it means we're heading in the right direction."

"Have you been looking at the stones?" Sarah asked. "Rock formations, maybe stones that look like hands when viewed from a distance, or from a higher elevation, or anything like that?"

"I wasn't paying attention to the stones," Thinian admitted. "I was more interested in looking for exotic flowers."

"Do you remember seeing anything that might qualify as a hand?"

"Hands," Steve reminded her.

"Right," Sarah said, nodding. "Thanks, dear. Thinian, does anything come to mind? Anything at all?"

The Fae shook his head. "I am sorry, no. I would have remembered anything standing out like that."

Sarah smiled at her husband and looked up at the distant northern peak ahead. As they walked around the large lake, the terrain turned rocky, much to Sarah's delight. Large and small stones alike were pushing up through the ground, forming a myriad of strange and unusual shapes. Sarah pointed one out.

"I'd say we're on the right track. Look at that. What do you think that circle of rocks looks like?"

"A shield," Thinian answered.

"A pizza," Steve suggested.

Sarah shook her head and giggled. "A pizza? Really?"

Her husband grinned at her and pointed at the closest rock. "Sure. See those pock marks on the surface? Reminds me of pepperonis. Those could be sausages over there."

"I do not understand," Thinian began. "What is *pizza?*"

"It's a type of food," Sarah answered. "According to Steve, it's single-handedly the most important discovery the human race has ever made."

"Of course, it is," Steve retorted. He looked over at Thinian and nodded. "It is my world's super food. It's a perfectly balanced food. It's got your bread group, meat group, sauce group, veggie group…"

"Veggies?" Sarah laughed. "Pineapple does not qualify as veggies. And 'super food'? You're delusional, dear."

"I'm talking about tomatoes, thank you very much," Steve quipped, ignoring the look of incredulity that was on Sarah's face. "And we mustn't forget the most important group: the cheese group. You can't get a more balanced meal than that."

"I do believe I'd like to try this pizza," Thinian decided. "I believe I would enjoy it."

"Of course you would, pal," Steve jovially told the Fae. "Everyone loves pizza."

"Well, I don't care for it that much," Sarah informed him.

"I know you don't. You're *weird.*"

Sarah felt a gentle tap on her cheek and glanced down at Thinian. The Fae pointed to the right, at a second group of rocks.

"Behold. Another formation. Does that look like hands

to you?"

Sarah shook her head. "No, not really. Do they to you?"

"Possibly," Thinian shrugged. "That could be a palm and that could be a thumb."

"So where are the rest of the fingers?" Steve asked, looking at the misshapen mound of rocks. "Those really don't resemble hands in any way, shape, or form."

"The problem is, we don't know if we're looking for rocks," Sarah reminded him. "It's just a theory that would fit Shardwyn's prediction."

They emerged into a clearing with a small river flowing south. The river, Sarah decided, had to be fed by a natural spring that carved the deep trenches into the surface.

The ground sloped steeply up, eventually rising well over a thousand feet to form the southern side of the barren mountain they had seen earlier. Sarah craned her neck to look up at the distant mountaintop and gasped with surprise. The river, it would seem, did not emerge from within the heart of the mountain, as she had originally surmised. The water was the excess flow from a waterfall near the top of the mountain. Sarah groaned. While she couldn't quite tell if the stony outcropping resembled hands, she just *knew* they had found what they had been searching for.

Chapter 9 — Pool with a View

"Anyone got any bright ideas?" Sarah heard her husband ask. She glanced over to see him staring up at the mountain towering high above their heads. Craning her own neck to estimate how high up the side of the mountain they were going to have to go, she groaned. It was at least three, maybe four-hundred meters, easy. She might not be able to see any fingers—or hands—but her instinct was screaming that they had found what they were looking for.

"It's up the side of the damn mountain," Steve groaned. "Of course, it is. Why would it be otherwise? We should've just searched for the most inaccessible area of this island and saved ourselves a lot of time."

"You complain a lot," Thinian observed.

Sarah stifled a smile as she watched her husband's eyes narrow.

"Dude, I will flick your tiny butt right off this island."

She glanced down at the miniature figure on her shoulder. The Fae, it would seem, felt that he was more than a match for her husband and was preparing to jump off her shoulder to launch his own attack.

"Take it easy," she told the Fae. She looked over at her husband and frowned. "And you. Now's not the time, dear. We have a bigger problem to solve."

"You're certain that we need to get up there?" Steve asked, frowning. "I don't see any hands."

"Neither do I," Sarah admitted.

"Then how do you know the orbsceia flower is up there?" Thinian asked, genuinely confused.

Sarah smiled at the Fae. "Woman's intuition."

Steve sighed and looked at Thinian. "You know this place better than I do, pal. Do you have any suggestions for getting up there?"

Thinian sadly shook his head. "Like you, I am grounded. I cannot get up there any easier than you."

Sarah sat down on a nearby stump and stretched her back. "There must be a way we can get up there. We wouldn't have been sent here if we couldn't handle it."

"Are you sure you can't teleport?" Steve asked. "Your jhorun would come in mighty handy right about now if you could."

Sarah closed her eyes and ordered her jhorun to provide her with a mental picture of the top of the waterfall. As before, she was unable to bring up any place on the island. She looked at Steve and sadly shook her head.

"It just isn't going to happen. I couldn't teleport a dozen feet away on this island, even if I wanted to. This place just won't let it happen."

"Well," her husband said, "what if…"

"If you're going to rephrase your original question and ask me, yet again, if I can teleport something then I will personally help Thinian push you off this island. Steve, I can't teleport. Stop asking me, okay?"

Steve jammed his hands into his pockets. "You're upset. I get that. Look, I'm trying to brainstorm here, alright? We know you can't teleport. I'm not asking you to try. But what about the telekinesis facet of your jhorun?"

"Her what?" Thinian asked, from his perch on Sarah's

shoulder.

"She has the ability to move things around without touching them," Steve explained to the Fae. "We've always viewed it as another extension of her jhorun. The ability to teleport an object from one location to another, while keeping the item in sight."

Thinian turned to look at Sarah, a look of wonder on his face. "You can do that?"

Sarah nodded. "Yes. I don't know if I can do it here, though."

The Fae cleared his throat. "I, er, hesitate to side with *him*," Thinian began, hooking a thumb in Steve's direction, "but perhaps he is right? Could you try?"

"What if I end up angering the island?" Sarah asked. "What if the island disappears, or turns back into that cloud, and we all plummet straight down? Do you really want to risk it?"

"You're right," Steve conceded. "It's not worth it. We'll think of something else."

"She's a teleporter," Thinian recalled, giving Sarah's earlobe a friendly pat. The Fae turned to Steve and smirked. "What can you do? Can your jhorun be considered useful? Can you do anything worthwhile to help us out?"

"You really ought to find out what he's capable of before you insult him," Sarah quietly whispered to the Fae.

"Why?" Thinian whispered back.

"Because I'm a fire thrower," Steve nonchalantly told the small figure as he approached. "Before you ask, yes, my jhorun will undoubtedly work here. However, I don't want to piss anything off, either. So, my hands are just as tied as hers. Besides, I fail to see how blasting out jets of flames would help us in this situation."

"Thanks to you we were able to make it here," Sarah reminded him.

"True. I wouldn't want to push my luck, though. *Our* luck."

"I agree," Sarah agreed. "So, here's what we do. We brainstorm. Thinian? You're up first. Give me a suggestion, no matter how bizarre it may sound."

"We, uh, scale it?" The tiny Fae's voice trailed off, as though he was uncertain he should have said anything.

"No, don't question yourself," Sarah scolded. "I asked for ideas, no matter how bizarre. You suggest we climb it. That would be one way to get up there but there's no way the three of us could scale *that*. Steve? You're up."

"Well, I could call for help."

"You mean Pryllan?" Sarah clarified. "There are a couple of things wrong right off the bat. First, I doubt very much the island would let her approach. Second, and most important, she's currently nesting. Her egg isn't due to hatch for several more months. You remember what Pravara told us the last time we saw her, right?"

Steve nodded. "You're right. I forgot. Pryllan won't be any help until her egg hatches. It's for the best, really. Even if she wasn't tending her egg, there's no way Kahvel would let her come up here. Alright, dear. You've heard our suggestions. What's yours?"

"Well," Sarah slowly began, "we are on an island populated by griffins. I say we ask them to fly up there to check out the top of the waterfall. Let's see if they can spot anything resembling hands up there."

"That won't work," Thinian instantly responded.

"Why not?" Steve asked.

"Because griffins don't fly here," the Fae answered.

"Because they can't or because they won't?" Sarah wanted to know.

"Either. Or both. Does it really matter? In all the days I've spent here not once have I seen a griffin in the air."

"I wonder why that is?" Steve wondered aloud.

"I would imagine it has something to do with the simple fact that this island is *moving*," Thinian slowly explained, as if to a child.

Sarah shrugged. "It makes sense. Why risk it? Whether it is an unspoken rule or whether it's just basic, common sense, the griffins don't fly. Where does that leave us?"

Steve glanced up at the sun. He swallowed nervously. The sun was inching ever closer to the western horizon. They were running out of time.

"Let's go ask them for help," Steve suggested.

"Let's ask *who* for help?" Sarah wanted to know.

"The griffins. This is their island. Maybe they'll have a suggestion or two that might help us out."

"I doubt it," Sarah muttered, more to herself. She raised her voice. "You heard Thinian. They can't fly. What do you think they're going to be able to do? Climb?"

Steve shrugged. "Why not? They might be able to make it to the top. You never know until you try."

"You're right," Sarah conceded. "It's worth a shot. Has anyone seen any griffins lately?"

She felt a tug on her right ear. Thinian was pointing back the way they came.

"Go that way. You'll find a large gathering by the lake. New arrivals have a tendency to loiter there until they get their bearings."

They rushed back to the same clearing where they had first arrived. Steve, Sarah noted, was wheezing like an out-of-shape chain smoker and was clutching his side. While somewhat out of breath she was nowhere near as incapacitated as her husband. She felt Thinian tap her ear to get her attention.

"Is he well?"

"Just give him a moment," Sarah whispered to the Fae. "He'll be okay."

"Are you sure? He sounds as though he's suffocating."

"It's what happens when you work at a job that doesn't require you to move around too much," Sarah quietly explained. "I keep telling him he should exercise more."

The wheezing stopped.

"I heard that," Steve grumbled. "I'm fine. And I get plenty of exercise, thank you very much."

"Really? You don't sound fine. Even Thinian was concerned."

"Let's just focus on the problem at hand, shall we?" Steve indicated the serene lakeside environment. "We're here. There are griffins everywhere. Now what?"

"Do you see Tesur anywhere?" Sarah asked, peering anxiously around the glade.

"No. I don't see his mate, either."

"Any of them will do," came Thinian's exasperated comment from within her inside jacket pocket.

Sarah cleared her throat and nervously eyed the numerous griffins lounging about. She took her husband's hand and pulled him close. She could see at least two dozen griffins in the area. They were reclining in trees, stretched out in the soft grass, and even sitting complacently by the water's edge. All, however, were staring directly at them. She couldn't help but feel a bit like a deer who had wandered into a sleeping pride of lions.

"Hello again. It's us. We, um, need to ask you for some help. Do you know that big mountain at the edge of the island's forest zone? There's something near the top that we need to get. We're just not too sure how to do it. Can someone give us some help?"

Not one griffin moved a feather. Several dozen pairs of avian eyes silently regarded them.

"Anyone? Anyone at all?"

More silence.

"This isn't working too well," Steve mumbled.

"Ask them for a favor," Thinian's voice quietly suggested from inside Sarah's jacket.

Her brow furrowed. It had almost sounded like the Fae had been suppressing a laugh when he had made his suggestion. What could that mean?"

"Go on," Thinian urged. "Ask them for a favor. Watch what happens."

"What will happen?" Sarah urgently whispered back. "What do you know that you're not telling us?"

The Fae fell silent. Cursing silently to herself Sarah turned to face the closest griffin. Suddenly finding her mouth dry, Sarah gave a slight cough. "Would one of you be willing to do us a favor?"

It was as if someone had taken a baseball bat to a hornet's nest. Suddenly the griffins couldn't react fast enough. They were jumping out of trees, leaping off the ground, and surging toward them from the other side of the lake. One griffin brushed up too close to another and a fight ensued. Within seconds the entire scene had switched to a griffin free-for-all as everyone began fighting with their neighbor.

Alarmed, Sarah clutched her husband's arm and the two of them slowly backed away.

"What the hell just happened?" Steve quietly asked. "Why are they all fighting?"

"All I did was to ask them for a favor," Sarah breathed. Her shocked eyes were glued to the quarreling griffins. Tufts of tawny fur and broken feathers dotted the landscape.

Steve nudged her shoulder and pointed north. "Look! More are on the way. I don't get it. What's going on?"

Sarah angrily smacked her jacket. "Thinian! Get out here this instant. What have you done?"

"I didn't do anything," Thinian insisted, as he climbed back up to Sarah's shoulder. "You're the one who asked, remember?"

"Was it Tinkerbell's idea to ask for a favor?" Steve wanted to know.

"Yes," Sarah nodded. "And don't call him Tinkerbell. I thought something was up when he suggested it because it sounded like he was trying not to laugh."

"If you want to see what it's like to be a toasted marshmallow, then keep it up," Steve warned, as he dangerously eyed the Fae. "Out with it. What's going on over there?"

Properly cowed, the Fae swallowed nervously. "They're fighting to see who will win the favor."

"What's the big deal about asking for a favor?" Sarah asked, perplexed.

"You will owe them one in return. Think about it," Thinian said. "If you're a griffin, and you're here on Ranal, that means there's no leaving. What if you have unfinished business? What if there was a message you wanted to send? How would you go about doing it?"

"You couldn't," Steve decided.

"That's right," the Fae agreed. "Once you're here, then all contact has been cut off. *But…* what if the impossible happens? A newcomer arrives, and it isn't a griffin? What's more, what if they do have the ability to leave? What then?" Thinian pressed. "I'm willing to wager everyone fighting over there has unfinished business that they would love to have resolved."

"Fighting griffins aside," Steve began, "how exactly are they supposed to help us? If they don't—or won't—fly then what good are they to us?"

"They know this island better than anyone," Thinian answered. "If there's a way to reach the top of that waterfall then they should be able to tell us what it is."

"Do you think they could climb it?" Sarah asked.

"Perhaps," Thinian said. "The mountain may be solid stone but it isn't smooth. They might be able to scale it."

"But all of us need to go there," Steve pointed out. "If that's where this flower is then we need to be together the moment it's harvested 'cause I'm pretty sure the island is gonna evict us the moment we do."

"Let's just see what they suggest," Sarah said. She pointed at the ruckus. "Looks like it's breaking up. Hey, how is it possible that after all that fighting it looks like no one got hurt?"

"Seriously?" Thinian asked, turning to look up at Sarah. "What do you think could happen to them? They're already dead."

The victor of the melee squawked victoriously and strutted his way over. Once the griffin arrived it extended a foreleg and gave them a small bow. Thinian darted back inside Sarah's pocket. Just to be safe.

"I have won the right to grant the favor," the griffin exclaimed, surprising them both with its voice. It was a female. And, contrary to what they'd seen on virtually all the griffins on Ranal, this one didn't have any white feathers or any silver streaking its tawny hide.

This griffin, Sarah realized with a start, was young.

"What's your name?" Sarah asked the griffin.

"Loryss."

Sarah introduced herself and Steve.

"What do you require?" Loryss finally asked.

"We need to scale a mountain," Sarah told her. "There's something we need near the top. Do you know of a way to get up there?"

Loryss shook her head. "Aside from flying? No."

"Do you think you could climb it?" Sarah hopefully asked. "No."

"Well, that's what we require," Steve told the griffin. "The two of us have to make it up to the top of that mountain."

"I could climb it," another voice suddenly chimed in. A second female griffin appeared next to the first. "I can take you there."

Loryss turned to face the newcomer and squawked angrily. "You didn't win the right to ask for a favor, Nyx. I did."

"If you can't perform the task they require, then you must forfeit your claim," Nyx stated as she ruffled the feathers on her wings.

"I will do no such thing," Loryss snapped. She pawed at the ground with one of her avian front legs. "I just said that I couldn't climb it. There must be another way to accomplish their task."

"There is no flying allowed," Nyx reminded her. "There is literally no other option to explore. Either you climb or you will allow someone else to earn the favor."

"Like you?" Loryss angrily squawked.

"Aye. Like me. I can scale it."

"You've never even seen that mountain," Loryss pointed out. "You've only been on the island for a few days. You have no idea how to scale it any better than I."

"I have the motivation to try," Nyx softly answered.

"You are no match for Usol," Loryss retorted, lifting her beak and staring down at the smaller griffiness. "Besides, it's irrelevant. I won the favor, not you."

"Usol?" Sarah repeated, puzzled. "What is that? The name of the mountain?"

"Usol is Ranal's creator," Loryss explained, lowering her voice to a whisper. "He is a powerful being who was rumored to be so old that he witnessed the birth of time itself. It is said he favored the griffins, and he proved that by creating this island as a sanctuary."

"How?" Steve wanted to know, not bothering to hide the disbelief in his voice.

"Usol selected islands from all over the world," Loryss quietly explained. "He lifted them from their watery beds and pushed them together until a land with a wide variety of environments had been created. As you can see, he succeeded. Every clime a griffin has ever lived in is represented here. We can freely choose which is the most comfortable."

"Except for the mountain," Nyx added.

"What do you know about that mountain?" Loryss fired back. "You're too new. You've never even seen it."

"I know what I'm told," Nyx answered. "From the moment I awoke here I was told that the mountain is off limits."

Loryss clucked approvingly. "Well, you'd be right. It has long been known that Usol reserved the right to use that mountain for his own purposes."

"Does that mean you can't even step foot on it?" Sarah worriedly asked.

Loryss shrugged. "Unknown. There has never been a need to try."

"Well, back to ye olde drawing board," Steve mumbled. "We'll have to find another way to get up the side of that thing."

"I said I never stepped foot on the mountain," Loryss corrected. "I never said that I wouldn't."

"I don't want to make you do something you shouldn't be doing," Sarah told the griffin. "We'll find another way."

"You don't understand," Loryss said, dropping her voice even lower. "Some things are worth the risk. I need that favor."

Nyx stepped forward. "As do I. If Loryss is unable to earn the favor then consider me. I'll get you to the top of that mountain."

"Close your beak," Loryss angrily snapped. "If you can climb that mountain, so can I."

"What favors could the two of you possibly need that each of you would consider breaking the island's rules?" Steve asked with a bewildered air. "If this Usol person is the one responsible for protecting this island and keeping undesirables out, aren't you worried about what will happen to you?"

Loryss briefly shared a look with Nyx. "I do not know what her circumstances are, but my own are dire. I will gladly resign myself to oblivion if I can right the wrong that befell me."

Nyx nodded. "My needs are just as strong. I will gladly suffer the same fate as Loryss."

"I won the favor," Loryss sadly reminded Nyx. "I will be the one who will benefit from the humans' help, not you. I'm sorry."

Nyx's head fell. Sarah gave a quiet cough and waited for the smaller griffin to look up.

"Both of us need to make it up the side of that mountain, and since there's no way my husband and I could be carried up there by just one griffin, we're going to need two. As much as I don't want either of you to get into trouble, our plight is just as desperate as yours. We *have* to get up there. From the sounds of it, I think we could all help each other."

Loryss nodded her head toward the north. "Let us go. We will discuss it. Nyx, this is indeed your lucky day. Come. We have much to talk about."

Husband and wife followed the two griffins away from the lake and the clearing. Once she was sure they were out of earshot of the rest of the griffins, Sarah increased her pace until she was walking alongside Loryss. Steve hurried to catch up.

"So, let's start with you, Loryss," Sarah began. "What sort of favor do you need from us?"

"As you may have guessed," Loryss slowly began, "there aren't many young griffins here. What would that suggest to you?"

Steve scratched his head. "I'd say that means all the other griffins lived out their normal lives back on the ground and then chose to come here when the time was right."

"And you've noticed I don't have a single white feather anywhere on my wings, haven't you?" Loryss asked, turning to look at Steve.

"It means you're young," Steve decided. "Your life was cut short, is that it? Was it an accident?"

"No," Loryss spat. "I was denied the honor of my final Journey. I didn't get to feel the Pull. How would you feel if you were a griffin in the prime of your life and one morning you woke up here instead of next to your mate? It's embarrassing. Everyone here knows I used the Fool's Pool."

"The Fool's Pool?" Sarah repeated, confused. "What's that?"

Loryss gave Sarah a neutral look. "I. Was. Brought. By. Pool."

"I take it griffins don't like to swim?" Steve asked.

"Only an invalid would resort to using a Pool to get here," Loryss said, sounding bitter.

"Or the infirm," Nyx added.

Loryss stepped around Nyx, taking the lead. A path seemingly appeared out of nowhere, and without missing a beat, both griffins increased their pace as the mountain neared.

"Aye," Loryss continued. "An invalid or an infirm. How do you think that makes me feel?"

"I am the same," Nyx reminded the larger griffin. "I was denied my final Journey, too."

"What does a pool have to do with anything?" Sarah asked, as she shared a look with her husband. Both were walking fast in order to keep up with their guides. "What are we missing?"

"You've no doubt noticed the number of pools on this island," Loryss began, looking over at Sarah. "Would you care to speculate why there are so many?"

Sarah shrugged. "I don't know. This place gets a lot of rainfall?"

"A plausible explanation," Loryss decided, but then shook her head no. "However, I personally have yet to see moisture fall from the sky."

Steve held up a hand. "That doesn't make any sense. How does the island stay so green without rain? Who waters the plants? Who makes sure the trees don't dry out?"

"Usol," Loryss said, in a matter-of-fact tone. "That's not the point. Have you ever stopped to consider the pools may be here for a different reason?"

"Like what?" Sarah curiously asked.

Loryss shrugged. "I have only been here a few months. I realize that I haven't seen that much, but in that time, I've witnessed peculiar behavior from anyone who immerses themselves in the Pools. Some are transported between zones. Others have become older while others have become younger. Some of the smaller pools have even been known to change your appearance."

"Ooo, this has promise," Steve chortled, rubbing his hands together. "Dare I ask in what way?"

"Changing the color of our feathers, our fur, and even the number of talons on our front legs."

"The number of talons?" Sarah looked down at Loryss' avian front legs.

"Early griffins had an extra talon on their feet," Nyx explained. "My sire told me that when I was a cub."

"I wonder what would happen if one of us were to fall in," Steve mused, nudging Sarah's shoulder with his.

"Get that thought out of your head," Sarah scolded. "Not only are we not going to try, we don't have the time. Focus. We have a mission to accomplish, remember?"

"You're no fun. Fine. Loryss, you said you're not supposed to be here, right?"

Loryss nodded.

"Do you have any idea how you ended up in a Pool?" Steve asked. "Did one just happen to appear underneath you?"

"Unknown. I fell asleep that night and the following morning, when I awoke, I was shocked to discover myself emerging from a Pool. I knew instantly what had happened."

"I still don't get it," Steve grumped.

"Perhaps we're not meant to," Sarah told him. "We didn't have any idea where Tesur was going when he took us to the Arch. We couldn't see the island for what it was during our approach. I wouldn't worry about it. Besides, did you hear what Loryss said? Ranal has some type of Fountain of Youth on it. Boy, would I like to find that Pool."

"Didn't you just say that we don't have time to check out the Pools?" Steve teased, grinning at her.

"I'm not suggesting we look for it. I'm just saying it would have been nice. That's all."

"Mm-hmm. I believe you. Ow!"

Sarah had punched him on his arm.

They passed by several small pools that were as still as glass. Everyone was quiet as they hurried by. Steve hesitated to lean over the closest pool. "I wonder what that one does."

"Perhaps nothing," Sarah suggested.

"I thought every pool did something different," Steve argued.

"Most do," Loryss agreed. "I was advised upon my arrival to use the Pools at my own risk because only a very select few were nothing more than they appear. Water."

"So why put them here?" Steve demanded. "What's the purpose?"

Loryss' wings rustled against her back.

"I have an opinion, if you'd care to hear it."

Steve nodded. "Go for it."

"Entertainment."

"What? Really?"

The griffin nodded. "Aye. As you might have imagined, there's not a whole lot to do up here."

"If that's the case then this Usol character has a strange sense of humor," Steve softly muttered.

"Would you please keep comments like that to yourself?" Sarah hissed at him. "I'd just as soon not anger the being that not only created this island but is also more than likely still keeping an eye on it." She glanced back at her husband and smiled once she saw his face. His defiant look was gone and he was now nervously looking about. Good.

Steve noticed he was being watched and smiled sheepishly. A split second later the smile was gone and he was frowning once more. He increased his pace until he was walking next to Loryss.

"Wait. You're telling us that we can use the pools to jump from one area of the island to the other? Why in the world are we walking when we could be teleporting there? Look at the base of that sucker and how high we have to go. Wouldn't it be easier to just jump in one of these portal pools and zip up to the top?"

"That would anger Usol," Loryss answered, briefly glancing in his direction. "Pools are for griffin use only."

"What happens if we were to try?" Steve pressed.

Loryss turned until she was looking at Steve. "I would advise against it. However, I must confess I would be extremely interested to see what would happen to you should you insist. Therefore, after you."

Steve instantly veered off the path and angled toward a small pool less than a dozen feet from them.

"What do you think you're doing?" Sarah demanded. "That could be a teleporting pool."

"Exactly," Steve told her, squatting down near the water's edge. "What if it takes us straight to the flower?"

"What if it drops you straight off this island?" Sarah countered.

About to dip a finger in the pool, Steve hesitated. A look of concern spread across his features. He sighed, straightened up, and looked back at her.

"You're no fun. I've got a serious urge to do a cannonball right into the middle of that thing. I'd love to find out what it does."

"Well, keep wondering," Sarah told him. "We don't have time for this. We're not here on an exploration mission, remember?"

A loud cracking noise instantly silenced the group. Half a dozen more sounds followed, coming quicker and quicker. Both husband and wife swallowed nervously. The top of a huge pine came crashing directly toward them, taking out three others in a few seconds.

Her thoughts were cut short as both of their griffin companions squawked with alarm. She and Steve whirled around. She had been right. She could see the top of a huge pine tree, slowly pushing its way past its neighbors, on its way to the ground. Unfortunately, it was angling straight toward them and picking up speed. In just a matter of a few seconds, the towering tree crashed into its neighbors, uprooting three of them. Now there were at least four full-sized evergreens crashing noisily to the ground. There was nowhere to go.

Nowhere except…

Steve grabbed her by the arm and yanked her bodily out of the way, forcing both of them into the small pool. Sarah took one look at the trees careening toward them, made eye contact with her husband, and dove as far down as she could.

After what felt like an eternity —in reality, a few seconds— Sarah felt someone tapping her shoulder. Steve was frantically pointing up. Together they kicked toward the bright sunshine directly above them.

Sputtering, Sarah's head broke the surface of the supernaturally still pond. Even with their splashing about, there were barely any ripples in the water. A few seconds later Steve's head appeared next to hers, facing the other direction.

"If I didn't know any better, I'd say we were just forced into the water. Coincidence? What do you want to bet that…?" Steve trailed off as he finally spun around to look at her. His eyes widened. "Umm…"

Sarah felt the blood drain out of her face. Steve was looking at her as though she had just sprouted horns. He was giving her such a peculiar look that it made her want to run a hand through her hair and ascertain for herself that she hadn't grown a set.

"What's the matter? Why are you looking at me like that?"

The two griffins, who had leapt into the nearby trees, were at the water's edge. Each stared at them with unreadable expressions on their faces. Steve nodded toward shore and started swimming in that direction, being careful to avoid the two trees that were now partially blocking their way. Had Steve not pulled her out of harm's way, and into the water, then they would have most certainly been struck, perhaps even killed.

Sarah felt firm ground under her feet and stepped out of the water. Both Loryss and Nyx were staring silently at her. Steve appeared by her side and carefully turned her head until he was looking straight into her eyes. Sarah slapped his hand out of the way.

"What are you doing? Why are you looking at me like that?"

Her husband pointed back at the water. "Maybe you

ought to see for yourself."

Confused, and somewhat scared, Sarah leaned out over the pool to look at her reflection and almost screamed with surprise. The face staring back at her wasn't hers! In fact, it didn't even look human!

Sarah studied her face. Her reflection, containing decidedly feline undertones, studied her back. What was the term for her appearance? Anthro feline?

Sarah groaned and bit back a curse. While still humanoid in appearance, she now had a fine coating of pale fur covering her skin. Her nose shrunken and black; her cheeks rounded. The area below her nose thickened and her mouth half its size. Also compounding the problem were the existence of nearly a dozen vibrissae on either side of her face that were at least six inches. Good Lord, she had whiskers! Could this day get any worse?

She ran her tongue over her teeth and felt sharp points everywhere. That's just great. Of course, she had a matching set of fangs to go along with everything else. At least she didn't have any … Sarah's hands flew to the top of her head and gingerly felt around.

Yes, they were there. Protruding above her head were two very feline-looking ears. Intent on finding some way to place the blame on Steve, Sarah angrily extended an arm and pointed at the water.

"This is all your fault! Look what's happened to me! I look like a damn cat now!"

Steve stared at her with his mouth open. Finally, after a couple of awkward moments of silence, he shook his head. "I've got nothin', babe. I had no idea that was going to happen to you. Those trees were falling straight toward us. I had to do something."

Sarah looked at her hands. While still mostly humanoid in appearance, her fingers were covered by a fine coat of soft, pale fur. Ugh. This was something else she didn't need. What had caused that tree to drop right then? Was it this same mysterious force that tried to prevent them from arriving on Ranal? If she didn't know any better, she'd say someone was actively trying to drive them away.

Sarah scowled. In her current state it came out as a hissing growl. She started to clench her hands into fists, when inch-long talons appeared at the tip of each finger. Surprised, she turned to her husband. "Do you see this?"

Steve was already backpedaling. "Hey, it's not my fault. I didn't cause that tree to fall when it did."

"Then why didn't something happen to you?" Sarah complained. "Why am I the only one who has been affected?"

"Who says you are?" Loryss asked from nearby.

Sarah rounded on the griffin.

"What? What was that? Has something happened to someone else?"

"Perhaps you should ask your mate," Loryss advised.

"I don't have to," Sarah said, turning back to Steve. She watched him trudge out of the water. "He looks perfectly fine to…"

She trailed off as Steve finally extricated himself out of the water. Her mouth closed with an audible snap. She held a hand to her mouth and tried to stifle a giggle. "Okay, maybe I don't have it so bad."

"What's that supposed to mean?" Steve asked, stepping away from the pool.

Sarah felt the heat pouring off of him as he walked by, proving he was now working on drying his clothes. She shook her head. She could actually see the water lines receding from his shirt as the ambient temperatures continued to climb. By the time she made it to her husband's side, his clothes were dry.

"Loryss is right. You didn't make it out of that pool unscathed."

Steve held his hands up in front of them and turned them this way and that. Then he ran his hands over his arms and legs. Finding nothing she watched her husband run his hands through his hair. Confused, he met her eyes and shrugged.

"I don't know what you're talking about. I can't find a thing wrong."

Sarah spun her finger in the air. "Turn around. You'll find the problem."

Steve rotated in place but was then yanked to a sudden

stop, as if someone had tied a rope around his waist and anchored it to a tree. Confused, Steve twisted around to see that he *had* become attached to a tree. Kinda.

He had a tail! A long skinny brown tail—attached to his own butt—wrapped itself around the closest tree and was hanging on, as if for dear life. Steve stared stupidly at the tail. He followed it back with his eyes to verify *again* that it was physically attached to him. He even gave a few experimental tugs to see if it was someone's idea of a bad joke.

Sarah watched her husband wince in pain after giving his tail several sharp tugs. No, it certainly wasn't his imagination. Steve had a tail and it was real. And not cooperating, she thought with a giggle. From the way he was scowling at the tail she could tell that he wanted it to let go of the tree, only the tail didn't seem to be getting the message.

Steve looked over at her and saw that she was trying to suppress her laughter. He scowled, looked back at his tail, and tugged a few more times. He finally crossed his arms over his chest and glared at her.

"Alrighty, Ms. Chuckles. You seem to think this is so damn funny. How do I make it let go?"

"I could bite it off," Loryss casually suggested.

"Are you kidding me?" Steve sputtered, backing up against the tree in order to protect his newest appendage. "No biting, thank you very much. Sarah, stop laughing."

"I can't help it," Sarah wheezed out between breaths. "Your face is so funny!"

"I didn't laugh at you," her husband pointed out.

"Yes, you did," Sarah countered. "I could hear you."

"Check your hearing! I did not!"

Sarah tapped the side of her head. "I heard it up here. Okay, all hysterics aside, can you tell it to let go? We have to get going."

"Are you sure you don't want to jump back in?" Steve asked, frowning as he looked at the pool. "We might be able to fix this."

"And we could very easily make it worse," Sarah pointed out.

"You want to go around looking like that?" Steve asked.

"Not particularly, but we don't have a choice. We don't have time to deal with this. Besides, we've already wasted enough time as it is."

"I think I got the short end of the deal here," Steve grumped.

"You have a tail. I look like a cat. There's no comparison who got it worse."

"I'd like to weigh in here," a new voice disgustedly chimed in.

Sarah's eyes widened and she came to an abrupt stop. Thinian! The Fae had been in her pocket when she dove into the pool! Both she and her husband had been affected. What about him? Had anything happened to him? She waited until the griffins had looked away before opening her jacket to see about looking inside her pocket.

"Thinian? Are you okay?"

"That's a matter of opinion," came the Fae's sour response.

She felt movement inside her jacket. It felt as though the Fae was trying to extricate himself from the confines of her pocket but wasn't having any luck. Her clothes were still wet and it was making movement difficult.

A frog appeared, completely covered in warts. It stood up on two legs, comically crossed its front legs across its chest, and glared at Sarah with a look of utter disgust. The amphibian's mouth opened but before Thinian could say anything, the vocal sac expanded and a loud *ribbet* escaped his mouth. Horrified, Thinian slapped his two front appendages over his mouth. The frog then leapt off her shoulder and back into the pool. Surprised, Sarah stared at the surface of the small pool and waited.

"What was that?" Steve asked.

"Umm…"

"Come on. We need to catch up to the griffins."

"I'll be right there."

A few ripples appeared on the water's surface. A tiny form practically leapt out of the water, scrambled up her clothes, and dove headfirst into her inner jacket pocket. It had happened so fast that Sarah had been unable to get a good look at what Thinian had become.

"Thinian, are you—"

"Do not concern yourself with me," the faerie snapped. "I've dealt with far worse than this."

"But if you—"

"Do you wish to help? Dry your clothes. I'm freezing in here."

Sarah motioned Steve over and quietly explained what she needed him to do. Once Sarah's clothes were dry, Steve tried—unsuccessfully—to persuade Thinian to come out so he could see for himself what the poor Fae had been transformed into. He moved off, hurrying to catch up to the griffins. As soon as she was alone, Sarah gently prodded her pocket.

"Better?"

"Yes," Thinian grumped.

"So, what do you look like now? Is it any better than the frog?"

"I don't want to talk about it," Thinian snapped.

"Will you come out here? No one is going to laugh at you."

"Absolutely not."

"Suit yourself."

Sarah caught up with the rest of the group in time to see Steve strike up a conversation with the griffins, who up until this point, had been very tight-lipped.

"So, what are you in for?" Steve companionably asked. "What happened to you?"

Both griffins turned their heads almost a hundred eighty degrees to stare back at him. Loryss rustled her wings a few times, stretched them out, and then folded them flat against her back. Sarah thought for sure the griffin was going to ignore him, but surprisingly Loryss decreased her pace to allow Steve to walk beside her. The griffin sighed.

"I've had time to reason things out. I was poisoned."

"How would one griffin go about poisoning another?" Steve asked.

"I hadn't been feeling well. My mate brought me various things to eat, all in an attempt to help me regain my strength.

It was working. I was starting to feel better. I fell asleep and when I awoke, I saw several freshly picked seedpods in the nest."

Sarah detected movement in her peripheral vision and glanced over at her husband. He was staring at her with a confused look on his face. She shrugged and held a finger to her lips. Loryss looked up just in time to catch the tail end of Steve's confused expression.

"They were spiny coneflower seeds," the griffiness said, in a matter-of-fact tone.

"I take it they're toxic?" Steve asked.

"Those seedpods were harvested from the most poisonous pontal that existed in the forest. Of course, they were toxic."

Steve nodded. "I get it. In your weakened condition you... *drop it!* Drop it, or so help me I'll have Loryss bite you clean off."

Startled, Sarah looked over at her husband. Steve had twisted around and was scowling at his tail, which unfortunately was long enough to touch the ground. That was the problem. It had curled itself around a long branch he had just stepped over and now it was being dragged along behind them.

After a few moments, the prehensile tail uncurled and the tree branch fell away. Steve shook his head and scowled at the tail before turning back to Loryss. He shrugged dismissively.

"Sorry 'bout that. Going back to what I had said earlier, you didn't recognize those seed thingies for what they were and ate them."

Loryss' head fell and she nodded. "I just assumed Ceraeon had picked them for me. There were only two of them and I consumed both. Those seeds were deliberately placed in my nest. I just know it."

"By whom?" Sarah asked. What Loryss was suggesting was that one griffin murdered another!

"I suspect it was another female," Loryss answered. "Hemera. It has to be her. She was my biggest rival and coveted my status. You see, Ceraeon, my mate, was being groomed to be the next Prime of our flock."

"So what exactly do you expect us to do?" Steve demanded. "Walk up to your mate and ask him if he's been fooling around with another female since your death? I can't imagine that's gonna go over well."

"All I ask is you find Ceraeon. See if a griffiness with wings of black and blood red feathers has taken my place. If she has, inform Ceraeon of my fate and my suspicions. He deserves to have a better mate by his side than her."

The four unlikely companions pushed through the line of trees bordering the jungle and emerged into the forest. Sarah took her husband's hand and pulled him toward the eastern shore of the same small lake they had been at before. The two griffins automatically followed.

"So, after we find your mate," Sarah continued, "you want us to make sure your rival hasn't taken your place, is that right?"

Loryss nodded. "Correct."

"What if Hemera didn't poison you?" Steve asked. "What if she's innocent?"

"Then she wouldn't be anywhere near my mate until an acceptable mourning period has passed," Loryss told him.

"How long is that?" Steve wanted to know.

"At least a year, maybe two."

"And if she is?" Sarah prompted. "What then? How do we convince your mate that what you say is true? We can't make an accusation like that without proof!"

"The proof would be Hemera's proximity to Ceraeon," Loryss explained. "If she is by his side then she has completely disregarded my period of mourning and is guilty."

Steve hesitantly raised a hand. "I hate to bring this up, but, um, what if your mate is the one who is responsible for your current predicament?"

Both Loryss and Nyx instantly shook their heads no.

"You are not familiar with griffins," Loryss said, giving Steve a piteous look. "I admit I know nothing of the mating habits of humans, but when two griffins mate, we do so for life. One griffin will never choose a mate they didn't trust. I trust Ceraeon. Implicitly. Therefore, I know it wasn't him."

"Fair enough," Steve decided. He looked over at Nyx.

"What about you? What do you need us to do for you?"

"Save my cub's life."

Sarah gasped at the same time Loryss squawked with surprise. "Your cub is in danger? What happened? Why didn't you say something before?"

A fiery determination appeared in Nyx's eyes. She squawked angrily. "Loryss is right. I am new here, having arrived two days prior. I will be honest. I despaired once I learned this was Ranal. It could only mean I was dead, and without help, my cub will be, too."

"What happened?" Sarah asked. "Will you tell us?"

"It was foolish. I knew I shouldn't have strayed outside our borders, but to find an entire herd of typas? I couldn't pass up an opportunity like that."

"What's a typa?" Sarah asked.

"A feminine version of a typo?" Steve suggested, raising an eyebrow. Sarah didn't bother with her customary smack on the arm. She raised her left hand and, just like all the cartoon cats Steve had ever seen, claws began appearing, one right after the other. He hastily fell silent and offered her a sheepish smile.

"I can get used to these," Sarah softly murmured, looking at her claws.

"I've never had to describe a typa before," Nyx confessed, ignoring Steve's quip. She paused a few moments as she thought about how to best define her favorite food. "Hmm. A typa is a macropod of incredible speed and dexterity. They are rarely spotted and incredibly difficult to catch."

"A macropod?" Sarah turned to her husband. "What's that?"

"Umm, it's like a plant-eating marsupial," Steve told her. "Provided 'macropod' means the same thing here as it does in our world."

"Like a kangaroo?" Sarah asked.

"That's the only one I can think of at the moment," Steve admitted.

"I'm sorry, Nyx," Sarah apologized. "I didn't mean to interrupt you. Please continue."

"Typas are not only my favorite food but are also

Skeiron's, my mate. They rarely emerge from the safety of the trees, so when I encountered several dozen of them all at the same time, I had to pursue. I hid my cub, finished hunting, and returned to him later. We had a long flight ahead of us so we feasted on a few of my kills and prepared to depart."

"So far it sounds harmless," Steve mused.

Nyx regarded him with an unreadable stare, "Wait for it. It gets worse."

"Sorry."

"May I continue?"

"Uh, sure."

Sarah reached out and took her husband's hand in her own. Steve swallowed noisily and tried to pull his hand free. Sarah threw him a disapproving frown.

"As I was saying," Nyx continued, navigating around the slight rock formation that had reminded Steve of a pizza earlier in the day, "I had stashed my cub in a small cave at the base of a cliff. After we had eaten, we were about to depart when I heard a loud rumbling. I looked up just in time to see a rockslide heading straight toward us. I was able to grab my cub and shield him, but clearly, I didn't make it."

Sarah dropped Steve's hand and slapped both of hers over her mouth with a look of horror on her face. "You died saving your baby!"

Nyx nodded. "Aye. But don't you understand? He's not here. It means he is still alive! If he doesn't get help soon there'll be no hope for him! No one is coming to help him and even if there was, no one would know where to look. I thought for certain my cub was doomed until …"

"Until you saw us," Steve finished for her. "I promise you we'll do what we can. How much longer do you think he can survive?"

"There were three typas left. If he's smart then he'll be able to eat those and survive for a few days more. The problem is, I've already been gone for a few days. He'll be out of food shortly."

"Your cub is alone, frightened, hungry, and missing the comfort of his mother," Sarah breathed, horrified. "I'll agree to your favor right now. We'll find your cub. We promise."

Nyx described in as much detail as she could about what she remembered where she and her cub had been while hunting the small typas. The griffiness could only remember that there was a small lake to the west, open forest to the north and south, and the beginnings of a mountain range to the east. Sarah paled. Hopefully there wouldn't be too many places that fit that description.

Fifteen minutes later, they were back at the base of Usol Peak. Sarah shaded her eyes and stared up at the distant waterfall, trying to tell if the slight outcropping at the top resembled hands. She couldn't tell.

"Loryss—or Nyx—can either of you see the top of that waterfall?" Sarah asked, pointing up at the peak.

Loryss angled her head up and studied the mountain's distant summit. Nyx mimicked her. The elder griffiness finally nodded.

"Aye, I see it. What is the nature of your desire to reach the top?"

"Where there's water there's typically plant life," Steve told the griffin. "We suspect there's a rare flower up there. We know there are two specimens somewhere on this island and since all other areas have been searched, we're left with the mountain. It has to be up there."

"What did you see?" Sarah asked Loryss. "Was there anything resembling hands?"

Loryss nodded, eliciting a squeal of excitement from Sarah.

"Before I tell you what I saw," the griffiness began, turning to Steve, "perhaps you could tell me what you meant by having searched the entire island. You have been here less than a day. There's no way to search this island in a single day."

They all heard an audible groan coming from Sarah's direction.

"Is there something you're not telling me?" Loryss asked.

Nyx stepped forward and inhaled. "So *that's* it. That's why you smell the way you do."

Sarah frowned. "Excuse me? Are you saying I stink?"

Nyx approached. "You're carrying something. It's

emitting an odor that reminds me of what a fresh kill would smell like."

Steve had to bite his tongue to keep from laughing. Thankfully neither griffin noticed. Loryss stretched her avian neck toward Sarah and took a couple of cautious sniffs.

"Nyx is right. There is a nauseating aroma emanating from your person. It reminds me of carrion rotting under a full sun."

"Nauseating?" a tiny voice barked out. Sarah slapping a hand over her mouth in surprise. "Carrion? You think I smell? Do you have any idea how badly this place reeks to a nose as sensitive as mine?"

A tiny humanoid figure had emerged, but it certainly didn't look like Thinian or the amphibious form he had been. Small, squat, and just as wide as he was tall, the grubby figure had wild unkempt hair, thick bushy eyebrows, a belly that would make a beer drinker envious, and several warts on his face and chin. To make matters worse, Thinian's increase in size was now threatening to tear his clothes. The figure carefully climbed up Sarah's shoulder and peered angrily at the griffin.

Both griffins had jerked their heads back. Loryss looked at Sarah and then pointedly back at Thinian's tiny form.

"You appear to be suffering from an infestation of bravi. I would recommend bathing immediately."

Nyx squawked with alarm. "Bravi? Kill it! Hurry! Don't let it burrow under your skin!"

Sarah stifled a giggle. By now her husband had doubled over with laughter.

"Bravi? You cretins dare insinuate I am nothing more than a lowly bravi?"

"What's a bravi?" Steve asked in a hushed whisper.

Sarah shrugged. "Maybe it means some type of fat gnome thing with warts?"

Overhearing him, Thinian turned angrily to Steve. "They're scavengers and pests. They live in small tribes deep beneath refuse heaps. Those two ingrates are suggesting I am a foul-mouthed, dim-witted imbecile not worthy of being stepped on. I'm not, you pathetic pin-feathered excuse of a flying monster."

Intrigued, Loryss moved closer and stared at Sarah's shoulder. "It speaks? Nyx, I do believe we have discovered the first intelligent subspecies of the chrara family!"

"I'M NO BRAVI!" Thinian angrily shouted. "I'm a Fae!"

Both griffins stared at each other in shock.

Steve gave a slight cough, "Not right now you're not. Have you looked in a mirror lately?"

"Do you see a mirror around here?" Thinian snapped.

"Come on, Thinian," Sarah said in a soothing voice, "even you must know you're not yourself."

Thinian leveled a gaze at the closest griffin. "Forget about what I look like at the moment. Thanks to *him*," the transformed Fae pointed at Steve, "I now get to suffer in this bloated form."

"I'm not the one who caused the tree to fall," Steve reminded him. "You can thank whoever did. My guess is it's the same guy who tried to prevent us from getting here."

"You really are a Fae?" Nyx breathed. "I thought they were extinct. I never knew Fae were allowed on Ranal."

"They're not," Loryss quipped, raising her beak. "You have no more business being here than the humans do. Why are you here?"

"I'm here for the same reason they are," Thinian clarified. "Trust me, as soon as I find the orbsceia, I'll leave this wretched place far behind."

Steve cleared his throat. "I think you mean that when *we* get the flower. Remember, we are allowing you to tag along."

"You're *allowing*?" Thinian sputtered, turning to face Steve. "In your dreams, human. I will be returning that flower to my people. I will be the one to earn all the accolades from the king and queen, not you."

Sarah snapped her fingers a few times. Once she had everyone's attention, she turned to point at the distant mountaintop.

"Boys, boys. That's an argument best left for another time. Talk to me about the mountain. How are we going to get up there?"

Both griffins moved to the base of the mountain. Loryss

tentatively placed one of her front avian feet against the sheer rock wall and dug her talons in. Satisfied that she had a solid grip, the griffiness placed her other foot on the stone wall. She carefully lifted herself from the ground and waited to see if her grip held. It did. With a triumphant squawk, Loryss turned to look back at her audience.

"While dangerous, and not ideal, Nyx is right. It is possible. We will climb."

Chapter 10 — Usol the Outraged

The climb was, Sarah would always remember, one of the most unpleasant experiences of her life. What they were doing was dangerous, no doubt about it. The only way she was able to stay on Nyx's back was with a tight bear hug. She risked a glance down to see Loryss and her husband about a dozen feet below them, slowly but surely rising up the face of the mountain.

Steve was watching her. "Are we having fun yet?" he shouted up at her.

"Absolutely not," Sarah yelled back. "And don't even begin to tell me that you're okay with this. I know you don't like heights."

"I don't," Steve confirmed. "Don't let my impressive display of machismo fool you. Internally I'm screaming like a little girl. You just can't hear me."

Sarah sighed. She'd have to side with her husband. She didn't relish the fact that if she lost her grip, she'd end up plummeting to her death. Ten minutes after they began their ascent, Sarah had already decided that if either of them fell off their respective griffins then she'd have no choice but to teleport the two of them, ending their quest. And, Sarah sadly realized, that'd also end the hopes of the Fae, dooming them to extinction when their Tree died.

Determinedly, she vowed it wouldn't happen. The Fae had come to *her* for help, and by God, she would see it through. They *had* to succeed. She didn't know how she'd be able to cope with the fact that if they failed, the Fae would end up perishing.

She felt Nyx slip, sending small bits of stone tumbling down onto Loryss' head. The larger griffin flattened herself against the rock face and waited for the falling rocks to subside.

"Do watch what you're doing," Loryss snapped. "It is a long way down."

Sarah risked another glance at her husband. His eyes were now screwed shut and he was gritting his teeth. She sighed. Steve hadn't been lying when he said he was truly not enjoying the experience. She couldn't blame him. Her own arms were tiring and her back hurt.

"What happens if you get tired?" Sarah quietly asked Nyx. "I'm sorry I didn't think to ask that question sooner."

"You believe I will deplete my strength?" Nyx asked, puzzled. "Why?"

The griffin's response confused her. What an odd thing to say!

"Well, think about it," Sarah continued. "You're climbing straight up with at least a hundred and… let's just say some extra weight, alright? You have a number of extra pounds clinging to your back. It can't be easy on you."

"It's not easy," Nyx confirmed. "I have to be certain of my footing. However, I am more concerned about your welfare than my own."

"Why?" Sarah wanted to know. "I realize that if something happens to you then I will also be affected, but why aren't you concerned about what will happen to you? Let's say, for example, you slip and fall off. I can always teleport myself back to safety. Granted, it won't be on Ranal, and it would end my quest, but I would still be safe. What about you?"

"What about me?" the griffin curiously inquired.

"What would happen to you if that happened?" Sarah asked.

"Nothing. I imagine I would shake myself off and go about my business."

"After falling hundreds of feet? I don't think you'd be able to walk that off, Nyx."

"You're assuming I'd be hurt?" Nyx dryly asked. "Or perhaps killed?"

Sarah's eyes widened as she realized why her griffin friend wasn't worried about suffering any physical harm. "You're already dead. No wonder you're not concerned."

"I can't die twice," the griffin smugly told her.

Just then Nyx stumbled again. Once more, broken rocks hailed down on Loryss and Steve's heads. Nyx squawked with alarm. "Look out!"

One particularly large stone smashed into Loryss' right front leg, knocking it loose. Off balance, Loryss squawked in fear, trying to throw her weight forward to gain another foothold. However, the damage was done. Her front left leg was torn loose as the much larger griffin began to tip backward. Sarah watched helplessly as Loryss flailed about with her avian front legs, desperately looking for something—anything—that would arrest her fall. Her scared eyes locked on to her husband's. She was ready. She brought up a mental picture of their cabin. She wouldn't risk her husband's life. Ria and Tivan would have to understand.

Steve started to slide down Loryss' back, past her wings, when his long tail wrapped itself around a wing and brought him to a sudden stop. He extended his arms and blasted jets of fire from both hands, pushing the two of them back to the wall. Loryss sank her talons into the rock and shuddered.

Sarah gasped with shock. "You blasted fire out of your hands! You're not supposed to use your jhorun! We could be expelled!"

"I'm fine, thank you," Steve grumped, adjusting his grip on Loryss' back. He tried to pull his tail free but it remained wrapped around Loryss' wing. He smacked it a few times, as though he was trying to get its attention, and it finally released its hold. "There was no time to think. I decided to risk it."

"I am grateful," Loryss told him, turning her head almost completely around to look directly into his eyes. "That was quick thinking."

Steve gave the griffin a smug smile before looking victoriously over at Sarah.

"Did you hear that? She complimented me on my quick thinking."

Sarah remembered their predicament. Her husband had used his jhorun! Shouldn't there be some type of retaliation? Would the island disappear? Would they suddenly find themselves in the middle of a free-fall?

After a few uncomfortable moments of silence, she hesitantly looked around. They were still on the side of a mountain. Steve and Loryss were directly below her. She could see the ground and the base of the mountain several hundred feet below.

"Umm, not that I'm complaining," Sarah began, "but shouldn't something have happened? I thought for certain that the instant Steve blasted out those flames then we would have been kicked off this mountain. What happened?"

"Nothing, obviously," Steve answered. He shifted his grip on Loryss' back and looked up at her. "We're still stuck on the side of this damn mountain. Let's figure out what happened later, okay?"

Sarah shook her head. "Steve, this is important. We need to figure this out. Why were you able to use your jhorun here and not get penalized? I thought for certain this Usol character would have noticed that."

"He probably has," Steve finally decided.

"And?" Sarah prompted.

"Sarah, think about it," Steve answered. "If this Usol character truly wants us off the mountain then all he has to do is switch this place back to a cloud. Do you follow me?"

Sarah nodded. "Yes."

"Now, if that were to happen, yes, we'd be falling to our deaths. But what about the griffins? They have every right to be here. They belong on Ranal. We don't. Usol would be evicting Loryss and Nyx off of this sanctuary, too. Remember, he has an affinity for the griffins, right?"

"You're assuming everything we've heard about Usol is true," Sarah reminded him.

"For the sake of argument, let's assume it's correct. All of it. I think the last thing Usol would want to do is to cause any harm to the griffins. Us, sure, but not the griffins."

"What are you saying?" Sarah asked.

"I think that as long as we remain on their backs we're safe. If we lose physical contact with them then I think we will be ... what's the word I'm looking for? Oh, yes. *Screwed.*"

Sarah was quiet as she considered. Could her husband be right? Were they only still there because of the griffins?

"I'm surprised Usol isn't a little more annoyed," she decided. "Too bad there isn't a way to tell."

Loryss squawked with alarm. "He is. We have awoken the mountain! It trembles!"

"What?" Sarah gasped. She leaned forward, intent on touching the side of the mountain but was too far away. "Are you sure? When did it start?"

"Just now," the griffiness answered. "Nyx, do you feel it?"

"Aye," Nyx agreed. "The mountain shakes."

"Is it growing stronger?" Steve asked, trying to gauge the distance to the ground. "I don't feel anything."

The two griffins were silent as they waited. Loryss finally shook her head no.

"Fear not. Now it appears to be receding."

"Confirmed," Nyx reported. "In fact, I cannot sense it any longer."

"Nor can I," Loryss said.

"So does that mean the threat is over?" Steve asked. "That wasn't too bad. So, do you think it means we can use our jhoruns now? Sarah, can you tell if the restrictions placed on you are gone?"

Sarah closed her eyes and tried to visualize the lake shore where they had first arrived on Ranal. As before, nothing appeared. She let out an exasperated sigh. "I tried, and I can't."

She heard her husband grunt with frustration. "I don't get it. I can use mine but you can't use yours? How come… wait. Listen."

Sarah paused. Steve was right. It had suddenly become eerily quiet. Realization dawned and she sucked in her breath. The water! The ever present sounds of falling water had suddenly vanished. Were the griffins right? Did Usol really exist? Had he somehow stopped the flow of water? "I can't hear the waterfall any more. Why?"

Both griffins cocked their heads to one side. Nyx gave a tremulous squawk. Sarah could tell that the young griffin was scared. They all were. Falling water didn't suddenly switch off. Something was wrong. Terribly wrong. She looked down and suddenly the absence of water became the least of her worries.

"Ummm, we have a bigger problem! What happened to the ground?"

Steve's head jerked up. "*What?*"

"We started up on the right of the waterfall, remember? About fifty feet. We've been going up in a fairly straight line. How come when I look down I can't see the river anywhere?"

Both griffins paused in the midst of their climb and craned their necks to look down. Sarah heard Steve grunt with surprise. They could see a solid expanse of tree tops to their left, but directly beneath them? Sarah shuddered. It was proof that they were definitely on a floating island because now there was nothing directly beneath them but open air. This mountain was sitting on the northernmost point of Ranal, a vertical drop-off of thousands of feet of open air. From her vantage point she could even see small clouds far below.

"What do we do?" Nyx wanted to know. "Do we climb?"

"We still need to go up," Sarah decided. "Keep climbing. We'll figure it out later. We are on a serious time crunch here."

"We don't have a choice," Steve agreed. "What are the chances the mountain will move us around again?"

"Unknown," Sarah said. "It's anyone's guess at this stage."

Steve groaned. "My back is killing me. Loryss, let's keep moving."

The griffins resumed climbing. Astonished that the island floor had somehow vanished and they were now for all intents and purposes climbing up a different side of the mountain, Sarah started to consider the problem at hand. What had happened? Obviously, it had something to do with Steve helping to keep Loryss on the side of the mountain. Less than ten seconds later they had felt the mountain tremble. That's when they noticed the waterfall had gone silent. Only then had she looked down and noticed they weren't where she had expected them to be. If she didn't know any better, she would have accused the mountain of spinning them around so that they were now on the opposite side.

Sarah pondered the situation and twisted back and forth to locate the sun. It should have been on their left. Her eyes widened. The sun was now directly behind the mountain! The mountain had somehow spun them around and they were now on the eastern face of Usol Peak! How was that even physically possible?

"We're on the eastern side of the mountain now," Sarah informed them, raising her voice so everyone could hear. "Thinian, you've been quiet far too long. You've been on this island longer than we have. What's going on?"

"There's a reason why this mountain is called Usol's Peak," the former Fae said, poking his grubby head out. "I've heard many a griffin mention this mountain and not once have I ever heard of anyone ever stepping foot on it. If we've angered Usol, then I shudder to think what he'll do to us. Whatever it is, I know it won't be good." He looked down at the distant ground, belched, swallowed nervously, and then disappeared back into Sarah's pocket.

"That's very helpful," Sarah sarcastically said, as she briefly considered giving her pocket a thumping. "Care to offer anything useful?"

"Be prepared to return to the ground," Thinian advised, scratching his thick unruly beard. "I think you're right. Usol wants you off this mountain. He will eject us the instant he feels it won't harm the griffins."

"What about the fact that we're climbing up a mountain with no ground below us?" Steve asked.

"I would say Usol is trying to hinder your progress," Thinian answered.

"Perhaps we should descend," Loryss suggested. "We could try to return to the elevation in which the ground was as we remember it."

"We'd be wasting time we don't have," Sarah pointed out.

"We could just go down maybe twenty feet or so," Steve suggested. "If Usol wants us off this mountain then you'd think he'd help us down."

"Fine," Sarah reluctantly agreed, clearly not happy about giving up ground.

For the next ten minutes the griffins carefully backtracked, only coming to a stop once it became clear that the mountain was not going to cooperate.

Sarah sighed and looked up. She sucked in a breath. "He did it to us again! Look! The peak has changed! See how the mountainside bulges outward about a hundred feet above our heads? That wasn't there before."

Steve turned to scan the skies. He shook his head.

"Are you sure? The sun is still behind the mountain."

"I'm sure," Sarah confirmed. "Only the top half has changed. What that means, I don't know."

"It means that only part of the mountain turned," Loryss announced, "I have no idea how something like that is even possible."

"Think about it," Steve told the griffin. "If we go under the assumption that this Usol guy is real and could pick up several islands to squish them all together to make Ranal, then finding a mountain on that island capable of rotating in place really shouldn't be too much of a stretch."

"That really doesn't help us, dear," Sarah pointed out. Her grip was tiring and she was starting to feel dizzy.

"Let's just make it to the top of the waterfall and then we'll figure out what to do from there, okay?" Steve suggested. "My arms are getting tired and I've got a nasty kink in my back."

"You and me both," Sarah agreed. "However, there's a problem with that."

"What?" Steve wanted to know.

"We were climbing up with the belief that what we wanted was directly over our heads."

"Yeah? And?"

"Steve, look up there. I don't see the waterfall anywhere. It means that we'll have to climb around this stupid mountain until we're back on the right track."

"Fine. Let's do that first, okay? Let's get back to where we're supposed to be and then we'll continue up."

Loryss nodded her head. "Agreed. Nyx? After you. Start side-stepping to the left. Careful now."

"How far should I go?" the younger griffin inquired.

"Until we can hear the falling water," Loryss answered.

Nyx hesitantly took a step to the left and sank her claws into the stone, moving only when she was certain her talons were firmly anchored. Sarah looked down and watched her husband's progress on Loryss' back. Like Nyx, Loryss was cautiously moving to the left. She could only assume that climbing sideways was more difficult than climbing straight up. If they...

Sarah's thoughts drifted off. She suddenly smiled. The sound of falling water was back. It was working! Only ... Sarah's smile melted. That was too quick. And it was coming from the wrong direction. The waterfall now sounded as though it was on their right, when it shouldn't be. What was going on?

"Everyone hold up a second," Sarah called out. Both griffins came to an immediate halt. "Usol is messing with us."

"In what way?" Steve wanted to know.

"Can't you hear the water?" Sarah asked.

"Sure, I can," Steve answered. "We started moving toward it and we started hearing it again, only ... wait a minute."

"That's right," Sarah confirmed. "It's on the other side of us now."

Loryss gave an exasperated squawk. "How could we have made a complete circuit of the mountain in less than a quarter of an hour—?"

"We didn't," Sarah told the griffin. "The mountain moved again."

"Why?" Nyx asked. "What purpose does it serve?"

"If the purpose is to piss us off," Steve grumbled from Loryss' back, "then Usol is doing an admirable job."

"I have a theory," Sarah announced. "I'm fairly certain that all of us were looking left, in the same direction we were headed."

"You're suggesting that the mountain will change in whatever direction we're not facing?"

Sarah nodded. "Right."

"Then why didn't the mountain change when we were going up?" Steve asked. "We must have all been looking up."

"Well, perhaps it could be any direction where someone isn't looking," Sarah suggested. "Maybe one of us was looking either left or right. Either way, this should be easy enough to verify."

"We each look in different directions," Loryss guessed. "We'll pick a specific direction and agree to not look that way. If the mountain only changes in that direction, then we'll know."

Sarah looked gratefully down at Loryss and smiled. "Yes, that's it exactly. I'll look down. Steve, you look left. Loryss and Nyx, you look right. Hang on. Before we do this, we should check the surroundings. Do you see that indentation in the mountainside about three hundred feet up?"

"It looks like a dragon could have collided with it," Nyx decided.

"Right. Let's see if that depression is still there after this experiment. Alright, everyone. Are you ready? Look in the direction you're supposed to look."

"Now what? The mountain doesn't appear to be reacting."

"Start climbing up," Steve decided. "That'll get Usol's attention. Let's see what he does."

Both griffins began to climb. Less than ten seconds later they all felt the trembling. They gave it another thirty seconds before Sarah called for the griffins to stop. She looked up and gave a victorious shout.

"Haha! I knew it! The mountaintop has changed. That depression is gone!"

"So where are we now?" Steve cautiously asked. "I mean,

this is the same mountain, but now where are we?"

"Don't you get it?" Sarah asked, exasperated. "The rest of the mountain is still the same, only the top part has changed. Do you know what this means?"

"No," Steve admitted. "Do you?"

"Obviously. Assume this mountain is a complex Rubik's cube. It can spin on multiple axes. We can—"

"A Rubik's cube?" Loryss repeated, puzzled. "I'm not familiar with that term."

"Umm, it's a multi-layered puzzle from our world," Sarah explained. "The challenge is to twist and turn it until all sides are whole again. I don't think I'm doing a good job explaining it."

"Close enough," Steve assured her. He gave Loryss a smug look. "I actually *solved* it."

"You took it apart and put it back together in the correct order," Sarah said. "That doesn't count. Now, back to the problem at hand. If we really want the ground to come back then we should be able to make that happen."

"How?" Nyx asked.

"By looking in all directions but down," Steve guessed, finally catching on. "Nice one, babe. Alrighty then, we'll each face a direction other than down and we'll stay that way until the bottom looks like what we remember when we first started this."

Sarah beamed her approval. "Exactly."

"Your plan is to work on each direction until what we seek lies above us once more," Loryss deduced. "An excellent plan."

It took longer than Sarah would have liked, but eventually the waterfall was once more on their left. The outcropping they were angling for was directly above their heads and the river was where it should be.

The mountain trembled with rage. Pea-sized rocks shook themselves loose and rained down upon them, forming small welts whenever they made contact.

Sarah reached to rub a welt on the back of her head when Nyx slipped again. The young griffin scrambled to reestablish her footing, but Sarah was torn loose. She heard her husband let out a shout of alarm but there was nothing he could do. Nyx helplessly watched Sarah slide off her back and fall toward the thousands of feet of open air below.

Sarah's surprised brain had yet to focus on a safe zone, and before she could, she felt a sharp stinging sensation on her right shoulder. Something had collided with her, pushing her toward the mountain. It was Nyx, or more specifically, her tail. It shoved her into contact with the mountainside.

Sarah briefly wondered what the point was. She was falling and picking up speed. What was she supposed to do? Stop her fall? It's not like she had claws that could … But she did!

Sarah immediately grasped at the mountain with two hands and ten claws. She felt her talons bite into the rock and knew it was going to work. After she had finally stopped her unplanned descent, she looked up. What had felt like several hundred feet was only about two dozen. Steve was worriedly looking down at her.

"Sarah! Are you okay?"

Dangling by her fingertips, Sarah violently shook her head. She felt the strength in her arms waning and muffled a curse. She gave her companions an imploring look.

"Don't just stand there! Help me! I won't be able to hold on for much longer!"

"Nyx, get down there," Loryss snapped. "On the double!"

Only when she was safely sitting on Nyx's back once more could she relax. As Nyx started to climb once more, she noticed Steve and Loryss hadn't moved. Once the two griffins were side by side, clinging to the vertical rock face, did she finally look at her husband. His look spoke volumes.

"Are you okay?" Steve asked. "You scared the hell outta me."

"*I* scared the hell out of me," Sarah said, nodding. "If it wasn't for these new claws, I would have kept falling and would have had to teleport back to the ground. So, for that, I thank you, Usol."

"This tail has kept me from sliding off Loryss, too," Steve added. "I will have to admit that it is coming in handy for this oh-so-wonderful trek up the mountain. So add me to his list of admirers."

"Well I'm *not*," they all heard Thinian say from within her pocket. "I think I'm going to be ill."

Sarah extended a claw and poked at her jacket. "Don't even think about it, Paco. If you make a mess in there then you'd better be prepared to clean it up. There's no way I... oh!"

"Hey!" Steve cried, in unison.

"What is the matter?" Loryss asked, concerned. She twisted her head to stare at her rider. "Are you well?"

"It felt like someone just pinched my butt!" Steve complained, rubbing his rear. "And not in a good way. Hey, wait. My tail! It's gone! Sarah! Did you hear that? My tail is gone!"

Sarah looked down at her hands. Healthy pink skin met her gaze. Her fur was gone! So were her whiskers, her claws, and her mouth full of sharp teeth. Was this Usol's way of pouting? Was he upset that one of his pools had been responsible for saving their necks?

Sarah poked a finger into her pocket. "Thinian? Are you back to normal?"

Thinian's head briefly appeared, back to his customary Fae form. He took one look at the ground far below and ducked back inside the pocket.

"I don't know how you humans do it," the Fae muttered crossly. "How your species can manage without flying astounds me."

"Stop your complaining," Sarah scolded. "You're obviously back to your normal self. That's all I wanted to know."

"Looks like we're all back to normal," Steve said. "I don't know how and I don't know why, but I'm sure not gonna complain."

Sarah rubbed a painful spasm in her lower back. She wasn't complaining about her human form, but she would miss her claws. They had some serious potential.

Clearly Usol was a being of great power. Why, then, was he concerning himself with these trivial demonstrations of his power? Because of their proximity to the griffins? She could only guess Usol didn't want to risk hurting the griffins during their climb. The humans on the other hand, were another matter.

She'd hardly formed the thought when she realized her worst nightmare—the mountain had disappeared! She gripped Nyx in a death hold and summoned her jhorun, about to teleport herself and Steve to the ground when… why weren't they falling?

"What's the problem?" Loryss asked. "Why are you humans panicking?"

"The mountain is gone!" Steve exclaimed in a shaky voice. "It's a damn good reason to panic! Come join us, will you??"

"You cannot see the mountain?" Loryss asked, looking at her rider. "Is this true?"

"You mean you can?" Steve cautiously asked.

Loryss nodded. "Of course."

"Why the hell would he make the mountain disappear for only us?" Steve asked, looking up at Nyx and Sarah above his head.

Sarah cracked an eye, looked down at the ground many thousands of feet below her, and swallowed nervously. The mountain was nowhere in sight. Unhindered, Nyx and Loryss continued to climb. She gave a shaky sigh. In another second or two she would have teleported the two of them back to the safety of the ground and ended their quest altogether. Actually, she was surprised she hadn't teleported automatically as a reflex to hanging there in open air. Hmmm. It was almost as if…

"This was a direct slap to my face," Sarah announced, looking down at her husband. She quickly looked back up. A swirling sense of vertigo threatened. "This Usol character is really starting to get on my nerves. Steve, we can't see the mountain because of me!"

"Better 'splain yerself, little lady," Steve drawled, using his best John Wayne impersonation.

"I've said a few times now that I've been ready to teleport the two of us off this mountain and back to solid ground, remember?"

"Yeah. What about it?"

"I think Usol heard me," Sarah said, grimacing. "I think he's trying to freak me out and get me to teleport the two of us out of here."

"Well, it didn't work, did it?" Steve asked, giving her a smug grin.

"It almost did," Sarah argued. "If you only knew how close I was to getting us the heck out of here then you wouldn't be smiling."

"But you know not to panic now, right?"

"Steve, I can't see the ground. I'm really hating this. But, do you know what? You're right. I'm not panicking." She raised her voice and shouted up at the clouds. "You're not scaring us away! We're still here!"

The mountain suddenly reappeared. Spooked, Sarah turned to look down at her husband. Steve nervously cleared his throat.

"I, uh, guess that confirms that Usol is real."

"I wonder what he's planning for us next," Sarah said, worried.

A rumbling noise sounded from the south. A dark, ominous cloud was forming to their left. Flashes of lightning lit the cloud from within as it continued to swell in size.

"Oh, that can't be good," Sarah whispered. "Nyx, go! Keep your eyes directly up! I'll look left while Loryss looks right. Steve, keep your eyes looking down. Let's move! We need to get up there before that cloud hits!"

The griffins doubled their efforts. Progress was slow, but steady. Sarah looked back at the rapidly approaching thunder clouds and knew they weren't going to make it. It didn't take a rocket scientist to figure out who was behind it.

The rain started first. Within moments everyone was completely drenched. The griffins continued to climb.

"Well, I'm having the time of my life," Sarah heard her husband grumble. "How about you, babe?"

"I'm living the good life," Sarah called down to him. "Nyx, Loryss, how are you holding up?"

"I am fine," Nyx reported.

"As am I," Loryss added. "Wet or dry, the climb makes no difference to me."

It was, Sarah recalled later, the wrong thing to say. The rain doubled in volume and hurricane force winds whipped into existence. The griffins were hammered from above as they continued to climb upward. The progress slowed to nearly a crawl. Sarah, with her wet hair plastered to her face, turned to look up at the waterfall. The top was still at least two hundred feet away. The sun, unfortunately, was beginning to dip toward the horizon. They didn't have much time left.

"Steve! We need to hurry! We're almost out of time!"

"What exactly do you want me to do?" Steve shouted back at her. His voice was almost drowned out by the howling winds.

"I don't know! Do something! Anything!"

Nyx paused as she slipped on the wet stone. Sarah wished again that her jhorun would work here. All she'd have to do is teleport the two of them to the top and this whole ordeal would be over.

A brief burst of heat and light caught her attention. She quickly looked down at her husband. Steve had locked his ankles around Loryss' abdomen once more and had his arms extended. Sarah nodded. Loryss must have lost her footing and Steve had compensated by blasting out jets of fire to push them back into position. He saw her watching him and grinned.

"The cat's out of the bag, right? Usol knows we're here and wants us gone so I might as well. I figured at this point it couldn't hurt."

Almost immediately the winds shifted directions, threatening to blast the fire jets back at them. She watched her husband snap both hands closed and extinguish his flames. She shook her head in amazement. Even in circumstances as dire as this, her husband had the tenacity to turn and scowl up at the sky, as if that would help.

"Would you *please* stop trying to anger Usol even further than he already is? Wait. Blast your flames to the right."

"What?" Steve shouted back.

"To the right!" Sarah yelled at him. "Over there! North! Blast your fires that way!"

Steve angled both arms north and blasted away. The winds

shifted once more, immediately blowing from the south and threatening to envelop everyone in fire. Steve groaned.

"This must be Usol's way to counteract me helping Loryss staying on the mountain. Man, this dude isn't fighting fair!"

"No," Sarah agreed, thinking quickly. She pointed down at the ground. "We might be able to use this to our advantage. Shoot downward. Now!"

Steve held both hands out, palms facing down. He blasted out twin jets. Two seconds later he had to extinguish the flames. The winds had changed direction for a third time. The powerful blasts of air were now pushing up at them from below, threatening to once more blast Steve's flames back at their party. Sarah watched a grin quickly spread across her husband's face.

"Not bad, my dear. Not bad at all."

Sarah reminded everyone to keep looking in their assigned directions, to keep the mountain from moving. Steve continued the brief bursts of downward fire.

Battered, soaked, and bedraggled, both griffins pulled themselves up the final few feet to stand triumphantly before the source of the waterfall. The winds died off and again the mountain trembled with rage. Ignoring Usol's mounting anger, Steve whistled with amazement.

"Where exactly is the water coming from?" Still astride Loryss, Steve pointed up at the actual peak of the mountain, still about fifty feet above their heads. "You can't tell me that this is coming from somewhere higher up. There's no snow up there."

"This mountain spins in place, becomes transparent on cue, has thunderstorms that appear out of nowhere and you're worried about the source of the water?" Sarah asked, dumbfounded. "Forget about it. We're here! Finally!"

The four companions quietly stared at the smooth-as-glass water. Nyx appeared at Loryss' side, allowing husband and wife to sit side-by-side. Sarah nudged Steve's shoulder and pointed. The Pool appeared to be resting in a large rocky basin. To Sarah it looked as though two giant stone hands were cupped together. Water spilled from the 'V' formed by the fingers, forming a waterfall.

The pool was nearly seventy feet across and was being fed by four springs of water emerging from within a spider web of cracks running across the rock face directly behind it. Bright colorful flowers, thick green shrubbery, and a small evergreen tree covered the east and west sides of the pool. A miniature oasis.

Just as the thundercloud that had made their life a living hell broke up, revealing clear skies once more, the sun finally made contact with the horizon. The blue azure slowly began to bleed from the sky, replaced by burnt orange and cinnamon tones.

Sarah sniffed loudly. They were out of time. However, that didn't concern her any more. There, sitting on the western side of the pool, was a flower so beautiful that she had instantly begun to weep. A slender, graceful stalk nearly two feet long was capped with a large golden multi-petal flower. Sarah thought it looked like a huge golden rose. A 'cabbage rose', she heard her grandmother's voice say.

She blinked away her tears. It could only be the orbsceia flower. Ria had been right. Anyone who laid eyes on that flower was instantly reduced to tears. She glanced over at her husband and was pleased to see him quickly wipe the corners of his eyes.

"You didn't see anything," he accused. "I have allergies."

Sarah shook her head and waved her hands dismissively. She pointed at the exotic golden flower.

"Honey, we made it!"

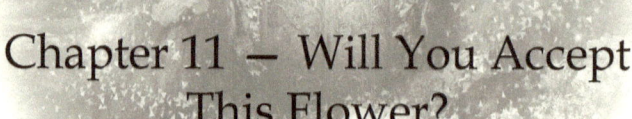

Chapter 11 — Will You Accept This Flower?

Usually, I wouldn't say something like this," Steve announced from his perch on Loryss' back, "but I have to admit that flower has got to be the prettiest one I think I have ever seen."

"And yet we have to pick it," Sarah reminded him, frowning. "It seems a shame to pick something that lovely."

Steve twisted around to inspect the plants growing nearby.

"I only see one of those flowers. Aren't there supposed to be two?"

"It must have been destroyed, too," Thinian observed, slowly emerging from Sarah's pocket. He caught sight of the blooming flower and fell silent.

"I thought you said you only found the remains of one," Steve asked, glancing over at the tiny Fae.

Thinian could only nod.

"The third must have been elsewhere," Sarah decided,

"and as Thinian suggested, it must have been destroyed, or harvested, or eaten, or whatever."

"It doesn't matter now," Steve happily exclaimed. "That's what we need, right there. Let's go get it."

Sarah held up a hand. "Hang on. How do we harvest it? If this is the last plant then we need to make certain we don't damage it. I don't think I could stand it if I knew I was responsible for destroying the last orbsceia flower. Not when it's that pretty. There must be a proper way to harvest it."

"It's a flower," Steve pointed out. "You harvest it like any other, right?"

"Not so fast," Sarah warned. "How do we know which part the queen needs? What if we don't harvest it correctly?"

"I thought she said she needed the nectar," Steve said, looking down at Thinian for confirmation. "Wouldn't that suggest we just need the head of the flower?"

"She said she needed the pollen," Sarah corrected.

The sun finally dipped below the horizon and the daylight began to fade. Both griffins seemed unconcerned by the growing darkness—being naturally able to see in the dark—but Sarah couldn't say the same. The last thing she wanted to do was to blindly fumble around on a mountaintop. Not to mention she didn't want to be anywhere near *this* particular mountain since she and her husband had managed to piss off its creator.

"How do you want to do this?" Steve asked her.

"I think we should… do you feel that? I can feel it this time. The mountain is shaking!"

"Usol is angry," Loryss reminded her. "And you have just announced your intentions. I would not have done that."

Both griffins carefully picked their way over to the western bank of the small pool. Sarah gazed down at the flower and contemplated the best way to harvest it. Should she just reach down and pluck it, as with any other flower? Or should she find a way to snip the flower off its stalk, thus minimizing potential damage to the plant?

She blinked. The sky was growing dark much faster than it should. What was going on?

A quick check revealed the answer: a new thundercloud

was forming directly over their heads. The mountaintop would be completely enveloped in less than a minute. Nyx, sensing her distress, moved as close as she dared to the edge of the pool. The orbsceia was growing less than two feet from a deadly vertical drop-off. No matter how Nyx tried to position herself, the flower was out of reach.

Sarah leaned out as far as she was able without losing her balance, but it wasn't enough. Her arms were simply not long enough. She pulled herself upright and gave her husband an imploring look.

"Come on, Loryss," Steve said, giving the griffin a friendly pat on the back. "Looks like it's up to us."

The larger griffin nodded. "Agreed. Nyx, fall back. Let us try."

"I might be able to get the flower in my beak," Nyx suggested.

Sarah shook her head. "I'm sorry, Nyx. We can't risk damaging the flower. We need it intact."

Nyx and Sarah moved back and Loryss carefully edged as close as she dared. Her avian front legs gripped the lip of the bowl and dug in. The griffin stretched her neck out, narrowing the distance to the flower.

"If I hook an arm around your neck, I should be able to reach it." Steve slid forward. "Sarah, as soon as I grab the flower, get us the hell out of here, agreed?"

Sarah nodded. "Got it. I've got my safe zone already lined up." She gave both griffins a feeble smile. "I just wish I could teleport the two of you back to the base of the mountain, too. I don't want either of you to come to any harm."

"We're already deceased," Loryss reminded her. "Nyx and I will be fine. Please remember our arrangement."

"Absolutely," Steve agreed. "We'll make sure your mate knows what happened to you."

"And you, Nyx," Sarah added, looking over at the smaller griffin. "I promise we'll find your cub."

Nyx bowed. "Thank you. That is all I ask."

Sarah looked back at her husband. "Ready?"

Steve nodded. "Yep. Let's do this. Loryss, Nyx, it's been a blast. Here we go."

Sarah watched as her husband looped an arm around Loryss' neck, leaned forward, and closed his hand around the orbsceia flower. A quick pinch from his fingers released the flower from its stalk. He quickly held his arm up to show Sarah he had the golden flower.

Almost immediately the mountain trembled with rage. Jagged bolts of lightning shot out of the fearsome cloud above their heads. Nyx and Loryss suddenly vanished; Steve and Sarah dropped straight down on their butts.

Sarah didn't wait to see what the mountain had in store for them. She instantly ordered her jhorun to move the two of them to the safe zone she had selected. In an instant, they were sitting on the floor in their cabin's living room.

"Man alive, did that hurt," Steve exclaimed, as he painfully regained his feet. "Usol dropped us right on our asses. How uncool was that? I didn't know he could do that. In fact, why didn't he do that before … wait. Was that you?"

Sarah nodded and gave him a sly smile. "Yes."

"You could have warned me that you were teleporting them out of there. Seriously. I think I bruised my tail bone."

"Usol was clearly listening to us," Sarah explained. She grasped one of Steve's outstretched arms and allowed him to pull her to her feet. Her own rear was stinging. "I had to create a distraction. I didn't know what Usol was going to do once you picked that flower. I think I surprised him."

"Well, I can't speak for Usol," Steve said, glancing down at the glittering gold flower in his hand, "but you certainly surprised me. I thought you couldn't teleport there?"

"That's what I thought, too," Sarah admitted. "Then it dawned on me. What if I was only restricted to moving *myself* on the island? Clearly I couldn't teleport us anywhere on Ranal. I wondered if I could teleport something already on Ranal to another part of the island. When I voiced my wish for them, for the first time since arriving on Ranal I received a vision. That was when I knew my jhorun would work. I just had to be careful to never once think about teleporting either one of us."

"Nicely done," Steve told her. He looked down at the golden flower. "Come on. We're not done yet. We need to get this to the Fae."

"Where's Thinian?" Sarah suddenly asked, gently patting her pockets. "Omigod! Don't tell me I left him up there!"

Steve went into the cabin's only bedroom, pulled one of his tee shirts from the dresser, and carefully set the flower down on it. He then approached Sarah and gently began prying her pockets open to peer inside. Sarah shook her head.

"He was in my left inside jacket pocket," Sarah whispered, still horrified at the notion she might have left the Fae back on the mountaintop.

Steve opened the jacket and peered into the pocket. He reached inside, carefully scooped up what he found, and then opened his hand. A tube of lip balm, and Thinian. Unconscious.

Sarah hurried over to the sink, poured some water from the pitcher, grabbed a nearby hand towel, and dipped the corner into the water. She gently ran the damp cloth over the Fae's head.

Thinian began sputtering, "What, in the name of all that's good, happened?" the Fae demanded, gaining his feet. He rubbed at a welt that was forming on his forehead. Thinian noticed the lip balm and angrily pointed at it. "And what is that?"

"The lip balm must have hit him when Sarah teleported the griffins," Steve guessed, looking back at her. "We landed hard on the ground. We've got the bruises to prove it."

Thinian looked puzzled and held up a hand. "Wait. You were able to teleport the griffins?" That's why you two fell? I thought you couldn't teleport on Ranal?"

While Sarah explained her discovery about her jhorun, Steve gathered up the shirt with the orbsceia flower. He took Sarah's hand with his left and then lowered his right hand for Thinian to hop on.

"Come on, buddy. We have work to do."

Thinian nodded appreciatively. "Agreed. We must save the Tree."

Thinian jumped onto Steve's hand and then nimbly ran up his arm to perch on his right shoulder. Sarah smiled at each of them, closed her eyes, and just like that they were standing before the Tree. Even in the fading light she could see that the Tree had turned completely brown, like a pine tree unlucky enough to have been planted in a desert.

Sarah glanced over at Thinian. The tiny Fae looked absolutely crestfallen. All the color had drained from his face and he looked as though he was going to be sick. Thinian turned to her and opened his mouth to say something only nothing came out.

"Thinian, hush," Sarah told him. "We're going to save the tree. Think positive. Hurry, this way."

"But it looks dead," Steve whispered in her ear.

"Don't you start, too," Sarah scolded.

They hurried through the open amethyst doors. Even the sparkling gemstone doors appeared lackluster to her eyes. Sarah valiantly fought a growing sense of despair. Were they too late? Had the Tree already died? Had all of their efforts been in vain? It couldn't be. There must still be time. They *had* to save the Tree!

Not bothering to see if she was being followed, Sarah hurried to the Throne Room. She found the King and Queen there, sitting on their thrones. Both unconscious, unfortunately.

Sarah started to rush to their aid when a hand fell on her right shoulder, drawing her to a stop. Her eyes widened. She knew Steve was standing on her left, too far away to be able to touch her. Then who...? Realization dawned. It had to be Thinian. He must have increased in size the same as the king and queen!

"Allow me," their Fae companion said. It was true. Thinian had increased his mass. Or they had decreased theirs. She still wasn't certain.

The Fae hurried to Tivan's side and gently touched his arm. When the king didn't respond the soft touch turned into a firm poke. Not even a solid shaking on both shoulders could rouse the sleeping king. Worried, Thinian moved to the queen. He took her hand and brought it to his lips.

"That only works in the movies," Steve quipped.

Sarah stared at him. "Not helping," she snapped.

The queen's eyes fluttered open. Her eyes widened in

surprise as she recognized the person standing in front of her.

"Thinian! You've returned! Does that mean…"

Ria trailed off as she noticed they weren't alone. She held a shaking hand out to Sarah. Ria's strength, like her husband's, was waning. Sarah took the queen's hand; it was freezing cold.

"Sarah! Steve! You've returned! That could only mean … could it be? Do you have it? Do you have the flower?"

Sarah motioned to her husband, who gently unwrapped the flower and held it up for Ria's perusal.

"We have it right here," Sarah told the queen. "Is there still time?"

Ria's eyes filled as she gazed upon the flower. A few moments later she shook her head, as if awakening from a trance. The corners of her mouth turned upward.

"I'm still here, aren't I? There is hope, but we must hurry." The queen held her other hand out to Thinian and allowed herself to be lifted to her feet. "There's a workshop we can use. Thinian, do you remember where Slilyn keeps her equipment?"

Thinian nodded. "Aye."

"Slilyn?" Steve asked, curious.

"She and her apprentices led the efforts to revive the tree," Ria explained, leaning heavily on Thinian as they left the Throne Room.

"Where is she now?" Sarah asked.

"I do not know," Ria sadly admitted. "She may be in hiding. She may have collapsed. She may even be dead. I can only hope that is not the case."

Thinian led them through a maze of dimly lit corridors until they approached a large arched doorway. The door, Sarah noted, was another gemstone door, and it was pale green. Not emerald but perhaps something different?

"Apatite," Sarah guessed, lowering her voice as she ran her hands over the glass-like surface of the door.

Steve glanced over at her, curious. "You're hungry?"

Sarah held the door open and allowed Thinian and the queen to enter.

"Huh?"

"I asked if you're hungry," Steve repeated.

Sarah cocked her head at him. "Why would you ask me that?"

"Hey, you're the one who mentioned you had an appetite, not me."

"A-pa-tite," Sarah slowly repeated as she tapped the smaller gemstone door. "It's another type of jewel. I think it's a lighter green than emeralds. They… never mind. I'm talking about this door."

"Right. I knew that. I was just testing you."

"Uh huh. Let's go."

Husband and wife moved inside the darkened chamber and saw that Thinian was busy setting things out on a large counter, including what looked like a large marble cookie sheet. The Fae had something tucked under his arm, something white and very fragile, like a rolled-up tube of sheer gauze.

"Done," Thinian reported, carefully unrolling the delicate white fabric across the marble tray. "What do I do now?"

"Retrieve the large pestle," Ria instructed, pointing at something neither of them could see.

Thinian ducked low and came back up holding a stone pestle. He held up a matching mortar. "What about this, Your Majesty??"

Ria shrugged. "I'm not sure. Set that aside for now. Sarah, please place the flower on the vyla mesh."

Sarah gingerly took the bundled shirt, moved to the counter, and unwrapped the flower, being careful not to disturb any of the petals.

"What now?" Sarah asked, gently placing the flower on the velvety white mesh. "I sure hope whatever we do doesn't harm the flower too much. I'd hate to mess up something this pretty."

"The petals must be plucked," Ria sadly told her. "Then each petal must be wiped along the vyla. We must have every last bit of pollen, including any that might have collected on the petals."

Sarah groaned with dismay as she looked at the exquisite golden flower. Not only was she disappointed the flower would be destroyed, but it had to have dozens and dozens of petals! Each one must be plucked and rubbed against the white mesh? How long would that take?

"Are you well, Sarah?" Ria asked, concerned.

Correctly guessing the nature of Sarah's concern, Steve jumped to her rescue.

"Uh, is there anyone that might be able to give you a hand with this?" he hesitantly asked. "There are a lot of little petals on that thing. That's gonna take some time and I can't imagine you're okay with this taking longer than a few minutes."

Thinian's head jerked up. Comprehension dawned behind his eyes as he nodded at Sarah. He approached the golden flower and bowed in front of the queen.

"Your Majesty, perhaps I could continue to be of some service? Would you like me to see if I can perhaps find some others who could come to our aid?

Ria, who up until now had been leaning heavily on the counter as she ordered Thinian to retrieve certain pieces of equipment, swayed dangerously as her strength continued to fade. Sarah rushed to her side and caught her before she could topple over. She glanced over at Steve and saw that he had been watching her with a worried expression on his face. Sarah pointed at a chair on the other side of the room. Steve nodded.

"Here," Sarah soothingly told the Fae queen as Steve slid the chair behind her. "Rest. Sit down."

Ria patted her hand and gave her an appreciative smile. "No one else is left to help."

Thinian swallowed nervously. "Then let's be certain we don't become the last. What do you require of me, Your Majesty?"

"Please assist Sarah in dusting all petals with the vyla mesh. And hurry. You're right, Thinian. There are precious few moments left. I ... Lady Sarah? What is the matter?"

Her emotions had finally caught up with her. With the fate of the Fae out of her hands, Sarah's thoughts had turned to the young griffin cub somewhere out in Lentari that needed help. She couldn't help it. She started crying. Steve was instantly by her side and put a protective arm around her shoulders. He looked at the Fae queen and gave her a helpless smile.

"We ran into some difficulties in getting the flower," Steve explained to the Fae queen, correctly guessing what was bothering Sarah. "We had to make a couple of deals, and one of them—and I'll bet I know which one—is eating away at her."

Ria's eyes had opened wide.

"I had no idea that … Thinian? Please begin working on the petals. Time is of the essence. Thank you. Sir Steve? Would you tell me what happened?"

He related the deal with Nyx. "Right now that little cub is still out there, buried under the body of its dead mother, both of them under a landslide, and we promised we'd find her cub and rescue him. Or her. Sorry, I can't remember what it is."

"What can I do?" Ria exclaimed, trying to rise to her feet. Steve put a hand on her shoulder and pushed her back into her chair.

"Nothing. You aren't going anywhere. You don't have the strength. Besides, you have something more important to deal with. You have a sick tree. Heal it. You told us that this nectar from this flower will do the trick."

Ria solemnly nodded. "You're right. And it's the pollen we're after. The fate of my people lies in my hands right now. I wish I could help you, friend Steve."

"I know you would," Steve gently assured the queen. "You're busy. I'm not. With that being said, I have a feeling that Sarah and I need to split up. I'll go see if I can find this cub, while she helps you harvest the pollen to save your tree."

"Actually I will be the one going," Sarah clarified. "I'm sorry, Ria. I have to leave my husband here with you, if that's alright."

"Of course," Ria immediately answered.

"Wanna run that by me again?" Steve asked at the exact same time.

"Steve, if you're the one doing the searching then it will take forever," Sarah explained, turning to face her husband. "We just don't have that kind of time."

"Excuse me? My sense of direction isn't the greatest, I will admit. However, I don't think it's as bad as you make it out to be, thank you very much."

Sarah gave him a fleeting smile. "Sorry, that's not what I meant." She caught Steve's expression. "I'm the teleporter. I'm the one who can jump from one side of the kingdom to the next. That gives me the best shot at finding the cub before it's too late. I can cover way more ground far faster than you."

Sarah watched the surprise on her husband's face be replaced by anger, and then almost as quickly, melt into resignation. Steve sighed and shoved his hands in his pockets. He glanced over at Thinian who was carefully plucking flower petals and delicately rubbing them along the white mesh. A faint smear of gold dust could be seen on the delicate white fabric.

He finished with the latest petal, dropped it on the growing discard pile, and gently plucked the next one from the flower. He carefully tipped it upside down and slowly wiped it along the surface of the mesh, like a mother wiping the face of her newborn baby. After making at least five passes to assure himself no more pollen remained on the flower's fragile petal, it was discarded and the process started over.

Sarah estimated Thinian had finished processing half a dozen of the petals, while possibly a hundred remained.

"Now, no using your jhorun," Sarah warned as she took Steve's hands in her own and gave them a squeeze. "You cannot run the risk of damaging anything. Watch Thinian and do as he does."

"But…"

"I have to search for Nyx's cub."

"But…"

"You're going to be fine, Steve."

"But … you want me to help them pluck flower petals? Seriously?"

Sarah smiled and gave him a quick peck on the lips.

"You're going to do just fine. Trust me."

"But I don't know a damn thing about flowers!" Steve protested. "What help am I going to be able to…"

He trailed off as Sarah blew him a kiss and vanished.

"…give them?"

A quick glance at Thinian confirmed the dread he was feeling was written all over his features. Thinian slid a second chair over and patted the cushion. Steve grudgingly sat on the stool and glared at his new friend.

"Not a word, dude."

* * *

Nearly an hour had passed. Sarah still hadn't returned, so he could only hope that she had found the cub and was now looking for Nyx's mate. Steve scowled. Sarah was out there in the dark, in the wilds of Lentari, while he was sitting here, wiping flower petals on what looked like a long piece of white toilet paper. His large, clumsy fingers had already knocked two of the petals to the ground—on accident, of course—rendering them useless, and unless he hunched over with both elbows on the counter to steady his hands, it would happen again.

"Are you sure we're doing this right?" Steve asked yet again, stretching his aching back, as he eyed the gold-stained vyla mesh on the counter. "This can't possibly be getting enough pollen to be considered useful. I mean, look at this. It looks like all we've done is wipe King Midas' nose."

"Who is King Midas?" Thinian wanted to know as he dropped a recently processed petal onto the discard pile. "I am not familiar with him."

"He's… someone you won't know. My point is, we've recovered only a tiny portion of pollen from all these petals and we're more than halfway done. How do you plan on collecting the nectar from this mesh thingy?"

"The queen has her ways," Thinian cryptically answered.

"You don't know, either," Steve guessed.

Thinian shrugged. "Correct."

They both glanced over at the queen, who was asleep in her chair. Steve glanced down at the flower, which looked like it'd had an unfortunate encounter with a weed whacker. He looked over at Thinian, who was hard at work processing another petal.

Steve let out a sigh. This wasn't his idea of fun, but then again, he couldn't allow anything to happen to the Fae. Even if it meant killing his back for an hour while they slowly plucked the petals from this large golden rose-looking-thing.

"Listen man," Steve began, using a soft tone so he wouldn't disturb the queen, "I gotta know. What happens if there's not enough nectar to revive the tree?"

"There certainly isn't enough time to find another griffin willing to make their Final Journey," Thinian told him, keeping a close eye on the queen. "I doubt very much we could find the third flower. More than likely it was destroyed, like the first specimen I found. Besides, do you really think Usol would allow us to step foot on his island again?"

"Probably not," Steve agreed.

"How do you know that name?" Ria quietly asked, startling both of them.

"A thousand apologies for disturbing you, Your Majesty," Thinian said, bowing low. "We should have kept our voices down."

"Your voices *were* down. I can barely hear you. Speak up, please."

Steve grinned. "You want to know how we know Usol?"

Ria nodded weakly. "Aye."

"We didn't meet him personally," Steve said, nodding at Thinian, "but we certainly figured out who he was. And he definitely knew we were there."

"He most assuredly wanted us off his island," Thinian confirmed, reaching for another petal.

"How did Usol interact with you?" Ria wanted to know.

"How do you know who he is?" Steve countered.

"He is one of the Ancients," the Fae queen answered. "It has been so long since I have heard any of their names that I had thought all of them to be extinct. Hearing you speak his name just now startled me."

"The Ancients?" Steve repeated. "Are you talking about deities?"

"No mere words would suffice when trying to describe an Ancient," Ria said, shaking her head. "They are beings that existed long before the beginning of time. One for each of the elements. Oros, Creator of Fire; Aeus, Protector of Water; Eion, Master of the Winds; and there's Usol, Guardian of—"

"Earth," Steve whispered. "I should've seen that coming. So how does it work? What will this pollen do?"

"The pollen will restore the essence of the Tree," Ria explained. She leaned back in her chair and sighed. "Once the Tree's life force has been replenished, it will once again begin sharing its jhorun with the Fae."

"Why did you ask the humans for help, Your Majesty?" Thinian asked. "Friend Steve, I mean no offense. I am simply curious why you didn't trust your own people to complete this mission. We are more than capable."

"It became clear after the Tree was drained of jhorun that we would need to seek outside help."

"Far be it for me to disagree with you," Thinian began, "but…"

"Then don't," Steve hastily interrupted.

Thinian shot him a dark look.

"As I was saying," the Fae continued, "we wouldn't have needed the help. I had located and was on my way to the mountain to get the flower when I encountered the humans."

"You didn't have a snowball's chance in hell of completing your mission without us," Steve told the Fae, to which Thinian harrumphed. "If you found a way to the top of the mountain—and you couldn't, by the way—then once you picked the flower how were you going to safely get back?"

"I would have found a way."

"How?" Steve pressed. "You couldn't fly. You were just as grounded as we were. You lost your companions, you were all alone, and you were completely out of time."

"I had no idea how dire the situation had become. Fine. I will admit I was very glad to see you and your mate up there."

Steve held out a hand. Thinian grasped his arm moments later.

"I'm glad we could help," Steve told the Fae. "And I do mean that. I just wish we hadn't ended up pissing off a god. That can't be good, no matter how you look at it."

"We're no longer on Ranal," Thinian reminded him,

plucking another petal from the flower. "We're out of his clutches."

"I just hope he realizes we had a good reason to do what we did," Steve said, wiping his petal on the soft white mesh. "I don't like knowing that an angry Earth Guardian is glaring down at me from up high."

Nearly an hour later Steve and Thinian were done. They had plucked every single petal, dusted each of the petals with the white vyla mesh, and handed the tray to Ria. After Thinian woke her up, of course.

The Fae queen, with Thinian's assistance, began the process of purifying the pollen.

"Be careful not to snap off the pollen sacs," Ria was saying, watching Thinian carefully reach into the plucked flower with a thin metal tool. "Gently swab the collector in a circular motion."

Steve stretched his back. He left Thinian and the queen to work on the primary pollen extraction while he stepped outside to pace about the silent corridor. It was going on two hours with no word from Sarah. It was probably pitch black out there. How in the world could Sarah hope to see what she was doing? What if something had happened to her? What if she needed help?

Steve angrily shook his head. He had to trust her. Sarah was a capable, grown woman. If she felt she was in danger she'd simply teleport herself back to Dynwe at a moment's notice. So why, then, wasn't she back? Was she not able to find the cub? Perhaps she found the cub but couldn't find the cub's sire?

Steve groaned. There were too many unknowns and he was getting a headache. If she wasn't back in fifteen minutes, he was calling out the cavalry. Of the wyverian sort.

Thinian suddenly appeared at his side. The Fae's expression was encouraging. In fact, he was smiling! "We have it!"

"It worked? The Tree has been saved?"

"Oh. No, I was referring to the pollen. The harvesting is complete. Her majesty has requested your presence."

Steve followed Thinian back into the workroom and saw

that the queen, smiling weakly at him, was holding a cauldron small enough to fit in the palm of his hand.

"Would you do the honors, fire thrower?"

Steve nodded. He pulled a stool toward him, plunked his rear down, and held out a hand. Once he was holding the small cauldron, he ignited his hand and gently increased the flow of jhorun.

The cauldron began to heat. Steve leaned over and stared at the bubbling golden liquid. "Umm…"

"Just keep raising the heat," Ria answered, before Steve could ask. "I'll know when you get it hot enough. Once you reach the right temperature, it must be maintained for a very specific amount of time."

"And how long will that be?" Steve wanted to know.

"I'm not sure," Ria confessed. "I'll just know it when it happens."

A few minutes later, as Steve was slowly increasing the temp of his flames, Ria suddenly smiled.

"There. That's what we need right … no, you've gone too far. Now it's too warm. Lessen the… perfect. Right there. Can you hold that temperature?"

"For how long?" Steve asked, peering down at the heated cauldron sitting in his flaming hand.

"Until I say," Ria answered. "It shouldn't be more than a few minutes. Provided you can maintain that precise level of heat. The more the heat fluctuates then the longer the pollen will take to process."

In actuality, it was less than two minutes. Steve's nose reported the purification process was done several seconds before Ria informed him the pollen was ready. He pulled his jhorun back from the cauldron, allowed it to cool, and started to hand it to the queen. Noticing the shakiness of Ria's hands, Steve switched directions and handed the cauldron to Thinian.

"Okay, what's next?" Steve asked.

Ria smiled gratefully at the two of them. She held a hand up and waited for Steve to gently pull her to her feet.

"Now it's time to save our…"

There was a sudden disturbance behind him. Steve and

the two Fae turned to see Sarah standing there, looking bedraggled and completely worn out. Cradled in her arms was something that instantly drew everyone's attention. Steve stared at the sight before him, trying to make sense of what he was seeing. Sarah was rocking back and forth, all while softly singing. Steve nervously cleared his throat.

"Umm, I think you've got some 'splaining to do."

Sarah looked up and smiled at him. She sighed, sank down onto the closest chair, and returned her attention to the small form she was carrying.

"Umm, there's been a slight change of plan, dear," she began to explain.

Chapter 12 – Unexpected Twist

Sarah had teleported herself straight to R'Tal. She wasn't too sure where to start looking for Nyx's cub, but she had a really good idea who to ask. She just had to hope he hadn't gone to sleep for the night.

Sarah looked around the Great Hall. Neither the king nor queen were present, which wasn't too surprising. By her estimation, it had to be past ten in the evening. In fact, the only people in the throne room were a few servants cleaning tables and two stationary guards positioned at either end of the room. Sarah motioned one of them over.

"Nohrin, what can I do for you?"

"It's imperative that I speak with the king. Do you know where he is?"

"His majesty has retired for the evening," the guard informed her.

"Well, un-retire him," Sarah ordered. "He gave me implicit orders to ask for help if I needed it. Well, I'm asking."

The guard nodded. "Captain Pheron gave us explicit

instructions that if either of the Nohrin were to appear then he should be notified immediately. A moment, if you please. I will send word."

The guard hurried off. Sarah began to pace around the room. What if she couldn't find the cub? What if she found the cub but it was too late? What if she couldn't keep her promise to Nyx?

Sarah angrily shook her head. She wouldn't allow that to happen. She *had* to find the cub. If that meant waking up every single person in this castle, she would. She looked around at the nearly empty Great Hall.

Thankfully the guard returned a few moments later, followed closely by an exceptionally tall soldier who was hurriedly donning his uniform. Sarah broke out into a smile.

"Pheron! Am I ever glad to see you!"

"Lady Sarah. A pleasure, as always. I am relieved to see you are well. What can I do for you?"

"Please, there isn't a moment to lose. I need to talk to the king and I need Gareth, Shardwyn's apprentice."

Pheron indicated she should head to the Antechamber.

"Does this have anything to do with the top secret mission I am supposed to know nothing about?"

"Umm…"

"Don't answer that. I'll fetch the king. Wait here, milady."

Less than five minutes later Pheron was back, accompanied by the king. He was still pulling on his robe as he hurried through the door. Kri'Entu inclined his head at his desk and promptly sat down. After running his hands through his graying hair, the king finally looked at Sarah and nodded appreciatively.

"Lady Sarah. Thank you for including me. How may I be of assistance? Captain, you are dismissed."

Sarah held up a hand. "Wait! This doesn't have to do with … what we talked about earlier. This is something else."

Captain Pheron paused, spun around, and waited patiently for Sarah to explain.

"I need information," Sarah hastily explained. "I need maps. I need to speak with someone who knows the kingdom's topography better than anyone. And I need Gareth."

Kri'Entu stared at her for a few seconds before turning to Pheron. The king motioned him over and indicated a chair next to Sarah's.

"Have a seat, Captain. Lady Sarah, please explain."

"Long story short," Sarah began, "there was a landslide. A female griffin sacrificed herself in order to save her cub. I promised the cub's mother that I'd find her baby. That's it, in a nutshell. Please, we have to locate this cub. I don't think he'll survive another night."

"Captain Pheron, send word to Mister Barrett, of cartography. Get him here, on the double. And tell him to bring a selection of his best maps. Go."

Pheron nodded. "Aye, Your Majesty."

Kri'Entu summoned one of the guards.

"You. Come here. Shardwyn's apprentice, Mister Gareth. His extended leave of absence is not due to start until tomorrow morning. He's spending time with his father," Kri'Entu gently explained, seeing the look of confusion on Sarah's face. "You'll find him in his quarters. Fetch him here at once. Oh, I would advise you to knock first. It's never a good idea to surprise a wizard."

The young soldier nervously nodded and departed. As soon as the two of them were alone, the king sat back in his chair and sighed. He looked over at Sarah and smiled.

"I'm sorry for waking you up," Sarah began.

The king dismissively waved his hand. "Think nothing of it. Can you tell me about your agreement with this cub's mother?"

"She offered to help us if we agreed to try and save her cub."

Kri'Entu stared at her for a few moments before chuckling and shaking his head. "I envy your experiences. How many people can say that they have visited other worlds, have journeyed to forbidden islands, and have a jhorun which could make a wizard envious?"

"It's not as fun as you might think," Sarah said. "All Steve and I wanted to do was have a nice, quiet vacation here. Did we get it? No. We're going to need a vacation after this. Talk about stress!"

"You have definitely earned your down time," Kri'Entu observed, with a smile.

"I would like to say again how appreciative we are that you built that cabin for us."

"Mikal was the one who suggested…"

The door to the Antechamber opened and the young guard appeared, leading one very groggy teenager. One look at the poor boy wearing a rumpled jerkin, trousers that were on backwards, and mismatched shoes had Sarah slapping a hand over her mouth. There was someone, she decided, who wasn't a night owl.

"Oh, Gareth, I'm so sorry to wake you up like this."

The guard plopped the teenager down onto the closest armchair, saluted, and promptly resumed his post in the darkened corner of the room. Sarah hurried to Gareth's side and gently shook his arm. When the young wizard still refused to answer her, Sarah put her hands on her hips.

"Gareth, I need you to wake up. I have an emergency and I need your help."

Gareth yawned, stretched his arms, and looked at Sarah with unfocused eyes.

"That does it. I really do hope you can forgive me for this."

The boy wizard disappeared. Moments later they heard a splash and a loud screech of indignation. In the blink of an eye, he was back. Dripping wet. The king's mouth quivered as he fought the urge to laugh.

"What the blazes did you do that for?" Gareth sputtered, jumping to his feet and hurrying over to the fire. "It's the middle of the night. I'm supposed to be sleeping. What did you expect me to be doing?"

"It's nowhere close to the middle of the night," Sarah disagreed. "My eighty-five-year-old grandmother stays up later than you. Now, are you awake or would you like another dip in the moat?"

Kri'Entu managed to keep his face supremely devoid of emotion.

"I'm awake!" Gareth cried, lunging forward to grip the hearth's mantle, as if that act alone would be enough to thwart her jhorun. "Sorry. I had a long day. Now, what's with all the urgency?"

The doors opened again, this time admitting a tall, stocky man lugging a bag full of rolled up parchments. He bowed as soon as he noticed the king. His eyes lit up with recognition as he spied Sarah.

"You must be Lady Sarah! It is a pleasure, milady. I am Barrett, head cartographer. How may I be of assistance?"

Sarah hurried to the king's desk and beckoned the other two over as well.

"Barrett, I have an emergency that I hope you can help me with."

"A map-making emergency?" Gareth stammered, trying to keep the disbelief out of his voice.

"Of sorts," Sarah agreed. "Don't laugh, Gareth. He's here to help me. You are, too."

"What do you need?" Gareth asked.

Sarah faced the cartographer and tapped the king's desk. "Can we see your most detailed map of the kingdom?"

Confused, Barrett looked at the king.

"Do as she says," Kri'Entu commanded.

Barrett nodded, rifled through his bag of scrolls, and selected one. He carefully unrolled it and placed the map on the desk. Sarah nodded. There was a reason Barrett was the best; his maps were exquisite. Sharp lines, stark colors, detailed mountains and landmarks; all were represented on the map.

"Will this do?" Barrett asked. "I'm still putting some finishing touches on it."

"It's perfect," Sarah assured him. She faced Gareth. "Okay. I need you and Barrett to listen. We need to find a very specific location and we need to do it quickly. I'm looking for a trapped griffin cub."

"Oh, my," Barrett exclaimed, surprised.

"Poor thing," Gareth murmured.

"Exactly. You two are going to help me find him. Now, the mother said that she had been killed by a recent landslide and it wasn't in her normal territory."

Gareth blinked a few times. "The mother was killed and

yet you—"

"Let the matter drop, Mister Gareth," the king quietly instructed.

Gareth nodded sagely. "It's dropped."

"Excellent. Lady Sarah, do continue."

Sarah nodded. "Right. As I was saying, the mother said she had stashed her cub in a cave at the base of some cliff while she hunted. She finished her hunt and returned to the cave. An earthquake hit, causing a landslide."

"An earthquake?" Gareth asked, frowning. "Is that another name for terra tremor?"

Sarah nodded. "Yes. A terra tremor. Nyx said something about a lake being nearby, trees to the north and south, and mountains to the east."

"Which mountains?" Barrett wanted to know. "The Bohanis or the Selekais?"

"I don't know," Sarah answered. "I would think it'd be the Bohanis, but she never did say. What do you think? Is this enough information to go by? Can you guys find out where I need to go?"

Barrett briefly glanced at Gareth before leaning forward to study his map. After a few moments, he sighed heavily and gave the king a frustrated stare. The king held up a hand and signaled the cartographer to wait.

"We know it isn't much to go on, Mr. Barrett," Kri'Entu began, "but hopefully it's enough to trigger your memory. You know the country better than virtually everyone. Can you pinpoint the griffin's location?"

"Well, it all depends on the size of the lake," Barrett finally decided, turning to look at Sarah. "Do you know about how big it is? How many gallons of water would you estimate it has?"

"Now how in the world would I know that?" Sarah asked, perplexed.

Barrett was silent, thinking. Sarah looked helplessly at the king but saw that Kri'Entu was staring hard at Gareth. She glanced over and saw that the young wizard had his eyes closed. He hadn't gone back to sleep, had he?

Gareth's lips were moving. He was chanting! She smiled,

hoping he was coming up with a spell that would help her pinpoint where the landslide had occurred.

"I need some markers," Gareth suddenly said, snapping his eyes open. He quickly stood and looked around the room.

"Markers?" Barrett repeated, horrified. "You are *not* going to desecrate my map with any type of marker, young man."

Having experienced several of Gareth's spells firsthand, Kri'Entu started searching his desk for some suitable objects. Three small figurines, like pawns on a chessboard, were placed on the desk. The king looked up, questioning. Gareth shook his head no and gathered up the objects, placing them just outside the map.

"What are you going to do?" Barrett hesitantly asked. "You aren't going to damage my map, are you?"

"If he does, I'm sure you can create another," the king told him, growing impatient. "Your work is exquisite, Mister Barrett. If something happens to the map then I will personally commission another. In fact, I will even commission … that is to say, I will officially request…"

After the king had trailed off for the second time, Sarah came to his aid.

"How about a map which shows all the islands off the western coast of Capily?"

Barrett gasped with alarm and gave the king a horrified look. "Do you have any idea how many islands there are?" the cartographer sputtered. "It would take weeks, if not months to properly chart."

Sarah paled. Dynwe was on one of those islands. The last thing she wanted was to draw extra attention to the Fae and their home. Thinking quickly, she decided she should add an addendum.

"Then perhaps just the islands that are visible from the shore. We saw the map that Constable Fensham had in his office. It was nowhere near as nice as this."

Kri'Entu nodded. "An excellent idea, Lady Sarah. Mister Barrett, consider that your next paid commission."

"But that will take…" Barrett trailed off as his eyes took on a wistful gleam.

"An exceedingly long time," the king finished for him.

"For which you will be compensated."

The cartographer finally smiled. "Maybe I could include a…"

"Got it," Gareth suddenly announced.

Sarah whirled on the young wizard. "You found the cub? That's fantastic, Gareth! Where do I have to go?"

"No, I haven't," Gareth quickly apologized. "I finished my spell and have the first set of results."

"What do you have?" Sarah eagerly asked. "What does your spell do?"

"I checked for recent terra tremors," Gareth explained, battling valiantly to hold back a yawn. "I checked back as far as a week. There have been six."

"Where?" Barrett asked, interested.

Before he could ask, Kri'Entu placed three more items on his desk. A pen cap, the stopper to a bottle of ink, and a ring he pulled off one of his fingers joined the three figurines. Gareth nodded appreciatively, closed his eyes, and chanted once more. All six items zipped across the map and stopped.

The small group fell silent as they studied the map. Two of the small figurines landed in the northern Bohanis. The pen cap landed near the Zylan River, almost dead center in the kingdom, while the third figurine, the ring, and the stopper ended up in various locales in the southern Selekais. Kri'Entu stared at the two figures located in the northern half of his kingdom.

"I would think it would be one of these two."

"That's assuming the nearby mountains are the Bohanis," Sarah pointed out. "Look at the map. There are three markers in the Selekais. The odds are the cub is somewhere south, provided we knew where Nyx's flock resides."

Gareth snapped his fingers. "Of course. The griffins. I can modify the spell to single out the locations with recent griffin activity."

"You can do that?" Barrett asked incredulously.

"Of course," Gareth scoffed. "It's easy. Anyone can do it. All you have to do is…"

"Perhaps explanations would be best left for another time, Mister Gareth," Kri'Entu suggested.

Gareth smiled sheepishly and cleared the markers off the map. His eyes closed and within moments he was chanting. Ten seconds later they watched as only two of the markers slid across the map, to the locations in the Bohanis.

"There you go," Gareth announced, opening his eyes. He looked at the map and nodded. "It's one of those two places."

Barrett nodded and tapped the first marker. "This one has potential. I don't see any lakes nearby but there are trees to the north and south."

"What about caves?" Sarah asked, leaning forward to study the map in closer detail. "We're looking for a cliff, remember?"

Barrett sighed. "Unknown, I'm afraid."

"And the other?" the king prompted. "What can you tell us about that location, Mister Barrett?"

"I don't see any lakes there, either," Barrett groaned. "In fact, there's not much detail there at all. I'm going to have to fix that."

Sarah pointed at a couple of squiggles on the map. "What are these? Mountains?"

"Hills," Barrett answered, after leaning forward to see.

Sarah hastily stood. "That's close enough. It's gotta be it. Barrett, Gareth, thank you. I have to get going."

The king's eyebrows shot up. "You're going outside at night? Alone? This I cannot allow. You will need help, Lady Sarah."

"I'll go," Gareth volunteered. "I'm awake. And I think I owe it to them to try and make things right."

"What things?" Kri'Entu wanted to know.

"Things I shouldn't have done when we first, er, met."

The king nodded. "Ah. Carry on, Mister Gareth. I leave her care in your capable hands. Mister Barrett, you have my thanks. You are dismissed."

Chairs were pushed back as everyone rose to their feet. Barrett rolled his map up, stashed it back in his bag, and hastily departed. Sarah looked over at the young wizard and smiled.

"Are you ready to go?"

Gareth gave her an unreadable stare. "Why would you

ask me that? I'm here. Obviously, I'm ready to go."

"Maybe you'll want to fix your pants before we leave."

"My pants?" Gareth glanced down at his trousers. "What's the matter with … what the…? How did that happen? Did I actually walk in here looking like this? I don't think I've ever put my trousers on backwards."

"I assumed it was a fashion statement," the king mused as he headed toward the closest exit. "Lady Sarah, I wish you the best of luck. Call upon me again if I can be of assistance. Good evening to you both."

Sarah waited for Gareth to correct his attire and dry his clothes with a hastily constructed spell before teleporting them as close as she could to the second marker. Gareth conjured several fireballs into existence so they wouldn't stumble blindly about.

"Which way?" she asked.

After a few moments of chanting, Gareth pointed east. Once the young wizard informed her that they were in the correct area, Sarah looked around. She could see the bases of several hills to the east. She didn't see any lake, nor could she smell any water in the air, but that didn't trouble her too much. Nyx could have been off on the lake's proximity.

"Can you tell if there are any griffins in the area?" Sarah quietly asked.

Gareth nodded. "Sure. Give me a moment."

While the wizard chanted, Sarah looked around. It was quiet. And dark. Without a moon to light the sky Sarah could see thousands of twinkling stars peeking over the treetops. She smiled wistfully. Steve would love this. Thousands of stars and no light pollution. She briefly wondered how he was doing with the pollen harvest. She definitely owed her husband a favor now. She was halfway into planning a nighttime picnic when Gareth cleared his throat.

"The closest griffin is less than a league away, due west. This must be the right place."

"Shoot," Sarah was saying. "I was certain this was the right one. Very well. We're on to … what is it, Gareth?"

Gareth had a frown on his face as he stared at her. "I just said the griffins were nearby. Isn't that good news?"

Sarah shook her head. "Nyx told me that she had gone outside her normal territory. If that's true, I would think the nearest griffins would be much farther away, unless you're telling me that your spell can look for a young cub?"

Gareth nodded. "Aye. I added in a layer to my spell which specifies the griffin we're looking for must be an age between newborn and six months."

"And aside from the cub, there shouldn't be any other griffins around him, right?"

"Unless he's been found," Gareth agreed. "Based on what you've been telling me, I have to assume that he hasn't been. Found, that is."

"So what can you tell me about this locale?" Sarah asked. "Is this the right one?"

The young wizard gave her an appraising look. "My spell has indicated that the nearest griffin falls outside of my age parameters. You're right. This cannot be the right place."

"I'm going to move us as close as I can to the other location. Put those fireballs out and get ready, okay?"

In the blink of an eye it was so dark that neither of them could see anything. Together they waited in silence.

"Well?" Gareth finally asked.

"Well, what?" Sarah returned.

"Are you going to do it?"

"What, teleport?"

Gareth nodded. "Aye. I'll relight the fireballs as soon as we arrive."

"Then get working on it. We're already here. I need you to tell me where I need to jump us to next."

"Oh. That was… Never mind. Just a moment."

The small clearing lit up as two huge fireballs flared into existence. Sarah looked around. The forest was quiet. Eerily quiet. The only thing she could hear was the occasional chirp of an insect. Gareth had his eyes closed. An arm lifted, finger pointing northeast.

"That way. I think we're getting close. There are four… no, make that five griffins that way which look like they're… no, sorry. There's six. It's hard to count them. They're all moving around, as though they're hunting."

"Maybe it's Nyx's flock and they're searching for her."

"Perhaps. That number is too small to be considered a full flock. I'd say our best bet lies in that direction."

"How far?" Sarah asked.

She was met with another shrug. She sighed. It looked as though they'd have to play the *hot potato, cold potato* game for a while. Hopefully it wouldn't be too long. She wouldn't be able to rest until she knew that Nyx's cub was rescued and safe.

Gareth sent one of the fireballs out in the direction they needed to go. Sarah zeroed in on the traveling orb of fire and jumped them several hundred feet at a time, keeping the speeding fireball within sight. She dared not risk trying to teleport any farther than that in the dark. She sighed. It was the best she could do.

Fifteen minutes—and six jumps—later Sarah and her young assistant came to an abrupt halt. Directly in their path were two adult griffins. Both were standing so still they could have been mistaken for statues. Sarah smiled as she pictured the hidden griffin safe back home in her husband's office. All that would be needed to complete that picture was to have the griffins raise their left foreleg. She glanced over at Gareth who was facing the other direction with his eyes closed and his mouth moving in a silent chant.

She tapped the boy on his shoulder. Gareth's eyes snapped open and she indicated he should look the other way.

"Are they, um, real?" Gareth hesitantly asked, staring at the two immobile griffins. "Why aren't they moving?"

"Are you friend or foe?" one of the griffins asked, in the high-pitched nasal voice prevalent with their species.

"Friend," Sarah answered.

"Identify yourself," the second griffin demanded.

"I am Sarah and my friend here is Gareth."

"What are two humans doing in the middle of the woods at this hour?" the first griffin asked.

"I could ask you the same thing," Sarah countered. "Griffins aren't typically nocturnal. What are your names? We gave you ours. What are yours?"

"I am Archadius," the first griffin said. "This is Thalian."

"What are you two doing here at this time of night?"

Sarah asked.

"We asked first," Archadius informed her.

Sarah nodded. "Very well. We're looking for signs of terra tremors. We believe a griffiness lost her life protecting her cub and now we have to see about rescuing it."

"Cub?" Thalian asked, cocking his head. "You search for a griffin cub?"

Sarah nodded. "Yes. Now, what are you two doing here?"

"How is it two perfect spheres of fire burn suspended in the air?" Archadius asked, looking up.

Sarah waggled a finger at the griffin. "Nuh-uh. That's not the arrangement. We answered your question. It's your turn to answer. What are you two doing out here?"

"Investigating *that*," Archadius answered, extending a wing and pointing it at the fireball. "When reports of fire in the forest reach our ears we investigate."

"Sorry, that's just us. We're only using it as light. Nothing is being lit on fire."

"What do you plan on doing with this griffin cub should you find it?" Thalian asked.

"The plan is to save the cub and reunite him with his father," Sarah said. "That's the promise I made to Nyx. Why? Is that a problem?"

Archadius jerked his head up and his wings snapped open.

"How do you know that name?"

"How do *you* know that name?" Sarah countered. "Was she a member of your flock?"

"Thalian and I are part of an exploratory team sent out to ascertain what has happened to her. She is overdue and no one knows where she went. Do you speak the truth? Has Nyx perished?"

Sarah sadly nodded. "Yes. She died saving the life of her cub. This was about three days ago. Will you help us? The cub is nearby."

"How do you know this?" Archadius asked. "We have been scouring the land for several days. Thus far, no traces have been found."

"She was killed by a terra tremor. Her body has been

concealed by a landslide," Sarah reminded the griffin. She pointed at Gareth. "Besides, I've got *him*."

The first griffin looked at his companion and started to squawk out orders.

"Thalian, bring the others. Notify them what we have found. Tell them I have decided we will aid the humans. Hurry!"

The second griffin disappeared into the darkness, heading rapidly south. Archadius turned to look at Gareth, giving him a querulous squawk, before turning back to Sarah. He pointed a wing at Gareth.

"Is he responsible for the floating fire?"

"Yes," Sarah nodded. "Gareth is a wizard. He's helping me look."

"And you're certain Nyx is somewhere in this area?" Archadius asked, turning to Gareth.

"I am, yes," he answered. "Within the last seven days this area has seen recent terra tremor activity. This has to be the place."

"And how do you know this?" Archadius asked.

"Oh, don't ask him that," Sarah quietly groaned.

Gareth grinned, "It's easy. All I had to do was look for recent terra tremor activity, cross referenced with localized griffin activity, followed by current griffin proximity, with a sublayer specifying the griffin's age between newborn and six months. Now, if you take…"

"You're a whiz with spells, no doubt about it," Sarah interrupted. She looked at Archadius and nodded. "If he says the cub is nearby, it's true. We just have to find him."

"Nyx's cub was buried in a landslide?" Archadius' wings rustled nervously. "I do not think we will find the cub alive."

There was a mad flapping of wings and in the blink of an eye four more griffins were standing before her.

"Where's Finndar?" Archadius asked. "Has he become lost again?"

"It was decided he should return to the flock," Thalian said. "More help may be needed."

"Is there a problem?" Sarah quietly asked.

Archadius gave her an unreadable look before giving her

the approximation of a shrug.

"Finndar would lose his own tail if it wasn't permanently attached to his backside. I fail to see how he'll find his way back."

"What was this griffin doing on your search team if his sense of direction is as bad as you say?" Sarah wanted to know.

"His father is the Prime," Thalian answered. "What choice had we?"

"How may we be of assistance?" one of the new griffins asked. "We understand you are searching for the same thing as we. We have already searched this area but have discovered nothing. We were planning on moving on at sunrise tomorrow. Where would you like us to search?"

Sarah turned to Gareth and gave him a questioning look. Gareth closed his eyes, was silent for a few moments, and then pointed east. Five griffins immediately turned to look.

Sarah nodded. "Perfect. Let's—"

"Just a moment," Gareth interrupted. "Before we go anywhere, we need to wait just a little bit longer."

Sarah blinked her eyes a few times, staring at the boy.

"What was that? Why?"

"We need to wait for another set of eyes."

"We're waiting for someone?" Sarah asked, perplexed. "Who? Who have you called for help?"

"Me," a strong female voice answered from behind them.

Sarah and the griffins whirled back around to see that a very large being was now sharing their small clearing. Sarah craned her neck to follow the massive form's shape up until she reached a pair of gold reptilian eyes. Those unblinking eyes were staring straight at her.

"Greetings."

Sarah smiled up at the sleek wyverian form. "Pravara! How nice to see you! My, you've gotten big. What are you doing here?"

The dragon, who had been sitting on her haunches, leaned forward until all four legs made contact with the ground. Her head lowered until it was resting on the grass-covered floor. A quick glance confirmed that all of the griffins had surreptitiously moved closer to the trees.

"I was in the area," Pravara explained, glancing over at Gareth. "I noticed the increased activity and decided a closer look was warranted."

"You are over exaggerating just a bit, aren't you?" Gareth asked, looking up at the large wyverian. "Why don't you just tell them the truth?"

"The truth?" Sarah repeated, confused. She looked at the huge form lying in the grass. "What does he mean by that, Pravara?"

"I, er, may have been eavesdropping," the large dragon sheepishly confessed.

"Are we to believe you are here to help us search for the cub?" Archadius suspiciously asked.

Pravara's gaze shifted from Gareth's to the griffins. She nodded. "I am. The death of the young one is nigh. If that is to be prevented, we must act now."

"Wait, you can see in the dark, can't you?" Gareth asked.

"As can we," Thalian hastily added.

"I can," Pravara announced. "A dragon's visual ac--"

"Whoa!" Sarah exclaimed, throwing her hands up into the air and leaping between dragon and griffin. "Did you hear what Pravara said?"

The griffins eyed each other but remained silent.

"What did we miss?" Gareth asked.

"Pravara said, 'the death of the young one is nigh'. Do you know what that means?"

"The cub still lives," Archadius excitedly exclaimed.

Sarah rounded on the griffin. "Exactly! Pravara, where is he?"

Everyone turned to watch Pravara stretch her neck out, narrow her eyes, and finally lower her head back to the ground.

"While I cannot give you the exact location, I can confirm that the youngling lies in that direction."

"Are you sure?" Sarah asked.

The huge dark green dragon nodded. "Aye. A strong scent of griffin emanates from that direction."

"You can smell the cub?" Thalian asked, impressed.

"No," Pravara admitted.

Thalian was confused. "Then what… oh."

Three griffins immediately launched into the air while the other two bounded forward, intent on covering the distance to the trees as quickly as possible. Sarah lunged forward, grabbed Gareth by the wrist, and teleported them to the other side of the clearing, just in time to see two griffins go bolting by them.

"Pravara says to continue in this direction for at least half a league," Gareth told her. "Once we find a 'thrice cracked boulder' then we need to head north for no more than a quarter league."

"How is it you can be so precise?" Sarah wanted to know.

"I keep several spells with me at all times," Gareth explained, reaching into his trouser pocket and withdrawing a handful of items. "Now, this looks like an ordinary pebble. Well, I guess it *is* an ordinary pebble. That's not the point. The point is it's my earth elemental. In case we need it. And this? This will summon a wall of water. And this is what I just used."

The young wizard proudly held up a … Sarah squinted at the object. What was it? It looked like a small figurine of a long sinewy snake with disproportionally tiny legs. Was it a skinny dragon?

"This is my nocturnal vision spell. You never know when you'll need to be able to see in the dark.

"We get it," Sarah told him, taking the boy's hand and curling his fingers around the contents of his pocket. "Everyone can see in the dark but me."

"Want me to create a spell for you?" Gareth casually asked. "It wouldn't take long. And we'd just have to find some little object to hold the spell. Any rock would do."

"You definitely know what you're doing, Gareth. No one can say otherwise. However, I think I just thought of something that will do the trick."

"Oh? What's that?"

Sarah held out an arm, palm facing up. She closed her hand, concentrated, and then opened it. Cupped inside her hand was a gold chain with a piece of broken jewelry looped through it. Gareth leaned forward to poke a finger at the misshapen pendant. Sarah whipped it away.

"Nuh-uh. I'm sorry, Gareth, I can't have you touching this. I've never liked using it and I really don't want to use it now."

"What is it?" Gareth asked, curious.

"An extraordinarily powerful talisman. Let's leave it at that."

"It looks broken," Gareth observed.

Sarah nodded. "It is."

Sarah looped the golden chain around her neck and gave the boy a cryptic smile. She looked uneasily at her half of the broken Amulet of Aria. She hadn't worn this wretched thing since she and Steve battled Celestia all those years ago. It unsettled her then as it did now. She could feel her jhorun traveling through her hands to investigate the object she was holding. The tingles she felt magnified into dangerous proportions.

Sarah swallowed nervously. As long as she was holding this piece of the amulet, she had to be mindful of her thoughts. If she tried to teleport something, she had to have a crystal-clear image of what she wanted to accomplish in her mind. The slightest deviation could—and probably would—have disastrous results.

Once the broken amulet had settled into place, she closed her eyes. As before, she felt the power of the amulet flood through her the moment it made contact with her skin. After a few moments her vision returned, as she knew it would. However, it wasn't the same as the griffin's nocturnal vision, or Pravara's. Thanks to the power of the amulet, she could see everything in vivid detail, as though she was standing in the middle of the clearing, in broad daylight.

However, the difference was her point of view. With her eyes closed she could actually see herself, as if from above and behind. Her vision would spin around and show her whichever direction she happened to be facing. At the moment, facing due east, she could see a thick copse of trees directly before them. Much to her delight, she could also see about three times the distance as with the light from Gareth's burning fireballs.

"Alright," she told Gareth. "Take my hand. It's time to go."

"But your eyes are closed," Gareth pointed out. "How can you see where we need to go?"

"I can see you just fine. In fact, if you were to extinguish those fireballs I'd still be able to see you. Their presence here makes no difference to me."

"What did you say that thing is, again?" Gareth asked, sidling closer to the amulet to get a better look.

Sarah instantly tucked the pendant into her shirt. "Let the matter go. Now, are you ready?"

Sarah took them to the farthest eastern point she could see, another group of trees. Getting her bearings, Sarah jumped them east again. And again. Then northeast. There, exactly as Pravara had described it, was the boulder with three cracks running through it. Sarah whistled with surprise. The huge stone was easily as large as her parents' old house in California.

"Her eyesight is impressive," Sarah breathed, running a hand along the stone's jagged surface. "Pravara could see this all the way from where she was?"

"She says yes," Gareth relayed. "She says she's watching us now."

"Where to next?" Sarah wanted to know.

"North. Pravara says no more than a quarter of a league."

"A quarter league north," Sarah repeated, turning to look left. The trees thinned somewhat and she could see several hills in the east. They had to be getting close!

Ten minutes later they found it. Pravara directed them toward a large glade situated within a break in the trees. There was a hill to the east, and Sarah could smell water! A lake! This had to be the right place!

Three griffins emerged from the trees. Thalian touched down next, followed closely by Archadius. Two of them eyed her, no doubt wondering how she beat them here. Together they stared at the hillside. While not exactly a cliff, as Nyx had remembered, she could easily see how there must have once been a formidable stone formation here. Strewn bits of broken rock were everywhere. Of the cave where Nyx had hidden her cub, nothing remained.

"Are you sure this is the right place?" Archadius asked as he eyed the mass of broken stone littering the eastern half of the glade.

"This is it," Sarah told the griffin. "It has to be."

"Confirmed," Pravara's voice chimed in.

Sarah risked a quick look back. Yes, there was the dragon, sitting complacently on her haunches and staring at the solid mass of broken stone. True to her wyverian form, the huge dragon had approached in stealth. Pravara, sensing she was being watched, looked down at her and nodded. Sarah felt a sudden thrill of excitement. They were going to make it! They found the cub! Only... only now what? Tons of rocks and earth would fill in any hole they dug.

The five griffins began to dig fervently. Bits of rock and debris went flying in all directions. Sarah wandered back to the dragon and gently tapped her claw. Once Pravara was looking her way, Sarah asked the question she'd been dying to know for the last thirty minutes.

"Are we too late? Is the cub still alive? Can you tell?"

Pravara sniffed the air. She stretched her neck up to see over the digging griffins. She sadly shook her head. Sarah's eyes filled with tears.

"I cannot tell for certain," the dragon softly told her. "I could hear the youngling's breaths before. I cannot now."

"Maybe you can't hear him because no one can hear anything while the griffins dig?" Sarah asked.

"Perhaps," the dragon conceded. "As long as the... do you hear that?"

Alarmed, Sarah faced the digging griffins. "What? What is it? What do you hear? I can't hear anything."

"As you feared, the hill has become unstable. Your griffin companions must stop digging. They'll cause more damage to the cub."

That was all Sarah needed to hear. She ran toward the closest griffin, waving her arms and shouting for all she was worth. However, as Pravara had noticed, when someone was moving as much rock as they were doing, as rapidly as possible, then the chances of being heard would become abysmally slim.

She was ignored.

Now she could feel it. The earth was trembling. She saw that more rocks were starting to gravitate toward them, careening into even more rocks that would eventually become a second landslide. Determined to not let that happen, Sarah looped a finger around the pendant's golden chain and pulled. She grasped the broken amulet tightly and felt her awareness expand in all directions.

Pravara was right. Another landslide had already started. She directed her enhanced jhorun to hold the falling stones in place.

The trembling stopped. The oblivious griffins continued to dig. Frowning, she looked at the griffins and easily levitated every single one of them. Using the amulet to hold them aloft, she looked over at Gareth and saw him staring, open-mouthed, at her.

"Don't just stand there, do something! I'm holding the rocks in place. Find the cub! Get him out of there! I don't know how long I can hold them!"

Gareth blinked once and nodded. He hurried past the floating griffins and began to chant. A disturbance appeared in the rocks. Something was rising up out of the rubble. It was a large form and it wasn't moving.

It was Nyx's body.

Sarah's eyes filled with tears as she saw the griffiness's lifeless form rise slowly out of the ground. Just then she felt the amount of jhorun she was expelling double. The landslide was getting worse, taking more of her enhanced jhorun to hold it in place.

The entire hill had collapsed! Several hundred tons of rocks were starting to make their way down the slope. It was heading straight toward them. The entire hill had collapsed!

"Gareth, you're out of time!" she shouted at her companion. "The whole damn hill is on its way down! Whatever you're doing, do it faster!"

"I'm trying!" Gareth snapped. He glanced irritably up at the nearest floating griffin and the huge mass of stones that were temporarily frozen in place. Gareth shouted, "Forget about them! Release them! You've got bigger things to worry about!"

Five griffins dropped unceremoniously to the ground. Gareth pointed at Nyx's still form, still partially buried.

"This whole place is coming down! Stop staring and lend a hand! Get the cub! Hurry!"

The griffins rushed forward. Three set about digging Nyx's body out of the rubble while the other two tried to ascertain the cub's location and condition. Gareth shouted orders; the griffins complied, and Sarah groaned. The amulet was drawing massive amounts of jhorun from her in order to slow the landslide. However, even with the power of the amulet, it was more than she could hold. She watched a large boulder break free and start tumbling down. Then another. And another!

"Gareth! I can't hold this any longer! Get everyone out of the way!"

The young wizard thrust his hand into his pocket, pulled something out, and hastily invoked one of his spells. He then threw something toward the madly scrambling griffins. A dust cloud enveloped the griffins just then, brought upon by the stones and boulders rushing down the hill. Then she saw something that caused a chill to run down her spine: movement. Something was moving in the heart of the cloud. Something big. And it was growing bigger. In fact, it almost looked like it was feeding off the rocks and boulders that were rolling toward it.

An ear-splitting roar rent the air. When the figure stood up and took a few steps, she stared at Gareth with shock written all over her features. He'd cast his earth elemental spell. It had to be!

The ten-foot-tall rock golem lumbered toward the digging griffins, who were still blissfully unaware of the danger they were in. Rocks and stones continued to hammer at them. A boulder, easily three times the size of an adult griffin, slammed into another and launched into the air, headed straight toward the griffins. Sarah screamed a warning but her shouts were drowned out by the approaching wall of dirt and debris.

The huge golem cocked its right arm back and struck the giant boulder, exploding it into a thousand gravel-sized pieces. The earth elemental stepped in front of the temporarily frozen-with-fear griffins and faced the onslaught of rock and debris. Within moments its massive stone arms were smashing through more of the tumbling boulders, swatting aside those too large to break, and shielding the cowering group from the smaller stones.

"Stop hitting rocks and get them out of there!" Gareth shouted at the golem. "Her jhorun is nearly exhausted."

The golem turned and looked down at the griffins. From her vantage point, Sarah could see that those that were digging had stopped. Several scrambled around Nyx's still form. One griffin darted in, grabbed something in its beak, and hurried off. The rest followed suit. The rock creature scooped up Nyx's body and ran after the griffins, not stopping until they were safely out of harm's way.

Sarah finally gave her jhorun the cease-and-desist order. Her right hand opened and she released the piece of amulet. Almost immediately, the ground shook as the tons of rock and stone she'd been holding back came crashing down.

Before she could even take a breath Sarah felt herself wrenched sideways and she was airborne. What happened? She tried to prepare her tiring jhorun for a jump, but before she could issue the order she was back on solid ground. Confused, she turned to see Pravara standing silently next to her. Sarah smiled up at her huge wyverian friend.

"Thanks, Pravara," Sarah said, raising her voice to be heard over the continuing clatter of falling stones. "Is everyone okay?"

"Everyone is accounted for," Gareth reported in from the other side of the dragon. "One elemental, one dragon, two humans, five griffins, and one cub."

Sarah saw that the five adult griffins were standing over a tiny form. A form that wasn't moving. She let out a cry and pushed by Thalian to kneel down in the soft grass.

"Gareth, light."

A dozen fireballs appeared, scattered throughout the glade. Sarah inspected the tiny form no bigger than her corgi,

Peanut. She swallowed nervously. This cub was young, not more than a week or two old. Why had Nyx taken a cub this young, this fragile, on a hunt? Why hadn't Nyx's mate been caring for the cub?

Sarah angrily blinked back her tears. She placed a hand on the tiny griffin's tawny chest. The heartbeat was there, but it was faint. So very faint! She didn't know anything about a griffin's physiology. A quick glance at the group suggested that no one else knew what to do, either. It was up to her.

"Alright, here's what I need. Food. Archadius, you and the rest of the griffins go hunting. Find something that this little one can eat. Gareth? See if you can find some fresh water."

"I'm not supposed to leave you unprotected," Gareth argued. "The king said you were in my care."

"Then leave your rock monster here. Hurry, okay?"

Gareth looked up at the golem just as the elemental looked down at him.

"Protect her," Gareth commanded. He hurried off just as all the griffins took to the air.

Sarah continued to run her fingers across the cub's body. She couldn't see any physical damage but that didn't mean there weren't any internal injuries. She couldn't take that chance. Closing her eyes she brought up the mental picture of their safe back home. She sent the amulet piece back and simultaneously teleported her medallion to her. She threw the thick leather cord around her neck, cupped the medallion in her hands, and gently applied pressure to two very specific points. The medallion's hidden compartment opened, revealing a tiny crystal vial of kaormac juice. The precious liquid was capable of healing practically any injury.

She gently applied a drop of the elixir to the tip of her finger, pried open the cub's beak, and wiped the drop across the cub's tongue. A few seconds later Sarah's breath caught in her throat. The cub started to stir! Not by much, unfortunately. Even she could see that the poor little cub was weak from hunger. The cub tried to push himself up off the ground and squeaked weakly when Sarah gently, but firmly, pushed him back down.

"Hang in there, little one. Help is on the way."

Gareth returned first. He held up a water bag. Sarah gently fed some of the clear liquid to the cub and smiled as the tiny griffin tried again to rise. His petite wings flapped uselessly before they were refolded. The cub's eyes opened and stared at her, unblinking. Sarah looked back into the cub's hazel eyes and smiled.

"It's okay. I'm here to help."

She extended her hand and allowed the young griffin to learn her scent. The cub feebly batted at her hand a few times before collapsing on the ground, exhausted. Sarah soothingly stroked the cub's fur and kept her voice just as friendly as possible.

"You just rest. Your brothers and sisters are finding you some food. Everything is going to be okay."

Archadius touched down in front of them, followed closely thereafter by Thalian and the others. Archadius had some type of small, furry creature dangling limply from his beak. A quick check of the others showed similar finds. Only one griffin was empty-handed. As one, all the kills were dropped at Sarah's feet. The cub, alerted to the presence of food, squeaked hungrily.

Sarah looked at the griffin baby, down at the kills, over at the adult griffins—who had all taken several steps backwards—and groaned. Once more it was up to her. She nerved herself and picked up the closest, least mangled kill. She dropped into a cross-legged sitting position, gently pulled the cub into her lap, and grasped the tail of a dead mouse-looking thing. She dangled it over the cub's mouth and prayed that the tiny griffin would know what to do.

It did.

The cub lurched forward, grabbed the kill with its beak, and happily pulled it out of her hand. Sarah averted her eyes and loudly hummed to herself. The last thing she wanted to hear were the crunching of bones as the cub enjoyed its meal. Within moments the 'food' was gone and the cub squeaked for more. Sarah selected another and fed it to the cub. Thankfully she only had to suffer through that second feeding before the cub, full and content, circled once on her lap and promptly went to sleep. Sarah was sure her heart skipped a beat. She crooned softly, stroking the sleeping cub's fur.

"So where can we find Nyx's mate?" Sarah quietly asked as she looked up at the watching griffins. "I can only imagine he wants to get his baby back just as soon as possible."

"What was his name?" Archadius suspiciously asked.

"What kind of answer is that?" Sarah demanded. "Nyx was a member of your flock. Obviously, her mate is, too. Don't you know him?"

"What was his name?" Archadius repeated.

Sarah thought back to their meeting with the two griffins up on Ranal. What had Nyx said her mate's name was? "Skeiron. His name is Skeiron."

Archadius and Thalian hastily shared a look with one another, a fact not lost on Sarah.

"What was that for? Why did the two of you just look at each other?"

"It is your intention to have Skeiron assume full care of the cub?" Archadius asked, using an unsettling neutral tone.

Sarah nodded. "Well, yes. That's what parents do, right? It's his cub. He's the father. Why wouldn't he?"

"Skeiron has no business raising a cub," Thalian angrily spat. "It would have been far more merciful to allow the cub to perish in the terra tremor."

Sarah felt sick. What were they saying? Was Nyx's mate a poor choice to raise the cub alone? Had she just doomed the poor young griffin to a life of misery?

"Skeiron is cruel and vile," Archadius quietly explained, confirming her suspicions. "If he is told that he must now care for his offspring, he will undoubtedly kill him."

"What about someone else?" Sarah asked. "This cub belongs in your flock. There must be something you can do."

"There is," Archadius admitted. "For the cub's sake, it must be believed that the terra tremor claimed the lives of both the cub and his mother. If any other griffin were to learn the cub lived then they would require the cub's sire to assume responsibilities. Trust me, you don't want that to happen."

"But that's insane!" Sarah cried, looking down at the tiny form. "What'll happen to him? Who's going to look out for him? There must be something you can do."

"There is, and I am already doing it," Archadius admitted. "I'm trying to save his life. If I take that cub back with me, he'll be given to his father. If anyone volunteers to look after the cub, Skeiron will view that as an insult. He will not allow any other to care for the cub, but if he's given custody then I predict the cub will be dead within a day or two."

"What if I take him?" Sarah quietly suggested. "What if the cub comes with me?"

"You're willing to look after the cub yourself?" Thalian asked, stepping forward. "This is no easy task. I don't think one human can do it alone."

"Her mate is the fire thrower," Gareth added. "If anyone can protect him, then it would be Lady Sarah and Sir Steve."

"Then it is decided," Archadius announced. "The cub now belongs to the human female. As far as anyone else knows, Nyx and her cub perished in the landslide. Are we all agreed?"

Squawks of acknowledgment sounded from all sides. Archadius looked up at Pravara. "Dragon, may we have your silence in the matter?"

Pravara nodded. "Of course."

"Good. Thank you. We'll be off."

"Wait!" Sarah exclaimed, rising to her feet. "What does he eat? How often do I feed him? What do I call him?"

"Nyx's cub has already been named," said one griffin, who up until that time hadn't spoken a single word. "I was there for the naming ceremony. My mate and Nyx were close acquaintances. The cub's name is Emerion."

"Emerion," Sarah softly repeated as she looked at the sleeping form of the cub. "It's nice to meet you."

By the time she looked up she and Gareth were alone in the woods. Gareth squatted next to her and gently ran a hand down the cub's fur. He looked up at her just then and raised an eyebrow. "What should I tell the king?"

"I don't want you lying to him. Tell him exactly what you saw here. Be sure to tell him about the dangers of returning the cub."

Gareth solemnly nodded. "I will. Are you leaving now?

Are you going back to your world?"

Sarah shook her head. "No. We're not finished yet. I've got to get back to Steve and the Fae. Do you need me to take you back to the castle?"

Gareth held up a hand. "No, don't worry about me. I can see you're tired. I can take care of myself. Good luck!"

"Gareth, thank you. For everything. I wouldn't have been able to pull this off without you. Now, repeat after me: *we're even.*"

Chapter 13 — Moment of Truth

S o, what's your plan here?" Steve asked, leaning over to stare at the young griffin, still asleep in her arms. "Are you actually considering taking it back to Idaho with us? I know you're aware of the severe lack of griffins in our area, right?"

"I know that, silly," Sarah answered, cradling the baby to her chest. She looked up into her husband's concerned eyes and smiled. "Don't worry, everything is going to be fine."

Thinian poked his head into the room. "We really must be going. I honestly do not know how much time we have left."

Sarah nodded. "Of course. I'm glad I didn't miss anything. After you, Thinian."

Sarah struggled to get to her feet. Even though the griffin was practically a newborn, he was still almost thirty pounds of dead weight in her arms, added to her own exhaustion and depleted jhorun.

"Can I give him to you?" Sarah asked her husband.

"Sure. Careful. I don't him to wake up and realize I'm

not you."

Steve took the sleeping bundle of fur and feathers and looked down at the motionless griffin. It had its paws curled up under its body and its two tiny wings were folded flat against its back. It squeaked a little but otherwise remained asleep. Sarah felt an immediate increase in heat from her husband and realized Steve must have increased his jhorun to help keep the cub warm.

"So what happens if it does wake up?" Steve wanted to know.

"His name is Emerion," Sarah told him as she rubbed the painful kinks out of her arms. "And I really don't know what he'll do. I'll stick close to you. I'm pretty sure he trusts me. No offense."

Steve nodded. "None taken. What are we supposed to feed him?"

"Well, he ate this dead mouse thing earlier, followed by some type of small lizard. I assume we can feed him things like that."

"You assume? You mean you don't know either?"

Sarah pushed open the amethyst front doors. "I really don't. We have to play this by ear."

"I thought the plan was to give the cub to its father?"

Sarah shrugged. "That *was* the plan." She repeated what the other griffins had said about Nyx's mate and his cruelty.

"To hell with that."

"Which is precisely why I brought him with me. However, that is a matter for the griffins. I will not let the cub be given to his sire. So, he's coming with us."

"But … you expect us to raise a griffin? In Idaho?"

"We have a lot of land," Sarah reminded him. "We have nearly five hundred acres of wide, open space. It's more than enough room to raise a griffin. Couple that with the absence of neighbors, and I'd say it's perfect."

"A lack of neighbors would be your doing," Steve said, grinning. "You're the reason everyone thinks the manor is haunted. Luther must've bought the neighbors' land."

"That's still a sore spot," Sarah confessed, giving him a frown. "What about those poor people that *were* living near us? They're all gone. We came back to find that there were no houses around us at all."

Steve sighed. "It's in the past. There's nothing we can do about it now."

She paused, held a finger to her lips, and pointed at the Fae queen. Ria was gesturing at the trunk of the tree and giving Thinian instructions. They watched as their Fae companion squatted down on the ground.

"Start there at the base," the Fae queen instructed, pointing at a spot on the ground near the middle of the trunk. "The pollen needs to be spread evenly around the Tree. Every reference state the pollen must be administered around the entire circumference of the Tree."

"There isn't much here, Your Majesty," Thinian reminded her. "The trunk is massive. I do not believe we will have enough."

"Use it sparingly," Ria instructed. "If it must be one or two drops every three feet then so be it. What's important is that the pollen circle be complete."

Thinian nodded, uncorked the small vial of golden liquid, and carefully tapped the side of the vial. Once a single pure drop had fallen onto the ground he took a step, administered another drop, and repeated the process until he had traversed the entire tree's huge trunk. He held the vial up to the queen to show that there was still some left.

Ria held up a hand to wait. Everyone held their collective breaths as they watched the tree with eager anticipation. Nothing happened.

"Circle it again," the queen instructed. "We went to such great lengths to retrieve the pollen that we shouldn't let any go to waste."

Thinian nodded and started again. The moment the Fae started on the second pass around the trunk, Sarah noticed the drops of pollen begin to glow. Within a few seconds, a glowing golden ring of light had appeared around the entire tree.

The glowing ring of light melted into the earth and disappeared from sight. Husband and wife shared a look. Was that it? Was it cured? Sarah squinted up at the huge tree. It was still brown and devoid of most of its foliage.

"Is that it?" Steve whispered. "Talk about being anticlimactic."

Sarah glanced uncertainly over at the queen. Ria was staring up at the tree with the saddest expression. The Fae queen must have expected more. Was it over now?

Sarah's eyes filled with tears. Steve nudged her shoulder but she angrily brushed him off. Now wasn't the time for her husband to offer some sarcastic bit of humor to lighten the mood. Her friends were going to die and it was their fault.

She felt a tap on her shoulder. Her tear-streaked face looked up into her husband's, but his eyes were trained on a spot near the trunk of the tree. Then she heard Ria gasp with surprise.

A tiny sapling, growing near the base of the trunk, was giving off a golden glow. In fact, the tiny plant looked as though it was made of pure gold. *And it was growing!*

The sapling wrapped itself around the trunk and began a helical ascent up the tree. The trunk of the Fae's home tree started to glow at every point the glowing sapling made contact.

Sarah hurried to the queen's side. Ria clasped her hand and they both stared. It was as if someone had begun adding color to the Tree, starting at the trunk and working their way upward, in time with the growth of the sapling. Then they heard something that made them giddy with excitement: the Tree was making noise. It was *swaying*.

Sarah hastily wiped her eyes with a corner of her sleeve. They had done it after all! The Tree was going to survive! It was getting its health back, right before her eyes.

"Houston, we have a problem."

Sarah's eyes snapped over to her husband's.

"What is it? What's the matter?"

"It's slowing down," Steve told her. "The rate of growth for the glow is decreasing. I hate to say it, babe, but it looks like it's not going to make it to the top."

"But it has to!" Sarah cried, looking up at the trunk. Her husband was right. The sapling had slowed as it neared the trunk's halfway point. In a few minutes she estimated that the sapling would halt its ascent altogether.

"So what do we do?" Steve asked. "We can't let it fail now."

"The Tree must be farther gone than we thought," Sarah whispered, thinking hard. "I'm guessing the pollen isn't strong enough."

"If it's not strong enough then what is?" Steve demanded. "There's gotta be something we can do."

"Not strong enough," Sarah slowly repeated. Her eyes widened. "Honey, that's it! We have to make it stronger!"

"Again, I ask, how? It's not like we can make the Tree use a jorii."

"Even if we did have a jhorun amplifier with us, you're right. It wouldn't do any good."

"Then why bring it up?" Steve asked.

"We need to make the sapling stronger. And who do we know who has the ability to enhance jhorun?"

"Mikal," Steve breathed. Her husband risked a glance at the tree. "If you're going to get him, you'd better hurry. The glow is starting to fade at the base."

Sarah muffled a curse, gave her husband a light peck on the cheek, and brought up her tiring jhorun. She visualized the Antechamber back in the castle and made the jump. The Tree, and its partially glowing trunk vanished. Kri'Entu's plush private chamber appeared. There were no guards present. In fact, no one was present at all.

She hurried over to the closed door and knocked a few times. The last thing she wanted to do was startle the guards she knew would be standing on either side of the door. She smiled as she heard a muffled explanation of surprise. The double doors were hastily pulled open. Two baffled guards were staring straight at her.

"I need the prince. Yes, this is an emergency. Please hurry."

The two guards eyed each other. One nodded and hurried off. He was back in less than a minute, escorting … Sarah scowled. That wasn't Mikal.

Captain Pheron nodded. "Milady. I had a feeling you might return. How can I…"

"Pheron! No time to explain! This is an emergency! I need Mikal, like *right now!*"

"You need to speak with His Highness?" Pheron asked, confused. "Perhaps if you could…"

"It's regarding that secret that you're not supposed to be privy to. Please, Pheron. Hurry!"

Pheron's eyes widened. He stifled a curse and hurried off. Sarah glanced over at the two guards, who were dubiously eyeing her back.

"Don't worry about me. You know, secret missions. Middle of the night? They're not as much fun as you might think."

"Are you really the teleporter?" one guard asked.

Judging by his voice Sarah pegged him to be in his late teens. She nodded wearily. The young soldier's helmet disappeared from his head and appeared in her arms. She tossed it back to the wide-eyed soldier.

"That's so cool," the soldier whispered to his companion. "I wish I could do that!"

Pheron returned with not one, nor two, but three people: Mikal, Lissa, and the king, who was once again hastily pulling on his robe. The guards gulped nervously and pulled open the Antechamber doors. Mikal followed his father inside. Lissa hesitated but Sarah forcefully pulled her inside. She indicated for the guards to close the door then hurried over to Mikal.

"I need you to come with me. Right now, no questions asked."

"Are you well, Lady Sarah?" Kri'Entu asked, alarmed by the urgency in her voice.

"I'm fine and so is Steve. Our friends are not."

"It didn't work," the king said quietly, letting out a sigh.

"What didn't work?" Mikal asked curiously, sharing a look with Lissa, who only shrugged.

"It won't if we don't help it," Sarah said. She hooked her arm through Mikal's. "Can I borrow him? I promise to return him as soon as I can."

The king nodded. "Of course. Just make sure he's back in plenty of time for tomorrow. We wouldn't want him to miss anything, would we?"

Sarah smiled. "Absolutely not. Rest assured, we'll return him to you in tip-top shape."

Kri'Entu nodded. "See that you do, Lady Sarah. I would hate to think that he'd be late for… well, we don't need to go into that here. You and Sir Steve will be there, correct?"

"Of course. We wouldn't miss it for the world."

"And the preparations you told me about earlier? Will those be in readiness?"

"Absolutely. I'll take care of it."

"Splendid."

"Your timing is excellent," Mikal said, the instant his father had left the room. "I don't know how much more I could have taken."

Lissa appeared in front of him and crossed her arms across her chest.

"What's going on? What are you two talking about?"

Sarah winked at Mikal and held out her hand.

"We're going west. Are you ready? Deep breath. And here we… Lissa? Would you like to come along? We might even need to use your skills, too."

"Is someone sick?" Lissa asked, rushing forward. "And don't think I've let this matter drop. You two are up to something. I want to know what you're planning."

"If you only knew," Mikal softly murmured.

Sarah had to bite her tongue. With all the excitement and stress of trying to revive the Fae's Tree, she had completely forgotten about other plans. She groaned. Her jhorun was going to require a good night's rest. With all the upcoming teleporting, she would need it at full strength.

"Lissa, take my left hand. Mikal, take my right. Are we ready? Here we go."

Just like that they were standing in front of the Tree. The glow, Sarah was dismayed to learn, was fading fast. There was only a ten-foot section of the sapling which had any glow left on it. As far as its ascent up the trunk, unfortunately, that had come to a complete stop.

"Where are we?" Lissa asked as she looked around. She spied Ria and Thinian on the ground, looking listless. She turned to Sarah "Can you tell me what's wrong with them?

I'll find something that will help. Oh. Sir Steve. Hello. I didn't see you there."

"Hey there, Lissa," Steve returned.

"We already know what will help them," Sarah stated, indicating the huge tree. "We have to fix *that*. Mikal, you're up."

Mikal spun in place and stared up at the huge tree. "What do you need me to do?"

She pointed out the situation. "We need to boost the sapling and we need to hurry. Can you help us?"

Without a second's hesitation Mikal rushed forward and slapped his hands on the Tree's massive trunk.

"I'm not sensing any jhorun in the tree at all. Then again, I don't typically sense jhorun in any pontal, so I'm not really too surprised."

Sarah frantically pointed at the golden sprout.

"Don't try to boost the Tree but rather boost the sapling! Hurry!"

Mikal knelt down and placed his hands on the base of the sapling. His brow furrowed as he concentrated. Lissa appeared next to Sarah's side. "Look! The tree is starting to glow!"

Lissa was right. The sapling had indeed started to glow again. As before, the glow gently spread to the trunk, making it glow wherever contact was made. The sprout slowly snaked its way up the trunk. It wasn't growing as fast as before, but at least it was growing.

Sarah sighed with relief. At least the Tree appeared to be out of danger. It had resumed its swaying and was in the process of growing new foliage on the lower branches.

She looked over at her husband. He had Emerion in his arms and was gently swaying in time with the tree. Nyx would be proud. Of her. Of Steve. Of her decision to keep the cub out of harm's way by raising him on their world. It would be a challenge, yes, but she was sure she and her husband could pull it off.

Then she remembered Loryss and the promise they'd made to her.

Sarah sighed. She was exhausted, both mentally and

physically. Could she ask her husband to handle this one? Would he be capable of locating Loryss' flock and subtly asking about a specific griffiness? What would he do if he *did* find her? Would he be discreet? How would he react if confronted by a mob of angry griffins?

Her arms and legs cramped at the thought of moving. And if she tried to coax her jhorun further, she'd jeopardize her plans for tomorrow's festivities. She had made too many promises already. Whether she liked it or not this one would have to fall to her husband.

"I agree," Steve quietly told her.

Startled, Sarah looked up to see him squatting down next to her. The young griffin was still sound asleep in his arms.

"I think you were dozing," her husband told her.

"Really? Wow. And what are you, a mind reader now?"

"You're tired, babe. It's not too hard to figure out you're thinking about Loryss. Mikal is taking care of the tree. What say I go find Loryss' mate and make sure the griffin who poisoned her isn't her mate's new girlfriend?"

"You don't know where—"

"And neither do you. I either have to do this tonight or it'll have to be done tomorrow morning. Something tells me you won't want me to be preoccupied tomorrow, will you?'

Sarah smiled at him, "You're right, I won't. Fine. You go see if you can find Loryss' mate. Do you have any idea how you're going to accomplish that? They're probably all asleep by now."

"Leave that to me. I'm going to call in some favors." Her husband gave her a cryptic smile, passed the sleeping griffin cub to her, and kissed her tenderly on her cheek.

"Don't wait up for me. I'll be back as soon as I can."

She sputtered, but without breaking stride, Steve turned to look at her. He winked.

"Trust me."

* * *

"Stop your fretting."
"Wearisome, it is."

"Sorry," Steve apologized, sighing as he stretched his back. "It's just that I've never ridden a dragon your size before. I'm not exactly a small guy. I don't want to hurt you."

"We have carried much heavier burdens than you," the first voice informed him.

"When?" the second voice asked.

"Do you not remember when our treasure horde was returned last year?" the first voice asked, casting a scornful look at his twin. "Our gold alone is heavier than he is."

"Not by much," the second voice grumped.

Steve stared at the owner of the voices with a bemused expression on his face. "Okay, listen. I'm sorry, I know you've already told me. Several times, in fact. Which one of you is Dirgath and which one is Tirgath?"

The zweigelan dragon turned both necks and stared back at him with four sets of eyes.

"I am Dirgath," the left head reported.

"And I am Tirgath," the right head answered.

"So what were you just saying, Tirgath?" Steve asked, raising an eyebrow.

"That I never believed humans could be so heavy," Tirgath admitted.

Steve laughed. "I do believe you're calling me a fatass."

"Promised his Lordship, we did," Dirgath reminded him.

"Aye, I know," the zweigelan's left head snapped.

"Promised who *what*?" Steve wanted to know.

"You have the ear of the Dragon Lord," Dirgath explained. "His lordship favors you. Treat you well, he made us promise."

"You're helping me out in the middle of the night," Steve reminded his wyverian friends. "That more than constitutes compliance in my book."

"Appreciated, it is," Tirgath admitted.

"Quite frankly I was surprised that Kahvel, er, the Dragon Lord even answered me. It was late. I could only hope that you dragons don't sleep as much as us humans."

"We don't," Dirgath confirmed.

"Meditate, we do," Tirgath added.

Steve blinked. Meditate? Dragons meditate? He shrugged.

You learn something new every day.

"So how have you two enjoyed being part of the Collective? The last time I saw you was when we were all battling to remove the curse that kept you dragons grounded."

"Remember that well, we do," Dirgath told him. The zweigelan's right wing dipped and they turned south. "Would prefer not to discuss the matter, we do."

"Agreed," Tirgath added.

"Enjoy contact with others, we will admit," Dirgath said. Tirgath nodded. "Never realized how lonely it was without the company of our brothers and sisters."

"I'll bet," Steve agreed.

He glanced up at the night sky. Thankfully the moon was out. Once more Steve's eyes were drawn to the stars. He shook his head as he scanned the heavens, looking for familiar constellations. As always, he failed. The night sky here was so different to their home in Coeur d'Alene, Idaho. He wondered yet again if there was some way to get from Lentari to his home world without the use of magic.

He shrugged. He probably wouldn't ever know.

"Ridden many dragons, have you?" Dirgath asked, breaking the silence.

"Never ridden the likes of us, I'll wager," Tirgath added.

"I've ridden plenty of dragons," Steve informed his traveling companion. "Never one as unique as you. Or as cool. I'm truly honored Kahvel assigned you as my guide."

"No one knows this area better than I," Dirgath stated.

"Except for me," Tirgath contradicted. "I know it better. I always have. Jealous of me, you are."

Steve stared at the two heads with a bemused expression on his face. "And you know where you're going?" he asked.

"You wish to speak with Ceraeon, is that not so?" Dirgath asked.

Steve nodded. "Right. You said you know him?"

Both wyverian heads nodded. "We do," Tirgath said. "Was being groomed to be the next Prime, he was."

"He may be Prime now," Dirgath added.

"How many Primes are there?" Steve asked. "The only thing I know about the griffins is that there is no main Prime."

"We know of only three in the northern mountains," Dirgath answered. "Ceraeon is a member of the largest."

Steve repeated, nodding. "Do I want to know how you know him? You know what? None of my concern."

"Many dragons live in the mountains," Dirgath reminded him. "Many have contact with other species. It is not unreasonable to believe that the wyverians would have business with the griffins."

Remembering Sarah's story about Emerion's father, Steve swallowed nervously. "What can you tell me about this Ceraeon character? Is he nice? Mean? Quick to lose his temper?"

"Unknown," Dirgath said. "Find out soon enough, you will. We approach griffin territory. Behold. We have already been spotted."

Steve sat up straight. "We have? Where?"

"Two sentries, nearly a quarter league apart," Tirgath growled. "Both have taken to the air."

"They are on an intercept course," Dirgath advised. "Be prepared, fire thrower."

"Be prepared?" Steve sputtered. "For what? It's too damn dark out there. I probably couldn't hit the broad side of a barn. Hey, what do we have to worry about? We've come in peace."

"Know that, they do not," Tirgath said.

They landed in a small glade and waited. Steve slid off the zweigelan's back and generated a large chaser.

"What do we do now?" Dirgath wanted to know as he looked cautiously around at the silent trees.

A loud squawk echoed thunderously throughout the small clearing. Steve flinched and automatically ignited his hands. With a curse, he flicked them out.

"Who are you?" one of the griffins called out to them, as he safely circled, high above their heads. "Be you friend or foe?"

Both zweigelan heads turned to look expectantly at Steve.

"Friend," Steve called out. "We've come in peace."

"Then extinguish your fire sphere," the second griffin challenged, joining his companion in the sky above them.

"I wouldn't be able to see a thing," Steve told the griffins. "You guys may have been born with nocturnal vision but I have not."

"You control the fire?" the first griffin asked.

In response, the fireball jetted over to Steve and smoothly separated itself into three smaller spheres, which he began juggling. He ended his pyrotechnical demonstration by tossing the three fireballs back into the air and merging them. The newly reformed fireball returned to its position in the sky.

"Very well," the first griffin conceded. "Your identity has been confirmed. We know who you are. What do you want, fire thrower? Why do you travel with a zweigelan?"

"Dirgath and Tirgath are here to introduce me to a member of your flock. I'm here to talk with Ceraeon. Can you tell me where he is?"

"Ceraeon is our Prime," the second griffin stated. "He is not to be disturbed."

"It's a matter of life and death. Well, mostly death. Loryss is already dead so... Look, we don't need to get into that right now. I know it's late but can you go get him for me? He'll want to hear this."

"I do not know if he'll wish to speak with you," the first griffin said, ruffling his wings.

"How do you know that name?" the second griffin suspiciously asked. It tucked its wings and landed in the clearing less than ten feet from Steve.

"Wasn't Loryss the name of the Prime's mate?" the first griffin asked, completely ignoring the others. "The one who died under mysterious circumstances?"

"Aye. It has never set well with the Prime. He wanted answers and found none."

"I have answers," Steve interjected, startling both griffins. "I know what happened. That's why I'm here. I need to let Ceraeon know."

"Go get the Prime," the second griffin told the first. "The human is correct. He would want to know."

The first griffin took to the air and disappeared.

Ten minutes later nearly a dozen griffins were standing

before them. One, larger than the rest and carrying his head high, approached Steve and inclined his head. Steve nodded back.

"Fire Thrower. You are known to us."

"That's just great," Steve muttered under his breath.

"What was that?" the Prime demanded. "Do you offer us insult?"

Steve held up his hands in the friendliest manner he could think of.

"No, sorry. No insult intended. I really don't mean anyone harm, yet it seems like all I'm remembered for is the guy who attacked a group of griffins several years ago. It was just a big misunderstanding."

"I was referring to your remarkable jhorun," the Prime clarified. "What is this about harming a griffin?"

"It happened years ago. I've since apologized. Humans and griffins have become friends. It's old news. Now, are you Ceraeon?"

The Prime nodded. "That is my name, aye."

"You obviously remember Loryss, right?"

The Prime squawked with surprise. "Of course I remember her. She was my former mate. We never knew any humans. How is it you know of her?"

Steve looked at the Prime's entourage and swallowed nervously.

"Can I speak with you alone, in private? I'll tell you how I know her but this is for your ears only."

"It's a trap, Sire," one griffin insisted. "I trust this not. Allow us to remain by your side."

Ceraeon turned to his companions. "He's the Fire Thrower. If he wanted to cause us harm, he would have done so by now."

Steve nodded. "That's true. And no, I wouldn't, by the way."

"I will speak to you in private. Leave us."

All but the Prime took to the air and disappeared into the night. Ceraeon looked over at Dirgath and Tirgath, shrugged, and turned back to Steve. He cocked his head and waited, silently.

"I've met Loryss, just a few hours ago," Steve told him.

"Impossible," the griffin scoffed. "She died months ago not one to be messed."

"Exactly. I, er, met her on, uhh … hoo-boy. I met her on Ranal."

As Steve had expected, the Prime's eyes opened wide and he squawked angrily. "What you speak of is impossible. No human has ever set foot on Ranal. Only those—"

"…that feel the Pull will be able to make their Final Journey," Steve finished for him, trying unsuccessfully to keep the exasperation from his voice. "I know. Look, I'm sorry. Usol is not one to be messed with."

The Prime continued to regard him as though he had sprouted feathers. Steve spent the next ten minutes outlining their experiences on Ranal, ending with the announcement they needed someone to do them a favor.

"Loryss won."

"She would," the Prime clucked to himself. "She has always been a tenacious one. It's what I admired about her. Wait. She wanted a favor from you? What was it, if I may ask?"

Steve nodded. "You may. It's why I'm here. She says she was poisoned."

Ceraeon shook his head. "Not possible. Never has such a heinous crime been committed by a griffin."

"These are her words, buddy, not mine. She believes she was poisoned and wanted to warn you."

"Did she say who she suspected?" Ceraeon asked.

Steve drew a blank. "Damned if I can remember her name but I do remember this griffiness had wings of black and blood red feathers."

"Hemera," Ceraeon whispered dangerously. "You accuse the one who will be my mate of murdering my former mate?"

"I'm sorry, pal," Steve apologized. "I'm just relaying Loryss' suspicions. She said you deserved a better mate than one who would kill to get what she wanted."

"Did she say how she was poisoned?" Ceraeon wanted to know.

Steve nodded. "Yes. Spiny coneflower pods. She woke

up and found them at the nest. She thought you had brought them. Knowing you'd never hurt her, she ate them."

"Without realizing what they were," Ceraeon groaned. The Prime glanced upward at the night sky and squawked three times. He looked back at Steve. "Those are serious accusations."

"I know they are. I wish I had better news, but that was our promise to Loryss. She helped us, in exchange for warning you."

Two griffins landed nearby.

"Bring Hemera here at once," Ceraeon ordered.

The Prime watched the griffins disappear before he eyed Steve once more.

"I should have known. Loryss was getting her strength back. She was getting better. I checked on her before I left the following morning and she was fine. I returned several hours later to find her dead. I *knew* something wasn't right."

"So, you believe me?" Steve asked.

"I found the remnants of a seedpod, but didn't think anything of it at the time. Hemera is one of the healers. She is very familiar with local pontal and its location. She would know where to find those accursed pods."

"But how do you know if she's ultimately responsible?" Steve asked. "We would need proof."

"We will allow Hemera to provide us with proof."

"How?" Steve asked.

"Watch and learn, human."

Ten minutes later the two griffins were back, escorting a third. Steve had let the large chaser dim as he and the Prime had been talking. Now that Loryss' suspected killer had arrived, Steve wanted to see the color of her wings for himself. Half a dozen additional fireballs flared, scattered throughout the small glade.

Steve caught a glimpse of the third griffin's wings--black and dark red. This *had* to be the griffiness Loryss had warned them about. He inadvertently clenched his fists, igniting both of them, flicking them out a moment later.

"What is the meaning of this, Ceraeon?" the female griffin demanded. "Why do you summon me at this hour?"

Ceraeon extended a wing and pointed at Steve. "This human has leveled some serious accusations at you."

Steve snorted. This wasn't what he had expected. Hemera started to advance on him.

"I will not allow a human, *any human*, to cast aspersions at me," the female griffin snapped. "Prepare to defend yourself!"

Steve ignited both hands; Tirgath and Dirgath growled a warning. The griffiness paused. Steve gave the silver zweigelan a friendly pat and continued to eye Loryss' killer. He decided to leave his hands ignited.

"What is a dragon doing here?" Hemera screeched. "What treachery is this?"

"There is no treachery," Ceraeon contradicted. "The dragon is the human's companion."

"We prefer to think of the human as *our* companion," Tirgath softly snorted.

Steve grinned and knocked a fist against the zweigelan's front talons. Tirgath turned to look at Steve with confusion written all over his face.

"It's a fist bump," Steve explained. "It's what friends do to signify their willingness to back each other up. You two have my back and I have yours."

Both wyverian heads nodded.

"Why have you sent for me?" Hemera asked again.

"Would you care to explain to me why you placed spiny coneflower pods into my nest several months ago?"

Steve might not have spoken—or understood—the griffin language but even he could tell that the noise from Hemera was an expletive. Ceraeon's mouth opened with surprise. One of the other griffins let out a tremulous squawk.

"Impossible," Hemera whispered, shocked. "There were no witnesses, except perhaps…"

"Loryss?" Steve casually asked.

"Aye, no one except … Ceraeon, let me explain."

"What is there to explain?" the Prime raged. "You coveted her position as my mate. You took it upon yourself to remove her from my side. You made yourself available to me the moment the flock learned of Loryss' passing. I should have seen this."

"She didn't deserve you!" Hemera screeched. Her wings extended and she took a threatening step toward Ceraeon. Every griffin present leapt to their Prime's defense. "I am a better match for you. I will serve you better!"

Ceraeon's head slowly pivoted toward Steve. "Human, we will take our leave of you. I do not require your assistance any further. I thank you for bringing this to my attention."

"Thank Loryss. In her words, you deserve someone better."

"I will honor her always," Ceraeon promised, bowing before Steve.

Steve nodded and gave the zweigelan a nudge. "Are you guys up? It's time to go."

"It's about time," Tirgath grumped. "Want to listen to more trivial griffin matters, I do not."

"I concur," Dirgath agreed.

Thirty minutes later, they were nearing the western coast of Lentari. Steve let out an exclamation of surprise. Since when did the western coast of Lentari have its own nightlight? He could see a bright golden glow that must have been visible for miles in all directions. Steve grunted. It had to be the Fae's island. Was that the tree that was giving off that glow? Did that mean Mikal had worked his magic on it?

Indeed, one island was giving off a healthy golden glow. Using it as a navigational beacon, they easily returned to the Fae's island. As expected, the glow was coming from the Tree. The huge evergreen looked to be coated in solid gold and luxurious foliage all the way to the top, several thousand feet off the ground.

The zweigelan set him down in the familiar clearing where Sarah had awoken only a few days ago. Steve gave the friendly two-headed dragon another fist bump, which Dirgath tried to clumsily replicate. After a few unsuccessful attempts, the zweigelan let out twin grunts and launched themselves back into the air.

Steve turned to study the clearing where Sarah had originally been brought and whistled with amazement. Had it only been two days? From the simple, but laughable, purpose of enjoying a few quiet days together in Lentari, his and

Sarah's excursion had become anything but that.

A firefly buzzed by his nose. Steve absentmindedly brushed a hand over his face. The blasted bug had been so close that he was briefly surprised that it hadn't done a visual inspection of his nasal cavities. He snorted. What an unpleasant prospect that would have been.

The bug dove by him again. Steve scowled. He took a swing, certain he was looking much like King Kong attacking encroaching airplanes. The bug flew off. He looked around the clearing, surprised to see fireflies everywhere–dancing through the trees, hovering just above the ground, some were being chased by hordes of others.

Odd. He didn't remember seeing any of the glowing bugs moment ago. He felt a slight tingling sensation on his arm. A quick check confirmed one of the bugs had landed on him. He'd be damned if he was going to let himself be bitten. Of all the infernal luck! He prepared to flick the offending insect off his arm when he paused. Since when do bugs stand up on two legs? He brought his arm up for a closer look.

A tiny human form, glowing with a blue-white light was waving excitedly at him.

It was a faerie! They were back, and they were flying!

Clearly Mikal and his jhorun had properly resuscitated that gold tentacle thing and enabled it to finish doing *its* job on the Tree. So where was Sarah now?

He eyed the faerie on his arm. It was female, and she was sitting down, swinging her legs, as if his arm was a log in the forest. She waved toward the flickering lights, and two other faeries joined her.

He shrugged. Fine. If they wanted a free ride, so be it. He had to find Sarah.

Steve headed toward the glow, thinking Sarah and the queen would be at the Tree trunk. When he got there, however, he was dismayed to see no one. He craned his neck to look up into the glittering golden foliage of the tree. He briefly wondered if the Fae's Tree would forever look like it was made of solid gold. In its brilliant state, it would surely attract the attention of the humans. If the Fae wanted to remain hidden, this wasn't the way to do it.

Another Fae landed on his arm, followed immediately by another, and another. Within seconds he had at least a dozen Fae sitting on each arm. One Fae on his right arm broke away from the group and quickly walked up to his right shoulder. A tiny hand gripped his earlobe and he finally heard one of the tiny winged figures speak.

"I bid you greetings, human!"

It was a voice Steve recognized. "Hey there, Thinian. How's it goin', pal? It's nice to see you up and flying around. I can only assume your Tree is back to full strength. Congrats! That was too close for comfort."

"Tell me about it," the Fae agreed. "I cannot begin to tell you how elated I feel, having full use of my wings again. When you're a Fae, and you've danced on the backs of the gentlest zephyrs, being grounded was the equivalent of a death sentence."

"Melodramatic much?" Steve asked, grinning at the Fae.

"I'm not familiar with that term," Thinian returned.

"Forget it. Where is everyone?"

"Their royal majesties are seeing to their people. Many were at death's door."

"Do you know where Sarah is? Or Mikal?"

"The human prince and his princess are seeing to the infirm. As for Lady Sarah, she awaits your return. Come. I will show you."

Thinian flew off his shoulder and headed into the heart of the tree. Steve followed Thinian's tiny glowing form as he vanished down a tunnel leading away from the entrance. Everywhere he looked he could see smiling faeries, now human-sized. Confused, Steve glanced through each open doorway and saw more of the same thing: full-sized faeries performing proper castle duties.

Steve rounded a bend and saw that Thinian had become human-sized. "Hey, I have a question for you,"

"Oh? What is your question?"

"What's the deal with your size? One minute I have nearly a dozen faeries sitting on my arm and the next we're passing the kitchen where people are cooking. And… I see wings, so I know they're all faeries."

"And you wish to know why I am not presently smaller than you? Or perhaps why we are not glowing?"

Steve nodded. "Well, yeah. When we were on Ranal you could sit on my shoulder. Hell, you were doing just that only a few minutes ago. What's the deal? Can you change your size at will?"

"How do you know you're not the same size as a Fae?" Thinian countered, trying unsuccessfully to hide a cryptic smile. "For all you know you were shrunk as soon as you stepped foot on this island."

"You were sitting on my arm. Try again."

"We can change our size accordingly," Thinian finally said, after remaining silent for a few seconds. "Whether we increase our mass to the equivalent of a human or shrink ourselves to the same level as the Alluin, our size is entirely of our own doing."

"The Alluin?" Steve repeated, puzzled. "Who are they?"

"A very peculiar species who only wish to… Ah. Here we are. Lady Sarah, your champion has arrived."

They arrived in a large chamber that Steve could see had been turned into a hospital of sorts. There were rows of cots filling the room with most of them holding patients. Faeries outfitted in bright yellow were tending them. There was Sarah, standing next to the queen. Sarah looked over at him as he entered the room and smiled warmly.

"There you are! We were beginning to worry about you!"

Steve started toward his wife, then turned back to Thinian and held out a hand. Once the Fae had grasped his forearm, Steve grinned. He gripped Thinian's hand tightly in his own and gave his jhorun the order to ignite his hands.

Thinian let out a yelp and tried to pull his hand away. Steve's grip was stronger and he held on. He let his flames burn for a few seconds before he extinguished them.

"Now we're even."

Thinian was confused. "For what? What have I done to you?"

"Who are the Alluin?"

Thinian nodded with comprehension, grinned, and gave him a small bow.

"I see your point. Thank you for all your help. I won't ever forget it, friend Steve."

"Take it easy, pal," Steve jovially returned. He detected movement in his peripheral vision and saw that Sarah was now standing before him.

"What was that for?" Sarah demanded. "I've half a mind to knock some sense into you. That was rude!"

"No, it wasn't," Steve argued. "It was just two guys getting even with each other. No harm done."

"What did he ever do to you?" Sarah asked, perplexed.

"What are the Alluin?" Steve countered.

"What was that?"

"What—or who—are the Alluin? Ever hear of them?"

Sarah shook her head. "No. What are they?"

"That's what Thinian was in the process of telling me when we made it in here and he dropped the subject. Little turd. Now I'm curious as hell."

Sarah giggled. "Curious enough to research it in the Archives?"

Steve vehemently shook his head. "Oh, *hell* no. You couldn't pay me to go back in there to see that old crone again. Where's Mikal?"

Sarah turned to point at the far corner of the chamber. Mikal was laying in one of the cots, resting. Lissa sat quietly nearby, reading a book.

"What happened? Is he okay?"

"He expelled a lot of his jhorun making certain that sapling finished the job," Sarah quietly explained. "He told me he hadn't ever felt so drained before."

"Did he have any problems?" Steve asked, curious.

"Only when he tried to take his hands off that sapling," Sarah told him. "Every time he did, the glow would start to fade. So, he had to sit there, hunched over, for more than an hour. Aside from a backache and a practically drained jhorun, he seems to be okay. What about you? Tell me about Loryss. Were you able to find her mate?"

Steve gave her a recap of everything that had happened, starting with the moment he stepped outside and contacted Kahvel and ending with discovering the faeries had regained the use of their wings.

"I am *so* glad you were able to warn him," Sarah said, sliding her arm into his. She led him toward the queen. "Did Ceraeon say what he was going to do?"

"I got the distinct impression it wasn't going to be pretty," Steve answered. "He promptly told me that it was now a griffin issue and he didn't need me hanging around anymore."

"Ah. Got it."

"Wish I could've seen the instant the Tree returned to health," Steve said. "Did you see it? What happened?"

"It was such a wonderful thing," Sarah wistfully sighed. "As soon as that sapling made it to the top of the Tree the whole thing began to glow. Ria was leaning against me because she didn't have the strength to keep herself upright. The next moment she was leaping to her feet as though she were a ballerina! Her wings appeared and she rose off the ground. And then I heard it."

"Heard what?" Steve asked, leaning close.

"Singing. I could only assume the Fae started to sing as they got their strength back. It was so wonderful and magical! I will never forget those voices. Ever."

"That was the voice of our Tree, Lady Sarah," a male voice said from behind them.

Husband and wife turned to see the Fae king and queen.

"Thanks to you," Tivan was saying, "our Tree will live to sing countless more songs. We are in your debt."

"Now and for all time," Ria agreed.

As one, the Fae king and queen bowed. Almost immediately all conversation ceased. Everyone who was able also bowed.

"Is your Tree going to be golden now?" Steve asked.

"If it is, I welcome it," Tivan answered.

"As do I," Ria added. "The health of our tree has been restored. I do not care what color it is."

"What about the outside world?" Sarah asked. "Isn't it bound to attract visitors?"

"Let them come," Tivan warmly answered. "We would welcome the company."

"Really?" Sarah asked, surprised. "I'm shocked, but in a

good way. Good for you, Your Majesty."

"Life is too precious," Ria added. "I never want to hide again. From anyone."

Tivan embraced her and they moved off, stopping at each cot. Steve pointed over at Mikal and Lissa. Mikal was now sitting up in his cot and holding Lissa's hand.

"What about tomorrow?" Steve asked, worried.

"What about it?" Sarah wanted to know. "He's not going to be needing his jhorun tomorrow. He'll be too preoccupied to notice anything else, trust me."

"Are you sure?" Steve asked.

"We certainly were," Sarah reminded him. "What do you expect? Weddings have a tendency to do that to people."

Chapter 14 — Off the Market

D on't forget to bring it. I get so little chance to wear it that I'm not about to pass up an opportunity. Especially when it's for something as cool as this."

Sarah groaned and rolled her eyes. "There's absolutely no reason to have that thing strapped to your back. Besides, you don't even know how to use it."

"Regardless, it'd be only proper," her husband argued.

Sarah laughed, crossed her arms over her chest, and sat down on the corner of the bed in their cabin.

"Proper? Explain yourself. When would it be *proper* to wear a sword on your back?"

"When you happen to be dressing up for a formal ceremony here. In Lentari. A land where it's perfectly acceptable to have a medieval weapon strapped to your belt. Or to your back. Lest you forget, I earned that sword fighting the guur. Besides, the dwarves are sending representatives. What if Maelnar is there? What would he think if I *didn't* have Mythrin with me? I think the least I could do is to wear it as an homage to our friends from Down Under."

Sarah shook her head in exasperation. "I told you to stop referring to them like that. Down Under refers to Australia, not the dwarven realm."

"If they're gonna call us Topside then I get to call them Down Under."

Sarah giggled. "You're just being a goofball."

Steve grinned and shrugged.

"If Rhenyon isn't wearing his, you're taking it off," Sarah decided. "Agreed?"

Steve's smile melted. He reluctantly nodded his head, but not before crossing his fingers behind his back. "Fine. Agreed."

Sarah pointed an accusatory finger. "No warning him, either. I know that sword allows you to contact each other."

"Fine, fine. You win."

Her husband fell silent as she returned her attention to her wardrobe. What should she wear? It wasn't every day a formal occasion presented itself in Lentari.

"Why don't you bring the dragon sword, too?" Steve idly suggested, clearly demonstrating that his mind was still elsewhere. "Then I could wear 'em both. That'd be cool, wouldn't it?"

"I am not bringing back both of those swords," she informed him. "You'll have to make do with just the one sword."

Grinning, Steve nodded. "Okay, just the one, then. You win, dear."

Sarah blinked with surprise. "Wait, what? Did you just sucker me into dropping my argument to get your green sword by trying to suggest I should bring back both of them?"

Steve nodded and tapped the side of his head.

"Don't even think you've won this one," Sarah laughed.

"Look, you have to go back and get Lia and Adam anyway, right?"

"What about your parents?" Sarah argued. "What about mine? What about Annie and Tristan and the kids? I have a lot of people I need to get from our world to here."

"All the more reason you should bring Mythrin on your

first trip. I've got all those mimets charged up. Something tells me you're going to need to recharge your jhorun a few times before all this is said and done. Wait. You know what? Why don't you just use the portal at our house? Why not just get everyone to the manor and then you can use our portal to bring them all here."

"Except the portal won't bring them to the right place," Sarah reminded him. "If we use our key, we'll get the forest. If I use the king's, I'll get R'Tal. The ceremony is being held in Capily. That's on the west coast."

"Oh. That's right. I forgot that they decided to have the ceremony in Lissa's village. Why are they doing that again? Mikal is the crown prince. The wedding should be held at the castle. Did I miss something?"

Sarah nodded. "Naturally. Don't you remember Kri'Entu telling us about Gareth's father? He's a water dragon, a shealk. Anyway, Gareth is already there, spending time with him underwater in shealk form. However, he and Mikal are friends. Mikal wanted to make sure he'd be there. So the site was moved from the castle to Capily. It's a good thing, too. From the sounds of it, the ceremony will have to take place outside."

"Are there that many people coming?" Steve asked.

Sarah nodded. "Of course, but that's not the question you should be asking."

"Alrighty. I'll bite. What should I be asking?"

"'*Who* is planning on attending?'" Sarah clarified. "Wyverians, griffins, and dwarves, for starters. Plus we have the shealk. Those are just the species that I know about. All are coming together to honor Mikal and Lissa's wedding."

Steve whistled. "Amazing. Who would've thought that the little boy we first met all those years ago would be getting married? And that we'd be there to witness it. Man alive, time flies when you're having fun."

"If I get everyone to the manor," Sarah suddenly said, surprising her husband into silence, "and use the portal to get everyone to the castle, then I could use the castle's portal to get everyone to Capily. Yes, that's what I'll do. That way I won't drain my jhorun. I wonder why I didn't think of it before."

Steve held up a hand. "Umm, excuse me? Didn't I just suggest that?"

"No, you suggested I use the portal to get to R'Tal and then teleport everyone to Capily. I made your original idea better, making it *my* idea."

"It's a good thing you're cute," Steve grumbled.

Sarah giggled, selected an ornate purple gown, and laid it across the bed. "This one. I think I'll wear this one."

"What time do we need to get going?" Steve asked.

"Like, right now," Sarah answered.

"Already? Okey doke. Let's get a move on. What do you need me to do?"

"You and Rhenyon will see to it that all the guests are on their best behavior. Dragons, dwarves, and griffins are all going to be in the same area. Their history isn't the greatest. They all need to behave themselves."

Steve nodded. "Got it."

* * *

An hour later, a familiar sound filled the smaller chamber adjacent to the castle's Great Hall. Large wooden frames began glowing while a high pitched—but not too unpleasant—chime started to ring. The surface of the portal rippled several times and then turned opaque. A scene of a comfortable sitting room should have appeared except this time all anyone could see was a large group of people in their finest attire. Sarah stepped through the portal first.

"Okay, quickly now. You don't want to get left behind. Mom? Stop staring. It's a portal. I told you it's a portal, even though I'm pretty sure you didn't believe me. Dad, Annie has her hands full. Grab Christopher before he knocks over that suit of armor. Come on, everyone. Don't be afraid. I'm pretty sure it won't close if someone is in the process of stepping through, but why chance it?"

A blonde-haired woman in her forties pushed by Sarah's dumbstruck parents, leaned forward, and snatched Christopher off the ground. The two-year-old squealed with delight.

"Come on, kiddo," the woman told the toddler. "Stick with me. Where's your brother? We're all going to have fun together. Whaddya say?"

Sarah smiled. At least that was one thing she wouldn't have to worry about. With her good friend Lia watching her nephews, it meant her sister, Annie, could rest. She really shouldn't have come, Sarah thought with a frown, as she was eight months pregnant with twins this time. However, her sister had pleaded to not be left behind. Therefore Tristan, ever the devoted husband, had refused to leave her side, even for a moment.

Once Annie and her family finally crossed over into Lentari, Sarah waved over Steve's parents, Stan and Bonnie Miller of Phoenix. The Millers, Sarah remembered, had been to Lentari once before. It had been the celebration of Celestia's defeat back when she and Steve had stopped being Mikal's bodyguards.

"This is all so amazing," Bonnie said, clutching her husband's arm tightly in hers. "We're going to a wedding on another world! Let's see if the girls at my bridge club can top that one!"

"You haven't told them about Lentari, have you?" Stan asked, shocked.

"Of course, I have. Oh, stop your fretting. No one ever believes me."

Sarah smiled. Her parents were the last to cross over. Her mother, ever since learning both her daughters had been to a magical land, had been desperate to be included. She was sure that Sue was secretly hoping she'd get her own jhorun the moment she stepped foot on Lentari, much like what she had thought had happened to Annie. Her father, Martin, had taken the news they had been invited to attend Mikal's wedding with aplomb. Sarah had shaken her head when, after informing her father that he was accompanying her and Steve to Lentari, he had only smiled and said, "Neat." Nothing seemed to rattle the man, Sarah thought. Perhaps seeing a dragon in the flesh? She nodded. That ought to do it.

"Everyone stay with me," Sarah ordered, as she noticed several members of her group had inched closer toward the door leading into the Great Hall. "We're heading to Capily next. Stay close."

"Where's the portal that'll take us there?" Stan asked.

Sarah hooked a thumb at the portal they had all just stepped through, which had just faded out. It now resembled nothing more than a large carving of the castle. Sarah opened her handbag and retrieved a light, sky-blue colored crystal key. She approached the carved relief of the castle, inserted the key into the keyhole disguised as a window, and activated the portal. Within moments they were looking at the inside of a large office. Visible through the large picture window was a wide open expanse of water. Rolling waves crashed against the shore, sending plumes of water high into the air.

Sarah frowned. The water was choppier than it should be. There wasn't any wind. There weren't even any clouds in the sky. If she didn't know any better, she'd say something large was thrashing about in the surf. Her eyes widened. The shealk! The water dragons were supposed to be in attendance. Was *that* why the waves were so choppy? Were water dragons already here? She risked a glance at her father and smiled. If this didn't surprise him, nothing would.

"Okay, everyone, follow me. The ceremony will be down at the shore."

"Where are we now?" Bonnie asked Lia in a low voice.

"Capily," Lia answered, shifting Christopher from one hip to the other. "It's a gorgeous seaside village. Just about everyone here is a fisherman."

"Have you been here before?"

Lia nodded. "A few times. We're now on the western coast of Lentari."

"Where were we before?" Martin asked, falling into step besides them.

"That was R'Tal, Dad," Sarah answered, overhearing the question. "We were at the castle. It's on the eastern side of the kingdom. Northeastern, if you want to get technical. It's where the king and queen live."

"So you're telling me that we just jumped from one side of the country to the other?" Sue asked, joining the conversation.

Sarah sighed. "Mom. I told you I'm a teleporter. I do this all the time here. You know this. I know you know this. Why are you acting so surprised now?"

Her mother fell silent. When she didn't get an answer Sarah looked over at her. Both of her parents had fallen silent and had come to a stop in the doorway of the Constable's office.

"Mom, Dad, you're blocking the way. Let everyone else out, okay?"

Her father pointed at something she couldn't see. She saw his mouth move but couldn't hear anything. Moments later her mother was pointing, too. Was it a shealk? Perhaps they had spied one of the shealk that were supposed to be in attendance?

Sarah eagerly pushed her way past her parents and came to a stop. She grinned. Well, that would explain the holdup. Nearly a dozen griffins were reclining on the ground a few feet away. Every single griffin had turned and was watching them intently, as though she and her group had just walked into a noisy bar to find it fall deathly quiet. Lying so still on the ground that he could have been mistaken for a statue, one griffin, larger and with a few streaks of gray coloring his otherwise tawny fur, rose to his feet and approached. The older fellow regarded Sarah for a few moments and then bowed his head.

"Lady Sarah. A pleasure as always."

"It talks!" Sue cried, clutching her husband's arm in a death grip. "Omigod! It's talking to us!"

Exasperated, Sarah turned to her mother. "Let's go over this one more time. You're in Lentari. Dragons live here. So do griffins. There's nothing to worry about. In fact, come meet Pheris. Dad, you, too."

Sarah had to resort to pulling her mother's left arm while her father pulled on her right. Once they were standing in front of Pheris, Sarah smiled and curtsied before her griffin friend.

"Hello, Pheris. It's good to see you!"

"And you, Lady Sarah," the griffin returned, bowing low. "Is this your sire?"

Sarah nodded. "Yes. These are my parents. This is Martin and this is Sue, my mother."

The griffin bowed a third time. "It is an honor to meet you all."

Sarah finished introducing the rest of the group before she herded everyone toward the water. There was a lot of activity down at the waterfront and she was anxious to meet her first shealk. She detected a presence by her side and glanced over. It was Lia.

"I can't believe that little booger is getting married," Lia observed. "Seems like only yesterday I was volunteering to help battle that bi— um, mean lady. It was hard to forget. I was accused of being an evil sorceress."

Sarah giggled. "Remember when the dwarves tied you up on that pole harness? Steve and I found you stretched across a giant hearth. I thought the dwarves were going to have you for dinner."

Lia's face soured. "It's kinda hard to forget. What's worse was I had to see your husband laughing at me, like he thought it was the funniest thing in the world."

Sarah tried to stifle a smile. "He remembers that fondly."

"I swear, if he asks me to juggle something, I'm gonna let him have it," Lia vowed.

Her friend moved off, joining her husband, Adam, as they neared the rows of piers. Sarah could see three huge galleons lashed to their berths nearby. Everywhere she looked she could see ships. Row boats, crude canoes, fishing trawlers, ferries, and even large, flat-bottomed boats were tethered. It looked as though not a single boat was out on the water. In fact, Sarah couldn't remember seeing that many boats all in one place before.

A commotion sounded on her right. She glanced over to see her husband and Commander Rhenyon directing traffic. A dozen griffins had just landed and Rhenyon was gesturing to an expanse of open grass to the north. An armed contingent of dwarves appeared next. Sarah traced the line of dwarves back to the Constable's office. They must have arrived right after her group.

Steve pointed at a section of the beach with a number

of chairs set up. One dwarf approached, went down on a knee, and began speaking to her husband. Steve was staring at the dwarf with a bemused expression on his face. He finally squatted down so that he could hear what the dwarf was saying. Sarah sighed. She was too far away to make out what was said. She saw the dwarf point at the beach and then point over at the griffins. Perhaps they wanted to be seated next to them?

Sarah shrugged. She didn't realize that the dwarves and the griffins were allies. She watched Steve shrug and nod his head. The lead dwarf said something to his companions. The rest of the dwarves rushed forward, grabbed the chairs, and hurriedly set them up in a semi-circular formation next to the griffins.

Sarah approached her husband. "What was that all about?"

Steve grinned. "Hey there! Would you believe they want to avoid the shore? Turns out dwarves hate water. They asked to move their chairs further away. Since the majority of the shealk haven't shown up yet, and I'm pretty sure the dwarves aren't allies of the shealk, I thought some distance was in order. Man alive, this is turning out to be a pain."

Steve caught sight of his parents and waved. They promptly waved back. He stretched his back and groaned.

"Let's do a recap, shall we?" Steve turned to point to the south. "The dragons are over there. Griffins and dwarves are okay with them, but guess what? We humans are apparently still scared to death of them."

Sarah frowned. "Didn't you tell the villagers that they're harmless?"

"Yeah, I did. So did Constable Fensham. So did all the king's guards It still didn't work."

"But the dragons are our allies!" Sarah protested. "They shouldn't have to sit apart from the rest of us just because the people are jittery."

"I agree. The dragons volunteered to leave. Holy cow. I've never seen the king so angry. He scolded the entire village. He accused every single villager of embarrassing him, the kingdom, and humanity in general. Kri'Entu went on and on, for at least fifteen minutes straight."

"And their feelings now?" Sarah asked.

"Still nervous, but they dare not speak against the king."

"Good."

"Now, over there," Steve continued, pointing over at a section of wooden boardwalk that stretched up and down the shoreline, "is where the shealk will be. I met Balthor. He seems nice."

"Who's Balthor?" Sarah asked.

"That's Gareth's father. Did you know the shealk have their own wizards? Apparently that's Balthor's role. He can transform himself into a human."

"Well, obviously," Sarah laughed. "Balthor's son is human, isn't he? Wait. Is he? Completely human, that is."

"Yep. I asked that, too. Gareth is completely human, but shares his father's jhorun."

"Which is?" Sarah inquired.

"Spellcasting. Apparently both father and son are whizzes at making spells."

Sarah nodded. "I've seen Gareth at work. So, when does the ceremony start?"

Steve shrugged. "I overheard the king talking to Rhenyon. I think they plan on getting things underway once the rest of the shealk arrive."

"How many more are there supposed to be?" Sarah asked. "Are they all transforming to humans for the duration of the wedding?"

"No. Only Balthor can do that. The rest will be right down there. Do you see that gap in the piers? Fensham had several piers dismantled so that the shealk would have enough room at the water's edge. Their eyesight isn't the best. They have trouble seeing out of the water," Steve explained. "Something about their eyes drying out."

"Got it."

"Looks like your dad was finally surprised."

Sarah clapped excitedly. "I know, right? I've waited a long time to see that."

"Want to see it again? Looks like your parents have caught sight of the dragons."

"Who's over there?" Sarah wanted to know. "Anyone we know so that I can introduce them? Is Kahvel here?"

Steve shook his head. "No. He sends his regrets. He and Pryllan are otherwise occupied. Guess what just hatched?"

Sarah gasped and clutched her husband's hand. "Their egg hatched? Oh, how wonderful! Is it a boy or a girl?"

"It's another girl. Pryllan broke the news to me about thirty minutes ago."

"Do you know any of the dragons that are here?"

Steve nodded. "I know two. Pravara is here, of course. Do you see her over there? She has her back to us at the moment."

Husband and wife watched the dark green dragon turn until she was looking straight at them. Pravara nodded. They nodded back. Sarah nudged Steve's shoulder and pointed at a large red dragon that was nearby.

"Is that Rhamalli?"

Steve nodded. "Yep. He's the other one. I was briefly talking to him earlier. You did know that he has a rider, didn't you?"

"Yes. Mikal told us."

"Rhamalli said that an additional five dragons have requested riders."

"That's good news, right?" Sarah asked.

"Kri'Entu told me just a little bit ago that he's creating some type of Dragon Rider Enlistment program. He said he needs to be certain anyone he recommends to Kahvel will have proven themselves worthy."

"It makes sense," Sarah said. "More dragon riders. That's wonderful! I … hey! Where's Emerion? Is he okay?"

Steve turned to point at a nearby tree. To Sarah's eyes it looked like a large red oak. Resting in the shade of the tree's ample canopy was the young griffin. She could see that he was awake and watching the proceedings with wide, unblinking eyes. Keeping a watchful eye on the cub was none other than Peanut the corgi. The little dog was stretched out in what Steve had called the Sphinx position and only had eyes for the young griffin.

"Peanut is watching him?" Sarah asked. "How in the

world did you manage that?"

"What? Peanut and Emerion? Those two took to each other like peanut butter and jelly. Somehow, and I don't know how, Peanut figured out that Emerion is just a baby. So she's being extra, extra protective. So as long as I keep Peanut in my sights then I'll know Emerion will be nearby."

"What if Emerion decides to get up and take a stroll? I don't want anything to happen to him."

"Corgis are herding dogs," Steve reminded her. "He's already tried a few times. She herds him back to that tree and keeps him there. It's fascinating to watch."

"Have the other griffins said anything?" Sarah asked.

Steve nodded. "As a matter of fact, yes."

"And?" she prompted.

"They all say how cute he is."

"Haven't they asked about his parents?"

"Pheris did. I told them that we are his parents now."

"And they were okay with it?" Sarah asked, dumbfounded. She had expected some of the griffins to have a problem with their adopting the young cub.

"If they were, they didn't say anything."

"I'm shocked. Surprised, even."

Her husband grinned and pointed at the water.

"You're about to be surprised again. Check out who just arrived. That has got to be the coolest thing ever."

Sarah turned to see for herself. Two long serpentine necks had just broken the surface of the water and were now staring at the proceedings. Each neck was at least twenty feet long and each of the shealk heads were silently regarding them. One had dark blue scales covering all of its body while the second had black scales covering everything but its undersides, which were a light blue.

A clamor broke out. Many of the villagers cried out in alarm. Children were snatched up by their parents and whisked safely away.

"We welcome the shealk delegation!" Kri'Entu shouted, raising his voice above all others. "So good of you to join us for these festivities!"

Those villagers in the process of fleeing reluctantly came

to a stop. Constable Fensham appeared at the king's side. He looked as upset and disgusted as the king did.

"My most humble apologies," Steve heard the constable say. "I never knew our people were so … so…"

"Courageous?" Kri'Entu muttered darkly.

Steve stifled a laugh, but not before he caught the king's eye. Kri'Entu sighed, winked at Steve, and faced the two swaying shealk.

"You honor us with your presence. Thank you for coming."

Neither aquatic dragon said anything. There was a pregnant pause as everyone turned to look at the king. Kri'Entu turned to Fensham.

"I'm ashamed to say that I never considered communication to be an issue. I had assumed that we would be able to talk to one another. Do you think they can they understand us, Constable?"

"Not without some help they won't," a new voice announced.

"Who's that?" Sarah quietly asked, pointing to a strange man that was walking toward the king.

"That's Balthor," Steve answered. "He's Gareth's father."

"Elucidate, Mister Balthor," Kri'Entu was saying. "I would like to say hello to your leader."

"Then you'll have to wait for a bit," Balthor informed the king. "Neither of them is my Lord. They are only scouts. Lord Phaedren will be here at any moment."

"Lord Phaedren, leader of the shealk," Kri'Entu breathed. "Please help me communicate with your Lord."

Balthor closed his eyes. His lips moved but no one heard anything. Standing nearly a dozen feet away, Sarah smiled. Like father, like son. Balthor was chanting. He must be formulating a spell that would enable shealk and humans to talk to each other.

Balthor finished, opened his eyes, and smiled at the king. "It is done. The spell will last for two hours. Use the time well."

Kri'Entu looked back at the two shealk in time to see the black water dragon pull its head back into the water. A moment later it reemerged. A few seconds later the second shealk did the same. Balthor tapped the side of his face, indicating his eyes.

"Their eyes dry out. They need to keep submerging them or they will be completely blinded."

Just then five additional shealk heads surfaced. Their long necks rose gracefully from the water. Three shealk spread themselves out on the left while four took the right. There, in the middle, was space for one more.

Right on cue a glittering ruby red shealk head rose from the water. The head rotated left and right as it took in the surroundings. Balthor looked over at the king and inclined his head.

"If you wish to say hello to his Lordship, now would be the time."

Sarah watched the king, along with a handful of his advisors, hurry to the water's edge so that he could introduce himself. Also making her way over, Sarah noted, was Pravara. Deciding she'd like to say hello as well, she hooked her arm through her husband's and pulled him to the water's edge.

"I bid you all hello," Lord Phaedren was saying.

Sarah blinked with surprise. The shealk's voice was soft, musical, and even somewhat enchanting. She immediately wondered what it must be like to live deep beneath the surface. Did they have nests? Did they live together in some type of community? Listening to the shealk's voice made her yearn to find out.

"I'm halfway tempted to jump in the water right about now," her husband said, startling her.

"Why do you say that?" Sarah whispered.

"It was just something that popped into my head. Makes me wonder what you'd find below the surface. That's the Erudian Ocean. Imagine what stories it could tell."

"I feel the same way," Sarah confided.

"We welcome the hospitality offered by the humans," Lord Phaedren said. "Young Pravara, it is good to see you again. Your natural form suits you better, young one."

Pravara nodded once. "Thank you, Lord Phaedren."

More introductions followed. Shealk were introduced to

wyverians. Wyverians were introduced to griffins. Even most of the griffins chose to meet the shealk.

"May we be included?" a deep gruff voice suddenly asked.

Heads turned. Dozens of hushed conversations erupted. Kri'Entu looked, smiled, and bowed.

"Master Maelnar. It is a pleasure, as always. Did you just arrive?"

The dwarf nodded and began pushing his way through the crowd of onlookers. He appeared in front of the king, took off his helmet, and bowed. A quick scowl at his companions had them doing the same.

"Aye. Didn't think we'd make it in time. It would seem a certain wizard we both know misplaced Capily's portal key."

Kri'Entu groaned. "Indeed? All four portal keys were misplaced? How unfortuitous."

Maelnar grinned, reached into his tunic, and held up a sparkling orange key.

"No worries. You granted me permission to commission my own. I suspected there might be a delay with the portal so I finished it only this morning."

Sarah stifled a giggle, drawing Maelnar's eyes to her own.

"Lady Sarah! Sir Steve! Damn glad to see you! Have you been here long?"

"Two days," Sarah said, smiling at their dwarf friend. "We've been here two days."

"Feels like a lot longer," Steve muttered.

"You should take a vacation, lad," Maelnar advised. "You look tired. You, too, lass. If you'd like to take a proper vacation, then may I recommend a wonderful relaxing stay in Foronlir? You haven't lived until you've gazed upon the wonders of the Crystal Caves of Creaphor, or…"

"We might just take you up on that, pal," Steve warmly told the dwarf. "It's been a busy couple of days."

"Is Breslin here?" Sarah asked. "I'd like to say hello if he is."

Maelnar turned and pointed toward the dragons. "He's over there. He told me he wanted to say hello to Rhamalli."

Sarah, keeping her arm looped through her husband's,

turned to head toward the wyverian encampment when a hush fell over the crowd. Griffins, dwarves, shealk, and humans all fell silent. Curious, Sarah turned and her eyes widened.

A large bright blue sphere of light was approaching from across the water, floating several feet off the surface, and was on a direct course toward them. Sarah's eyes filled. She couldn't help it. It could only be the Fae!

Ria and Tivan appeared the moment the sphere made landfall. Both were now human-sized. Ria was wearing a dazzling light green satin gown that seemed to glow with a light of its own. Her gossamer wings, typically hidden under a cloak or tucked out of sight, were extended and proudly displayed. Tivan was wearing a dark forest green suit that complimented Ria's nicely. His wings remained concealed.

"I can't believe they're here!" Sarah whispered excitedly to her husband. "Oh, the king is going to flip out!"

Husband and wife glanced over at the king. Kri'Entu had a shocked expression on his face. Sarah could see that he was looking for the queen, Mikal's mother. Steve nudged her shoulder and pointed up the path toward Constable Fensham's office. Sarah nodded. She could see Ny'Callé chatting with a dwarf, whose back was turned toward Sarah.

One of the queen's ladies-in-waiting leaned close and whispered something in her ear. Ny'Callé's head jerked up, saw that Kri'Entu was looking up at her from his position down at the waterfront, and looked imploringly straight at Sarah. The queen's eyes sought hers out and pleaded for assistance. Sarah nodded.

In the blink of an eye, Sarah's jhorun teleported the queen to Kri'Entu's side. The queen slipped her arm through her husband's and turned to the Fae king and queen. Both human monarchs bowed, followed moments later by the Fae doing the exact same.

"You must be Kri'Entu, human king," Tivan began. "I am Tivan, King of the Fae. I'd like to introduce my wife, Ria. I am sorry to, what's the phrase you mentioned before, dear?"

Ria beamed a smile. "The phrase was, 'crash the party.' I am sorry, but we could hear and feel your joy all the way from Dynwe. I do hope you do not mind."

Kri'Entu started sputtering. "No, er, not at all. You are more than welcome here. I, er, would like to present my beautiful wife, Ny'Callé."

She smiled warmly at the two Fae monarchs. "You are welcome here," Mikal's mother assured the two visiting monarchs. "If there's anything you need, you have but to ask."

"Would Lady Sarah and her delightful husband be here?" Ria asked.

"Did you hear that?" Steve whispered, nudging Sarah in the ribs. "Did you? I'm delightful."

"Oh, swell," Sarah softly groaned. "As if your head wasn't big enough."

"They're right over there," Kri'Entu answered, turning to indicate their direction. "My dear, would you escort her?"

Ny'Callé nodded. "Of course."

The two queens began walking along the wooden sidewalk to where Steve and Sarah were standing. Both husband and wife noticed that Ria seemed anxious to reach them. Tivan elected to stay behind to chat with Kri'Entu.

"I wonder what's on her mind," Steve murmured quietly.

"I hope everything is alright," Sarah agreed.

The queens arrived just a few moments later. Ria caught Sarah's arm with her left hand and snagged Steve's with her right. She pulled them into a three-way hug. The Fae queen surprised them both by bursting into tears.

"I don't think I've properly thanked you for all that you've done for us," Ria tearfully told them. "We would be dead by now if it wasn't for you."

Ny'Callé turned to go but Ria let go of Steve's arm and pulled her to a stop.

"No, please stay. What I have to say can be heard by your ears, too."

As was the case whenever Sarah was exposed to someone else crying, her own eyes filled. A few moments later the Lentarian queen was also dabbing at her eyes with a silk handkerchief. Caught in an awkward three-way hug, Steve looked over Ria's shoulder at Mikal's mother. Ny'Callé was smiling at the three of them and waiting patiently to find out why the Fae queen wanted her present. Steve gave Ria a few awkward pats on her back before he gently pulled back. Thankfully, Ria must have decided she had held the hug long enough and let them both go.

"It's over, Ria," Sarah soothingly told her. "Everything is good. Everything should be back to normal, right?"

Ria smiled and twirled about. Her wings fluttered a few times as she clapped excitedly. The Fae queen looked at both husband and wife and nodded.

"You have no idea how much I've wanted to … Ny'Callé, would you please step over here? I don't want to appear rude by having my back to you. There, much better. As I was saying, you have no idea how alive I feel right now. We've been in Dynwe far too long, keeping only to ourselves. It has been centuries since I've stepped foot off the isle. Now that I'm here, I want to make the most of it."

"How can I help?" Ny'Callé asked, smiling at the Fae.

"Officially invite us for a visit to your home," Ria said, not bothering to take a breath.

"You'd like to see R'Tal?" she asked, surprised.

"I want to see everything. I feel like I've been reborn! I told Tivan that I refuse to return to our solitary lives. I refuse to hide. I wish to make as many friends as I can! I want to see other cities, be they human, dwarf, griffin, or any other species in nature. I want to see how other inhabitants of this fine land live."

Ny'Callé regarded the Fae queen for a few seconds before clearing her throat. "Ria, queen of the Fae and resident of Dynwe, I officially invite you and your husband to be guests of honor in our castle in R'Tal. Would you do me the honor of accepting?"

Ria shrieked with delight and clasped Ny'Callé's hands in her own. "Of course, I will. I would be delighted! *We* would be delighted."

Sarah suddenly cocked her head. She could hear a soft, haunting tune that was rising steadily in volume. She looked back toward Constable Fensham's office. A young girl, dressed entirely in white, was standing, motionless, while she held something to her lips. Whatever instrument it was, Sarah decided, the young girl clearly knew how to play it.

The slow, soothing tones of the instrument switched to a faster tempo. The girl had started playing a lively tune that was now causing heads to turn. A few moments later two young boys and another girl joined the soloist. The boys each held something that looked like a flattened 'S' while the second girl held something resembling an animal's horn. Moments later all four instruments were playing together, harmonizing perfectly, and eliciting nods of approval from more than one onlooker.

"That's the sign," Ny'Callé announced. "The ceremony is about to begin!"

"Who's performing the ceremony?" Steve wanted to know.

"Shardwyn, of course," Ny'Callé answered. The Lentarian queen was already on her way back down to the king.

Tivan appeared by Ria's side. He nodded at each of them before he took Ria's arm and guided them toward the waterfront. Dwarves took their seats. Griffins settled onto the ground. The wyverians, after much insistence from Kri'Entu, had agreed to move closer, taking the stretch of land directly opposite the griffins. Granted, there were only four dragons present, including Pravara and Rhamalli, but their combined bulk was more than all the dwarves and griffins combined. Probably the humans, too, Sarah thought.

She swung by the tree where Emerion was resting. The young griffin, catching sight of his adoptive mom, sprang to his feet and launched himself at her. Peanut pranced alongside the griffin, keeping a close eye.

"Hello, Emerion," Sarah cooed to the little griffin. "Did you miss me?"

In response, the young griffin nuzzled his head into Sarah's chest and trilled happily.

"Would you mind if Steve held you? Or, if you prefer, would you walk alongside us?"

Emerion took one look at Steve and elected to jump down. He stayed close to her left knee, while Peanut paced them both on the left of Emerion. Sarah heard her husband grunt once, but thankfully he elected not to say anything.

She chose a seat near the front of the procession, on the left so Emerion could curl up beside her on the ground. Once both the griffin and corgi had made themselves comfortable, she turned to her husband. Steve took her hand into his and together they waited for everyone else to sit down. Maelnar, catching sight of them, immediately veered over and hopped up onto the seat next to Steve. In a matter of moments, the entire contingent of dwarves occupied the first three rows of chairs on the left. Kri'Entu and Ny'Callé and their huge entourage chose the right.

"We've come a long way, Master Steve," Maelnar whispered, leaning close.

"We really have," Steve agreed.

"You seem to have acquired yourself a wee griffin."

"We did," Steve agreed.

"How?" Maelnar asked. "Griffins do not typically give up their young."

"It's a long story. Let me see if I can sum it up. The mother was killed and the father is not fit to raise the youngling, so we're taking him back with us to our world."

"Commendable, Sir Steve."

"It was Sarah's idea."

"Good for her," their dwarf friend decided. "That will not be easy on either of you."

"We know. But it's something that had to be done. Hey, did you and Shardwyn ever bury the hatchet like you promised you would?"

Maelnar sighed heavily and grunted. "Longstanding grudges are hard to forgive, my friend. Especially when they're held by insufferable know-it-alls."

"You promised me, pal," Steve reminded him.

"You misunderstand," Maelnar added with a chuckle. "We get along fine. Neither of us will raise a voice to the other…"

Steve nodded, pleased. "That's what I want to hear."

"…while we're face-to-face," Maelnar finished, lowering his voice so Steve would be the only one who could hear him. "When we're out of earshot, it's an entirely different matter, I'm sure."

Eavesdropping, Sarah groaned inwardly. Maelnar and Shardwyn were still at each other's throats? Concerned, she glanced at her husband. Much to her surprise, Steve was laughing.

"I don't expect you to behave yourselves at all times," he was saying. "I only need to see you two acting cordial when you're in the same room together, agreed?"

Maelnar laughed and companionably slapped a hand on Steve's back.

"Excellent. Then we understand one another."

"Ladies and gentlemen!" a familiar voice announced.

Sarah noticed Shardwyn was now standing in front of the procession. His back was to the water as he held his hands up to signal silence.

"We extend our heartfelt welcome to all of our guests, including the dwarves!"

Three rows of dwarves all bellowed in approval.

"The griffins!"

A collective screech came from the griffins.

"The wyverians!"

Pravara, Rhamalli, and the other two dragons threw their heads back and roared.

"The shealk!"

The waters turned frothy as every shealk present, including Lord Phaedren, lifted a section of their tail from the water and slapped the surface.

"And the Fae!" Shardwyn cried.

Sarah breathed a sigh of relief. She didn't know if Shardwyn had noticed their arrival. The last thing she wanted was to slight the Fae at the start of a new friendship. A resounding cheer went up from everyone but the Fae. Ria and Tivan bowed politely while waving to the crowd.

"If everyone will please stand, I do believe there are two young people who are anxious for these proceedings to start!"

Everyone rose to their feet. Nearly two dozen teenagers appeared, each holding a peculiar-looking instrument. Each of them was wearing robes of white. The four young musicians, each holding the same instrument they had been playing before, were amongst them. A lone adult appeared and motioned for everyone to get ready.

"It's Quinn!" Sarah excitedly told her husband. "I was wondering if we were going to see him. He looks so much better, don't you think?"

"I knew he was a teacher but didn't know what subject he specialized in," Steve said, watching as Quinn led the youngsters into the Lentarian wedding march. "To be honest, I saw him as more of a history teacher than a music teacher."

"He is the schoolmaster," Sarah reminded him. "He undoubtedly teaches everything, including music. He probably volunteered the kids to play for this wedding. It was nice of the Kri'yans to accept."

A hush fell over the crowd. Everyone turned to see that there were now two people making their way down the aisle. Sarah could see Constable Fensham, outfitted in a dark leather jerkin with a white long-sleeved shirt and black trousers, complete with calf-high leather boots, escorting his daughter down the aisle. A sword was buckled to his left hip.

Lissa, clutching her father's right arm, was a sight to behold. She was wearing a sparkling light blue gown that had a high back and a square front neckline. The upper sleeves of the dress were fitted, the lower sleeves very full and double layered with velvet and lace. As the father and daughter duo passed her Sarah also noted that Lissa's dress had lacing on both the front and back.

"How did Lissa handle the news when she was told it was her wedding today?" Steve whispered in her ear.

"Surprisingly well," Sarah answered, keeping her voice low. "If you ask me, I think she knew. She's a very bright girl."

"It's a strange custom," Steve added, "not telling the bride when her wedding day will be. That wouldn't go over well back on our world."

"True," Sarah decided. "It all worked out. Besides, I think she might have been tipped off."

"By whom?" Steve asked.

"The queen. Did you see them just now? Ny'Callé just winked at Lissa."

Steve nodded. "Nice. Good for her. Look at the grin Mikal has on his face. They make a good pair."

Mikal had appeared and was beaming his approval as Lissa and her father approached. Fensham swatted aside Mikal's outstretched arm and pulled him in for a bear hug. Wiping the corners of his eyes with the back of his hand, the constable lifted the veil covering his daughter's face, kissed her tenderly on her cheek, and took his seat next to Ny'Callé.

"Friends and family," Shardwyn began, raising his voice so that he could be heard, "we are gathered here today to witness the union of these two young people, Kre'Mikal, son of Kri'Entu and Ny'Callé, to Lissa, the lovely daughter of Constable Fensham of Capily."

The wizard paused for a few moments to give his audience a chance to applaud.

"The union of two souls is not an arrangement to be taken lightly," Shardwyn intoned, clearly reciting from memory a script he had recently memorized. "Your companion will be standing by your side, throughout your worst times and your best…"

Steve leaned close and started whispering.

"Have you ever noticed that music played at weddings often resembles the music that is played for soldiers going into battle? Oooof!"

Sarah had elbowed him in the gut. Hard. Maelnar, sitting nearby, snorted loudly. Sarah gave the dwarf a neutral stare.

"Allergies," Maelnar sniffed, rubbing his nose.

"Mm-hmm. Keep quiet."

"Sorry," Steve apologized.

"And I," Maelnar agreed, winking at Steve.

Sarah sighed and reached out to take her husband's hand. Steve, alerted to imminent danger, promptly sat on both of his. She tapped his leg and waited for him to put his hand in hers. The moment he did she dug in her nails. Steve's eyes began to water.

"Is that necessary?" Steve whispered.

"You're missing the ceremony," Sarah coolly informed him. "Mikal is about to take his vows."

"Kre'Mikal. Will you have this woman to be your wedded wife, to live together as a joined couple?"

"I will," Mikal answered as he smiled at Lissa.

"Will you love her, comfort her, keep her in sickness and in health, and hold her in the highest honor for she will one day be your queen, for so long as you both shall live?"

"I will," Mikal vowed.

"Young Lissa," Shardwyn began, turning to Mikal's fiancée. Lissa repeated the same vows.

"I will, always and forever," Lissa answered.

"You may exchange your rings now," Shardwyn announced.

"What?" Steve whispered again. "They exchange rings at the same time?"

"This is Lentari, not Idaho," Sarah scolded. "Things are clearly different here. Now shush!"

"Kre'Mikal, repeat after me," Shardwyn intoned. "I, Kre'Mikal, take thee Lissa to be my wedded wife, to have and to hold…"

Mikal carefully repeated the words.

"…to love and to cherish, until death do us part…"

As Mikal repeated the words, Sarah smiled and released her death grip on Steve's hand. She nudged him and indicated Mikal's face. Both Mikal and Lissa only had eyes for each other. Steve smiled, nodded, and kissed her hand.

Husband and wife watched and listened as Shardwyn walked Lissa through the same dialogue. Once she had repeated her vow for Mikal to hear, Shardwyn leaned forward and whispered something to each of them. Mikal grinned while Lissa giggled.

"By the powers vested in me, I now pronounce you husband and wife. My prince, you may kiss your princess!"

A round of applause went up as Mikal and Lissa embraced and shared their first married kiss.

"I present to you Kre'Mikal and Kre'Lissa, the prince and princess of Lentari!"

Applause thundered from all sides. The dragons roared their approval, the griffins squawked, and the shealk…

The applause continued well past the departure of the happy newlyweds down the aisle. Sarah looked anxiously down at Emerion, afraid that all the loud cheering and clapping might frighten the little griffin. Griffin and corgi were lying comfortably side by side.

"Now what?" Steve asked. "I assume there's going to be some type of reception?"

"The likes of which Topside has never seen," Maelnar assured him.

The dwarf hopped down from his seat and gazed admiringly up at the two of them.

"Who better to supply the food for a feast than the dwarves? Trust me, my friends, no one can spit a roast better than us. Surely, you'll stay?"

Right on cue a roar of applause sounded from behind them. Emerion immediately jumped up into Sarah's arms. Maelnar clucked approvingly and held up a hand for the young griffin to sniff. After a few moments, Emerion nuzzled the dwarf's hand.

"Maybe it's me?" Steve softly grumbled.

"It would appear that the party has started without us," Maelnar said. "Come, my friends! I hear that our wyverian friends are giving us a treat! Dragon races!"

Steve perked up. "Really? How cool! Who's racing?"

"Rhamalli and his rider were challenged by Bastillius."

"Who's Bastillius?" Steve wanted to know.

"Apparently he's the top wyverian flyer," Maelnar explained. "He'll be the bronze dragon sitting by himself in the back."

Sarah shaded her eyes and peered at the unusually colored dragon. "I don't think I've ever seen a bronze dragon before."

"He's the only one," a new voice added.

It was Maelnar's one and only son, Breslin. He was wearing the same dark armor as the rest of the dwarves of the Kla Guur, but differentiated by a dark red, dual-bladed battle axe and a hammer. The hammer, none other than the famous Narian power hammer he had helped discover, swung lightly on his belt, as though it weighed no more than a feather.

"Hey there, Breslin," Steve greeted. "It's good to see you, buddy."

Breslin bowed. "And you, my friend. So, are you wagering?"

"On which dragon will win? Sure! I have to go with

Rhamalli, being a dragon rider myself."

A cough sounded from nearby. Everyone looked over to see Maelnar reaching into his money pouch and withdrawing several coins.

"Five gold pieces."

Breslin grinned. "You're making a wager? Excellent, father. Which dragon?"

"Rhamalli, of course. A dragon with a rider will win every time."

Hearing peals of laughter and lively music coming from just up the hill, Sarah wrapped Peanut's leash around her wrist and called for Emerion to follow. With Steve keeping an eye on the young griffin, they decided to mingle with the guests. She knew her husband wanted to meet a shealk in person so she automatically veered toward the water. Several of the shealk had gone, but most were still there, including the sparkling red water dragon who was their leader.

The red shealk had just reemerged from the water after rinsing his eyes when Sarah and her procession stopped in front of them. The shealk leader's eyes flicked over to hers and stayed there. "Greetings, humans."

Sarah curtsied and her husband bowed.

"Lord Phaedren. It is an honor. I am Sarah, and this is my husband, Steve."

The red shealk's eyes widened with surprise. "You are the Nohrin. I have heard of you."

Steve blinked a few times before he shared a look with his wife. "You have? If you don't mind me asking, how? You're a water dragon. It's not like we run in the same circles."

"We shealk have a wizard who can't seem to keep his tail in the water," Lord Phaedren said. "Balthor's son, Gareth, is a human wizard, who happens to be friends with the human prince. So, that would mean … it would mean…"

"It would mean you really don't care one way or the other?" Steve guessed, finishing the red shealk's train of thought.

"Not one bit," Lord Phaedren admitted. "Don't tell anyone I said that."

"Your secret is safe with us," Sarah assured the water dragon.

"Say, how fast can you guys swim?" Steve asked as he caught a glimpse of the water dragon's sinewy body underwater.

"We are unmatched in the water," Lord Phaedren assured him. "The only exception being the great serpents who thankfully live far to the east."

"The oskorlisk," Steve agreed. "I've seen those things up close. Way too close, if you ask me. You're right. You don't want to tangle with one of them."

"You've encountered an oskorlisk in person?" Lord Phaedren asked, stunned. "In what regard, may I ask?"

"Pryllan and I once participated in the Hunt. It would seem a wager had been cast, namely who performed better? Dragons with riders or dragons who didn't carry riders."

"This Hunt was *not* sanctioned by me," Sarah told the shealk, throwing her husband a dirty look. "Nevertheless, they did end up winning the bet. They even found a red oskorlisk and retrieved a silver fang. I think that was probably the main reason why more dragons are interested in riders lately."

"Fascinating," Lord Phaedren breathed. "I have often considered devising a competition for my own shealk, only I have no idea what."

"An obstacle course," Steve immediately answered. "You say you're fast swimmers? Throw some obstacles in the way and see how well you do."

"Obstacles?" Lord Phaedren repeated, curious. "Like what?"

"Oh, how about swimming through a shipwreck? Or swimming through an underwater canyon? I'd look for that type of thing. Then, whoever can do it in the quickest time would be the winner."

"An interesting idea, human," Lord Phaedren decided. "I will reflect on the matter. Out of curiosity, why do you want to know how fast a shealk can swim?"

"Water skiing."

Sarah smacked his arm. "What? Water skiing? You can't ask a shealk to pull you through the water like that. That'd be insulting, dear."

"Spoilsport."

"You're that fast in the water?" Steve asked again, suddenly smiling.

"Aye," Lord Phaedren confirmed. "Why?"

"I have a proposition."

Sarah groaned. "Oh, Lord. This ought to be rich."

* * *

"The first wyverian to land a strike is the winner!" Breslin was shouting. "The contest is over if after ten minutes neither shealk have been touched."

"Do not be offended if our winged brethren are unable to hit anything," Lord Phaedren chided. "No one can match a shealk in our own element."

"We'll see about that," Rhamalli vowed. He lowered himself to the ground and allowed Pheron to climb up his back. "My rider and I will score the first hit. There's no way a riderless wyverian will strike first."

"Challenge accepted," a deep voice thundered.

Everyone turned to see a large bronze dragon *strut* his way to the front of the procession. Comments were thrown about. Wagers were cast. Nearly a dozen different conversations erupted all across the waterfront.

"You're sure a strike by the wyverians will not hurt you?" Breslin asked for the fifth time, looking up at the glittering shealk leader. "I've witnessed firsthand the power of a wyverian blast."

"We are as armored as our winged brethren," Lord Phaedren assured him. "Fear not. No one will be scoring a hit on any of my shealk."

"Are you ready?" Breslin asked, pulling his hammer from his belt. He was standing next to a large metal gong that had been suspended from a pole set in the ground. "On your marks."

The two dragons, bronze and red, crouched low. Their muscles bunched as they waited to launch themselves into the air. The two shealk, one black and one dark green, readied themselves just past the piers, facing open water.

"Remember, no submerging," Breslin hastily reminded

the two shealk. "You must stay on the surface."

"Yes, yes, we know," Lord Phaedren said impatiently. "Do get on with it. I cannot wait to tell Kahvel the outcome of this contest."

"Of that, I have no doubts," Breslin smirked. "And now, I'll say … go!"

The surface of the water turned choppy. Of the shealk, there were no signs. It was if both water dragons had simply dipped below the surface. However, Sarah knew that wasn't the case. She figured the shealk were good swimmers, only she never realized how good. Both shealk were already nearly a half mile out to sea and, incredibly enough, gaining speed.

Rhamalli and Bastillius launched themselves into the air, spread their gigantic wings, and took off after the shealk. What followed was an impressive aerial demonstration as each dragon fired blast after blast at the fleeing shealk, only to see each blast bounce harmlessly off the surface of the ocean. Lord Phaedren was right. His shealk were more than a match for their aerial cousins. Not one wyverian landed a hit.

Ten minutes later Breslin announced the end of the contest, much to the delight of the shealk. Rhamalli was unconcerned. Apparently, he had been impressed by the dexterity of the shealk and their amazing speed in the water. Bastillius was somewhat more annoyed, but he took his loss with a grain of salt. He politely congratulated the two shealk before departing for the Bohanis.

More games followed. The dwarves introduced their favorite pastime, rebekar, a type of tile and dice game of chance. Surprisingly, the griffins excelled at the game, being able to watch the rapid hand movements when shuffling the tiles. Naturally, the dwarves were less than amused.

As soon as the dwarves called for a rematch, Sarah felt a presence behind her. She turned to find Mikal and Lissa standing quietly nearby, watching the game between the dwarves and the griffins. Lissa looked up, met her eyes, and gave her a hug.

"It's all so magical!"

"What is?" Sarah asked. "Being married or seeing all these species interacting peacefully with one another?"

"Both. If it wasn't for you and Steve, I would never be here."

"Sure you would," Steve contradicted, coming up to lay a friendly hand on the young bride's shoulder. "You would have caught Mikal's eye, regardless."

Lissa shook her head. "No, silly. I meant that you brought me out of the past when you rescued Sarah. For that, I will be eternally grateful."

"For the record, it was a group effort," Sarah reminded the young woman. "But you're welcome all the same."

Mikal looked down at Emerion, squatted down next to the young griffin, and held out his hand. Peanut was instantly on her feet. Curious as to what his packmate was doing, Emerion cautiously rose and sniffed at Mikal's outstretched hand. After a few moments, both griffin and corgi were darting playfully between Mikal's legs, pausing only long enough to hide behind Lissa's dress.

"Isn't he just the cutest thing!" Lissa exclaimed, leaning down to pet the young griffin.

Emerion squeaked contentedly and rubbed up against Lissa's leg.

Steve frowned. "Okay, it's definitely me. That griffin lets everyone else come up to him. What, do I have B.O.?"

"B.O.?" Lissa repeated, confused.

"He thinks he stinks," Mikal translated.

Lissa and Sarah burst out in giggles.

"I never said I did," Steve argued, "only that maybe there was a teeny tiny chance that I did."

"Where'd you get him?" Mikal asked.

"It's a long story," Sarah said.

Just then there was a shout—a warning. A quick check of the area showed people pointing down at the marina. Round Two of the shealk/wyverian battle was happening and one of the shealk had just swum through the piers at high speed. The resulting wave was tossing some of the smaller ships around like toys. A wave washed over the piers and headed their direction. Thankfully the wave only made it a few feet up the embankment.

"My apologies," Lord Phaedren was saying. "I challenged

my shealk into showing off a little. I shouldn't have suggested he come so close to the shore."

"No harm done," Kri'Entu assured him. "It's only water."

"As I was saying, about Emerion," Sarah continued, turning back to Mikal once the hubbub died down, "it's a long story. His mother was killed and his father wasn't in any position to care for him. So, Steve and I are going to take him back to Idaho."

Mikal's eyes widened.

"This is the griffin I heard you talking about with the Fae last night, isn't it? Something about the mother dying but yet you actually talked to her somehow?"

Sarah nodded. "That's right. I didn't realize you were listening."

"Sorry," Mikal apologized, looking contrite. "I shouldn't have, but I was bored."

"It's okay," Sarah assured him.

"So what is Ranal?" Mikal asked.

"Hmm, that's not okay," Sarah corrected, thinking hard. "Ranal is where the griffins go to die."

"I never knew such a place existed," Lissa said, lowering her voice to a whisper.

"It's considered bad form to talk about such a place," Steve said. "It's governed by an entity that is a lot more powerful than any of us. As a griffin, you don't want to anger him. He will prevent you from feeling the Pull, which will deny the griffin his Final Journey. Trust me, for a griffin, that's bad."

"How do you know?" Mikal asked.

"Because I inadvertently pissed him off," Steve sighed. "Royally. I didn't mean to. He was just doing his job and protecting his griffins."

He gave the highlights of their adventure to the newlyweds, then looked up. "Usol, if you're listening, we're sorry. *I'm* sorry. We only harvested that one flower, and I only took the flower head, so the plant should still be alive. I know it angered you and I'm sorry. We didn't have a choice. We did it to save a civilization."

Thunder rumbled loudly. Mikal and Lissa glanced up at

the sky. There were a few clouds overhead but none of them were rainclouds. Sarah looked at her husband and mouthed, *he heard you!*

"You'd be proud of us," Steve continued, glancing up at the sky. "We just adopted a griffin. We essentially saved his life. Remember Nyx? This is her baby."

The rumbling thunder stopped instantly.

Epilogue

The party lasted well into the night. Balthor ended up renewing his communication spell three more times so that the shealk wouldn't feel left out. Kri'Entu and Ny'Callé stayed until the last guest finally went home, which in this case were Maelnar and his band of Kla Guur.

The dwarves offered to help clean up, but were turned down. Constable Fensham assured everyone that he and his team of workers would tidy up the following morning. The wyverians left, having been completely unsuccessful in five rounds of races with the shealk, but each species had developed the utmost respect for the other. Lord Phaedren had admitted that each of the participating shealk were barely able to stay ahead of their flying counterparts. One even attributed the wyverians' tenacity to that of a pursuing oskorlisk.

Lissa and Mikal departed on their honeymoon just as soon as they were sure no one was looking. Sarah later found out that the newlyweds were planning an extended visit to their southern neighbors, the Straosians. She knew the king objected, but in the end, it was Mikal's decision.

It was just past dusk when the occupants returned. Shadows were creeping in, enveloping the tiny log cabin in a comfortable blanket of darkness. The soothing sounds of Greenquill Falls could be heard as the forest's residents retired for the night, paving the way for the appearance of the nocturnal creatures. In a matter of moments, the small clearing was inundated with trills, hoots, chirps, and nighttime activity.

Tucked safely away inside the cozy cabin, in its only bedroom, slept the inhabitants. Draped across the cabin's only bed, as though they had collapsed from sheer exhaustion before having a chance to change into their sleeping clothes, were Steve and Sarah. She was sleeping on the extreme edge of her side of the bed while Steve did the same for his. Nestled between the sleeping humans was one corgi, on her back with all four paws in the air, and one griffin, in the exact same position.

Author's Note

I cannot believe this marks the 9th fantasy story that I've released. What's even crazier is, with the release of my 2nd mystery novel slated for later this same month, my total number of books will be pushed to 11. And... I've already got #12 planned out. It will be a mystery novel, the 3rd in the Corgi Case Files series. If any of you enjoy a good cozy mystery, I would encourage you to give them a try. It's something completely different from epic fantasy and it's considerably shorter.

Now, I'll clue you guys & gals in on something. Don't hold me to it, but I'm going to try and modify my schedule one more time. I've been watching how fast I write, and how long it takes me to prep a title to get it published, and I'm thinking I can increase my releases. Essentially, if I buckle down, ignore distractions, and just write, I can typically write one of my mystery novels in about a month. Make it an epic fantasy and the time increases to two. So I'm going to shoot for alternating releases. Coming up will be the 3rd mystery, aptly titled Case of the Holiday Hijinks, just in time for

Christmas. Then it'll be a fantasy, encompassing January and February for writing time, then March for the next mystery, and so on. So, members of my Posse, are you ready to be put to some serious work? :)

I'm often asked which books I'd recommend if by chance I'm taking too damn long in releasing my next title. Anyway, here are a few that I personally enjoy, having read all of them:

The Blue Moon Detectives series by JH Sked
The Klondaeg series, by Steve Thomas
All of Dan Brown's novels (you know, the DaVinci Code author?)
The Charlie Parker cozy mystery series, by Connie Shelton

I still do enjoy chatting with the fans. For anyone who'd like to look me up, ask a question or two, or would perhaps like some advice on releasing their own novel, feel free! I can be found on Facebook, but more often than not you'll find me keeping an eye on my blog, www.AuthorJMPoole.com. Ask away!

I'd again like to remind you, the reader, of the importance of reviews. Nothing will help an indie author out more than by leaving a review wherever you purchased the book. I certainly would appreciate it, whether good or bad.

That's it for now! Stay tuned to the blog for news on announcements, contests, and book releases. There's also a newsletter signup, in case you'd like me to notify you whenever something of note happens.

Thanks again for all your support!

J.
October 2016

Submissions

I didn't use too many fan submissions this time, but there were a couple of them:

Archadius — Tanner Erb
Thalian — Toni Trick
Finndar — Wendy Egan
Emerion — Marie Howells
Bastillius — Deb Shapiro

Have you ever wanted to name of fictitious character? Keep an eye on the blog. You never know when I'll ask for help naming a human, or dragon, or griffin, or...?

ABOUT THE AUTHOR

Jeffrey M. Poole is a professional writer who writes in both the fantasy and mystery genres. His series are listed below. Jeffrey lives in picturesque Southern Oregon, with his wife, Giliane, and their Welsh Corgi, Kinsey. His interests include archery, astronomy, archaeology, scuba diving, collecting movies, collecting swords, and tinkering with any electronic gadget he can get his hands on.

In March, 2015, Jeffrey became a proud member of SFWA, the Science Fiction & Fantasy Writers of America! Jeffrey encourages readers to connect with him on Facebook (facebook.com/bakkianchronicles). Fans can also follow him online at: www.AuthorJMPoole.com.

Scan the QR code to sign up for his newsletter!

BOOKS BY JEFFREY POOLE

Epic Fantasy
BAKKIAN CHRONICLES
The Prophecy
Insurrection
Amulet of Aria
Disneyland Debacle (short story)
Winter Wonderland (short story)

DRAGONS OF ANDELA
Harness the Fire
Strike the Spark
Clear the Water*

TALES OF LENTARI
Lost City
Something Wyverian This Way Comes
A Portal for Your Thoughts
Thoughts for A Portal
Wizard in the Woods
Close Encounters of the Magical Kind
The Hunt for Red Oskorlisk (short story)
May the Fang be With You (Pirates trilogy #1)
The Hammer is Strong with This One (Pirates #2)
These are Not the Stones You're Looking For (Pirates #3)
Blast from the Past

Mystery
CORGI CASE FILES
Case of the One-Eyed Tiger
Case of the Fleet-Footed Mummy
Case of the Holiday Hijinks
Case of the Pilfered Pooches
Case of the Muffin Murders
Case of the Chatty Roadrunner
Case of the Highland House Haunting
Case of the Ostentatious Otters
Case of the Dysfunctional Daredevils
Case of the Abandoned Bones
Case of the Great Cranberry Caper
Case of the Shady Shamrock
Case of the Ragin' Cajun
Case of the Missing Marine
Case of the Stuttering Parrot
Case of the Rusty Sword
Case of the Secret Staircase (short story)
Case of the Unlucky Emperor
Case of the Ice Cream Crime